BUKHARA EXPRESS

Also by William Smethurst

Night of the Bear
(with Julian Spilsbury)

BUKHARA EXPRESS

William Smethurst

HEADLINE

First Published in 1994
by HEADLINE BOOK PUBLISHING

10 9 8 7 6 5 4 3 2 1

British Library Cataloguing in Publication Data

Smethurst, William
Bukhara Express
I. Title
823.914 [F]

ISBN 0-7472-0867-0

Typeset by Avon Dataset Ltd., Bidford-on-Avon

Printed and bound in Great Britain by
Mackays of Chatham PLC, Chatham, Kent

HEADLINE BOOK PUBLISHING
A division of Hodder Headline PLC
338 Euston Road
London NW1 3BH

To my daughter, Henrietta

Murmansk
Arkhangel'sk
DEMOCRATIC FRONT
2nd Guards Motorised Rifle (Taman) Division
22nd Kantimirovsky Motorised Infantry Division
106th Guards Airborne Division
KOTELNIKOV'S 2nd SHOCK ARMY
Oslo
Stockholm
St Petersburg MD
NATO RAPID REACTION FORCE FORWARD HQ
Moscow MD
Berlin
Anglo-German 3rd Army Brigade
Kaunas
POLAND
Tula
Ryazan
Warsaw
14th Airborne Division
NATO ALLIED COMMAND EUROPE
COSSACK 7th GUARD TANK ARMY
UKRAINE
201st Motorised Rifle Division
Odessa
BLACK SEA

THE FALL OF MOSCOW
Final Phase
17 March to 26 March 1998
SIBERIA
MILITARY DISTRICT
URALS
Novosibirsk
Ishim
Perm
Omsk
Yekaterinburg
Kulunda
Semipalatinsk
Ufa
Karaganda
Gates of Dzungaria
Kuybyshev MD
Orenburg
KAZAKHSTAN
Alma Ata
Tashkent
AMERICAN 82nd
AIRBORNE DIVISION
UZBEKISTAN
Bukhara
Baku
105th GUARDS
(PARATROOP) REGT.
SEA
MD = Military District

HINDU KUSH, AFGHANISTAN, 1983

Apricots were warming in the afternoon sun, and the boy plucked and ate them, sitting on the crumbling wall of the bombed-out government rest-house.

Above him, carved in the rock cliff of the valley side, towering massively over the abandoned village, was the great stone Buddha, its face disfigured by Tartar hordes in some long distant holy war.

Beside him, in the ruins of the rest-house, was a white porcelain lavatory pedestal of French manufacture. It had been sent up from Kabul some ten years ago and placed proudly in the washroom. Visitors could either admire or use it as they would – the valley had no sewers.

Over the shattered washbasin was a grubby cardboard sign, written long ago by a Peace Corps girl who was having a mental breakdown: '*For God's Sake don't drink the water and don't BRUSH YOUR TEETH IN IT EITHER. Do you WANT hepatitis*?'

The village, high in the Hindu Kush, had been a favourite destination – 'way station' they had called it – of the hippies. But it was three years, now, since the last hippie had packed his rucksack and hitched his way back to Kabul; three years since the sitar strains of *Sergeant Pepper* had been heard on the rest-house's ancient record-player.

The boy ate the apricots. He was tired and dirty, but felt no self-pity: he had always been tired and dirty. He was a messenger for *Jammiat-I-Islam*, an envoy of Massoud. He was sixteen years old, but was not just an ignorant village boy. He had seen the world. He had seen the rich carpets glowing in the light of the paraffin lamps at Herat market, he had seen hashish exchanged for arms with the Iranians on a desolate icy frontier, he had seen the old cannons in the square at Kandahar, captured long ago from the British and celebrated still in song.

A distant sound: an aircraft. Not a Hind or an Su-25, a heavier throbbing, a transporter perhaps. The boy froze, then slipped down from the wall and into the derelict building. A transporter could be carrying Soviet special troops, *Spetznaz*, on an operation. If so, it would be followed by the Hind helicopters that swept up the valley floors with their nose guns slaved to target anything in the gunner's sight.

From the shadows he looked out, down the valley. He looked beyond the mountain-ash trees by the river, and the thin stripes of green cultivation, now abandoned. He looked beyond the deserted track to Kabul, and the faded, psychedelic mural on the wall of the chai-house.

After a few moments the plane appeared. It was huge and fat-bellied, flying low. It had little to fear in this autumn of 1983, for the Mujahideen had not yet captured Soviet RPGs or recoil-less rifles; they had no AK 47s from Egypt; they did not yet possess Stinger missiles.

The plane turned over the village, and the boy put his head under his arms and waited for the bombs, the unguided rockets or tactical air-to-surface missiles to tear into the ruins around him.

Twice it circled over the settlement. Then it departed.

Silence returned.

The boy left the house. He plucked a final apricot, golden green in the clear mountain light, and hurried up the hillside, away from the valley where the Buddhist faith had been born, scrambling along a remote path he believed was not yet known to the Spetznaz, into the fastness of the Koh-i-Baba. He trod carefully because, in recent months, new and more ghastly weapons were being deployed – seismic Octopus mines with long creeping tendrils and explosives at the end of every tendril, and a central brain that could *think*, could listen to approaching footsteps or vehicles, and work out the most deadly explosive charge to detonate; new anti-personnel canister bombs filled with needle-sharp flechettes that would slice the flesh of a boy or a donkey.

Ascending the valley side as the light was fading he stopped for a moment to rest and to eat the apricot.

It tasted bitter, its skin stung his lips, and he spat it out in disgust.

Then he became aware that his skin was itching. His arms and neck were blotched red, his face felt puffy, and his eyes were watering so that he could hardly see.

In December, World Health officials in Peshawar heard reports of widespread outbreaks of skin irritation and inflammation in the valleys of the Hindu Kush. A note on possible Soviet biological warfare experiments was sent to the United Nations. It was impossible to check on the ground, and no further reports were received. No action was taken. World Health teams had enough problems to tackle in the refugee camps of Pakistan; the Mujahideen had the Soviets' new helicopter gunships to deal with.

Five years later (by which time the boy had forgotten the strange inflammation, the apricots, and the plane in the Bamian Valley, and had grown to be a feared and ruthless mujahideen leader in the military district of Uruzgan) NATO Intelligence at Spandau, Berlin, related the 1983 outbreaks of skin disorders in the Hindu Kush to the first experiments of *Chernobog*, a weapon named after the ancient Slavonic god of darkness, chaos, and death.

NATO ACE FORWARD HQ, KAUNAS, LITHUANIA 17 MARCH 1998

The MIG-55 Foxbat had climbed sixteen miles, high over the Arctic, and swept over the roof of the world, transcribing a broad curve from Siberia to the Baltic, from the Urals Military District to St Petersburg Military District, before coming in to land at 02.00: the dead hour of night.

Two men emerged. They were a Russian Army brigadier and a staff captain. They stretched their cramped limbs. The Foxbat 55, even with half its banks of electronics removed, was not designed for passengers.

In the near-darkness, a G2 NATO intelligence officer saluted crisply. He shepherded them into a car with discreet, dark-tinted windows.

Ten minutes later they were in the Kaunas army complex, the old home of Third Shock Army in the days when Third Shock Army was destined to spearhead the Soviet attack through Poland and loose its tanks on the fat and populous North German plain. More lately the barracks had been the base of the *Vozdushno-Desanatniye Voiska*, the elite Soviet 7th Guards. Now the complex was the forward base for NATO's Rapid Reaction Force (Central Europe) Command.

The G2, Patrick Littlehales, a captain on secondment from the Prince of Wales' Own Regiment, poured coffee and offered food. There were warm croissants, butter, smoked ham, cheese, and black cherry jam. The Russian brigadier looked at the buffet on its crisp white cloth for a moment, then shook his head.

The staff captain – regretfully, thought Littlehales – also shook his head. The two Russians moved to the window and stood by a radiator staring out.

'I hope you had a good flight?'

Brigadier Alexei Filatov, who for the past twenty-four hours had been the second most powerful man in Russia, did not bother to reply.

Beyond the perimeter fence a train moved south. Littlehales could see, through the diamond pattern of the wire, into empty, clean carriages. On the road beyond the railway track a neon sign shone on a Wyoming pizza house; red reflections bleeding on the wet tarmac.

Lithuania's acceptance of the West had been total. Filatov, the old Lion of Afghanistan, stared out expressionless.

His staff captain kept glancing at the tray of food.

At 02.30, Littlehales led them to the Secure Room. It had been adapted from the Red Army command centre, the place where, in the days long before electronic surveillance and electronic bugging, the generals of Third Shock Army had planned their route to the English Channel.

General Hoepner, NATO Supreme Commander Central Europe, and his staff, were waiting. Filatov and his staff captain sat where it was indicated that they should sit.

There was a moment of silence. Then Filatov said: 'We have taken Moscow.'

Untrue, thought Littlehales. They'd taken Vladimir. By tomorrow they'd reach the northern suburbs of Moscow – providing the Federal Forces did not hold them, and NATO did not intervene.

Filatov looked round the group, waiting to be challenged.

'Congratulations,' said an air-force general, an American, drily.

Filatov nodded, then said something quietly, half to himself, in Russian. In Littlehales' ear the voice of a female NATO psychologist said, 'I didn't quite catch that.'

Littlehales said distinctly, for the hidden microphones, 'The agony is over.'

'Yes,' said Filatov in English. 'The agony is over.'

He looked round the room, smiling faintly. Here were the generals, air marshals and admirals of a dozen nations, who were publicly pledged to support the Federal democratic government of Russia – a government that his own Second Army had all but destroyed, a government at this moment struggling through the refugees on the motorway to St Petersburg.

'The integrity of all nuclear strike facilities,' said Filator, 'will be respected.'

There was a perceptible release of tension. Filatov smiled again. 'I can smoke?'

Hoepner slid his packet of Burmese cheroots across the table.

'Old comrades,' said Filatov. He had worked with Hoepner two years previously, on joint manoeuvres along the Chinese border. They had both been members of the committee that integrated Russia's Kurdish forces into the NATO command structure.

'Old comrades,' said Hoepner.

Filatov lit his cheroot. He said: 'My message from General Kotelnikov is as follows. The present Nato/Russian security forces will be allowed to continue to guard nuclear strike bases designated under the Amsterdam Agreement, and the programme of decommission will continue under United Nations supervision. In return we require an undertaking that all military assistance to the former government of the Russian Federation will cease, all western flights over Russian territory will cease, all interference in Russian internal affairs will cease. We require a public affirmation that what is now happening in Russia is no concern of NATO.'

Hoepner said: 'Talk to the politicians if you want public affirmations. This meeting is designed to arrange practicalities.'

'The practicalities,' said Filatov, 'are arranging themselves.'

There was a pause.

Hoepner conferred quietly with an aide. He said: 'It is not as simple as you think.'

Filatov smiled faintly, politely, understanding the need to pay lip-service to alternative action, alternative proposals. He had been a major in the 105th Guards Airborne Division when it brilliantly seized Kabul airport, and a brigadier when it withdrew, clumsily, a decade later. He had helped to build the new Federal Army, and had watched it disintegrate. There was nothing anyone could teach him about the organization of defeat, although he would not be defeated this time.

'Twenty hours,' he said. 'You have only twenty hours.'

A Dutch brigadier's eyes subconsciously moved to his watch.

Hoepner said: 'That's impossible.'

Littlehales thought: So the democratic government of Russia is finally being abandoned. The experiment is over. The Petersburg politicians will chatter for a few days more, no doubt, issuing PR statements, fretting over their parliamentary allowance claims and their satellite bookings to NBC and the BBC – but their voices will soon be lost in the Russian steppes. For the old Red Army is on the march: four million men, a hundred and forty motorized and tank divisions, and still the world's largest nuclear arsenal.

'*Do you know who are the only God-fearing people on earth, whose duty it is to regenerate and save the world in the name of a new god?*'

'*The people of Russia.*'

Dostoevsky, in *The Possessed.*

'Twenty hours,' repeated Filatov. 'In the space of twenty hours we require the removal from Moscow MD of all NATO personnel, the personnel of all Western agencies, including the EC Commission for Aid and all so-called "joint venture" enterprises; the removal of all non-Russian citizens, including those of the Ukraine and the Baltic Republics, other than those with specific travel or residence documents issued by General Kotelnikov; the removal of all non-Russian *media* representatives.' Filatov imbued the penultimate word with profound distaste.

It would be an unfortunate Western media representative, thought Littlehales, who wandered up to Filatov in the Moscow Hilton and offered him a large Scotch.

Hoepner said: 'I don't see that it is possible or reasonable to evacuate Western personnel in the space of just twenty hours.'

'Anyone left can argue it out with the Army of Moscow,' said Filatov. 'Don't blame General Kotelnikov.'

So Russia was heading back into purdah, into its secret hell, its age-old agony.

But the nuclear bases were safe: the decommissioning programme was secure. Nothing else mattered; nothing else would cause a ferment in the war departments of the West.

Except perhaps . . .

General Hoepner was looking down at the sheet before him, at an item placed there by the British C-in-C Defence Staff, Northwood.

He paused for a moment then said casually: 'It is felt desirable that certain non-nuclear weapons systems other than those specified under the 1995 Amsterdam Agreement be also placed under joint NATO-Russian custody.'

'*Niet*,' said Filatov.

It was agreed that Western personnel would be evacuated within thirty-six hours. The Foxbat took off an hour before dawn; before Russian military satellites could reveal, to the Federal Democratic Government, the West's betrayal.

PART ONE
MOSCOW

Though the enemy was nearing Moscow, Muscovites were not inclined to regard their situation with any greater degree of seriousness: on the contrary they became even more frivolous, as is always the case with people who see a great catastrophe approaching.

Tolstoy, *War and Peace*

ONE

British Embassy, Moscow. Evening of Sunday 17 March 1998

Up until a week ago, the room had been the embassy creche. Posters for ITV Playtime still decorated the walls, next to recognition pictures of Russian troops in different orders of dress. A silhouette chart of Russian battle tanks had been pinned up next to a cardboard rabbit that said *I'm Flopsie Bunny – I'm a bunny what eats her carrots*. The men liked Flopsie. 'I'm a soldier what eats his carrots,' they chirruped.

Simon Morrell went over to the noticeboard where the orderly clerk had pinned up the post. There was a copy of the Methodist youth magazine his mother still sent him every month, and there was a brown internal envelope from army personnel: '*Lt Simon Morrell, 1 R Merc*' and in handwriting '*D coy Moscow embassy*'.

He dropped the magazine into the bin and looked fixedly at the letter for a moment. Then he put it, unopened, in his pocket.

It was just past 18.00. He went to a table, opened a bottle of beer, and poured it into a cut-glass tankard. He sat in an armchair and drank deeply. A moment later Clive, the embassy's civilian head of security, poked his head round the door.

'What can you tell me,' he asked, 'about some more soldiers arriving tomorrow?'

'Soldiers?' said Simon. 'They're nothing to do with me, are they?'

'That's what I'm asking.'

'Christ, I hope not. Want a beer?'

'That's very kind . . .'

Clive came politely, as befitted a civilian, into the Royal Mercians' temporary mess.

'I'm bloody shattered,' said Simon. 'It took me three hours to get out to the cattery and back.'

'He won't like it. He went there before once, and didn't like it. It's the American catfood. It's too rich. It makes him shit everywhere.'

'There are people in this city,' said Simon, 'who would give all they possessed for a dinner of American catfood.'

He turned on the television. A girl's head and shoulders appeared on the screen.

'. . . *in a city that is dying*,' she was saying, '*a city that waits for the final blow to fall.*'

'That's Kate Delacroix.'

'Oh yes?' said Clive, pouring his beer and sitting down.

'*In public, government officials claim that Moscow's defences are secure.*

In private, they concede that Second Shock Army is west of Orekhovo-Zuyevo . . .'

Her freckled face was lightly tanned, her cheeks flushing faintly in the cold of a March afternoon. She looked to be in her early twenties. She had a shock of reddish hair that would probably, Simon thought, be called auburn – or was it Titian? She was sexy, but it was not her sexuality that most fascinated him – no, not even the heave of her breasts under her British Army dark blue bulletproof vest. It was her confidence, her assurance, her clear, self-evident belief that she was a proper and competent person to stand, neatly framed against Moscow International Airport's departure lounge, and tell the world about a nation tumbling into civil war.

'Tickets to Belorussia and the Ukraine are changing hands at ten thousand coupons. One way only – but who would want to come back? General Kotelnikov is through Vladimir. The Federal Government is fleeing to St Petersburg. The Western perfumeries, the casinos, the luxury car showrooms are closed. But here at Sheremetyevo 2 Airport the touts are still selling tickets, the Japanese are still running the catering, and the Irish the duty-free. This is one place where the capitalist instinct is alive and well. This is Kate Delacroix live from Moscow.'

'Very nice,' said Clive.

Simon flicked over to the pop channel.

Major Innes-Chator came in. 'Simon, the coat of arms? What are you doing about the coat of arms?'

'Clive says to leave it.'

'Leave it? You want it left, Clive?'

The royal coat of arms was fixed to the panelling of the hall. The lion and unicorn, *Dieu et mon droit*, glowing richly against the dark wood next to the embassy visitors' book.

'It's been there since before the War. It'd be a shame to risk damaging it, Major,' said Clive, who thought of himself as a bit of a diplomat. 'Anyway, word is we'll be back in a fortnight.'

'We weren't back in Kabul in a fortnight.'

'Ah well, Kabul,' said Clive. 'We should never have left Kabul in the first place.'

'An instinct, I suppose,' said Simon, finishing his beer. 'Over the centuries we've been conditioned to being kicked out of Kabul. It only needs a whisper of "Kill the British ferangee" in the bazaar, and we're off hell for leather—'

'Simon,' said Innes-Chator dangerously, 'will you get off your arse and do something?'

Simon got up. Innes-Chator said: 'Have you done a vehicles check with REME?'

'No, not yet—'

'Do it. Then do a full weapons check. Don't tell me thirty soldiers and thirty rifles don't need checking, because they *do*.'

'Yes.'

Innes-Chator lowered his voice. He spoke urgently. 'You've got to get a *grip*, Simon. I keep telling you you've got to get a *grip*. See if the diplomats need any extra help. See the duty roster is *typed.* Do it yourself if you have to. I'm sick of seeing it scrawled on a bit of bogroll by Sarn't Gough. And get that coat of arms taken down. I'm not leaving it for Kotelnikov's rabble to take family snaps in front of.'

He went, his boots echoing on the polished wood floor.

'It'll never come off the wall,' said Clive. 'Not without chipping. Perhaps you ought to do the other things first.'

Simon liked Clive. He remained unflustered, whatever the panic of the moment, and always looked neat.

It was after supper, and he was on duty at the back of the immigration cabin, when Kate Delacroix came in person, in the flesh, through the door. She was pushing her way through the pimps and the profiteers, waving her press pass over her head. Then Colour-Sergeant Gough, doing his stint with five solid blokes from 2 Platoon, was making an opening for her – but standing firmly in the way of the Russian youth she was trying to drag through the barrier.

Not possible, more than his job was worth, Simon could see Gough explaining. She was gesticulating and tossing her hair, and her clear cool Cheltenham voice floated like a mountain stream over the keening sound of Russia's woes: 'Oh, for fuck's sake . . .'

'That's Kate Delacroix,' he said to Chaffinch.

They were behind the 'Redoubt': two office desks that blocked the doorway into the Embassy garden and compound.

'Sir?' said Chaffinch.

'The television reporter. She used to present the news on *Mercia Today* and do their *Weekend Walk* series. You know – tramping over Wenlock Edge or Offas's Dyke. Then she'd sit in a pub garden, drinking beer.'

'That right, sir?' said Chaffinch stolidly.

Chaffey was from Wolverhampton, where they watched Sky Sport and the Terror Channel from dusk till dawn.

'I'll just go and see if she needs help.'

'Sir.'

A dull bugger, Chaffinch.

Simon edged a desk to one side and squeezed through, then crossed the floor. She was speaking loudly but calmly; a girl used to getting her own way.

'Look, I need this man, right? I need him to carry my stuff. I need his car for my satellite gear and camera. I can't operate in Moscow on my own. Would you like me to go out there on my own? Well, would you – Oh Christ,' she yelped, as Gough yanked her through and closed the gap, leaving the Russian youth staring desperately at her from the other side.

'Sergei?' she commanded. 'Sergei, you just stay there. OK?'

Sergei nodded, a look of intense desperation on his face.

'You don't move a centimetre, right? I'm going to sort this out—'

'Miss Delacroix?'

She turned. 'That's my fixer. He's been so bloody loyal, you wouldn't believe. Is this the way we treat people? Well, is it?'

Actually, of course, it was.

'Sorry,' he said, 'but you're all being taken out by helicopter, and space is limited.'

'I can't just abandon the poor bugger!'

'This is his home, this is where he lives. The rest of the press are in the main building. If you come with me, I'll take you over there.'

'I'm not going anywhere. Not without him.'

'We can't let him through, not if he's a Russian citizen.'

'Christ almighty—'

'You can talk to the Press and Information people. They might be able to help—'

'No. Never mind them helping. *You* help.'

'Now, look—'

'You can let him through. Come on. Who's checking passports, for Christ's sake? It's an emergency. The place is in chaos. Listen' – she lowered her voice, pleading, intense – 'he will be killed. I'm not talking shit here. It'll be that or a fucking death camp. In Kotelnikov's eyes he's a collaborator first-class. You know they've already opened one of the gulags—'

'I can't let any Russian national into the embassy,' said Simon firmly.

'He's not Russian. He's Welsh. Oh come on! He's Chinese – he's from Uzbekistan. I'll sign a letter guaranteeing that, OK?'

They exchanged looks.

'Oh, for Christ's sake . . .'

She turned back.

'Sergei? Sergei, I'm sorry. It's no use.'

She held out her arms in a gesture of helplessness. Sergei smiled hesitantly across the barrier. He was in his early twenties – Western anorak, hair slicked back in the trendy style of a French *jeune homme*.

'I'm sorry,' she called again, 'I'm going. I'm going now.'

He nodded and smiled.

'I'm going, Sergei.'

He smiled some more, as if he thought that by assuming that everything was going to be all right, then it somehow would be.

She turned abruptly. Simon led her back to the Redoubt.

'Wait!' she said suddenly, 'What about my gear? What about my stuff?'

They turned back.

Sergei, desperately helpful, passed her gear across the counter to a soldier who said: 'Cheers, mate.'

'Bye, Sergei. Thank you.'

She took her gear under both arms, turned away again, stumbled against Simon. He put out his hand and she shook it off angrily.

He led her back to the Redoubt.

Behind them, Sergeant Gough suddenly bellowed: 'We must ask you to leave. We must advise you that this building is not part of the Embassy. This part of the building is not subject to diplomatic protection . . .'

The sound of Russia's woes fell, then rose again, its anguish greater than ever.

'Coffee or champagne?' he asked. 'We're going a bit wild.'

The press corps was spread around like scatter cushions: nests of brightly-coloured parkas and padded combat trousers, lightweight zip-bags and aluminium camera cases, ENG cameras, satellite transceivers and mini editing-booths. A six-man Korean TV crew was in a rage, the soldier at the gate having said 'Sod off' to them several times, believing them to be Mongolians seeking asylum. 'That man has had it,' a Korean was still shouting, pointing a trembling finger at the soldier hovering in the doorway. 'That man is dead meat.' The soldier was looking round indignantly. 'It wasn't my fault,' he said. 'What if everybody said they were Korean?'

'Would you like champagne,' repeated Simon, 'or some coffee?'

Kate Delacroix looked at him blackly, then asked for champagne. He went to get it.

Some reporters were asleep, and he had to step over them. Some were drinking champagne opened by the press attaché's over-excited girl assistant. Some were tapping into word-processors. A very old, very drunk man stopped him and said: 'I was in Saigon. I was on the last Aussie chopper out of Phuoc Tuy. I've had enough of this.'

'Saigon?' said an Australian voice, 'How long ago's that now, then?'

'It was when the world was young,' said a middle-aged English reporter in a dirty pink shirt. 'Miniskirts and *Good Morning, Vietnam*.'

The press attaché's assistant, only three months into the job, said: 'Champagne anybody? Champers, champers? A drop of the old shampoo?'

'I don't suppose there's such a thing as a pot of tea?' This from a weary, middle-aged female from the BBC.

'I wouldn't have thought so,' said Simon, who would have had to make it himself.

When he got back, Kate Delacroix was saying to a man: 'I couldn't get through to Foreign News Traffic. INMA was clogged solid. What time do we have an uplink to UTel?'

'Give over, love,' the man said. 'We're excommunicado. We're having a well-earned rest.'

He was EuroTV's Moscow agent and was looking at her with a peculiar expression – an expression she had come to recognize ever since she was fifteen. It was the look of a man speculating about her breasts, and the sort of bra she might be wearing.

Simon handed her her drink. 'I'm Simon Morrell, by the way,' he said.

'Hi, Simon.' She smiled wearily.

'I'm sorry about your chap,' he said awkwardly. 'Your fixer.'

She leaned against the wall and closed her eyes. He stood and admired her freckles. She opened her eyes after a bit, blinked at him, then remembered who he was. 'So, what are you lot doing here?' She peered at his shoulder badge. '1 R Merc. What's that?'

'First battalion Royal Mercian Regiment.'

'I thought it was the Marines that guarded embassies?'

'You're thinking of American embassies.'

'Oh,' she said. 'You do this all the time, do you?'

'God, no. We came to look after the diplomats when things got sticky – help them drink up the booze, you know, keep it out of enemy hands – cart stuff from the filing cabinets to the shredder.'

'How long have you been in the army?'

'Three years.'

For some time he had noticed, out of the corner of his eye, Innes-Chator edging his way purposefully towards them. Innes-Chator now arrived.

'My Dad, Miss Delacroix,' he said, grinning beefily, 'fancies you something rotten.'

How extraordinary it was, thought Simon, that Innes-Chator should have a dad – pottering about somewhere, presumably calling his son Frederick instead of Major Innes-Chator.

Kate said nothing.

'Ha, ha, ha,' said Innes-Chator, then: 'We always used to like it when you sat in the pub garden after your walk and raised your glass of beer and said "Cheers". In our house we always used to say "Cheers" back.'

Kate, a pained look on her face, stared urgently at Simon.

'Freddy,' said Simon, 'Didn't you say you wanted to talk to brigade at Kaunas?'

'I don't think so.'

'I thought you said you had to finalize details of the convoy.'

'There's no hurry,' said Innes-Chator icily. After a moment, though, he gave Simon a codfish stare, mumbled something to Kate Delacroix, and went.

Kate was looking broodingly into her glass.

'Is he your boss?'

'For the moment. Are you looking forward to getting home?'

'No. I've only been here four days. I haven't done anything. I suppose we're abandoning them all – all the poor sods who helped us, who believed in us, who trusted us, who took our word.'

'And took our money.'

'No. You're wrong. It was more than that. Oh well . . .' she shrugged, and drank champagne.

A reporter, Australian, was shouting at the press attaché's girl. 'Yes, but why can't we *stay*. I mean, why are we being . . . BUSSED around like . . . LITTLE children.'

He was emphasizing his words in a way peculiar to television journalists, pausing in unusual places and giving his words a rhythmic eye-glazing-over quality.

'You can stay if you insist, I suppose,' said the press attaché's assistant, upset, 'but we can't be responsible for you.'

'Did anyone ASK you to be responsible for me?'

'All I can tell you,' she said loudly, 'is that the rest of the press corps are being airlifted out from the American embassy at 15.00 hours tomorrow, and if you choose not to go, then that will be your concern.'

'If it was up to me,' whispered Simon, 'I'd leave him here, no trouble.'

She smiled mechanically. A man from the *Daily Telegraph* pushed past, asking: 'Anybody seen Art? Anybody seen Art Finkel?'

'OK,' yelled the press attaché's girl, whose good humour had finally gone. 'Ladies and gentlemen, you are shortly to be bussed from here to the American Embassy. I don't think I need to tell you that we do not have time for messing about . . .'

'It's all panic, isn't it?' said Kate Delacroix. 'I mean, what's Kotelnikov likely to do to us, for God's sake? He's not going to start stringing up the Western media. Reporters in Saigon weren't lynched when the North Vietnamese took over. They didn't put Western reporters in front of a firing squad, did they?'

'Yes.'

'What?'

'Yes they did. Anyway, Moscow is not going to be very safe. Not until things settle down.'

'Not very safe, eh soldier?'

'Yes well,' said Simon, 'there we are.'

'OK, ladies and gentlemen, if you will please follow me.'

'I think,' said the *Daily Telegraph* man, 'we've lost Art Finkel. Has anybody seen Art Finkel?'

'Get some of that champagne,' said somebody, 'for the coach.'

'See you,' Kate said. She joined the crocodile of reptiles, a bag slung over her shoulder, her mini-transceiver and satcom terminal powerbook under her arm. She did not, noted Simon, even say thanks for the champagne.

'Was it her then, sir?' asked Chaffinch. It was nearly midnight, and they were carting boxes of files to the shredder.

'Yes, it was, actually.'

'What was she like then, sir?'

'Very nice.'

'*Very nice,*' parroted a soldier.

'All right,' said Simon. 'Let's get on with it.'

It was around this time that Kotelnikov's Second Army crashed through the barricades round the Zladski terminus, the furthest north-easterly reach of the Moscow Metro. The Federal officer commanding the anti-tank platoon, a young lieutenant, fought a desperate holding action that crippled two tanks, before pulling his troop down into the metro itself. Some soldiers escaped along tunnels; others died waiting for a metro train that did not come.

Kotelnikov's men crept into the system like a virus.

TWO

United States Embassy, Moscow, midnight, 17 March

'Listen, I want to get out with a patrol. Just me. Nobody else. Can you fix it?'

'We don't patrol.'

'You don't patrol? Not at all?'

'We don't leave the compound.'

'Why not? Don't you want to know what's happening out there?'

'Honey,' said the marine, 'there are a lot of not nice things happening out there.'

'No there aren't. It's nothing like as bad as they say. You've been reading the papers too much. Can't we go in a truck? You must have a truck, a Land-Rover, a Jeep? You could be on television. They'd see it back in the States. Your mom would see you. Think how excited she'd be.'

'Wouldn't you like it better,' the marine said, seemingly indifferent to his mom, 'if we went and found somewhere more comfortable?'

'I didn't come here to be comfortable. I came here to do my job.'

'It's not very nice here, honey.'

'No, I know it isn't.'

The stairwell was dark and cold. From above came the crash, crash of doors slamming. The dim electric light wavered and flickered: the embassy generator was almost out of oil. On the metal stairs, over their heads, was the hack-pack: photographers and journalists, camera-crews and TV reporters – the Western media world spiralling upwards.

The *Daily Telegraph* man came out of the press department's subterranean burrow. He said: 'Art Finkel hasn't shown up, has he?' Then went away again.

In the gloom the marine was swaying in towards her, his mouth opening, as if about to attempt to kiss her.

'Oh, for Christ's sake, *lay off*, buddy!'

She had a First in Russian, and would have known how to put a Moscow lad in his place without any trouble. What was she doing with this suddenly sex-crazed marine?

She obviously wasn't going to get to Red Square.

Champagne, champagne – she'd drunk too much champagne. She remembered that everybody had drunk champagne in the German Ministry of Information in April 1945, when Berlin was falling, before sending their final communiqúe: *Sauve qui peut.*

'How about . . .' she said. 'You giving me your flak-jacket?'

'There's no Russkies shooting at you in here, honey.'

'Oh come on . . .'

She began gently to unpick the blue fabric ties, rather as cavaliers of old had lazily unlaced the bodices of girls they were about to tumble. The marine's hands started wandering. 'Don't worry, we'll get you out, honey,' he mumbled. 'Don't you worry about a thing.' His hands were trying to find a way under her sweater, fingering her breasts through the *broderie anglaise* of her bra.

'Ow,' she said.

She was suddenly aware of the EuroTV agent watching her from the shadows of the press office. She pulled away.

'I'm sorry. I'm going to sleep now.' She pushed past him and went quickly clattering up the stairs.

Behind her, the marine cried out 'Hey, honey, come back . . .' A sorry voice, a soldier boy far from home.

In the canteen she drank thirstily from a water fountain. Then she went and lay down between two BBC engineers. There was, she knew, a considerable risk that they would spend hours discussing Navsat frequencies and transponder wobble and Z-transmission codes over her recumbent body, but they were unlikely to venture on anything else. She used her anorak as a pillow, and lay on two blankets supplied by the embassy and marked with the words RUSSIA AID – A GIFT FROM THE PEOPLE OF THE USA.

She awoke at around two o'clock. The marine's bulletproof vest was covering her. She smiled in the darkness. Around her the hack-pack was sleeping, but on the edges shadows prowled: watchers, not threatening but comforting. It was like a hospital ward, and had the same sort of smell: stale cooked food and disinfectant. She clutched the flak-jacket to her bosom, and went back to sleep again.

Away to the south, beyond the Kremlin and the Moskva River, four vehicles arrived quietly at the back entrance to the British Embassy. Simon Morrell was awakened by the security guard and went down. The convoy's officer gave the British Army's Central Europe password for the night. Simon authorized admittance. There were thirty men – wearing uniform, but without badges or insignia. They parked their vehicles next to the kiddies' playground, on the grass tennis court used by the diplomats in winter for broom-polo. They unloaded their weapons and carried them into the embassy building.

Their weaponry included exotics: XM 203 'D' Armalites and Hecker Kock MP 6 submachine-guns, some of them still in their cardboard transit boxes. Not the sort of toys the Royal Mercians were given to play with.

Before he went back to his dossbag, he went to the embassy's 'telegraph office' and got the duty signaller to put through a call to ACE Rapid Reaction Force intelligence at Kaunas.

The latest word from Ukrainian intelligence – generally considered the most reliable – was that Second Army tanks had reached the bus depot at the northern end of Prospekt Mira.

Kate Delacroix awoke at eight o'clock. Around her the snakepit was stirring. Kotelnikov had reached Babushkin. Everybody knew it for a fact. Some Amsterdam boys, just arrived, claimed to have footage of Red tanks on Prospekt Mira, but nobody would believe that – not until the American press and information officer came out to the stairwell and shouted upwards: 'Ladies and Gentlemen. Second Army is moving faster than anticipated. A helicopter evacuation will begin at thirteen hundred hours.'

They grabbed Cokes and drank thirstily. They ate stale bread-rolls and peanut butter. Then they poured through the canteen's massive plateglass French windows, into the damp dawn light. Editing booths sprouted like mushrooms. In moments the grounds were dotted with engineers and reporters setting up lightweight ENG cameras, opening channels to the INTel and UTel satellites. Small black matt dishes were connected and aimed at the huge Bell Corporation leapfrog transceiver south of Moscow on the Sparrow Hills.

Kate had been working with a freelance Russian crew. She looked bitterly at what seemed to be hundreds of BBC engineers. Was there anybody *left* in England? Did they *have* to do Gardeners' World and The Clothes Programme from Moscow at a time like this?

She looked round for the EuroTV agent, but he was never there when he was wanted. She carried her transceiver to the gates by the ornamental railing, setting the mini-ENG so that the flagpole with the Stars and Stripes would be behind her.

Only a couple of years previously, a live satellite insert had needed a large van with special stabilizers, a bank of equipment, and two technical operators.

Now everything had changed. As long as she was within range of the Bell relay transponder, she could practically carry her equipment round in a briefcase.

She put on the bullet-proof vest given her by the marine, and checked her appearance in a small mirror.

Behind her was a red dawn. She wondered if she ought to talk about the new Red Dawn for Moscow.

Sam had once said 'Don't be *ornate*. Don't be clever. Just tell it straight.' But nobody ever made a name for themselves by being boring, and there was old Sam still toddling over to the BBC Pebble Mill bar every evening at five-thirty, his only claim to fame being that he was the man who discovered Kate Delacroix.

On the day she got the job at EuroTV, he'd said, 'So your big blue eyes bowled them over' – the bastard. As if she'd never won a Young TV Journalist of the Year award. 'Not so much my eyes; more my tits,' she had replied witheringly.

* * *

There was the whir of rotors. From inside the northern end of the Kremlin fortress a line of helicopters were rising like geese. They hovered, turned, and headed westwards towards St Petersburg.

Kate wondered if perhaps she ought to wave goodbye to the President. Nobody else was bothering, which seemed a shame.

She checked her satellite booking on her powerpad. 10.00 hours. If they airlifted out at 13.00, this would be her last chance to send a story. She felt irritable and tense. It wasn't going to make her famous, a piece to camera from an embassy compound.

Where were CNN? Tucked away in a Moscow suburb, by all accounts, with their cameras poised ready for action.

She called INMA, the International Marine Satellite used for telephone communications. She waited to be connected to the vision satellite operator. She waited some more, and shivered in the cold.

The operator came on. Kate said: 'Can I switch on?' and the operator said mechanically: 'Do you have permission of your host country?' and she said yes, she had, EuroTV to confirm, and she waited around some more until the blinking light on her monitor told her that her test pictures were going through to BBC Foreign News Traffic via SCAR, the Spur Central Apparatus Room. The BBC had the contract for EuroTV's Satellite Newsgathering Service.

'Katie! Katie!'

Russian faces were pressed against the gates, along the long wall, peering in through the ornate metal railing. It was Sergei. He was waving at her, jumping up and down, shouting over the sound of the helicopters and the babbling of a Japanese reporter.

'Hi, Sergei!' she shouted guiltily, her heart sinking because they weren't going to give him a place in the chopper, no way.

They stared at each other.

He waved again. His hand fell.

On a sudden thought, she ran towards him across the grass.

'Sergei?' she called. 'Sergei, can you take me to Red Square?'

What the hell, she'd be the last British reporter in democratic Moscow, or the first in the Kotelnikov terror.

THREE

'I'm going out. Nobody needs to worry about me, nobody needs to look after me,' she told the marine at the gate.

He replied, surprised: 'Nobody's going to.'

She ran across Tchaikovsky Street. Sergei's ancient Fiat was a time-warp, a car from a Sixties film, with brimming ashtrays, a colour transfer of a nude girl on the dashboard, and no seat belts.

She climbed into the back. 'All right, let's go!'

She had her transceiver dish, her mini-ENG, INMA phone and powerpack, which was enough for any girl who believed in travelling light.

Sergei was speaking as he drove, turning and waving his arms, imploring her to understand. He wanted money, coupons; he was going to his brother-in-law's family in Tula, but needed a hundred coupons for petrol.

'Red Square, Sergei,' she said.

No, he was saying, it was impossible. Since yesterday everything in Moscow had changed.

'Red Square, Sergei, then the coupons,' she said brutally, naively, for what was to stop him driving round the corner, stopping the car, and taking the money?

'*This is Risky City. Stay in the compound*,' an American security chief had warned, but to her Moscow was a second home, and Risky City just a place where a girl didn't walk alone through the subways after dark.

'Red Square. Then the coupons . . .'

They headed down Gruzinskaja, past the zoo. She'd stayed in a flat near here, in her year at Moscow State University. 'Krushchev flats,' Muscovites scornfully called the damp, crumbling apartment blocks put up in the Sixties – but there had been pink geraniums on the window, and she had inherited a cat, and it had been late spring, with powder-blue skies and blossom on the wild crab-apple trees, and she had been in love with a nice Moscow boy. In the afternoons, lying in bed, they had listened to the sound of the animals in the zoo, and the building work on the new American embassy residence block down the street. In the evenings they had gone and listened to nightingales in the birchwoods that ran down from the Sparrow Hills.

Sergei swore as a lorry blocked the way. She tapped her story into her autocue, the words coming smoothly, precisely. She pictured herself against St Basil's cathedral, with the government entrance to the Kremlin behind her, visible on camera.

The last German and French helicopters have taken off from the Kremlin helipad, from behind these walls, carrying the President and his cabinet to the doubtful safety of St Petersburg. They have left an eerie calm over the Kremlin, over the empty, desolate centre of government. Moscow is awaiting her new masters. Democracy has died. Five governments since Yeltsin, years of humiliation and privation at the command of Western banks – it's over, and the ordinary people of Moscow don't care a damn. The Army of Moscow might be at the gates, the profiteers might be fleeing in their BMWs and Mercs – as I speak, what's left of the Western press corps is being evacuated under the protection of American marines . . .

Get that last bit in, and shaft the opposition – what an operator. She looked at her watch, she had lost her INTel booking, she would have to send it by North Star, expensive but nobody would query a satellite charge, not on a story like this.

The car was stopping. Sergei was shouting. The way forward was blocked by army lorries: Federal troops establishing a cordon.

'Go another way,' she said. 'Please, *please* . . .'

'OK, OK.'

He spun the wheel, then they were jolting through back streets. They passed a line of Volkswagens and Moskviches, nose to nose, filled with families staring out, some resentfully, others in fear. There was an obstruction, a portable brothel. Dozens of them had sprung up to serve the tent cities of the suburbs. The cheapest prostitutes in town, they said at the International Press Club – if you fancied sex on the back seat of a Lada with the windows blacked out.

The vehicle, with its crudely-daubed pink heart, had once been a wedding hire limo. The two intertwined gold rings, traditional on Moscow wedding cars, were still on the roof ('Some call them wedding rings,' her girlfriend Svetlana had said laconically, 'and some call them chains'). It was blocking half the narrow alley, but nobody felt inclined to interfere. Two pimps sat on the bonnet, bouncing gently, nursing Kalashnikovs.

They edged past. She saw some Azeris on a corner, nervously guarding the edge of their patch. The various mobs held wedge-shaped territories pointing towards the city centre, so that each group had a slice of the Western hotels, a slice of the hard-currency tourist action. The mobs also specialized in types of trade: Azeris sold flowers and drugs, Georgians ran the prostitutes, Chechens stole cars. The London-based Criminal Intelligence Unit had described the Moscow mobs as being low on sophistication but high on cunning: great believers in the purity of violence.

Azeris, Georgians, Chechens – they were all southerners, or from east of the Urals, all hated by Muscovites. *Kosoglazyi* – slant eyes – the Muscovites called them , or *zheltoe gavno* – yellow shit.

The car spun round a corner.

They were now behind the Hotel Pekin. If they could get on to Tverskaja, they'd be clear straight down to the Kremlin.

'Great, Sergei, great!' she shouted.

He turned briefly and grinned, caught up in the excitement, forgetting his family, extravagantly using up the petrol that would get him part way, at least, to Tula.

They shot out into Majakovskaja Square. He spun the wheel and revved, and mounted the pavement to avoid an abandoned tramcar. Then they were heading down Tverskaja, weaving between the cars and the burnt-out trams, crossing the pedestrianized area by the Ring of Gardens – a twenty-thousand rouble fine, she shouted; that's what *that* offence would have cost him in happier times! – and then he slammed the brakes on. She grabbed hold of the seat-back to keep her balance and swore as her camera clattered to the floor.

Another roadblock.

She said: 'Offer them money. Say we have to go through.'

Sergei was sitting, not moving. Men were surrounding the car.

She got out. 'I'm a television reporter,' she said, pushing through them, pushing them out of the way.

She climbed on to an ornamental concrete flower-tub, the survivor of some mid-Nineties urban-renewal programme. From here she could see down Tverskaja, down the long boulevard: the old, elegant czarist road to St Petersburg.

At its end, in the smoky-red March morning, she could see the Hotel Moskva and the Kremlin walls, and the cross glinting on the golden dome of the Cathedral of the Annunciation.

People were milling around the road block. Fires had been lit during the night. Small groups of people were gathered round them and staring dreamily into the smouldering embers. As always, there were people selling bottles of home-brew vodka.

The Metro was closed. People crossed to the Majakovskaja subway entrance, then turned back, confused: like ants distracted from their preordained journeys.

There was a shout of excitement. People were pointing down the hill. At the bottom of Tverskaja, next to the Hotel Moskva, an armoured personnel carrier had appeared, and was slowly manoeuvring.

Second Shock Army? Or Federal troops?

The APC stopped, its machine-gun pointing not up to Tverskaja, but down Ogareva, the broad boulevard that ran by the Kremlin, towards the tomb of the Unknown Soldier.

She jumped down, and pushed her way back to the car. The men surrounding it were Yakutis, the last regiments of the old Soviet empire, lingering on in the capital for a decade because nobody could afford to pay their back wages and send them home.

'OK, Sergei. We'll do it from here.'

She reached into the car for her power-pad and INMA phone.

'Oh my God,' said Sergei, still frozen at the wheel.

'Come on,' she said. 'You're the fixer. The best fixer in town, remember?'

'Oh my God,' he repeated.

'Fix them, Sergei. The ciggies are in my bag.'

She stood with her back against the car and dialled. Sergei climbed slowly out. He talked to the men on the roadblock, gave them his usual spiel, his usual routine, made them laugh – *Crazy English girl, what can you do, she needs a good Cossack husband to take the strap to her.*

He gave them three packs of Marlboro. They offered him vodka.

She was through to the Television Centre, to Foreign News Traffic at the Spur.

'Kate Delacroix, EuroTV . . .'

She told them to book access to the North Star transponder. Had she been a BBC correspondent they would have queried the authorization, but she was a client, so there was no problem.

Twenty minutes passed. Engineers at North Star would be talking to engineers at ICR, the BBC's International Control Room. There was nothing speedy about setting up a live satellite broadcast. It normally took an hour, they reckoned, to set up a channel. She had told them this was urgent news priority from a battle zone.

Some of the Yakutis tired of their roadblock and went over to the hard-currency groceries-by-order shop on the corner of Kozickij. They smashed in the windows. A few minutes later they emerged with vodka and packets of biscuits.

Not very bright, these Yakutis, thought Kate. They should have thought of doing that before now.

Another ten minutes went by. She put on the American marine's green bulletproof vest. Sergei rootled in the car for a pack of Marlboro he'd stolen from her bag two days ago, and lit a cigarette. He inhaled nervously.

She said: 'Do the car, Sergei.'

He went round the vehicle, and stabilized it with the bricks he carried for the purpose. He linked the ENG camera to the dish. The tiny red pulse showed that the huge transceiver on the hill by the university was relaying the signal.

'Can we switch on?' she asked North Star.

The operator asked if she had permission, from the host country, to broadcast. She told the operator, sweetly, that permission from the host country would come retrospectively. She wanted to scream: 'Who do I ask for permission. Don't you know there's a civil war on?' But screaming never did any good; it only made them slow and bad-tempered.

Colour bars came up. They would use BBC World Service TV to give a cue.

The Yakutis were throwing empty vodka bottles at a Mercedes truck that was forcing its way through their roadblock.

'Katie,' said Sergei, 'you have got to hurry. You have got to hurry . . .'

She nodded.

'Hurry, hurry,' said Sergei.

He didn't like Yakutis, but who did? Officially attached to the anti-mafia paramilitaries, they scandalized Muscovites by using their patrol vehicles like dodgems and shooting the rocket launchers like fireworks.

A truck had pulled up against the Pizza Hut. Two men were standing on the back, holding on to the roof, waving guns.

'Oh my God,' said Sergei . . .

They were Chechens.

'We have got to get away from here—'

'London's coming through—'

'Now. *Now*! You don't understand—'

'Stay by the camera, keep it steady, give me the cue, and watch the background.'

A Chechen was waving a Makarov pistol and shouting: 'Twenty coupons!'

Thirty American dollars. Two days ago the price of a Makarov pistol had been fifty dollars, a Kalashnikov automatic twenty-five dollars – and if you bought ten, you got an extra one thrown in. For six hundred dollars in the Arbat, an impressed Canadian reporter had told her, you could buy a grenade-launcher with night-vision sights.

What would it cost now? Half that, by the sound of things.

A voice said: '*Intake.*'

Thank Christ!

'This is Kate Delacroix in Moscow.'

'*What time are you booked for, Kate*?'

'Put me straight through, you stupid git.'

A second later the studio director of the 24-hour roll-over bulletin said: '*Kate, where the hell have you been*?'

'I'm on Tverskaja Boulevard looking at the Kremlin. I'm the last British reporter in Moscow. I've asked for clean feed into the programme. Just take me, OK?'

Shots rang out. Her head whipped round, blood pounding suddenly through her brain. Yakutis were firing in the air with automatic rifles. The crowds suddenly cleared. She could see down the hill. She could see the APC by the Hotel Moskva revving and backing, turning to face up Tverskaja.

'*Hold on*,' said the studio director. '*John's coming.*'

'I can't hold on—'

The Yakutis were manhandling a car, trying apparently to strengthen their roadblock.

She turned back to face the camera. Sergei was staring at her, petrified, one hand on the ENG which was attached to the roof of the car, the other gripping her autocue.

In London they would all be watching and listening – the engineers in the International Control Room, in Foreign News Traffic, in the studio gallery.

'*Kate*?' It was the senior editor. '*Why aren't you at the embassy*?'

'Will you take my piece, for fuck's sake? Are you going to wait till I'm run over by a tank?'

She was almost weeping.

'*We're putting you on live.*'

A single pistol shot rang out behind her. Sergei was shouting, but she had her earpiece in one ear and her hand over the other. Another pistol shot; she heard a man cry out.

Sergei had left the camera, and was running towards her. He pulled her hand away from her head and shouted: 'We've got to go, we've got to go—'

She pulled herself away. 'I'm on air, you stupid bloody—'

A PA's voice, bored, thinking about shopping at Tesco: '*Kate Delacroix on four, caption on one. Kate Delacroix in five from now, five, four, three . . .*' And, more distant than the PA, the voice of the studio presenter '*Live from Moscow, Kate Delacroix . . .*' and the director, '*You're on,*' and the PA's '*Forty-eight seconds to the break.*' Forty-eight seconds, Jesus! A stupid bastard was sitting on her autocue, sobbing. Blood was running down his face from a gash across his forehead. If he would get up from the autocue box she might be able to angle him into the camera.

'All hell's let loose,' she said, speaking too quickly. 'Western agencies have all pulled out. Reporters are at the American embassy. I think the Kremlin itself has fallen. I don't know, but I saw a tank or a troop transporter. I believe Red Forces are in the Kremlin. Behind me you can see—' A million viewers saw the Chechen coming up behind her, saw Sergei try to stop him, and fall clutching his stomach.

'*Kate, look behind you,*' said the director's voice in her ear, and then the PA, '*Fourteen seconds to the break*', and the director's tense '*Go back to Tom*', as the satellite dish was pulled away from the car and her earplug went dead, and she hit out with all her might at the face coming down at hers, and screamed as her hair was pulled back with a pain she would not have believed possible.

FOUR

At school she had once played Montrose, the tragic marquis. 'He either fears his fate too much, Or his deserts are small . . .' she had declaimed bravely, a tartan plaid over her shoulders, a spotlight on her red-gold hair, 'Who will not put it to the touch, To win or lose it all.'

Cheers. Bully for Montrose.

What happened to Montrose?

He was hanged.

She was in the shelter of a shop doorway, lying on broken glass, her head bleeding from where she had hit the cobblestones, her arm stiff, her scalp throbbing.

Some old women had saved her. *Babushkas*, Moscow matrons, stout and respectable in their black woollen coats. They had shouted and pushed the Chechens, and the Chechens, who had a sentimental streak and came from a society that revered the family, had retreated.

It had been her bullet-proof jacket they wanted: her US marine jacket.

With luck the sod who stole it would be shot through by a 16mm cannon.

The babushkas had pulled and carried her round a corner. They had shouted at her, and poked her until she crawled into the doorway.

'All right, all right. I'm hurt. Can't you see I'm hurt . . . ?' she had wept.

They had scolded her, then left her.

There she lay, pulling her brain together, puzzling out a logic from what had happened, thinking back to the split second when the rules of normal life had ceased to apply.

There had been a moment when you did not grab somebody's belongings, or hit them, or rape them. At that point there had been chaos, but a sort of *ordered* chaos, a chaos which still acknowledged certain basic rules of human behaviour, when she could walk through a crowd of Yakutis, knowing, if she thought about it, that they would all *like* to tear her clothes off and rape her, but confident that it would not happen . . .

A moment later, the conventions had disappeared. Anarchy had taken over.

She had to get up. If she got up, she would not be defenceless. If she got up, she would be Kate Delacroix, a Western television reporter, and the shattered conventions would reassert themselves and people would spit and shove perhaps, and call her an *Amerikantsy* whore, but they'd move out of her way. They wouldn't take her on.

Sergei?

She got to her feet. She swayed for a moment, then she left the doorway and turned back along the pavement towards Tverskaja. Then she stopped, her heart thumping, her legs refused to move.

She couldn't do it. She couldn't go back.

'Bastards!' she yelled in English. She stumbled forward quickly, and rounded the corner of Tverskaja.

The Chechens were gone. Sergei's Fiat had been pushed over on its side to form part of the roadblock. There was no sign of Sergei. The Yakutis were standing round a fire. They had piled it high with cardboard packaging from the shop they had looted. They looked up at her when she called out.

She demanded to know where Sergei was. They ignored her. She screamed at them, called them *chernozhopi* – black arses. They shouted angrily back: told her to go away before she got hurt. She leaned against the wall and sobbed.

Where was Sergei? Where had he gone to?

After a few seconds she turned and walked towards Majakovskaja Square and the Pekin Hotel. A gang of youths came running towards her. She flinched back, but was too slow and was knocked to the ground. Someone was grabbing at her, hands prying for money, seeking a purse. She clawed at them with sudden fury, and they let go, and she pulled herself against the wall of a building.

It wasn't supposed to happen like this. It was going on for too long, the punishment was too great. OK, I was a stupid bitch, but I've learned my lesson, she cried silently. No more! I don't need any more.

She climbed slowly to her feet.

The Pekin's plateglass doors were smashed. The crew-cut mafiosi guards who stopped unauthorized whores from entering had vanished. The hotel entrance was a dark, open hole. The neon sign for the casino bar was unlit. Somebody was lying on the pavement in the entrance, his limbs twitching spasmodically. She watched for a moment, fascinated and horrified, then turned away.

She found and tried a dozen telephone kiosks. They were all smashed or dead.

She saw a helicopter – perhaps an evacuation helicopter from the American embassy – its lights winking, and she cried, snuffling with self-pity.

As darkness fell, the early dusk of March in Moscow, she found herself again on Tverskaja. She crossed the boulevard and stumbled round a corner, away from the crowds that were coming out on the streets with nightfall. She was in Dolgoruki Square. She could see the statue of Yuri of the Long Arms, Yuri the 'Landgrabber', the warrior chief who had founded the city of Moscow back in the twelfth century.

There was a restaurant here: the Aragvi. She had been here two nights ago with Selsdon of the BBC and Finkel of the *Sun*. The Aragvi had been Stalin's favourite restaurant. The three of them had raised a toast to him: Uncle Joe, the old devil who was being reborn. They had dined on borscht, and venison roast with juniper berries, and puffy warm bread and caviar, and 'rost duck mit garnishe', and plums in brandy. Georgians had played gypsy music. Art had insisted on paying by credit card, even though they pleaded for coupons or dollars. 'I don't have any dollars,' he had said smugly, waving his Amex card, pointing to the notice that said it was welcome. They had taken his card and gone through the ritual, but everybody knew there would be no time to get the money from American Express, not before Kotelnikov conquered Moscow.

To carry an American Express card when that happened, it was said, would be a bit like carrying your own death warrant.

The restaurant was closed, its windows shuttered.

She felt dizzy and thirsty. She was bleeding from the cut on her head. She collapsed wearily in the doorway of the restaurant. She wasn't even sure what time it was, but she guessed around five o'clock. The air was full of acrid smoke.

'At least I haven't been raped,' she said out loud. Then, being a practical girl, a realist, she added to herself: 'Not yet.'

FIVE

British Embassy, Moscow, afternoon of 18 March

'Follow us as soon after 17.00 as you can. I don't like splitting up, but they want the diplomats out of the city before nightfall. You should be all right. The freeway's clear west of Govorovo.'

'Yes,' said Simon, who had also listened to FM Radio Maximum's traffic report.

They were on the front step of the embassy, under the egg-yolk and white plaster of the portico, in the spot where the ambassador stood when he welcomed guests to the Queen's birthday party.

Innes-Chator was muffled in his combat parka. He looking out bleakly over the small formal square garden with its flowerbed and flagstaff, over the wrought-iron railings to the Maurice Thorez Embankment.

In the gloom, two soldiers were lowering the Union flag, catching it carefully so that it did not touch the ground, so that it could not be said to have been lowered in defeat.

Colour-Sergeant Gough stood watching, eagle-eyed.

'All right, lads, roll it up. Careful now . . .'

'Have a good journey,' said Simon graciously.

'For Christ's sake, Simon,' said Innes-Chator, whose temper was at breaking point.

'Sorry.'

'You're to follow us at 17.30 at the latest. You've got that in writing.'

'Yes.'

The French and Germans had already airlifted their staff out of Moscow. The British ambassador had refused to abandon the embassy Rolls Royce and the Range Rovers. 'First in, last out,' she had said vigorously, virtually ordering the Canadians to pull out before she did. The English, she claimed, had established their Moscow embassy in the time of Ivan the Terrible, before any other Western nation, in a house just off Red Square that was still called the English Inn.

'Really, ma'am?' Innes-Chator had said, pretending amazement, totally intimidated.

The convoy was ready. Innes-Chator would escort it out through Govorovo, down the M12 motorway and across the Dnepr.

'You realize that's the way Bonaparte went?' said Simon. 'I've often thought it would be fun to follow the route. In the summer, with an open-topped car, a pretty girl, and a case of iced Chardonnay.'

'Yes,' said Innes-Chator. 'Very tempting.'

A diplomat came out and said: 'Flag down? Bugger Kotelnikov. Bugger him to hell and damnation. It took me two years to negotiate the Moscow telecom contract for BT. Remember to turn the generator off, won't you?'

Simon was surprised. He had assumed that the remaining diplomats were intelligence agents. If so, this one was carrying his subterfuge to extremes.

'I'd like to move off if you're ready,' said Innes-Chator. He looked up at the sky as if he feared Kotelnikov's gunships might arrive at any moment.

'We're all in the vehicles,' said the diplomat. 'HE's on her way out to the courtyard now.'

He shivered and looked round the garden. It was bedraggled after the winter, with yellow grass and glistening wet flower-beds. 'It's the local staff I feel sorry for. The poor sods from secretariat and immigration.'

He went back inside.

Innes-Chator said: 'Right, then.'

'Yes.'

Would Innes-Chator implore Simon, as a final valediction, to get a grip?

They walked round the back, to the compound. Innes-Chator indicated upwards, to where a light was shining on the fourth floor. 'When you're through, clear that lot out from up there. Then lock up, and don't hang about.'

Simon said: 'Don't worry about us.'

Innes-Chator looked as if he was going to worry quite a lot. He swung up into the cab of the leading Centaur armoured vehicle. He looked down on Simon and hesitated.

This was it . . .

He leaned down. He said, with the confidential leer he might employ to tell a dirty story, 'By the way, I heard several of our chaps got the old redundancy bullet yesterday.'

'Yes,' said Simon. 'I was one of them.'

It had come in the brown envelope pinned to the noticeboard, next to Flopsie Bunny's cardboard carrot.

'Sorry to hear it,' said Innes-Chator, not trying to sound surprised.

Two soldiers opened the compound gates. The convoy – three Range Rovers, the Rolls, and two Centaurs with machine-gunners muffled against the wind – turned out into the dusk. If he was in a film, Simon thought, he would salute. He stood and watched with his hands in his pockets. The gates swung closed again.

The coat of arms had been taken down, but the visitors' book still lay on the small writing desk. Who was supposed to sign it next – Kotelnikov? Or some drunk trooper from Second Army?

Simon stood for a moment, enjoying the silence.

A shadow appeared on the cream-painted wall above the panelling.

Simon said: 'I thought they'd never go. How about tea and toast in the ambassador's study?'

Clive was coming down the ornate stairs. He smiled mechanically.

They stood and looked round the hall, at the English country-house oak panels, the gleaming brass light fittings, the rich red carpet. There was a faint, dusty outline where the royal coat-of-arms had been taken down. Simon thought the place looked better without it. It had always reminded him of the logo of a Forte heritage hotel.

'We won't come back,' said Clive, apparently moved. 'Not here. We won't see anything like this again. We're finished; we might as well stop pretending. We'll be a department in some Euro-embassy next time. They've been talking about it for years.'

'I don't think Nelson would like being in a Euro-embassy.'

'You're bloody right, he wouldn't.'

Nelson had been booked into the American cattery for six weeks. Simon suspected he would be reinvented as a marmalade muff by the weekend, but he had said encouragingly: 'Holiday time, Nelson. See you soon, old chap.'

Clive said: 'What do we do about that lot in the Secure Room?'

'No idea. Come on, let's get on with shutting down.'

It was a bit like making a final check through a house you were selling, but in this case there were no polite notes to leave for the new owners, no helpful hints about milk deliveries and window-cleaning.

That afternoon the Apple-Macintosh had turned out fifty notices: '*BRITISH EMBASSY. Entry forbidden by order of Her Britannic Majesty's Secretary of State for Foreign Affairs*', in English and in Russian. The Royal Mercians had stuck them on boards round the perimeter. The notices might, it was thought, survive for a week or two. The Russians could not sell them, or eat them, although they could of course burn them. A further fifty notices were run off and stuck to the walls.

They went from room to room, turning the lights out, locking doors. The Intelligence Section was already locked. The ciphers and coding machines had been quietly shipped out a week back, at the same time that the Foreign Secretary was assuring the House of Commons that Her Majesty's Government had full confidence in the Russian government's ability to survive, and in the Russian army's loyalty to democracy.

They ended up in what an Edwardian brass plate indicated was the *Telegraph Office*. The signaller, Beddoes, already had his parka on, his kitpack on the table by him, and was putting down the phone as they entered.

'It's PUFO, sir. That was the Yanks letting us know they're scarpering.'

PUFO – the soldier's signal: Pack Up and Fuck Off.

'Get me Kaunas, the adjutant,' said Simon.

Beddoes called up the battalion HQ at Kaunas, was put through to the orderly room, asked for the adjutant, then said: 'He's not available and Mr Pendred's gone for tea, sir.'

Simon took the phone.

'Lieutenant Morrell here. Get Mr Pendred for me.'

Jamie Pendred was the senior subaltern. Two minutes passed.

'Jamie, it's Simon.'

'Where are you?'

'Moscow.'

'Still? I've got you down for duty tomorrow.'

'I'm still at the embassy. I was told to evacuate by 17.30, and it's that now.'

'Better get a move on, in that case.'

'Look, I've got some SAS in the Secure Room.'

'Oh?'

'You don't know what they're doing here, do you?'

'Haven't a clue. They're nothing to do with us. You haven't met a bird called Kate Delacroix, by any chance? A reporter for EuroTV?'

'I saw her yesterday. She went to the Americans.'

'She popped up somewhere near the Kremlin and tried to send a story to London. People are worried about her.'

'She isn't here. What do I do about the SAS?'

'Any silver they could pinch, anything in the way of fine old wines that we could be held accountable for?'

Ever since Waterloo the battalion had been sensitive about charges of looting.

'No. Anyway, the Reds are hardly likely to complain.'

'In that case leave them to it, I should. You could try raising Innes-Chator. He's still technically in command I suppose.'

Simon said: 'Kate Delacroix – what's going to happen to her?'

'Christ knows, unless she can get back to the Americans. You know the Reds are in Perovo?'

'So everybody keeps telling me.'

'We're all watching it in the mess. If I were you, I'd get moving.'

'Thanks, Jamie.'

'Keep your head down and have a good journey. Oh, by the way, I suppose you've heard about the redundancies . . . ?'

'The letter came yesterday.'

'Oh, right.'

A slight pause.

Jamie said: 'It's a bastard. We'll talk when you get back.'

Simon said; 'Yes, see you, Jamie.'

He put the phone down. 'OK, Beddoes. Close down and get out to the truck.'

He said to Clive: 'I'll go up and talk to them.'

He went out into the corridor. 'Colour-Sarn't!'

'Sir!'

'Ready to move in five minutes.'

* * *

He went back up to the second floor, past Chancellery, through the library, into the ambassador's private rooms. Two soldiers were using the ambassador's desk to service a GPMG, setting the gun's gas regulator and the recoil buffer. A private was standing outside the Secure Room. He watched, alert but expressionless, as Simon approached.

'I want to speak to your boss.'

The soldier hesitated, then said 'Hang on,' and opened the door. Simon heard a voice saying, 'D force RV 2330.' The door closed. A few moments later a major came out.

'Yes?'

This was Langdon. Simon had met him the previous night, when the SAS mob had rolled in.

'We're off. No point getting caught in the rush-hour.'

Langdon looked at him blankly. This, of course, was why Simon's colonel had never taken him on one side and suggested he might like to 'go down to Hereford for a look round'.

SAS humour, if it existed at all, consisted in chopping the balls of Chinamen in the Malaysian jungles.

'Perhaps,' Simon added, 'you wouldn't mind turning the generator off and locking up?'

Langdon said: 'Aren't you leaving anyone here?'

'Not unless you're offering to take them along with you.'

That was an engaging prospect. He could sweep up a dozen old lags and send them into action with the SAS.

'No,' said Langdon, and, yes, this idea apparently amused him, judging by the way his lips were twitching. 'OK, you can go.'

Simon hadn't actually been asking for permission. 'Don't worry,' he said, 'about putting the cat out.'

Langdon went back into the Secure Room. Simon went back down the stairs. Beddoes, still in the Telegraph Office and looking fretful, said: 'There's been two more calls about the TV tart, sir, and this looks like another one.'

The phone had started blinking. Simon picked it up.

'D Company Royal Mercs. Morrell here.'

It was the adjutant. He said: 'I was hoping you'd gone. This girl Delacroix – all hell's been let loose. She's hurt and holed up somewhere near Majakovskaja Metro. Now, listen, there's absolutely no possible way you can exit Moscow via Tverskaja. You are now confirming that to me, and I'm confirming it to Brigade. All possibilities have been explored and regretfully ruled out. OK? Get a move on then, Simon. We've had some ScanSat pictures, and the M12 is clogging up.'

'I could take a section over there on foot.'

'No, you bloody couldn't.'

'It's only just across the bridge.'

'Simon, Second Army is at Perovo. Get moving. Get on the motorway, and don't stop.'

The line went dead.

Simon stood in thought. Beddoes said: 'Can I shut down, then, sir?'

'Yes, shut down and get to the truck.'

Colour-Sergeant Gough said, 'All clear, then, sir?'

Beddoes was quietly calling his opposite number in Kaunas, giving the embassy communications code.

'No,' said Simon. 'I'm going to have another word with the blokes upstairs.'

This time Langdon showed no sign of humour. 'What do you think we're doing here, laddie? Second Army are at Perovo, I'm up to my ears in shit, and you want me to send – look, get your men out. Go where you're supposed to go. Do not, for fuck's sake, bother me again.'

Clive and Gough found Simon, his face flushed, at the window of the ambassador's study, looking out across the Moscow River to the long line of the Kremlin Palace, the spires of the Cathedral of the Assumption.

Gough said: 'Men are in the trucks, sir.'

Beyond the bridge leading up to St Basil's there was an explosion: a crack of light, a burst of small-arms fire. A car skidded into the embankment, its headlights pointing wildly up into the air.

The city was almost in darkness, a deep gloom picked out by dim, dangerous lights.

Gangs were on the loose: rats up from the sewers of Moscow.

'The twilight administration', the British ambassador had called it – briefly in power before Kotelnikov would send it back down to the sewers again.

An English girl was out there somewhere in the dark, stumbling about, terrified, lost.

What the hell had he joined the army for?

'Colour-Sar'nt Gough,' he said, embarrassed by his patriotism, selfconsciously aware of the heroic stance he was taking, but not knowing what else to say. 'I want half-a-dozen volunteers.'

They lined up in the dark shadows, under the embassy wall. Each man had his Bergen on his back, with his dossbag tied to the top and his bumroll in its waterproof case. Mess tins – stuffed, in most cases, with spare pairs of socks – were slung from webbing, as were ammunition pouches and kidney pouches. Black water-bottles were hung from belts. Each man had a rifle, the British Army regulation SA80, with two hundred rounds of ammo. Lance-Corporal Gates, with the 7.62mm light machine-gun, was in the centre; Colour-Sergeant Gough was bringing up the rear.

A row of steady eyes gleamed in the darkness. The entire platoon had volunteered: fired possibly by the chivalrous desire to rescue an English lass in distress, or possibly by the fear of being left out of a bit of excitement.

In the end, he had selected Colour-Sergeant Gough, Corporal

Pullin, and eight men. Scanning them, he now looked doubtfully at Chaffinch, who was not as intelligent as he might have been; at Ferneyhough who was only a lad; and at Mace who was evil and who, he suspected, rather wanted to shoot someone.

'The trucks go in exactly one minute. Anybody want to change his mind?'

The two Bedfords were waiting in the rear compound, their convoy lights on, their engines running. Soldiers would be sitting there, hunched in their parkas, lost in their private thoughts in the way that soldiers, accustomed to interminable delays, were used to losing themselves: dreaming impossible dreams of gorgeous women, of inheriting a pub, of Wolves winning the Premier League.

Mace said: 'Can't let you go wandering off on your own, sir.'

Corporal Pullin said: 'Shut it, Mace.'

'All right, let's go,' said Simon.

SIX

She was cold, she was sick with cold, but it was her brain that was wrong somehow – fragmented, incapable of decision. She ought to be moving, getting to her feet, making her way through the darkness, using the cloak of night to reach safety.

Beyond the cold, shallow refuge of the Aragvi restaurant's entrance, beyond the square, she could see fires burning on Tverskaja.

She wondered where CNN was holed up. She tried to remember which of the embassies had declared for Kotelnikov. The North Koreans, Iran . . . The French were supposed to have done a deal. That had been the rumour. The bloody French had a *secret pact.* It had been the scandal of forty-eight hours ago – the start of the latest great Euro-row, with the French counter-attacking, bitterly accusing the Americans and the Brits of mounting a joint evacuation, the old Anglo-Saxons ganging up to save themselves.

Sod the French. She didn't even know where their embassy was.

She tried to think of Russians who could help her, but it had been three years and a hell of a lot of blood had since flowed under the bridges, and the two boys she could have turned to were far way – one with the naval nuclear decommissioning programme in Murmansk, the other at the United Nations in New York. She had lost track of Svetlana, her Russian girl friend, more than a year ago. She assumed she was back in Kuybyshev.

A sudden rattle of gunfire made her shrink back. For a moment there was silence, the murmuring complaints of the refugees was stilled. Ears listened in the darkness.

Nothing . . .

The murmuring started up again.

Here, there was an illusion of safety. The refugees were huddled in doorways, occasionally passing bottles of what she imagined was vodka.

She was offered a swig – and enjoyed her first taste of aircraft brake fluid.

This is Kate Delacroix, at the fall of Moscow.

A girl crawled into the doorway beside her. 'My boyfriend's a fighter pilot in Siberia. I worry. Oh God, I worry. Where's your boyfriend? Are you alone?'

After a while the girl crawled away. The square quietened. Kate dozed – and woke stiff and shivering, and feeling terribly sick.

A sudden thought: perhaps the phone kiosk in the square was still in working order!

She knew it was hopeless – but she had a wild hope, a surge of energy. She crept out from the restaurant doorway, leaving her cold little space, and ventured out over the cobbles. In the sky to the north-east there was a dull red glow. Against it the tall houses were silhouetted like a fairytale outline. Any moment now, she thought hysterically, Mary Poppins would twinkle over those rooftops on a broomstick, over the statue of Yuri the Landgrabber.

She stumbled over something, and a woman yelled. Kate yelled back in sudden rage.

On the far side of the square she found the kiosk.

Its glass was shattered, but the handset was connected and there was a dialling tone. She listened for a moment, stunned, then dialled the Foreign Press Club, the only number she could remember. She wept with relief as the number rang out. A recorded voice said: '*Your call is being rerouted.*' An American voice said: '*United States Embassy.*'

Oh Christ, she had no coins. She broke down and sobbed. The voice said: 'OK, take it easy.'

Then she remembered telephone calls were free. Hyperinflation had long since made it pointless to collect the money.

She told him who she was. 'For God's sake,' she said, '*help me.*'

The embassy had officially closed down three hours ago. Second Army was in Perovo. He would tell the British authorities where she was, he said in the voice of a man offering to inform her next of kin.

What should she do?

Stay there, he advised, already distracted by somebody in the background. Wait for the daylight. Try to get a Russian family to give her shelter.

Where were the CNN crew? Wait. Please don't ring off . . .

CNN, he informed her, had pulled out at 15.00.

She went back to the Aragvi restaurant, the bleak doorway that was already a sort of home. Somebody else had moved in, but when she spoke sharply in English they moved away.

She curled up, her hands between her knees. She thought about Sergei and wept hot tears at her own stupidity, her criminal arrogance. Time passed.

She was recording a piece to camera. Her piece on the fall of Moscow.

'In truth, Moscow fell a decade ago,' she was saying, her eyes looking through the transparent autocue into the camera lens, into four million homes in Britain and Holland.

'It fell when it became the "Wacky City", and had two English-language television channels, and two English-language newspapers, and announced its first Russian "dollar millionaire's club", and there were advertisements for 4x4s at the Moscow "Off-road" Centre, and the Marko Polo Hotel opened its "Speakeasy" . . .

'It fell when the mafia took over the taxis, and the railways, and the prostitutes. When the new-rich played the casinos and bought live lobsters and swordfish steaks from the Moscow Lobster and Fish Company.

'When the police made extra cash by giving tourists taxi rides on their

way to the scene of a crime, and the soldiers sold their guns on the street corners.

'*When corruption became so refined, so sophisticated, that five billion dollars of hard currency* vanished *from the Moscow State Bank in one year alone.*

'*And when the Muscovites who did not manage to get their snouts into the dollar trough stood in the streets, in their thousands, selling their possessions, their ornaments, anything they owned, for a few apples, a few rotten potatoes – or went to the soupkitchen run by the American* Moscow Times.

'*The fall of Moscow.*

'*I can date for you the fall of Moscow.*

'*The victors placed banners around the city, in illuminated glass cases, lighting up the night. There were three of them close to Red Square itself, one by St Basil's Cathedral.*

'*Each case had the same illustration: a black-and-white picture of a man and a woman. And the words:*

OBSESSION
By Calvin Klein

'*Few Muscovites understood this at first. They thought the signs had been placed by the city council, and bitterly condemned the expense.*'

'She's here, sir. I think she's asleep.' A thin slit of light from a torch.

A voice, faintly familiar: 'Miss Delacroix?'

She could not speak.

'Colour-Sar'nt Gough!'

'Sir?'

'Who's in charge of first aid?'

'Mace is down for it, sir. His sister's husband's a vet in Sunderland.'

'Post a sentry on the corner of Tverskaja, and check on the other exits.'

'Sir.'

Gently now: 'Miss Delacroix?'

A jacket, still warm, was round her shoulders. Tea from a flask. It was all going to be all right after all.

SEVEN

'I'm through, sir,' said the soldier.

The officer who had given Kate his jacket stood up and took the phone and said crisply: 'Morrell.'

She heard a voice reply, distantly: 'Yes?'

'We've found her. We're taking her to the RV.'

'Roger.'

He gave the handset back to the soldier and squatted down next to her again.

'Miss Delacroix? I'm afraid we've got to get moving.'

'I'll be all right. Don't worry about me,' she said, shivering uncontrollably. 'I'll be fine.'

'Here, have some more tea.'

She gulped it down.

Two Russian women, babushkas, were pointing at the radio and mumbling in soft, Slavonic voices. The sergeant said: 'Now come on, mother, off you go.' The girl with the pilot boyfriend had come back. She was talking earnestly to one of the soldiers, while his mates stood and watched and grinned.

The officer, crouching beside Kate, said: 'So we meet again.'

'Yes,' she said vaguely.

She had seen him before, recently, but such was the confusion in her mind that she could not remember where. In the dim torchlight she saw a thin face. Intelligent, young-looking.

'Sure you're OK?'

She nodded.

A soldier came up. 'The road's clear, sir.'

'Right, let's go.'

The girl with the pilot boyfriend in Siberia said quietly: 'Yea, let's move. Let's get out of here.'

A soldier said, 'Not you, love.'

They helped Kate to her feet. They left the square, their feet echoing on the cobbles round Yuri of the Long Arms. In the darkness they filed up Tverskaja and crossed Majakovskaja Square. A crowd was gathered in front of the Hotel Pekin. They were waving burning torches and shouting. Kate turned in sudden panic and found herself pressed against the young officer.

'It's all right. It's all right . . .'

He put his arm around her.

She said: 'I'm sorry. I'm OK, really.'

She pulled back, pulled herself together. The crowd was drunk.

Everybody in Moscow was drunk. This lot, unbelievably, were having a party. There were bursts of music from Korean battery CDs, the essential designer accessory of every Muscovite.

'OK, let's keep moving. Keep on this side of the square. Keep in the shadows.'

On the dark side of Majakovskaja, a group of youths were selling old razor blades, discarded syringes, small pieces of tinfoil. (She'd done a story, once, on the Birmingham drug scene. The joke there had been that the junkies bought Kit-Kat bars and threw away the chocolate.) Somebody offered her a plastic bottle, already punctured for smoking crack, and asked for a hundred coupons.

A soldier pushed the man back. 'Not tonight, thanks.'

They had to step over a man using a piece of rope for a tourniquet, while he slowly injected himself.

The sergeant in front of her stopped suddenly.

'Sir . . .'

A gang of youths had appeared from behind the metro. They stood in the flickering light of the torches. Lean, clean-shaven faces and cropped hair.

Then they charged silently towards the crowd.

'Lyuberi,' said a voice. It was the girl from the square, who had followed them in the darkness.

Lyuberi – thugs named after the district of Moscow where they had first sprung up. Moral vigilantes wiping out the decadent Western youth of the capital. Kotelnikov's fifth column, if he needed one.

There were screams of panic. The thugs were among the crowd, wielding batons.

The small group moved quickly away from the square, along the ringroad towards the planetarium. After a few minutes they stopped again.

'Thank Christ we weren't mixed up in that,' said the officer.

'Yea, thank Christ,' said the Russian girl in the darkness.

'Now you hop it,' said a soldier.

The girl said: 'My name's Anna. Hello. How are you.'

'It's no use, love. You'd best just go home.'

'What are you doing with that tart, Lacy?'

'What do you think he's doing?'

'For fuck's sake . . .'

'Language,' said another soldier.

'Quiet,' said the sergeant tersely.

The officer, who had been looking at a map, said: 'OK, we'll have to cut through the back streets.'

Kate felt terrible. She didn't want to move. She would never drink aircraft brake fluid again, she promised herself; not as long as she lived.

The officer turned to her and said: 'There's an RV – a rendezvous – at the Zoological Gardens in twenty minutes. They're sending a chopper from Smolensk. A Puma, a bit of an antique, but better than walking. Do you think you'll be all right?'

'I'll be fine.'

She could feel the bruise across her forehead pulsing. She was shivering uncontrollably. He suddenly put his hand on her forehead, then turned irritably: 'Mace!'

'Sir?'

'She's got a temperature. What can you give her?'

Mace looked at her helplessly. He could inject a syrete of morphine, he said, but wasn't too sure about dealing with a headache. 'I think there's some paracetamol—'

'Well, get it out.'

'I can't swallow,' she said. 'I can't swallow.'

'Have a swig of tea, miss,' said a soldier.

They gave her tea and tablets.

'All right?'

She nodded.

'Gates!'

'Sir?'

He turned to her. 'Corporal Gates is a married man – aren't you, Gates?'

'Sir.'

The entire world was crazy.

'Gates, I want you to stay with Miss Delacroix, whatever happens. Help her along. Let either me or Colour-Sar'nt Gough know if there are any problems.'

'Sir.'

'By the way,' he said to her, suddenly embarrassed, 'I'm Simon, Simon Morrell, in case you'd forgotten.'

'Of course not,' she lied.

She remembered him now. He was the officer who wouldn't let Sergei into the embassy.

The Russian girl spoke from the darkness. 'My name's Anna. Happy to meet you.'

Simon Morrell turned to the rest of the soldiers:

'Right, listen. We've got to get to the Zoological Gardens. There must be no trouble, no fighting. There's half a million armed men in Moscow tonight, and we can't rely on more than fifteen or sixteen of them being on our side. Nobody fires a shot without a direct order, or unless I do, whatever happens. OK?'

'OK,' said the Russian girl quietly from the darkness. Eyes nodded in the gloom.

They slipped into the dark side streets.

It took twenty minutes to reach the zoo. Kate was almost back at the American embassy, almost back where she had started from.

'All right, close up.'

They closed up. Around them lay the park, the jungle. The young officer spoke again on the radio phone.

The helicopter was coming in. They scanned the sky and listened. Men took up positions with torches. 'Ten metres apart – count them out,' the sergeant was shouting. 'Now angle them into the wind . . .'

Now there was a droning noise, the beat of rotors.

'Switch on!'

The torches shone upwards. Above them the helicopter's navigation lights were suddenly switched on, and a searchlight bathed them in a pool of light.

Around the park, people started shouting.

Gates took hold of her arm. 'It's all right, miss.'

The helicopter was coming down. She could feel the wind from its rotors. Suddenly, from the far side of the gardens, there was a burst of automatic fire.

'Henshaw, Lacy—'

Men were going down on their knees, raising their rifles.

'Hold steady. Target less than five hundred yards. Aim low.'

'Two hundred half-left four o'clock—'

'Seen!'

'Wait for the order.'

More shots. A line of tracer crackling through the bare trees.

'Fire!' shouted Simon.

'Christ, what's that—'

A vivid red flash as a rocket soared. Above them the helicopter reared upwards, wheeling, its engines screaming, its searchlight darting across the sky, then all its lights vanishing.

'Anti-tank, 66 mill—'

Simon was shouting into the radio.

'Pull out, do you read me, pull out. You are being targeted by an anti-tank battery. Pull out.'

'Fucking RAF, why didn't they send an army chopper?'

The Aragvi was the fallback position. They went back the way they had come. There were Chechens outside the Hotel Pekin this time, pretending to act as security guards, blocking the way through to Tverskaja.

She leaned against the wall as Simon went forward. He was talking to them. He was cracking jokes.

'Those bastards nearly killed me,' she said suddenly. 'What's he doing?'

In the darkness a soldier said: 'Saving your fucking life.'

She froze.

Simon was laughing, slapping a Chechen on the back, offering him cigarettes.

The soldier spoke again in the darkness: 'If it was up to me, I'd trade her in for a bottle of vodka.'

Another voice said: 'Shut your gob, Mace.'

'If she hadn't been such a stupid cow—'

'Mace!'

'Corporal.'

Simon came back. 'OK, let's go. As fast as you can.'

They hauled her across the road, one on either side, practically frogmarching her.

'Hey,' she heard herself squeak – then they were past the Chechens, who shouted after them in atrocious Russian.

Simon turned. 'The same to you, mate!' he shouted cheerily, 'Whatever it was you said.'

'They said,' said Kate, ' "Good luck with your tart. I hope she fucks well." '

There was silence for a while.

A voice behind her said: 'What happened to that other tart?'

'Given you up as a bad job, Chaffey.'

'Transferred her allegiance to the Azerbaijanis, Chaffey.'

'Is that what they were?'

'Christ knows.'

'You all right, miss?'

This was Gates, breathing in her ear. She stopped.

'Sir!' called Gates.

Simon came back.

'I'm sorry,' she said. 'I'm really sorry.'

'It's all right, I've got you,' he said, as she fell into his arms.

EIGHT

British Embassy, Moscow, 22.00 hours, 18 March

The SAS left the embassy in four SOV Land-Rovers that had been fitted with turbocharged V7 engines. Each vehicle was equipped with machine-guns and grenade pistols. In the back of the lead SOV was a security radio and satellite communications centre. The equipment was tracking a moving green dot, picking up a signal that had been relayed from the American spy plane *Aurora* via Filingdales in Yorkshire.

At the moment, the green dot was still in the northern suburbs of Moscow, but moving slowly eastwards. Spiderweb lines on the screen showed the Moscow orbital railway line.

They headed out of the city, south-west to Govorovo, then doubled back, coming in from the north-west at Tusino. Shortly after 23.00 they reached the Federal FEBA: the Forward Edge of Battle Area. An exhausted Federal officer wanted to argue, but took one look at the cannon pointing at his chest and wearily waved them through. They were going into no-man's land, he said; they were heading into anarchy. Second Army was in Perovo.

Yes, they too had watched CNN news.

They crossed into the FEBA. There were no cars, no vehicles moving. Twice they came under fire from looters, but did not return fire. Weaving round roadblocks and burning shells of buses, they headed towards Zeleznodoroznyj – the railway district. Shortly after midnight the lead Land-Rover came to a halt. The others pulled in round it.

Soldiers with SA80 assault rifles moved swiftly to set up a defensive perimeter. Others quickly unloaded their gear.

'All right. Move off.'

John Hoodless, young at twenty-four to be a full sergeant, was leader of Four Group gun team. He was the gun controller. Behind him came Jarvis, his observer, and behind him Gallagher the trigger man, carrying the GPMG itself. The fourth man was Corporal Buck. He carried the tripod, weighing thirty pounds, and one thousand rounds of link ammunition: half of it round his waist, the other half in his Bergen.

Each member of the team carried rations, water, belt kit, and personal weapons. Hoodless also had a self-loading rifle.

The amount of kit carried per man was part of the eternal military problem, part of the equation military and naval draughtsmen had struggled to reconcile for generations. Speed versus armour, firepower versus speed.

The SAS were trained to move swiftly, but nobody could run with a 130-pound Bergen on his back.

'Wait.'

Four Group paused, familiarizing themselves with the darkness. Other teams were disappearing into the gloom. One Group was heading towards the signals box.

Four Group's objective was beyond the wire-topped wall.

'One-four to Sunray, moving now.'

'Roger One-four.'

Ten minutes later they were scrunching on gravel by the rail track. From the distance they could hear occasional artillery fire, but everything was quiet round the railway yards. They started to build a sangar, a protective circle using stones, clumps of ice-frozen earth from the embankment . . . anything they could lay their hands on.

Then the Gimpy's cradle was levelled, and the front mounting pin withdrawn. The rear pin was slotted into place, the gun lifted into position.

A belt of two hundred rounds clicked smoothly into position. The top cover was slipped back.

The gun targeted the faint gleam of the track. Gallagher, the trigger man, knelt in position.

Hoodless said: 'OK, Para?'

Gallagher was ex-parachute regiment, ex-maroon machine.

'OK.'

Hoodless smiled to himself. 'The train arriving on platform four . . .'

NINE

They were inside the Aragvi, Stalin's favourite restaurant.

A soldier had shattered the door lock. They had first looked at, then rejected, the ornate caverns and cellars with their wall murals of Georgian village life. They had climbed to the first floor, and were barricaded in the room where, two evenings ago, she had eaten roast duck, and violins had played, and where an old man had shuffled from table to table selling carved wooden bears that played little wooden balalaikas.

She was lying in a sleeping bag, on a piece of foam called a bum roll. Simon was standing over her.

'When did you last eat?'

She thought back. 'A roll and peanut butter,' she said, 'this morning at the American embassy.'

'That's no good.'

'I drank something.'

'Booze?'

'Airline brake fluid, the man said.'

'Not a good idea.'

'He didn't say it till after I'd drunk it.'

'They don't.'

End of conversation. She closed her eyes.

He said: 'Do you want me to explain the situation to you?'

She would rather have gone to sleep. But she opened her eyes and nodded.

He crouched down beside her. He was drinking tea from a black plastic mug.

'The Ukrainians are still operating a refugee centre on Kalininskij Prospekt. They might take us in, but it's really intended for their own nationals. The Iranian embassy is still staffed, but that would be a bit of a desperate measure, and we've no reason to suppose they'd give us protection. Anyway, it would be a bit embarrassing. We can't expect another helicopter. As far as we know, all other Western agencies and embassies have pulled out. The basic problem is that half a million armed men are roaming round Moscow, and nobody can guarantee to control them.'

'What about the Feds?'

'We could try to link up with a government unit, yes. But a lot of them are going over to Kotelnikov, and other units are just disintegrating. Officially, the Federals are still holding a line running down through north Moscow. The FEBA runs through a place called the Park of Economic Achievement—'

'I know it.'

'You do?'

'I've spent a lot of my life in Moscow. I took a degree in Russian.'

'Right, that should be useful. I speak bugger-all Russian myself, and most of the lads are still struggling with English.'

'Yes,' she nodded agreement.

'That was a joke,' he said. 'Anyway, the military situation is changing by the hour. I'm due to talk to our HQ at Kaunas at 02.00, but we don't have a secure phone. I'd get as much rest as possible, if I were you.'

She nodded. He got up.

'Thanks,' she said, earnestly because she meant it. 'Thanks for everything you've done.'

He smiled. He looked suddenly pleased. She lay back and closed her eyes.

At her school there had been a series of pre-Raphaelite prints on the library wall, from paintings by Burne Jones, showing the perilous journey to a convent made by the good maiden Frideswide. Though pursued by soldiers, Frideswide had been looked after by God. '*Safe beyond a little brook*' said a caption, '*she shelters for the night in a pigsty.*'

As a sixth-former she had made love in the darkness under Frideswide's saintly visage, curled on a leather library seat with her escort to the Summer Ball, the tall windows thrown open to let in the flying beetles and the moths and the smell of night-scented stock, the distant sound of a very small band playing the hits of two years back.

'Who has taken the key to the library?' – the irate voice of a senior mistress, the rattling of the door.

Kate had possessed a reputation. In her fourth form's SLAM book (there had been a craze for American teens literature at the time) she had been voted *Girl Most Likely To End Up A Prostitute*. So it didn't really need anybody to explain: 'Kate Delacroix and her boyfriend.'

A week later she was sharing a flat behind Camden Lock, with a fake tattoo of a Japanese fish on her arm, and a new boyfriend who wanted her to get her nipples pierced.

She dozed now, thinking of the good maiden Frideswide, chased by soldiers and hiding in pigsties. After a bit she opened her eyes. She could smell food. She realized that she was ravenous.

'Rice Bolognese,' said a soldier, coming towards her with a paper plate. On it was a mound of wet rice and thick orange sauce.

She sat up and ate quickly, down to the very last grain of rice, unable to believe it was gone so fast. Other soldiers were now sitting eating.

'I hope I didn't take anybody's rations,' she said, watching them hungrily, wondering if they'd offer her some more.

'We put all our rations in the pan, miss, and shared it out.'

'You had a nice bit of my rations, a nice meaty bit.'

'Shurrup, Mace.'

'As I was saying earlier,' said Gates, the man who had been told to look after her, 'We got the army flat, and kept on with it. Our Julia's got the Wives Club. She likes the company there when I'm not about. I'm not saying we haven't had our ups and downs—'

'It's been a long time,' interrupted Mace, 'since I had an up and down.'

'But it's not like over here. Bloody hell. Half the marriages in Russia end within a year. Do you want to look at a photo of our Jenny?'

They all ate Mars bars.

Later, when Gates was on sentry duty, or 'stag' as they called it, another soldier squatted down beside her and said, confidentially: 'His missus was going with another bloke. What Gatesie did to him is a matter for the record.'

Soldiers were settling down to sleep. On the ground floor below them, Russian refugees could be heard scrabbling like mice, muttering quietly to themselves. They must have crept into the restaurant after the soldiers broke down the door. At the head of the staircase, which was blocked with chairs, a soldier was on sentry duty. Another looked out of the window, his gun cradled in his arms.

What a pity, she thought, that Frideswide didn't have these lads to look after her when she fled to the convent.

She wondered if her parents knew what had happened. She wondered what they were saying at EuroTV.

She felt tired and ill, and her scalp throbbed mercilessly. The aircraft brake fluid had not only made her pass out, it had done terrible things to her insides. The rice and Bolognese sauce was now rumbling uneasily in her stomach.

She remembered what the man at the American embassy had said. *CNN pulled out at 15.00.*

She was the last Western reporter in Moscow.

She was *definitely* the last Western reporter in Moscow.

She smiled to herself. Then a black rock of sleep rolled over her.

TEN

Moscow Cosmos Posthouse Hotel, 22.00 hours, 18 March, 5k from Forward Edge of Battle Area

He'd filed his story. *Moscow rock musicians flee Red Terror. Jimi Hendrix revival hits Moscow – too late! Primal Scream tour cancelled: fans in torment.*

You could rely on Art Finkel to nose out the *real* stories, the stories of human emotion and human endeavour, the stories squeaky-arsed *Independent* hacks always missed.

'What about the Reds? Are they there yet?' his Newsdesk wanted to know.

'No, and they won't be,' Art said. 'The top-shots are doing a deal. *You* told me they were doing a deal.'

'That is no longer what the BBC is saying,' said Newsdesk.

Art shook his head in despair – pointlessly since Newsdesk couldn't see him.

Newsdesk said: 'Or anybody else for that matter. Are you at the American embassy?'

'Near enough,' Art said, peering out of the phone-booth, which was in the hotel lobby. From here he could just see the Embassy Rooms Casino, up on the mezzanine floor.

'Didn't you get our message? You should have been at the embassy twelve hours ago.'

'Listen, I have it on the very best authority that the politicians are doing a deal. People always do deals.'

'Pol Pot?' said the Newsdesk.

'Pardon?' said Art, distracted by a passing whore, the first he had seen that night.

'Pol Pot didn't. Pol Pot shot everybody.'

Art reflected on what it was like to work for a paper where the lad on newsdesk was educated and knew about history. They were all graduate bloody trainees, of course, straight from a varsity rag to the newsdesk of a national newspaper. But what experience of life did they have? Three years screwing some tart at the taxpayer's expense, and writing 'articles' in poofy arts magazines. It made you want to cry.

'Don't play the hero, that's all I'm saying,' said Newsdesk, sober and responsible.

As Art wasn't safe at the American embassy , playing the hero was the only viable option. 'I'm just doing what I was sent here to do,' he said.

He had been sent originally to write a series – 'Who's Sorry Now?' – about the fate of Russian girls who had travelled to England to 'wed' lonely Englishmen, and had subsequently fled back to Russia after, typically, enduring 10.3 months in Swindon with a bearded sci-fi buff with a non-existent sex drive. 'We Russian women are passionate, *passionate*,' a runaway wife had told Art, as she plied her sorry trade in Arbat Street (selling fur hats and little painted boxes to tourists, but Art made it sound rather more sordid).

Newsdesk said: 'Have it your own way, but the news team left Moscow this afternoon. They say they were the last out.'

'The news team,' said Art, who was in Features, 'are arseholes.' He put down the phone, feeling less confident than he sounded. He left the little kiosk and looked round.

The Heineken bar was open, but the German-run hard-currency store was closed. The hard-currency souvenir shops were also closed. Even the poky little cafe that accepted roubles was closed.

There were fewer miniskirted tarts than usual leaning on the rail of the mezzanine, and no pimps on patrol. The business centre was in darkness. No longer, it seemed, could he take a personalized helicopter trip, with champagne and caviar round the 'Golden Circle' of Russia's ancient cities.

Only a crone, an old *babushka*, was on duty. She stood by the elevator, moving a switch to make it go up or go down.

It had been livelier than this even half an hour ago, he thought, feeling a small twinge of worry.

He went over to the hotel entrance and looked out.

Opposite, in the darkness across Prospekt Mira, was the Park of Economic Achievement. The Russian economy itself was normally to be seen assembled in front of it: a row of men and women selling single Western cigarettes, home-brewed vodka, poisonous beetroot liqueur, ornaments, bags of apples, and disposable razors. At night there were usually little lights that seemed, from a distance, to be tiny religious shrines lit by candles – but were, in fact, plywood and plastic boxes where flower-sellers displayed their goods.

All was in darkness. Even the flower sellers' candles were unlit. Whether or not the Russian economy was still operating in the darkness, he could not tell.

He hesitated. It might be best to pull out. He could see a couple of taxis sitting in the hotel car-park, their mafia 'minder' walking up and down. Bugger the Yank embassy – he could be across the border into Belorussia inside twelve hours. He could be lunching tomorrow in the Minsk Hilton.

But it was cold outside, and the taxi-driver would smell. There hadn't been any soap in Moscow for three months; they all stank like ferrets (he gave them bars of Posthouse courtesy soap, but they just flogged it off on the black market; they didn't dream of *using* it) and even if he made the driver come inside and take a shower, his taxi itself would smell of greasy unwashed bodies.

No way. Art turned and made for the escalator. Instinct was best; and his instinct, when in a foreign place, was to stay in the warm – or, depending on circumstances, in the cool. You didn't usually get robbed, mugged or raped (yes, Art had been to some funny places) if you stayed quietly in your Intercontinental or Forte Crest. He'd covered the Second Kurdistan War from the Ankara Moat House, and been commended on *What The Papers Say*.

The escalator was moving in a downward direction. The aged crone moved her switch, and the stairs reversed and started to move upwards.

'Ta, mother,' he said, stepping on to it. He went up past the massive chandelier and the polystyrene mobile of *Sputnik 1*. At the mezzanine he stepped off, and went into the black leather and chromium interior of the Embassy Rooms Casino.

'Well, now, sweetness,' he said.

Sonia, his favourite tart, was wearing her low-cut crimson dress that pushed her tits up.

She leaned over the counter, sexy as you like (he liked, he liked) and said in a mechanical voice: 'Well, hi there, stranger. You may think we play only Russian roulette in Russia, but at the Embassy Rooms we play Black Jack, Punto Banco, and dice.'

He said: 'You say that every night.'

She said: 'It's what I say. Tonight I say something else. We've got this special offer. Supper at the Caviar Station, including tiger prawns and lobster. Then an eggs Benedict and fresh pastry breakfast in the wee small hours, and of course a courtesy limo to take you home.'

'The wee small hours?' he said in a Scottish accent.

She said it was 350 coupons or a twenty-ton transporter full of roubles. They'd burn the roubles in the furnace, and use the transporter to ship in fridges from Latvia.

'OK,' said Art, not laughing (he'd heard the joke before), passing over his American Express.

'No cards. *Money*,' said Sonia, not quite as sexily as before.

'You don't take American Express?' he said, astounded.

'Not tonight. Two hundred coupons. Special price.'

Coupons were bonds based on the value – or at least on the existence – of Russian land. They were a last-ditch attempt by the Democratic Government to invent a new, non-inflationary currency. The armed forces and miners had been paid in coupons for the past six months. It was said that Kotelnikov would honour them.

'Dollars,' said Art, 'I'll give you US dollars.'

She waved her hand contemptuously. She said: 'Fifty coupons and two hundred dollars by card.'

'Fifty coupons, and five hundred dollars by card,' he said, frivolous, naughty.

Her hands closed round the coupons. He offered his Amex card, she again waved contemptuously. He went through into the casino. About twenty men and women were playing. They were laughing and shouting to each other, but he detected an air of tension (he had a reporter's instinct, even if he was Features) that had nothing to do with the spin of the dice. An acquaintance, Georgy, was standing nervously by the roulette wheel, immaculate in his white evening jacket.

'Art!' he called, seemingly surprised.

'Where is everybody? This place is dead.'

'You got here OK?'

'Got here? I live here. I don't go out of here if I can help it. Listen,' he added, 'they won't take dollars. What's wrong with dollars?'

Georgy's face contorted into a peculiar smile. He lowered his voice. 'They say Kotelnikov's in Perovo.'

'But they're doing a deal? The Feds and the Reds are doing a deal?'

'Of course they're doing a deal!'

'You're not pulling out?'

Georgy said: 'Me? And let some other bastard move in on my patch?'

'Ridiculous,' said Art.

Georgy was a financial operator. He placed adverts every day in *Commersant* and *Isvestia.* For ten thousand American dollars he set up offshore havens in Cyprus for Russian businessmen who wanted to move their hard currency and their land coupons.

'Of course they're doing a deal,' said Georgy. 'Listen, they're doing a deal right now as we speak. Don't worry.'

'I'm not worrying,' said Art.

The croupier said worriedly: 'OK, gentlemen . . .'

At midnight the croupier said, 'OK, that's it.'

Art said: 'Don't be a sherbert, Herbert,' but the man was already on his way through the door. Art looked round, surprised. The casino was empty: they were the last. Georgy, who had won four thousand dollars, sat looking blankly at the tokens, a glass of vodka in his hand. Art went out into the reception area in search of Sonia, but Sonia was not there.

'Sonia!' he called. 'Sonia, Sonia, Sonia!'

Feeling pleasantly fuzzy from vodka, he went through into the supper room, looking for a spot of caviar (the red stuff was delicious eaten, as the Russians ate it when they got the chance, on bread warm from the oven).

The Caviar Station was a gleaming white cloth with nothing on it but a stack of empty plates. The Lobster Bar was empty of lobster. There was not a tiger prawn in sight. Art, who had been raised in a hard school of disappointment and disillusion, knew instantly that he would not be getting his eggs Benedictine and fresh pastries.

Georgy was letting his dollar tokens fall through his fingers. He let them lie, unwanted, on the green baize. 'I tried to get to Sheremetyevo today,' he said, 'but the roads were blocked. I was told there was a plane leaving for Paris, but I couldn't get past Daroga. I had fifteen thousand dollars in a case. Would you believe fifteen thousand dollars wouldn't get me on a plane to Paris?'

Art said: 'Oh Jesus . . .'

A dozen soldiers were in the lobby, sprawled on sofas, looking tired. A man at reception said to Art: 'Go home.'

Art said: 'I live here. I'm a resident. This is not what I expected from Posthouse International.'

The man on reception said: 'Go away. Leave the hotel. Goodbye.'

Art said: 'Where's my courtesy limo?'

Behind him, Georgy laughed.

'Well, what a bugger,' said Art indignantly.

'Bye, Bye,' said Georgy. 'Take care of yourself.'

'Hang on. Wait for me,' said Art, who did not like to be out and about alone in a strange town. 'Wait while I pack. It'll be better if we're together.'

'Five minutes, OK?'

Art went up to the ninth floor. The key lady was in her usual place, at her little desk by the lift. She was a girl in her late twenties, and had been absorbed in a long and serious-looking novel ever since he arrived. She had a houseplant growing in a KP salted nuts tin, and he imagined that she inhabited an inner world of peace and tranquillity. He had been planning a colour piece about her for the *Guardian*.

Tonight she was agitated. She jumped when he tumbled out of the lift. She took his card and handed him his key, murmuring '*Danke*' without giving her usual serene otherworldly smile.

He went to his room and packed his stuff. On *Radio Maximum* an American voice said: 'Do you find yourself wasting time sprinting back from meetings to your office to make those essential international calls? The next time you call someone, call us. We're Moscow Cellular . . .'

He grabbed his bag and, as was his custom ('Remember that, as a member of the Press Corps, you are an ambassador for your country'), took a gift to the key lady: on this occasion a half-empty tin of Austrian wild boar pâté and three Posthouse individual shampoo sachets that he had intended for taxi-drivers.

She had gone. Her desk was abandoned.

He glanced quickly at his watch, hesitated, then seized an opportunity of a lifetime and grabbed a handful of keys from the open drawer of her desk.

Dropping his case, he headed back to the bedrooms.

Ten minutes later he was back in the lobby. It was full of soldiers. Georgy was nowhere to be seen.

He ran down the stairs to the lower ground floor to where the taxis normally queued. Lights were being rigged from an emergency generator. The grisly equipment of a field dressing station was being laid out. Two ambulances were creeping in, their flashing yellow lights strobing the concrete walls.

He returned to the lobby. Soldiers were pouring in, setting up some sort of office, pulling tables out into the centre of the reception area. A Chinese or Korean cameraman was shooting the scene. Art tried to say hello, to find out what transport the 'snapper' had got laid on (photographers and cameramen were known as 'monkeys', but not, if you worked for a politically correct newspaper – and who didn't nowadays – when referring to Blacks or Asiatics), but the cameraman pushed him out of the way and hopped over the back of a sofa to get a shot of a general coming in with his entourage. Outside the plateglass doors an armoured personnel carrier pulled up in a roar of diesel noise. More soldiers came in, ignoring Art, parting to flow past him, as if he was a piece of furniture.

Suddenly, from outside, there came a noise he associated with television news bulletins: a crackling of automatic fire and the rattle of artillery and, Jesus, yes, the thud of mortars.

The floor moved under his feet. Wall tiles crashed. The huge chandelier shivered violently over his head, and set up a tinkling noise that for a brief moment drowned the sounds of gunfire.

A Russian officer shouted a warning: tables were pulled hastily out of the way. Chunks of dusty glass had fallen like huge diamonds.

It was time to pull out. Time to move on.

He looked round for the snapper, but the bastard had disappeared.

He took out his International Press Card and a wad of coupons. Carefully he looked round at the Russians for a few moments. He chose a middle-ranking officer who was giving orders and looked as though he expected them to be obeyed. He marched up to him and said: 'Speak English? International Press. I need some transport. This is priority. I've an urgent dispatch for NBC in Washington.'

ELEVEN

The Russian girl, Anna, who had followed them to the helicopter pick-up point, had crept up the stairs an hour ago.

'You can't come up here. Go on, hop it,' the man on stag had said in a low voice. 'Go on, you silly tart.'

Simon, lying awake in the darkness, had heard her sobbing very quietly, like a child.

'I'll shoot you if you come any further.' Not a lot of conviction there, thought Simon.

The stairs had creaked as Anna crept up higher.

'Sir?' the sentry had appealed in an urgent whisper. 'Sir, are you awake?'

'All right, let her come up,' Simon had said, although he knew it would mean them giving her food.

Now she was lying, still as a frightened mouse, on the threadbare carpet next to Kate Delacroix, covered by a soldier's combat jacket.

He had given Kate his own sleeping-bag. She had buried herself into it, only her hair visible in the faint light. It was funny thinking of Kate Delacroix inside his sleeping-bag; her warm body where his body ought to be.

The whole thing was bloody funny when you got down to it: three years in the army without seeing a shot fired in anger, too late for Kurdistan, passed over for Hong Kong, one balls-up, seemingly, after another – 'the sub who's always in the shit' his friends chorused wearily – redundancy, and then this . . .

He couldn't sleep. He got up, quietly, and went over to the window and sat by it, looking out. Below him was the statue of Yuri of the Long Arms, Yuri the Landgrabber. The square was quiet, as was Tverskaja beyond. Moscow was dozing fitfully, uneasily. There was the occasional sound of automatic fire from the distance, from the northern suburbs, but nothing to excite the Moscow homeless, the drunks and drug addicts, the refugees from Second Army who had poured into the capital in the past week, and who were camped out on the streets.

Simon was wide awake. He was elated.

Somehow he would get his section out unhurt, he would get Kate Delacroix out safely – and that would teach the buggers something. After a while he dozed, his head slumped against the cold window.

At 02.00 Colour-Sergeant Gough woke him. Beddoes was on the

tiny musician's platform, fiddling with the radio. It was Brigade coming through on the NATO comsat. Simon expected to hear the irritated tones of Innes-Chator, but it was a voice he recognized as Littlehales, G2 to Chief-of-Staff Joint Intelligence Central Command.

Littlehales said: 'How's the girl?'

'Fine.'

'What's happening outside? Any sign of Second Army units west of Prospekt Mira? Any sign of Specials? We think they're sending Spetznaz commando groups through the metro.'

Simon said: 'For Christ's sake, I'm not Intelligence.'

'It's important. We're getting a confused picture. Some suburbs seem totally normal; apparently they've still got electricity in Vladikino and Babushkin. Last we heard, the FEBA was holding north of the old Hotel Cosmos.'

Simon gave what information he could. 'What about us?' he asked.

Littlehales paused, then said: 'Kazan Station, 04.45.' He sounded unhappy. The radio link was not a secure means. There was a small if distinct possibility that Kotelnikov's intelligence people would be listening by now.

'Do we have a contact?' Simon asked.

Littlehales said: 'We'll wait to hear from you. If anything goes wrong, don't try the Iranian embassy.'

The link cut.

Simon was now fully awake, and freezing cold. He reached for his map, pulling the lamp towards him. Ferneyhough, a boy soldier at Bulford only three months ago, brought him coffee. Simon drank it gratefully, wondering what had happened at the Iranian embassy.

He said loudly, 'Colour-Sarn't!'

'Sir!'

'We move out in thirty minutes.'

'Sir.'

Corporal Pullin said: 'OK, come on, lads. Get moving.'

Men emerged from their dossbags, yawning and farting, comfortable among friends. Ferneyhough put the cooking pot back over the two blazing hexamine blocks. He poured in bottled water, then added eleven individual packets of sweetened instant porridge and vacuum-packed raisins. Milk powder was added from a tin that emerged from his Bergen. Nobody would touch army-issue milk powder; it refused to dissolve, and floated to the top of tea like dandruff.

'Ferneyhough, after this meal we go down to half rations.'

'Sir.'

Each man had been issued with three 24-hour ration packs when they left the embassy: nine meals and three army 'snacks'. They were now eating their second meal.

The hexamine blocks gave the illusion of warmth, of cosiness even. Ferneyhough doled thick grey porridge into mess-tin lids, and handed it out. Simon ate rapidly, shovelling the food into his mouth. It was habit; he couldn't help himself. He had spent two winters in arctic

Norway, where it takes ten seconds for your hot dinner to develop shards of ice in the mashed potato.

Gates shambled past him, an extra plate of porridge in hand.

'Where are you going, Gates?'

'I'm looking after Miss Delacroix, sir.'

'*I'll* look after Miss Delacroix.'

Officer's perks: it hadn't been Gates who gave up his dossbag.

He took the plate over to Kate, shook her awake, offered her a plastic spoon. She ate a mouthful, dropped the spoon, and quickly fell back asleep.

'Come on, wake up,' he said awkwardly. He shook her shoulder and she groaned.

'Come on, Kate!' He realized that the rest of the platoon were watching him intently, their breakfasts forgotten.

'Kate!'

'Yes, all right. All right!'

Not a morning person. He let go of her shoulder. Her eyes closed.

He said loudly, 'Get on with it, then. We haven't got all day. Colour-Sar'nt Gough! Corporal Pullin! I want to look at the map.'

He took the plate of porridge to the Russian girl, Anna, who had somehow moved herself close to the stove and was trying to look inconspicuous but hungry at the same time.

'Here. After this, you go. Understand?'

She took the plate and smiled. Then she began to eat, slowly, politely.

'Ferneyhough,' he said grimly, 'give her some tea.'

'Sir.'

He joined Gough and Pullin. He said: 'We've a new RV. Kazan Station, 04.45. It's about a mile and a half from here.'

'We're going out by train, sir?' Pullin was incredulous.

'God knows.'

They plotted a route. A few moments later Beddoes, who was fiddling with his tiny satellite TV receiver, called: 'Bulletin from the Yanks, sir.'

They all gathered round to watch it. The American television crew was airborne: on an Air France airbus that had been held up with engine trouble at Moscow's Sheremetyevo 2 for the past twenty-four hours, and had been repaired just in time.

There were interviews with Japanese catering managers and Irish duty-free staff, all as drunk as lords; with a PR girl from the European Trade Centre, crying with relief into her champagne.

Simon went back to Kate, who was sitting up in her dossbag looking like death.

She said: 'Was there some porridge?'

'Yes.'

She looked round.

'I expect there'll be some more,' he said. 'Tomorrow morning.'

She said: 'Oh Christ, I'm sorry.'

'Here you are,' he said, relenting, and gave her a bar of chocolate.

She said: 'What time is it?'

He told her.

'I don't suppose there's any way I can send a story?'

'A story?'

'If I could get through to London – if your bloke could get me a line through to EuroTV or the BBC.'

'Afraid not.'

'Oh. Right.'

'We're on a military net, and anyway the call might be picked up by an enemy listening post.'

'Would that matter?'

'It would if a Spetznaz patrol turned up.'

'What, here?'

Well, no. He realized that Spetznaz, even if they were creeping through the metro tunnels, would have better things to do than hunt down a girl peaceably chattering her way through an item for *From Our Own Correspondent*.

'Probably not. But you getting your story out isn't the first priority.'

'I didn't actually think it was.' A note of irritation. A pause.

'How do you feel?'

'Terrible.'

She had dropped half the chocolate bar.

'I'm sorry.'

'If you want my advice,' she said, 'Never drink aircraft brake fluid on an empty stomach. Go through life remembering that, and you won't go far wrong.'

He said: 'We've got to walk a mile and a half to a new rendezvous. I'll try and fix you a radio link there, OK?'

She nodded, shivered, hugged herself in the dossbag.

'Would you like some more paracetamol?'

She shook her head.

As he stood up, she said: 'How long before we start?'

'Five minutes.'

She looked at him in horror.

'I can't leave things any longer.'

'No, of course not. Don't worry about me. I'll be all right.'

She slowly started to unzip the sleeping-bag.

'All right, Colour, let's go.'

'OK, lads.'

The Russian girl, Anna, was already standing by the stairs, looking purposeful and ready. He went over to her.

'We're going now. You won't be able to come with us. It's military only from now on. I'm sorry, but you're better off staying here, OK? Thanks for everything. Good luck.'

She looked at him, expressionless.

'All right, let's get moving.'

They clattered down the stairs. Anna stood and watched them go.

A soldier called back: 'Bye, Anna.' Another said: 'Take care of yourself, love.'

They left the restaurant. They picked their way carefully over people sleeping in the doorways, past Yuri of the Long Arms, and on to Tverskaja. Here Simon stopped. The broad boulevard was quiet, but that did not mean it was safe.

Shadows moved.

A neon advert over the Nina Ricci perfumery flickered green, and the shop below had lights in its windows. The building must have had a generator that started up automatically when the main power supply went off.

Suddenly, from the north over Babushkin, there was a crackle of noise and a line of tracer sparkled across the sky. A second later, a white flare silhouetted the Intourist Hotel and illuminated a poster: MOSCOW RELOCATIONS. LET US FIND YOUR OFFICES APARTMENTS AND DACHAS. THERE'S NO PLACE LIKE HOME.

He hesitated. Their direct route would take them towards Babushkin and the Prospekt Mira, skirting the danger zone.

There were two hours to the RV. It would be better to detour to the south, round the Kremlin walls.

He looked back at his men. Kate Delacroix was in the centre.

'You all right, Kate?'

'I'm fine.'

'Colour, you bring up the rear.'

Corporal Pullin and Chaffinch went ahead to check the approaches to the Kremlin. He was moving his men like a fire team, assuming a hostile environment, ready to turn on an attacker at any moment.

TWELVE

They moved south down the boulevard, hugging the walls, stepping over the drunks. Voices called, begging mechanically, or abusing them angrily. On the corner of Prospekt Khudozh, the Estée Lauder perfumery had all its windows smashed, and for a moment the night air was delicately scented.

'Spread out. Get ready to move on the order. Gates!'

'Sir.'

'Take care of Miss Delacroix. Kate, you're going to have to move quickly. Right, go!'

They crossed the intersection, no longer moving in single file, but in a line: five metres between each man. By crossing simultaneously, they would be halfway across before an enemy sniper – if there was one – could register that they were even there: gone before he could adjust his sights.

On this occasion, though, a shadow slipped across the road behind them.

Mace and Chaffinch stood waiting by the Moskva Hotel.

There were no cars on the inner ringroad, no people moving.

Simon looked south, down the old Marx Prospekt. As he did so, the moon emerged from behind the scudding clouds. The tomb of the Unknown Warrior was a dark mass where no flame burned. Over the Kremlin walls, the moonlight caught the highest golden dome of the Cathedral of the Annunciation.

Kate said: 'That is lovely.'

'Yes,' he said absently.

He had just seen Anna join the end of the line. The men bringing up the rear were letting her hide behind them.

'Anna,' he called quietly.

'Oh, sir . . .'

'She's all right, sir.'

'She's our mascot, sir.'

'Better than fucking Ninja.'

Ninja was the regiment's Shropshire ewe that ate its head off in Shrewsbury barracks.

'Unless you happen to be Mace,' said a voice libellously.

'You fucking shut it—'

'Quiet,' said Gough.

Well, it wasn't Simon's responsibility. She could go where she liked; it was a free country – just.

'OK,' he said, 'single file, as before.'

They moved round the corner of the Arsenal Tower, and filed quietly into Red Square.

'Halt.'

The moonlight reflected on the cobblestones, on the towers of St Basil's Cathedral.

The square was deserted.

Simon thought: this is where the Red Army, the greatest armed force in the world, once paraded in all its power. This was the heart of an empire that stretched from the Baltic to the Sea of Japan . . .

He raised his SA80, turned on the IWS night-sight, listened to the low whine as the battery connected.

' "My name is Ozymandias," ' Kate said quietly, ' "king of kings; Look on my works, ye Mighty, and despair!" '

The IWS multiplied natural light by five hundred times. The conifers round Lenin's former tomb sprang clear. He raised the weapon and scanned the balcony, seeing in his mind's eye the ghosts of Stalin, Krushchev, and Gorbachev.

'I'd give anything in the world' – her voice trembled – 'to send a story from here, right now. I would give anything to be able to do that.'

'OK,' said Simon, 'in single file. Keep in the shadows.'

Looking back, he saw Gough motion to Anna to go ahead of him, in front of Gates who had the machine-gun; under their collective wings.

They slipped round the square, cautiously hugging the walls of the buildings. They did not know what eyes, if any, might be watching from the windows of the Great Kremlin Palace.

They entered Dzerzinsky Square. Ahead of them, immense and squat, was the Lubjanka prison, the old home of the KGB. Next to it was the Moscow Children's World department store. As they went past, Simon's torch flickered over stacks of toys, displays that depicted scenes from Russian fairytales: the Princess with the Rabbits, the Witch in the Woods.

In front of the Lubjanka was the plinth that had once held the statue of some notorious head of the security services: Beria perhaps – Simon could not remember. The statue had been torn down in Gorbachev's day.

In the dim light from Simon's torch they could see that the base of the plinth was scattered with flowers: single roses still in their twist of wrapping paper, a small bunch of pink carnations in cellophane. Tributes from unknown admirers. The voice of the people. Kotelnikov's friends.

'Two minutes' break,' he said.

They poured tea from their flasks.

Kate said: 'It started off as the headquarters of the All Russian Insurance Company.'

'What?'

'The Lubjanka. I did a piece from here two days ago. The KGB have offices down most of these side streets. The place was never big enough, so they had to keep on taking over extra buildings. A bit like the BBC in Portland Place.'

'How are you feeling?'

'I'll be OK.'

She didn't sound it. Her teeth were chattering again, and she was shivering.

'OK, Corporal Pullin, Chaffinch. Fifty yards, no further.'

The two soldiers slipped ahead, into the shadows of the Lubjanka; into Kuzneckij Street, the narrow dark street behind the prison.

'That window,' said Kate, 'that small window at ground level in Kuzneckij, which looks like a railway ticket office, is where people had to come when their relations had been arrested. That's where they queued to find out which prison camp they should write to.'

'You must keep quiet. We're not safe here.'

'I'm sorry.'

Silence.

He didn't like letting Pullin and Chaffinch out of sight, but there was no choice; not in these dark winding streets.

Anna said: 'Excuse me.'

'Be quiet,' said Simon, listening intently.

After a few moments his radio hissed.

'Clear.'

He said: 'OK, move out.'

'Not that way,' said Anna.

'What?'

'We don't want to go that way.'

How did she know where they wanted to go? He was suddenly incredibly tired, his temper frayed. 'Now look here . . .'

A shot from up ahead, from the alleyway, its sound reverberating round the buildings. Then a burst of automatic fire, and a second burst – this time from an SA80.

They dropped into defensive positions, dragging the girls down with them.

'Shit,' said Kate, her voice muffled.

'Colour!'

'Sir?'

'Take three men forward and give cover. Gates and Mace, get the LMB—'

Pullin's voice on his intercompany radio: 'Contact. Snipers. Semi-automatics. We're coming out.'

Gough said: 'Lacy, Gates, Ferneyhough—'

They were on their feet.

'No, wait.'

Pullin and Chaffinch came running from the alleyway.

'Cover them.'

There was no need. The two men flew across the open ground, threw themselves down, their boots slithering on the wet cobblestones, turning as they fell so that their rifles were ready in the command position.

A minute passed. The chill night wind blew insistently from the open boulevard behind them. There was the sound of Gates and Mace quietly setting up the light machine-gun.

Kate said quietly: 'I'm freezing.'

Anna said quietly: 'You want to tell me where we're going to?'

Simon lay with his rifle barrel resting on a rose, the oily stock against its pink petals.

Kate said: 'For Christ's sake, tell her.'

Here he was, in Moscow, with his section, in contact with enemy snipers, at dead of night outside the Lubjanka, and he was being got at by bloody women.

He said, nicely: 'Kate?'

'What?'

'Whose stupidity got us here?'

Silence.

He said: 'Kazan Station.'

Anna said: 'We're going to Kazakhstan?'

'God knows.'

A pause. She said: 'This is a bad area you're going through.'

'Colour, we'll go back south round the GUM department store to the Ring of Gardens, and turn east again from there. Corporal Pullin, you and Chaffinch take the lead. Colour, you and Mace bring up the rear. OK, now, Anna?'

'That will be better.'

'Jesus . . .'

A sudden barrage of artillery fire from the north, from Babushkin; for the first time in several hours the thud of mortars. The uneasy calm was broken: something was happening, God only knew what.

'We've got one hour and forty minutes to the RV. It's almost certainly our last chance to get out of Moscow. Let's move.'

In Lithuania, in Kaunas, Littlehales was listening again to the taped report that had come from Moscow via St Petersburg.

It was from Ukrainian intelligence. It said that in the late afternoon, in the diplomatic enclave, outside the locked gates of the Iranian Embassy, four American aid workers had been hanged by Lyuberi, the anti-Western thugs.

Units of Kotelnikov's Second Army had watched, without interventions, from their troop transporters.

Iranian diplomats had shot the scene on video.

THIRTEEN

Kremlin escape tunnel, Khodynskoye, 03.50 hours, 19 March

They said that in the days of Stalin even the KGB did not know about the vast command centre under the Kremlin, with its secret entrance to Sverdlov Square metro station.

They said the KGB was kept totally in the dark when Stalin constructed an escape route for the Politbureau, along a metro line that was built specially for the purpose – Majakovskaja station, Belorusskaja, Dinamo – and then along a secret tunnel connection to Khodynskoye: the vast sports-field that was used only once a year to rehearse the Red Square military parades, and which for the rest of the year lay empty.

They said that the KGB, in all innocence, tried to buy a plot of land at Khodynskoye – Lubjanka was full – but every application they made was refused, and eventually they had to build their gleaming tower (the headquarters of Fourth Directorate, so fondly known in the West as SMERSH) out beyond the ringroad.

They said – the Moscow chatterers – that the KGB did not know about this escape route, but the evidence indicates otherwise. For overlooking Khodynskoye is the sports complex of the Moscow Dynamos football team, which was sponsored for three decades by the KGB . . . an act of generosity that gave them a standing excuse to be prowling about Khodynskoye.

And way back in November 1941, when the celebrations to mark the anniversary of the Russian Revolution were held in the Majakovskaja metro station, and the line was closed to the public, the metro train that arrived from a station that officially did not exist carried Stalin, Molotov . . . and Beria, the KGB head.

So the KGB probably knew all along that Khodynskoye was not a sports-field but an airfield, and that the Aeroflot terminus so incongruously placed there was really a station of First Task Force, an elite airforce unit responsible for the speedy evacuation of the Politbureau from the centre of Moscow to Khodynskoye, and then by fixed-wing aircraft to the nearby airfield at Podlinpki, and from there to the Russian government secret headquarters at Zhiguli.

And now, sitting in their tower block beyond the ringroad, the KGB were probably the people who told Kotelnikov that an aircraft had taken off from Khodynskoye . . . that Stalin's secret metro, built by thousands of prisoners from Zhiguli, had been used for the first time – by the last senior officials of the democratic government fleeing to Petersburg.

Or perhaps Marshal Kotelnikov heard the news on the BBC World Service, which was putting out non-attributable '*sources close to the Russian President*' reports from 03.30 hours on the Wednesday morning.

Hoodless, in his sangar by the railway track, heard it on his intercompany radio. 'The Eagle has Flown' – a code chosen by a whimsical commander who knew of the President's desire to restore the czar as a constitutional monarch.

'Roger,' said Hoodless softly into his radio.

There had been the possibility that the last government officials would flee on the presidential train, a move that would have stopped all non-essential train movements on the northern orbital, and would have ruined the SAS operation.

He massaged his hands, stiff with cold. On the other side of the track, he saw movement in the signal box, which was lit by a faint glow. The Royal Signals boys would be in there, changing the traffic route plan. The signal arm was still up and showing green. He could see the sangar of 5 Group, the stubby nose of a GPMG in the sustained-fire role.

The FEBA was coming alive. Artillery had opened ten minutes ago. There was firing of automatics to the east of them now, from Vladykino as well as from Babushkin. Lines of red tracer shot across the sky, and he watched, worried. They were in somebody else's war, all right; the sooner they got this over and got the hell out of it the better.

Once Second Army moved – once the battle tanks rolled forward – the Federal defences would disappear. Nobody was in doubt about that. You couldn't hold Second Army for ten seconds with a rabble of drunken Yakut mercenaries and a dozen regiments of Guards.

04.50. The train was late.

He nursed his shotgun – his personal favourite, this. You could get dazzled by fancy firepower, by grenade launchers and machine-guns, but, come the emergency, you couldn't beat a 12-gauge pump-action shotgun, not for close-range firepower.

He could hear the roar of engines. Tanks or troop carriers – he could see the dim shapes beyond the cinder track and the sports-field. He reached for his binoculars, turning on the StarlightScope battery, pressing the eyepiece firmly to his face to stop light escaping.

'Christ!'

A row of BMDs – parachute troop war machines. Not moving forward, but forming up.

'Zero to four, five and six,' said the voice of Langdon calmly, enjoying himself. 'Hold your fire.'

Hold your fire . . . !

Each Russian BMD was equipped with rockets, an automatic 73mm cannon, grenade-launchers and three machine-guns!

Langdon again: 'They're not interested in us. If they move, let them through.'

'He's a mad bugger,' said Gallagher admiringly.

They always were mad buggers in the SAS. He'd been led by mad buggers ever since he transferred from the Cheshires.

05.05 hours. They should have pulled out already: 05.00 was the outer margin of time allowed; that was what they had been told on the plane from South Cerney, at the briefing in the embassy.

'If it doesn't show by 05.00, we pull out. We don't risk Second Army rolling over us . . .'

The radio buzzed. 'Stand by.'

This was it. The train from Perm: the 'objective' that had brought them on a Cabinet- authorized mission from England. He could hear the hum of the diesel, the slow clatter of the carriages over points.

The signal arm thudded to red.

3 Group were moving out of the goods sheds. He could just see them: shadows running like rats; in their hands L 24 sniper rifles with the new lightweight night sights; the boss himself somewhere in the lead.

The train was stopping. The black shapes of 3 Group were running alongside, swinging up with small explosive packages to stick to the wagon doors. Sixty seconds and it would be over: already the shunter with SAS Royal Engineers in the cab was backing out of its siding.

Flares lit the sky, the goods yard, the train and the shunting engine – exposing the sangars and the men inside them against the pale gravel.

'Shit!'

Thud, thud, *thud* . . .

Mortars.

The world exploded.

You do nothing under mortar attack; there is nothing you can do as the bombs fall, except hug the ground and wait for the explosions to end. As he waited, he calculated that there were six or seven mortars, and that they must be dug-in somewhere beyond the scrubby skyline of thorn bushes. Looking up, he thought he saw a distant green flash that could have been their tubes as they briefly lit up their basepads.

Someone had seen the SAS. Somebody had decided to take them out.

More bombs shrieked.

Langdon's voice on the radio: 'Observer spotted—' his voice was half drowned as he gave the coordinates. The Browning opened up from 5 Group's sangar. Hoodless was opening his mouth to shout an order to Gallagher to train round the machine-gun, when a massive explosion lifted the train engine from Perm from the track and sent it toppling—

'Zero to all units. Zero to all units. Get that observer.'

The mortar was always the Russian weapon, big and crude and easy to make. It was a primitive weapon – just a tube resting on an iron plate, supported by two legs. The most stupid Azerbaijani, the thickest Tartar from the Siberian steppes, the most cack-handed intellectual from the university could learn how to use it in minutes. It fired cast-iron bombs that were cheap to manufacture, and that would splinter in a dense and satisfying fragment pattern when it exploded.

'Rapid fire,' yelled Hoodless, his head still ringing from the mortar explosions, tearing his eyes away from the huge train engine lying on its side. The enemy observer was in a building overlooking the goods yard. Gallagher pulled the trigger: thirty rounds, a close pattern of shots on line, but too high. Buck was already adjusting the elevation drum, feeding in another 200-round belt. Five Group had the upper windows of the building in range now, a stream of fire shooting out from their sangar.

Then Gallagher had the target. He fired. As he did so, a barrage of automatic fire opened from across the scrubby skyline, and, turning, they saw the muzzle flashes of RPD light machine-guns and the single flashes of AK 47 rifles moving forward under covering fire.

And from behind them he heard the roar of the BMDs.

Second Shock Army was moving south from Babushkin and Vladykino. The Fall of Moscow was entering its final phase.

FOURTEEN

Kazan Station, Moscow, 04.15 hours, 19 March

Simon had sent out three patrols. Colour-Sergeant Gough and Foster had come back first. Now Pullin and Lacy were struggling back through the crowds.

'Nothing up that way, sir,' said Pullin.

Only Gates and Mace had yet to return.

The station was filthy and freezing. The damp-stained walls dripped with condensation. The green-and-white plasterwork of the roof vault was like an iced cake smeared with dirt.

He looked round for the fat-cats, the spivs and currency profiteers fleeing Kotelnikov – but if they were here they were well disguised. There was no electricity, but he could see by the flickering light from bonfires outside, from candles and lamps. People were huddled on the floor in groups – Kazakhstanis trying to get home, he guessed; Muscovites desperate to escape to their country relations till the fighting was over.

There was a constant noise of shouting and screaming. Only the children were quiet.

There was a smell. Somebody had described the smell of Russians en masse as being like that of a laundry basket on weekly collection morning. That had been back in the days when Russians had soap.

He looked at his watch, the first stirring of panic in his stomach. It was 04.20.

'Beddoes?'

'Sir?'

'Get me Brigade.'

'No chance from in here, sir.'

Oh Christ. His head was thick with weariness. He would have died for a cup of hot coffee.

'We'll go outside, then. Colour, you come with us. Nobody else goes anywhere. Whatever happens, everybody stays together. Got it?'

They moved out into the crush: the others closed up the gap. They had seized a number of tangerine plastic chairs and piled their Bergens on them and then gathered around them, an island in a sea of moving humanity.

Small boys and girls, not more than eleven or twelve years old, wove their way through the mass of would-be travellers. A woman jumped up, shouting angrily; a small boy vanished through a door.

'Gotta pick a pocket or two,' said Kate. 'Little devils. There'll be a mafia boss around somewhere. Not that we haven't got one of our own. Where's he gone?'

'Having a pow-wow, miss,' said Chaffinch.

'Why can't we all pow-wow together? What is it with you soldiers?'

'It's terrible,' said Anna. 'And they don't stand up for old people on the metro anymore.'

'I do,' said Chaffinch.

'The children. When I was a girl, everybody stood up for old people on the metro. Last week there was an old man with medals, coming back from appearing in a TV quiz show – you like "*What? Where? When?*" on Channel 1? – with all the medals on his chest, medals from the Great Patriotic War, and they made him stand. The kids just sat there and made a hero of the Great Patriotic War stand on the metro, while they played Shoobah Doobath Blues tapes. Well, General Kotelnikov will sort that sort of thing out.'

'What's your job, Anna?' asked Kate.

'Intourist,' said Anna. 'I'm a very important guide. I spent three years at college.'

Kate shivered. 'Christ, this place is awful.'

'I don't see,' said Anna, 'how they'll get a helicopter to pick us up from here.'

'No.'

'The captain is very nice. I like the captain.'

'He's a fascist,' said Kate. 'Have you seen a loo anywhere?'

'A what?'

'Lavatory. Toilet.'

Anna looked at her doubtfully. 'I had better take you.'

'Right. Now, which hero of the Great Patriotic Peace,' she said looking at the soldiery round her, 'is going to be our escort?'

'Can't go anywhere without the OC's say-so, miss,' said Chaffinch.

'Oh, great,' said Kate. 'So we go by ourselves. Come on, Anna.'

They went. Simon came back a minute later, with Beddoes and Gough.

The time was 04.30. Fifteen minutes to the rendezvous. Outside, he had heard the thud of mortars firing to the north-west, seen flares lighting up the sky over Babushkin.

Beddoes had failed to raise Brigade at Kaunas, but had managed to pick up BBC World Service, with its report of the American aid workers hanged outside the Iranian embassy.

'Sir! Sir!'

It was Lance-Corporal Gates and Mace, the last patrol, pushing their way back through the crush.

'There's soldiers over the bridge, sir. Federals. They've opened a door to a platform, and civilians with tickets are getting on a train.'

'All right, get your Bergens on. Sling your rifles and let's go.' He looked round; suddenly his expression changed. 'Where are they?'

'Gone for a crap, sir.'

'Christ almighty!' he yelled, 'Christ almighty! Who the fuck let that happen?'

'They went on their own, sir—'

'Go and get them.'

'Me, sir?' said Chaffinch, outraged, querying a direct order for the first time in his life.

'Go and shout in the doorway. Oh, for Christ's sake, Corporal Pullin, Gates, go with him. Follow us as soon as you can. Right, let's go.'

Word that a train was loading had spread, a whisper running through the booking hall like a breeze through corn. People were scrambling up, grabbing their cheap cardboard suitcases, their boxes and carrier bags.

He put Mace in the lead. Mace was a hard bugger, a Walsall man, not possessing the ingrained instinct to stand back politely and wait his turn. They pressed through into the next hall, up a wide staircase and across a covered bridge.

'Make way, make way,' shouted Mace, his fist jabbing insistently forward, knowing where to twist a hard knuckle into a flabby lower back. A Russian stumbled to one side, a look of pain, indignation and surprise on his face.

'Thanks, mate . . .'

Simon could see the blue fur caps of Federal soldiers. The crowd pressed forward and the soldiers fell back, abandoning the swing doors.

The Royal Mercians tumbled through along with the crush. Federal soldiers were forming up in a new line behind a wooden barrier, trying to stop the crowds getting past. These were Russian Guards, disciplined, an officer standing calmly behind them shouting orders.

A train's lights came on. There was the loud hum of the diesel engine.

'Follow me!' Simon moved ahead of Mace, shouldering his way forward to the barrier. A Russian soldier raised his rifle butt, then saw his British uniform and deflected the blow down on to the shoulder of the man next to him.

They tumbled through like peas squeezed out of a pod, dragging their Bergens, clutching their rifles for dear life.

'Colour-Sar'nt! Get them on the train!'

'Sir.'

Simon ran to the Russian officer. 'I've five more personnel coming,' he shouted, hoping to God that the man spoke English.

The officer nodded, his eyes glued to the line of his soldiers that was giving way, being forced back. One soldier stumbled to his knees; a comrade pulled him to safety.

The officer yelled a single word, backing away as he did so, pulling Simon with him. The line of soldiers turned and ran back down the platform, then, on a whistled command, they turned and re-formed their barrier.

The officer had abandoned three carriages to the mob: easing the pressure, and enabling his new line to hold.

Simon stared back down the platform, his eyes searching the gloom for sight of a British uniform.

He swore a silent stream of obscenities.

He'd taken the only option open to him, but he knew, with cold clarity, that he could not himself escape from Moscow if it meant abandoning Kate Delacroix and three of his men. It was not nobility; he didn't pretend it was *that* – no, it was fear of a lifetime of self-justification and self-analysis, fear of the judgement of his fellow officers.

'Colour-Sar'nt Gough,' he shouted.

Gough swung down to the platform.

'Sir.'

'I'm going back. You stay on the train. Whatever happens, keep the men together—'

'You're not going back on your own,' said Gough. 'No way, sir.'

'Do as you're told and don't argue,' Simon snapped, as near to breaking point as he had ever been in his life.

'Sir, they're coming!' It was Beddoes, hoarse with excitement, leaning out of a carriage window. He was pointing back over the heads of the crowd.

'Chaffey! Come on, Chaffey!'

Soldiers were leaning out, waving and shouting. 'Get a bloody move on, Chaffey!'

'Come on, Gates, you silly bugger!'

'Come on, Anna!'

'Move, you dozy bint—'

The Guards let them through: the pressure had eased as refugees were deflected into the end carriages. Anna and Kate ran up the platform, the three soldiers behind them.

'What, the fucking hell,' Simon yelled, advancing to meet them, 'do you think you're playing at? I have never met two such stupid bloody women in all my life!'

Anna stared at him, wide-eyed, turned and dived up the steps into the train. Kate stopped, her mouth opened to speak.

'Get on that train!'

'Now, you listen—'

'Get on that train you stupid cow, and from now on do what you're fucking told or I'll fucking well lock you up.'

'You arrogant, arrogant bastard,' she spluttered.

'Jesus Christ! Corporal! Carry her on to the train and keep her under guard.'

Kate got on the train. The three Royal Mercians followed her up the steps. The Russian soldiers were also climbing aboard. A blast from the diesel's horn and the train started to move.

Refugees cried out, some of them jumping down to the platform to rejoin their families and friends, others clawing up to take their places, others running up the platform to try to find an easier way to climb aboard.

Simon swung up before they reached him.

He noted, before he did so, that the carriages were dark blue. And on each of them, illuminated in gold, was the legend *Bukhara Express*.

FIFTEEN

Art Finkel had reached Kazan Station an hour before the Royal Mercians. Hurrying through the vast booking hall, he had looked bleakly at the sea of suffering humanity.

'Piccadilly in a power cut,' he had said bitterly, and the Russian officer who had escorted him from the Posthouse Hotel had replied: 'Piccadilly Circus, London?'

'I was thinking of Piccadilly Station, Manchester, but you could be right.'

He, himself, would shoot all politicians at birth. It was just about the only thing he believed in. Shoot all politicians, he felt, and kill every baby that showed the slightest desire to tell other babies how to behave – and then, perhaps, we'd finally have a world where small thin-faced children with huge expressive eyes did not have to huddle at night on the dirty floors of railway halls, too tired to cry, too exhausted to shiver.

The platform was nearly empty. A keen, persistent wind blew across the wet concrete. They stood in the dark and waited. Soldiers appeared and, by torchlight, put up a wooden barrier. His Russian officer went and talked to another officer. Art watched him nervously: he didn't like being left alone.

His officer came back.

'I now have to go. The train is here soon.'

'Right you are,' said Art, his heart sinking. How often had he been told. 'It'll be here soon', on how many foreign railway stations – British railway stations, too, for that matter, except most of the time the bastards in England didn't even *pretend* the train was coming.

'Thank you,' he said. 'You've been very kind.'

The officer began talking, though his English wasn't very good. He was asking Art to remember them to the West, to remember them about the loyal regiments, the Guards, to remember them who held the flame for democracy and freedom, to remember they were not all mafioso, to remember to lands who spoke English which was the language of freedom.

'Don't worry. You won't be forgotten,' said Art, confused but getting the drift. 'I'll see to that.'

He offered the thick wedge of coupons. The officer shook his head. He saluted.

Art said: 'Cheers.'

Ten minutes later the train came in. It was empty and dark, but it was a train, and it was there. Art felt an overwhelming warmth towards his officer – an honest man, a man in three hundred million – who would probably be killed by the morning, dead so that one politician rather than another might warm his arse at the presidential fireplace.

The problem would be identifying the baby politicians. They'd be *cunning* little rats, even in the cradle.

He noticed that Russian civilians were being processed through a small door in quiet, secretive little groups, their tickets checked a second time at the barrier. It was time to secure himself a seat. He climbed on the train, which was still in darkness. A woman, large and solid, her face a pale full moon, asked him for his ticket. He ignored her, turned the other way, and wandered into a compartment. He put his bag on one seat, and sat on the other. The woman followed him in and stood over him, talking volubly, waving a list.

He was, he presumed, in somebody's reserved compartment. He wearily got up. He struck a match and, by its tiny light, gave her the thick wedge of coupons.

She went quiet while she counted them.

The money could have been the means of saving the Russian officer's life. Instead, Art mused sadly, it would buy him, Art, a bit of peace and quiet.

He asked her where the train was going to, but she spoke no English and sign language was tricky in the dark. He shooed her out and closed the door.

She came back ten minutes later with a glass of tea for him. It was good Russian tea from a samovar. She also gave him a wedge of tickets: poorly printed pink and blue tickets. God knew what he was supposed to do with them.

He was slowly drinking the tea, quietly thinking that life wasn't too bad, not for an old campaigner, when there was a lot of shouting and screaming and he had to move with agility to lock his door and pull the blinds down.

He climbed into his bunk, inserted into his ears the little foam muffs he bought from Boots before any foreign trip, and slept.

He did not hear the train start, or the banging on the door of his compartment by the mad woman who claimed it as her own. Seasoned foreign travellers learn to live with these noises, and Boots' earmuffs are effective.

Even later, he only awoke when the machine-guns started.

SIXTEEN

'Bloody hell,' said Henshaw, impressed, looking round the compartment. It was walled with dark wood veneer. It had a grey and blue carpeted floor. It had bunks that folded down, and tiny solid wood tables that swung out.

'Bloody hell,' he repeated, finding and clicking on and off a little twentieth-century-technology reading light.

Mace put his booted feet up on the opposite seat.

Chaffinch said uneasily: 'Not in here, Mace.'

Mace took his boots off and put his stockinged feet up. 'This all right Chaffey? This how we do it in your house, is it?'

'Have you still got foot rot, Mace?'

'Have a look for me and find out.'

'Where's the tarts gone?'

'Next-door with the OC.'

'What, both of them?'

'I wouldn't have minded that Anna in here.'

'How about a brew, then?'

'Go on, Ferney.'

'Yea, go on, Ferney . . .'

'The trolly'll be round in a bit,' said Ferneyhough.

Lacy said: 'I'm knackered. Wake me up when we get to Andover.'

He folded his coat, leaned his head against it, and closed his eyes.

The train moved slowly through the dark suburbs. Nobody thought to look out of the window. Mace pulled out a pack of cards. The door opened. It was a middle-aged, plump Russian woman in a pink shellsuit. She was crying.

Chaffinch, the kindly one, said: 'Hello, love. You back, then, are you?'

She stared round at them, tears staining her cheeks. She held up a piece of paper, pointing to the carriage number.

'*No comprendo,*' said Mace.

Chaffinch said: '*Parlez-vous anglais?*'

After a bit she went away.

'Pull the blinds down.'

They pulled down the blinds on the corridor side of the compartment. A minute later the door opened. Corporal Pullin looked in and said coldly: 'Get those boots on, Mace.'

The door closed. Lacy snored. Mace slowly put his boots on. He dealt out the cards.

'Pontoon?'
'Fifty p?'
'Go on, then.'
'Ferney? I'm gagging, Ferney.'
'Go and find the restaurant car, Ferney.'
'Yea, go on, Ferney: See if they have any crisps.'
Ferneyhough stood up. 'I'm not going on my own.'
'Bloody hell. Come on, then,' said Henshaw.

Ferneyhough took teabags from his pack, and collected plastic mugs. The door opened. This time Simon looked in and said: 'OK, you're stood down, but keep your weapons at the ready. Ferneyhough, put those bloody teabags away. Corporal Pullin will tell you when you can brew up. Lacy, you're on stag, so get to the front end of the corridor. You'll be relieved in an hour. We're still in Moscow and it's still bloody dangerous, you all understand?'

Yes, they said, they understood. He went. Lacy took his rifle and followed him.

Mace said, innocently: 'Chaffey, have you ever played Blind Man's Pontoon?'

Chaffinch said: 'I'm not betting. You're wasting your time. You'll get nothing out of me.'

Simon opened the door of the next compartment, the one he had designated Section HQ, and said: 'Anna, this train, what do you know about it?'

Anna said, startled: 'Pardon?'
'It's not your ordinary Russian train, is it?'
'Oh, yes, I think so,' said Anna.

'What? With all this . . .' He indicated the wood veneer, the carpets, the discreet vellum lampshades.

'We have good trains in Russia.'

Kate said: 'It's the Bukhara Express, sister train to the Bolshoi Express, renovated in 1996 at a cost of twenty million sterling. Some of its carriages originally belonged to the imperial train that carried the Czar on his final journey to the Urals. You remember the Czar?'

Simon said to Anna: 'Anna, how far is it to Bukhara?'
Anna said: 'To Bukhara?'
'How far is it? How long will it take us?'
Pause.
Anna said: 'It's a long way, Bukhara.'
'I know it's a long way. Come on. You work for Intourist.'
'I never went to Bukhara.'

Kate said: 'It's about two thousand miles. Tashkent, Samarkand, Bukhara, where red lilies blow.'

'Thank you,' said Simon politely.

'And Oxus,' said Kate, ' "by whose yellow sand, the grave white-turbaned merchants go." Oscar Wilde. You remember Oscar Wilde?'

'Thank you again.'
'You're welcome,' she said, cold and unsmiling.

He really ought not to have rescued her. He really ought to have kept his platoon together and followed Innes-Chator to Kaunas. By now he would be having a hot bath, and thinking about a full breakfast in the mess: steak and onions, three or four eggs, and a nice pint of beer to wash it down. Kate Delacroix could have dealt with Second Shock Army. It would have been tough on Second Shock Army, but Russian shock armies boasted they could deal with anything. They were the boys who took Berlin, after all, and finished off Hitler.

'Would you like to come and sit down?' asked Anna nervously, wondering what he was thinking about, worried that he was still angry and might suddenly say 'Anna, I'm sorry but we have to leave you here' and dump her by the railway track.

'Not now, Anna. You don't have a timetable? You don't know how long it is before we cross into Kazakhstan?'

'We're going to Kazakhstan?' she said, dismayed.

He left.

Anna said: 'He looks angry.'

Kate said: 'He's a fascist.'

'OK, Corporal Pullin, you and Beddoes go forward. Find the officer in charge of the Russian Guards. Give him my compliments. Ask him where the train is heading for. Tell him I'd like a word. He speaks English, so you'll be all right. Colour, you stay here with me.'

The two soldiers went. He'd have liked to go himself, but didn't dare become separated from his main group.

'How are they?' he said to Gough.

'Lads are all right, sir. It's all a bit of a lark.'

Simon nodded. Moscow, Aldershot, it was all one to a squaddie, as long as he got his dinner and wasn't being fucked about too much.

They stood in the corridor. Civilians were squatting on the floor, or curled up trying to sleep. The ticket-holders who had secured compartments had, for the most part, locked themselves inside. The ticket-holders who hadn't found seats were complaining to each other.

Simon peered out of the window. Through the blackness he just could see the darker loom of buildings. They were still travelling through suburbs. There was the noise of artillery fire. He saw the flash of heavy guns. Again there was the boom of mortars. Surely the noise was louder than it had been before?

'I think we're going into it.'

'That's what I was thinking, sir.'

Kate Delacroix came out of Section HQ. She gave Simon a brief, tight smile as she passed, stepping her way over sleeping bodies. He thought of calling her back, but didn't. Her face was yellowish, but her cheeks were flushed red.

Bizarrely, over the sound of the mortars, came the beat of pop music – a Tasmin Archer track from the first CD he had ever bought, when he was in the fourth form. He remembered listening to it on

Phillimore's CD Walkman in the Shrewsbury McDonald's, eyeing up the waitresses.

He stepped over sleeping bodies and peered into the compartment next to Section HQ. In it were two girls, slim, pretty, wearing '*Arbat Street At Midnight*' T-shirts. And a man, late twenties perhaps, wearing jeans and a dirty white shirt, a gold medallion round his neck. Expensive suitcases, western. Acoustic equipment piled up on one bunk.

One of the girls – purple lipstick, a thin Slav face with high cheekbones – gave him a friendly smile.

The man looked up at him sourly.

Simon went back to Gough. 'A trendy type and two of his tarts,' he said, wondering where he himself had gone wrong in life.

Gough said: 'Any idea where we're heading for, sir?'

'Bukhara and Tashkent, it said on the carriages.'

'Seems to me we're going north.'

'I know.'

Kate was making her way back along the corridor.

'Excuse me,' she said when she reached them.

'Yes?'

Her mouth opened and closed. She sighed an embarrassed, irritated sigh.

'There's somebody in the loo.'

They looked at her.

'I mean, there's somebody asleep in the loo. Two people in fact. Men, lying down.'

'I thought,' said Simon, 'you went to the loo at the station.'

'Oh well, for Christ's sake, if I have to ask permission now every time I go to the loo—'

'Yes, all right,' said Simon. 'Colour-Sar'nt, send somebody to clear the bog for Miss Delacroix. No, on second thoughts, let's do it ourselves.'

They evicted two men: lifted them and dragged them, unprotesting, into the corridor. Simon peered around. Rosewood panelling, Edwardian light fittings, a mirror, a white washbasin from Limoges with brass taps. The lavatory itself was Russian. A cold and howling wind blew up the pan, which opened directly on to the railway track below.

'Now if that doesn't cause piles . . .' he said, trying to be friendly.

'Thank you. You can go now,' said Kate.

He positioned himself in the corridor, outside Section HQ. It was an hour, at least, to dawn. Several times the train had stopped: now it was moving again, creeping slowly forward. Outside he could see the faint outline of houses by the track, the sky behind them lit by the glow of fires.

Two people came down the corridor, stepping over the bodies, looking for a place to put themselves. They were elderly, and looked like Kazakhstan peasants. They had their belongings in plastic bags.

They nodded politely at Simon, who said, 'Good morning,' and made way for them. Spotting a fractionally open door they turned into it. There was a scream of rage. The woman in the pink shellsuit was trying to push them out again. Behind her, Simon saw a weary-looking man who was sitting on a bunk in his vest and trousers. The intruders gently pushed their way in and sat down. The shellsuited woman burst into tears.

'Dear, oh dear,' said Gough. 'We've already moved the lady once.'

'Have you?' said Simon dully. He was desperately tired. Until now he had thought the most weary moment in his life had come during a three-day NATO exercise on Lüneburg Heath, when, sleepless after a twenty-hour forced battalion withdrawal, his mind so fogged he could scarcely work out what two-plus-two equalled, a brute of a major had fired mental arithmetic questions at him – 'You have to move your platoon from zero alpha 0469 to 7856, so give me the bearing. Well, come on!'

But he knew now that he had then only been *playing* at being tired; that he had never ever been as tired as this.

Gough said: 'I could get one of the lads to bevy up.'

'No. Not till we're out of Moscow.'

The train's brakes slammed on sharply. Simon grabbed hold of Gough to steady himself. There was the crack of automatic rifle fire directly outside the train's windows.

SEVENTEEN

'Stand to! Stand to!'

'Corporal Pullin!'

'Sir—'

'Get as many civilians as you can into compartments. Post a man at every third window. Tell them to lie on the floor.'

'Gates, Mace, Lacy . . .' shouted Pullin.

'What about the LMG?' said Gough.

'Leave it.'

If they needed to use a machine-gun, they would really be in trouble. The train had stopped. Simon crawled up to a window and looked out. Black tower-blocks, railway sheds, lit by a red glow in the sky. They must kill the lights; they were sitting ducks. As he turned to shout an order, the train's lights went out.

'Everybody keep down. Keep your head down,' he spoke loudly but slowly, hoping some of the civilians might understand him.

A building was on fire beyond the railway tracks. No, not a building – a train on a different line, its carriages blazing.

Mortars were firing a steady barrage beyond the sheds, a thousand, perhaps fifteen hundred metres away.

Beddoes, from behind him, said: 'Miss Delacroix, sir?'

'Tell her to keep out of the way.'

'She went to the bog—'

'I'll get her,' said Gough.

'No, leave her.'

Another burst of automatic fire from outside the window, then the deep crump of mortars.

Those bloody mortars! The ground under the train was shaking; the carriage was rocking.

Mace's voice: 'Shall we return fire, sir?'

'You do and I'll fucking kill you.'

Men were spreading along the corridor, crawling to their allotted places, then sitting, rifles cradled in their arms.

Simon called to Gough to join him. He said: 'All right, what do you think?'

'I don't like all this glass.'

Simon said: 'Oh Jesus. Try to get the civilians to lie on the floor.'

Gough shouted: 'Corporal Pullin!'

Kate's voice came from the end of the corridor. She called, frightened, 'What's happening? What's going on?'

He called back: 'Just come back to your compartment and lie down and protect your face.'

She came slowly back down the corridor, stumbling over bodies, and disappeared into Section HQ.

'OK,' he shouted, 'now remember that nobody fires without a direct order from me.'

Five minutes passed.

The mortars suddenly stopped.

The music in the pop-singer's compartment changed from Tasmin Archer to Mike Oldfield.

Tubular Bells. Loud.

'Tell them to turn if off.'

'I was quite liking it, sir,' said Mace, wriggling along the floor.

'There might be a Russian gunner somewhere who doesn't.'

The music stopped.

Another burst of automatic fire – this time returned from the trees beyond the blazing train.

They were in the FEBA – had to be – caught between two armies; stuck fast in no-man's-land.

Section HQ's door slid open. It was Kate again, crawling out on hands and knees.

'Look, I've been thinking. Can't we make contact, explain who we are, tell them what happened?'

He said: 'No.'

She said: 'General Kotelnikov's not a barbarian. I met him once at a Kremlin reception. They're not going to do anything to us. It's all press hysteria, believe me.'

'That's all right? That's OK, then?'

'He's got nothing against *us*. He's got no reason to hurt us—'

'They killed four American aid workers, yesterday afternoon. They hanged them. The mob hanged them while Second Army units watched. I've got ten men here. What the fuck do you think I can do with ten men?'

A pause.

She said: 'I could be the only Western reporter to go into Moscow with Kotelnikov's forces.'

'Pardon?' he said, incredulous.

'Sir?' a quiet voice from the far end of the corridor. Lacy, a steady lad, in line to be promoted lance-jack.

It was Pullin and Beddoes returning. Behind them was a shadowy figure: the Russian guards officer. He walked slowly down the corridor, stepping politely round the Royal Mercians, over the civilian refugees.

Simon said: 'Simon Morrell, 1st battalion Royal Mercians.'

'Andrei Nikolaievich Bulygin, 44th Cavalry Regiment, attached to the Presidential Guard.'

He leaned down and extended a hand. Simon wondered if he ought to get up. He didn't see any reason why he should get shot.

The Russian, apparently realizing his difficulty, crouched down on his haunches.

Simon said: 'You're the train commander?'
'Yes.'
'Where are we heading for?'
'Kazakhstan.'
'Do you know where we are now?'
'North Moscow. Near the Sportkompleks Dinamo.'
Something stirred in Simon's memory . . . something he had been told about a goods yard near the Sportkompleks, something from an intelligence cadre at Ashford.
'Near Khodynskoye?' he said. 'Near the Kremlin tunnel?'
'Yes.'
'Why are we stopped?'
'The line is blocked. I think it's the 111th Motor-rifle Division, they were in this sector just before midnight.'
Next to him, Kate jumped as a flare cracked in the sky outside. In the sudden bright light the Russian officer was revealed clearly. He was a lieutenant, about Simon's age: twenty-two perhaps.
'Will they attack us?'
The Russian did not reply.
'Are they with Kotelnikov – with Second Army?' asked Simon, although he already knew the answer.
The Russian said: 'They are part of Second Army.'
Simon said: 'What do we do?'
Kate said: 'Have a pow-wow, I should.'
Jesus . . .
'Well,' she said, 'I can leave you chaps to get on with it. Good-oh.'
She crept back to the Section HQ compartment.
A moment later there was a sudden jolt, as if a wagon had rolled into the back of the train, or an engine had been clumsily shunted against them. Section HQ's door opened.
Kate, on the floor, said: 'OK it's not my business, but can't we at least *ask* the engine driver to get his finger out? I mean I know I'm not a military genius and all that—'
He said: 'Kate, just sod off, all right?'
The door closed.
Simon said: 'We ought to try to get the train moving. We ought to try to get out of here. Look, I suggest . . .' But what did he suggest? That they take on a motor-rifle division?
The train was moving.
Imperceptibly at first – now picking up speed.
They both peered out of the window. They were passing the burning train. Another train was beyond it; they could see figures running – then they were past both trains. A moment later the red glow in the sky fading to blackness. The train lights came on.
'Kill those lights!'
Gough grabbed Beddoes' rifle and smashed the butt into a corridor light overhead. Down the corridor, Fisher and Pullin did the same.
Simon leaned back against the inner wall of the corridor, the wall through which, with luck, no high-velocity bullet would come. The

train was still moving; he could feel the wheels turning, picking up speed. The earth was no longer shaking. The mortars had stopped, or they were pounding some other poor bastards.

Thank Christ, he thought. Thank Christ . . .

He could see a faint lightening of the sky outside. Dawn was not far off.

The Russian officer said: 'I think something was joined on to the end of this train.'

'Yea?'

'I think so.'

Simon said: 'Shall we go and look?'

They pushed their way back through two carriages of civilians. They passed through into the end carriage.

The corridor was empty. The compartment doors were open. The refugees had been ejected. God only knew by what persuasion, or by what means.

After a moment his eyes made out a figure standing at the end of the corridor: a vague shape in the gloom.

It was a Russian soldier holding a submachine-gun.

As they stood, still and silent, he slowly raised his weapon and pointed it at their stomachs, their lower abdomens.

Simon said tensely: 'Ask him his unit.'

The guards officer called something in Russian. The soldier did not respond.

Simon said: 'What is he? Second Army?'

The guards officer said, 'The uniform's Spetznaz: special services.'

He called again. In the dim light Simon could make out the sailor-striped shirt of the Spetznaz trooper, and a pale, smudged face smeared with cam cream.

'He won't tell me his unit. Most Spetznaz are with General Kotelnikov.'

Simon said calmly: 'We go back, very slowly. All right?' but knew, as he said it, that it was no use . . . that if the train had been taken by Spetznaz, there was nowhere to run to.

'OK,' said the guards officer. He started to move back. Simon knew that if he turned round, the Russian would shoot him, fire a stream of shot into his back, blasting his kidneys, his stomach . . .

'OK, go now!' he said, turning.

'Wait!' shouted the Spetznaz trooper.

They stopped.

The trooper said: 'I think the sergeant would like a word.'

It was not his words, or the fact that he spoke English, but his thick Welsh accent that took Simon by surprise.

They had taken over a compartment, the last on the train. On the floor were two GPMGs. Ammo pouches were flung everywhere. A soldier was setting up a communications console, unwinding a radio aerial.

Two men were wounded. One sat holding a blood-soaked arm against his chest, his good hand clenched and pounding his knee as he swore a stream of obscenities.

Another man lay unconscious, breathing noisily, his Russian camouflage jacket stained with blood that was alive, moving, pumping.

A soldier was leaning over him, injecting a syrete of morphine into his arm. He looked up briefly and said: 'It was a fucking mess. How many men have you got? Are any of them medics?'

In Section HQ, Kate said to Beddoes: 'Beddoes, do you realize you could now be sitting in the very seat the Czar sat in when he went to meet his doom?'

'I hope I don't meet mine, miss.'

'I hope not, too, Beddoes.'

She looked out of the window, bored.

EIGHTEEN

NATO ACE Forward HQ, Kaunas, Lithuania, 03.30 hours, 19 March

Until a month ago the hut had been the barracks of thirty Lithuanian army conscripts, and it still smelled of the potatoes and the cabbage soup that they had lived on.

Their bunks had filled one end of the hut. Beyond a chipboard partition had been their mess area.

Privacy had been unknown to them. The Lithuanian army lived by the old Red Army regime, and there is no word for privacy in the Russian language. When the conscripts inhaled raw alcohol fumes, as they had most evenings, they had done so twenty men at a time, under a groundsheet.

Littlehales looked at the clock: 03.30 hours. Christ, but he was tired. His desk was littered with plastic cups. If he drank any more coffee his nervous system would disintegrate.

The phone rang. His clerk answered it, and then said: 'Major Biggin, sir, arriving 07.30. He'll want to see you.'

Biggin was part of *Catchphrase*, the SAS operation that promised to be the biggest operational disaster since the Gulf.

Thank God, Littlehales told himself with deep sincerity, he wasn't anything to do with it.

His job was intelligence. His job was to know what was happening in Moscow. Was the Federal line still holding? Had Kotelnikov reached the Kremlin? Were university students really, as Radio Tula claimed, barricaded inside their Stalinesque building high on the Sparrow Hills?

Was the Gastronome No 1 foodstore, with its mountains of first-quality beluga caviar, Georgian smoked hams, wines and spirits, being sacked, or (a straw in the wind, if he had the answer to this!) was it being protected by Kotelnikov's troops for the use of the new party bosses?

Was *Isvestia* being printed? Were the bakeries working?

Were all British subjects out of Moscow?

'He wants to see me *when*?'

'Soon as he gets here, sir.'

Nobody was getting any sleep. Not tonight. A steady stream of faxes came in: from the deciphering machines, from other huts by messenger.

Four television sets gibbered quietly to themselves. Just after 02.00 the Chinese had shown newsfilm from the Hotel Cosmos, the

Federation forces' new battle HQ on Prospekt Mira. Petersburg channels 1 and 2 were putting out endless government statements that Littlehales had to keep an eye on, though it was clear that Petersburg knew less than anybody. Moscow 1 was playing as safe as it knew how, putting out endless repeats of *Love at First Sight*, the Russian domestic version of the show *Blind Date*. The other Moscow stations had closed.

There was a knock at the door of the hut. It was a middle-aged thin man: sports jacket, lemon-coloured shirt and matching tie, an army parka.

He said he was Clive Preston, head of security at the Moscow embassy, just arrived by convoy with the ambassador and the last of the diplomats.

'They said you might know what happened to Lieutenant Morrell.'

Littlehales told him about the failure of the helicopter evacuation.

'He's still there? Bloody hell . . .'

Preston sat down. Unasked, the clerk brought him coffee, knowing that here was another fly in the intelligence-gatherer's web.

'He should have come out with us, but he fancied this girl – a television reporter.'

'Kate Delacroix?'

'Bloody daft, but there you go. Didn't seem old enough.'

'What.' said Littlehales, surprised, 'for the girl?'

'To be commanding a platoon of soldiers.'

Morrell was twenty-two. There'd been acting brigadiers of twenty-two in the Second World War.

Clive said: 'You reckon he'll be all right?'

'We're doing what we can.'

'But we've pulled everything out of Moscow?'

'Yes.'

'So there's fuck-all you can do?'

'I wouldn't say that.'

'Bloody daft. Chasing skirt in Moscow at a time like this. Nice lad. Good-natured. He couldn't stand his boss, Innes-Chator. A bit of a prat, Innes-Chator: always buggering the poor lad about, telling him to get a grip.'

Clive Preston's background, Littlehales guessed shrewdly, was ex-UK police or fire service.

'Well, at least *you're* out,' he said. 'What was the traffic like on the M16? Did you see any evidence of Guards units deserting? Petersburg say they can hold the Sparrow Hills, and move loyal units up from Tula and Kuybyshev, but all our sources say that Fed units are disintegrating . . .'

But his best source of information during that night, that final night, was Moscow's *Radio Maximum* English-language station.

It was broadcasting from its studio in Arbat Street, in the heart of the old city. He was monitoring its 103.7 FM waveband through GCHQ at Cheltenham. Easy enough – GCHQ Cheltenham could monitor a sparrow farting in Siberia.

The disc-jockey was a girl who sounded as though she was sixteen.

At 04.30, when intelligence reports from the Ukrainians and the CIA said that the Federals had fallen back from Babushkin and Vladykino, abandoning the Kremlin and the city centre, she was playing Beatles records.

At 04.45 she said that units of Second Army had been seen in Red Square, just a block away – then she played adverts for American VideoRental and the Moscow Off-Road Centre.

She played the music that would infuriate General Kotelnikov the most – the decadent new wave: the bands from the Rock Laboratory, successors to Krematory and Pyotr. *Love is a Disease*, she played, and *Shoobah-Doobah Blues* by The Source of Infection.

At 04.50 she informed Littlehales (who was hoping to be informed about the Federals new FEBA, if indeed one existed) that a Dark Mu song – *This Boy is Unchained and Let Loose* – was a rework about the guy in a Soviet fragrance factory forced to smell shit instead of perfume.

'The funniest nightmare in Moscow,' said the girl, with mordant humour.

Littlehales hoped she had an exit worked out, a hole to hide in, that somehow she would get across the river to the university.

The door opened. His clerk came in, bringing sandwiches from the canteen.

The girl was saying: 'Today there will be no "Moscow Business World", but "Moscow in the Morning" may well have an unexpected guest' . . . music faded up, then back. 'A general from Siberia' . . . the music faded up then down . . . 'A *five-star* general from Siberia . . .'

'That girl's dead meat,' said the clerk.

At 05.50 they were back with the classics. 'For all you romantics,' said the girl, the voice of a kid taking her GCSEs, 'all you lovers in Moscow tonight, wending your way home along Arbat Street, gazing up at the moon, kissing under the stars.'

Moon River . . .

'Good morning, Moscow,' said the girl suddenly.

The signal was cut off.

It was 05.52.

Moscow had fallen.

PART TWO
KUYBYSHEV

O Lord, Who didst call on Thy disciples to venture all to win all men to Thee, grant that we, the chosen members of the Special Air Service Regiment, may by our works and our ways dare all to win all and, in so doing, render special service to Thee and our fellow men in all the world, through the same Jesus Christ Our Lord, Amen.

Regimental Collect of the SAS Regiment

ONE

Buzuluk, Bashkir ASSR, morning of Tuesday 19 March

> ***This is an account of life in the Red Army and the army of the Russian Federation, as recorded by Major-General Vladimir Stephanovich Prosvirkin, presently commanding the 45th Division of the 9th Tank Army, Buzuluk.***
>
> ***First Russian and Ukrainian Rights: Dovstoy Agency, St Petersburg 14009. First European Rights: Curtis Browne, 162–168 Regent Street, London W1R 5TB. American Rights: Miss Maggie Tuttbinder, 204a East 87th St, New York, NY 10128.***

A thousand miles from Moscow, in a village in the scrubby pine forests of Bashkir, an hour's drive from Kuybyshev, Major-General Prosvirkin sat reading through the manuscript pages of his book.

He did not actually know anyone at Curtis Browne, or at the Maggie Tuttbinder agency, but had been given their names by the man at Dovstoy, and hoped that the recipients would be flattered, and interested. He read:

> *One day in 1995, when I was in Army Supply division (Procurement), I was ordered to negotiate a military equipment deal with a Near East country.*
>
> *I was ordered to negotiate the sale of 22nd Artillery Brigade.*
>
> *22nd Artillery Brigade!*
>
> *The 'Stalingrad' Brigade!*
>
> *This famous unit with its five battalions, its 180 mm S-25 guns, its new B-5M howitzers, to be SOLD – with or without personnel (who would not, of course, be forced to serve abroad, in a foreign service, but would, it was felt, jump at the chance!).*

His clerk knocked and entered, and told him that his car was ready, but no driver was available. The clerk had a seedy look. There was a shortage of vodka, and for several days men had been swigging eau-de-cologne and, of course, smoking hash.

Hash . . . the curse of the mujahideen on the soldiers of Russia!

Prosvirkin nodded. He said that he would not need his car today. The clerk clicked his heels, turned and went.

The office was desolate, the wooden desk scarred and unpolished.

He sighed, gently. His eyes returned to his manuscript.

At lunchtime I proposed to take the Iraqi military attaché to the mess on Grankovskogo Street (still, at that time, the best officers' mess in Russia, reserved for top generals and their whores). In the event, he took me to the Praga, at the end of Arbat Street, next to the Mothers of America 'Soup Kitchen'. We ate caviar and Georgian bread and lamb kebabs that were not slivers of meat but succulent thick chops on the bone.

When it was time to leave, a waiter appeared with my coat and put it round my shoulders. With shock, I recognized him as a former captain in the 103rd Airborne Division.

This man had been with me in Afghanistan!

He had been at my side when we fought our way up through the Tajbeg Palace – the paras and the KGB fighting side-by-side – until we captured the Afghan president and his mistress in the drinks bar on the top floor, took them down to the courtyard, and shot them.

This was the man who later stood behind the girl in the Kabul radio station (the photo-picture is available in the KGB Archive, University of Missouri), a pistol in his hand, as she read out those fateful words:

'The Revolutionary Tribunal has sentenced Hafizullah Amin to death for crimes against the noble people of Afghanistan. The sentence has been carried out . . .'

Now here he was, a man of sixty-five years, perhaps.

A waiter in a Moscow 'dollar' restaurant who timidly held out his hand for a tip, who said 'Thank you, thank you' to the man from Iraq.

Prosvirkin put down the manuscript. He stared sightlessly at the dingy cream wall of his office. In his mind's eye he was back in Afghanistan, on the night the 103rd Airborne Division crossed the Hindu Kush, and the paras landed in the moonlight round the Tajbeg Palace . . .

From the next office he heard a door bang, chairs scraping.

He got up and took his cloak from a hook. In the outer office the clerk was reading a novel about outer space. His aide-de-camp, a lieutenant with a red, raw face and his head shaved almost to the skull, was just sitting down to eat a plate of small squares of cheese – a lunch he had presumably brought back here to avoid the accusing eyes of the soldiers.

'Is there any news of Kuybyshev?'

'No, General.'

'From Moscow?'

'No, General.'

Prosvirkin went through the annex, out into the street.

His aide-de-camp could have driven his car. His clerk was probably hoping to steal the petrol, or had stolen it already.

The road through the settlement was unpaved: a sea of frozen mud that even the troop carriers had trouble negotiating. Two lines of barracks ran back, away from the thoroughfare. Their concrete walls were cracked and (he had seen the numerous complaints) let in a constant stream of water.

There was no restaurant, no cinema, no women except for the team of old hags whose job it was to mend the roads.

There were some pigs in a concrete piggery. There was the *banya*, or steam bath, a rusting corrugated-iron hut where once a week the men washed, and where the NCOs, the *praporshchiks*, inspected the white stripe sewn into their collars as a check on their cleanliness.

Smoke was rising now from the *banya*'s chimney. A conscript would be feeding wood into the furnace. They had plenty of wood, thank God.

This miserable village in the pine woods was Buzuluk. The home of his command: 45th division, 9th Tank Army.

A division that did not exist.

A division invented, in 1988, by the counter-intelligence gurus of the Frunzenskaja Embankment.

A division destined to live and breathe only in the computers of the Pentagon, Washington, and of NATO Intelligence at Ashford, Kent, where its strength would be assumed to be ten thousand men equipped with tanks, heavy guns, howitzers, multiple rocket launchers, and self-propelled anti-aircraft missiles.

A tank division that, in the cold reality of the pine forests, had exactly sixty men – a captain, four junior officers, a clerk, two drivers – and in command, as a great joke, a retired major-general.

No loaders, no tank commanders, no mechanics.

A phantom division.

He walked down the street. It was starting to snow. His aide-de-camp was following silently behind him, still chewing cheese, his face death-like, just like his clerk's face, from the effects of hash and cheap alcohol.

In the barracks a dozen men were having their midday meal. The mess room was steamy and full of noxious smells, the air tasting of macaroni and dried fish and rotten potatoes. The men stood to attention when he walked in, and saluted smartly enough. He was a hero of Afghanistan; as a cadet he had fought in the Great Patriotic War and had gone with 1st White Russian Army Group to Berlin. His wife was dead, and he was childless. They were sorry for him.

He saluted crisply in his turn, and made a joke.

'Men,' he said, 'today is bath day. There will be an official change of underclothing. Hut A will change with Hut B, and Hut C will change with Hut D.'

They smiled mechanically. It was an old joke, and too near the truth for comfort. He told them to get back to their potato soup, and wondered why he had come.

He returned to HQ through the driving sleet.

Were his men loyal to the Democratic Government? Or did they secretly support Nikolai Kotelnikov?

In the outer office the television set was on: satellite news from the Ukraine. Second Army had taken the centre of Moscow and pushed the Federal forces south of the River Moskva. General Kotelnikov had promised a Red Star on the highest spire of the Cathedral of the Assumption.

His clerk was breathing over the fax machine, watching a document scroll through.

'It's from America, General,' he said excitedly.

'Bring it to me,' said Prosvirkin, his old heart suddenly thumping.

He went through into his office, and the clerk bought him the fax. As Prosvirkin read it, he struggled with the English (his own book had been translated from Russian to English by a primary school teacher in a nearby town).

The telephone rang. His clerk, who had thought a fax from America the most extraordinary thing that could happen in one day, answered it, then said, even more amazed: 'A call from the Frunzenskaja Embankment, General, coming through now.'

'A call from whom at the Frunzenskaja?' he rapped, his head jerking up.

The clerk shook his head, his mouth still hanging open with surprise. The Frunzenskaja Embankment, Moscow, the headquarters of the Supreme Commander, was south of the Kremlin and was still in government hands, though the final evacuation was believed to be underway.

Prosvirkin's mind raced, assessing the implications.

Surely to God they were not calling up his skeleton division, his sixty depressed and despondent men, to fight Second Shock Army?

TWO

Near Kolomna, 100 kilometres south-east of Moscow, 11.15 hours, 19 March

A huge red star made out of plywood had been fixed to the front of the train's engine before the flight from Moscow – 'to confuse General Kotelnikov's intelligence service' the Russian guards told Simon wryly – and now it was being taken down. A young soldier was clinging to the front of the train and bashing at it with a small axe, having no spanner or not enough patience to undo the bolts.

Simon and Sergeant Hoodless watched for a moment, then walked away from the track and climbed the snow covered bank until they reached the edge of the birch forest. From here they could view the entire train.

When it had left Kazan station, it had pulled eight carriages and a dining car, all painted in the imperial blue-and-gold livery of the Romanovs.

Now it had an extra wagon tacked to its end.

It was windowless. Gunmetal grey aluminium. A railway wagon getting above itself, mixing in the wrong company, standing out like a sore thumb.

'OK, so what is it?' asked Simon.

Hoodless shrugged slightly: he did not know, his gesture implied, and he was too tired to answer.

'Was this supposed to happen? Were you supposed to hitch it on to this train?'

Hoodless nodded.

'Why?'

'What do you mean: why?' He sounded irritated, confused.

Simon said slowly, patiently: 'Why *this* train?'

'It's got special clearance. Kuybyshev, Orenburg, Kazakhstan, all the way to Samarkand. Government papers, financiers, ministers' wives – read tarts for wives, if you want to – the flight of the capitalist classes.'

'You're going to Samarkand?'

'Orenburg. Cross-border pick-up by chopper. Nobody knows that but me and the lads. I'd appreciate it if you kept that to yourself.'

The sergeant, Simon thought, was in a difficult situation: senior man in his own unit, but still only an NCO talking to an officer from another regiment.

Hoodless said: 'We should be there in twenty-four hours. Ryazan's the danger. Ryazan's the place I'm worried about. I wish they'd get a fucking move on.'

The Bukhara Express was pulled up against a long wooden platform. The Russian guards were busy ejecting passengers who did not have Ministry of Interior passes.

Clutching their belongings, heads bowed against the wind, the refugees walked along the unmetalled road to the village half a kilometre away. Through the birch trees Simon could see the tiny weekend dachas of Muscovites: little wooden huts scarcely bigger than garden sheds.

'What went wrong?' Simon asked. 'What went wrong with your operation?'

'The boss left it too late. We should have pulled out at 05.00. We were *told* 05.00 was the deadline, but he's a mad bugger . . .'

Yes, thought Simon, he would be. He might even be a dead mad bugger by now.

'Second Army advanced. They must have thought we were Feds. They opened up on us with 75-millimetre RCLs, mortars, rocket-launchers – you fucking name it, they chucked it at us. A mortar bomb hit the engine; knocked it out. You've never seen anything like it. We were told to get the wagon free, and the engineers hitched it to a shunting engine. The BMDs had passed on by then, heading south towards the Kremlin, but they left some troops behind to finish us off. They fired incendiary rounds and tracer, ratio four-to-one, I'd reckon. God knows how many men we lost. We had most of 1 Squadron on this job, as well as signals and engineers.'

'What happened to your boss?'

'Christ knows. I got my lads on board, with Taffy from 5 Group, a signaller and a REME bloke, then the fucking train moved off. I don't know who gave the order.'

Simon looked again at the extra wagon: the ugly duckling that was worth venturing 1 Squadron of 22 Special Air Service regiment to capture. It had a sliding door, bolted and padlocked, and red security seals.

'And you've no idea what's inside it?'

Hoodless said: 'Gold bars, some of the lads reckon. Ex-President's pension fund.'

'Hardly an SAS job.'

'Never know what you'll be doing these days.'

That was true enough.

'Your man Gallagher,' said Simon. 'He needs to be in hospital. He needs to be in intensive care.'

'Not in Russia, he doesn't. Orenburg, maybe. Then casevac over the border, there's a hospital at the BP oilfield.'

'Will he live that long?'

'I dunno.'

Simon shivered suddenly. The cold was becoming intense. The wind was blowing through his bones, despite the protection of his parka. The air was damp and raw: March on the Moscow plains – the misery month.

Hoodless seemed not to notice. He was still wearing blackened camouflage gear, his face streaked with camouflage cream. He stood swaying on the balls of his feet, tensed up, ready to pounce and break somebody's neck.

There was nobody's neck to break, not at the moment. Pine forests were behind them. Drifts of snow stretched alongside the track, stained black by smoke. A power-station tower could be seen over the treeline.

'Reminds me of Didcot,' said Hoodless. 'You know Didcot Parkway? We had a bit of bother at Didcot.'

Simon tried to imagine what sort of bother the SAS might have had at Didcot.

'Practice run,' said Hoodless, smiling at the memory. '17.20 from Paddington, but some bugger ballsed the signals up at Didcot. Bloody hell, you should have seen those stockbrokers running about that field.'

Hoodless clearly wasn't too fond of the capitalist classes, of whatever nation.

Blue smoke from the old Czechoslovak diesel engine was caught by the wind and blown towards them.

Hoodless said, slightly formally, 'What about you and your men, sir?'

'We're just finding our way home. We've got a reporter with us. A girl.'

'Any other Brits on the train?'

'Not that I know of. None at any rate,' he added sincerely, 'that I'm responsible for.'

Hoodless said: 'I don't suppose there's a Russian medic on board?'

'You want me to ask?'

Hoodless nodded.

A Russian soldier appeared at a train window and called to them.

They walked back, slithering down the bank of ice and slush. They climbed into the train. Hoodless said quietly: 'Orenburg midday tomorrow. You can lift out with us. If there's room for that fucking loot wagon, there's room for you and your lads.'

Simon returned to Section HQ. Anna was sitting in between Ferneyhough and Lacy, a contented look on her face.

'Anna . . .' he began.

'Yes?' she said, startled, terrified he was going to send her trecking off into the forest.

'There are two wounded men on the train, British soldiers, one of them hurt badly. Can you find out if there are any passengers who have medical training of any kind?'

He sent Gates along to look after her.

'Who's going to look after Gatesy?' said Mace wittily. 'That's what I want to know.'

'What about our dinner, sir?' asked Chaffinch.
'Your dinner?'
'We were going to get Anna to make it for us.'
'You can make your own bloody dinner, Chaffinch. Hasn't Colour-Sergeant Gough organized anything?'
'He's looking for you, sir.'
Chaffinch's eyes bulged with repressed indignation. It was 11.30 and nobody knew where their dinner was coming from. There was a bloody civil war raging for some three thousand miles in any direction he cared to look, but that was OK as long as some cookhouse was frying his chips or he could get at his twenty-four-hour ration pack.
Henshaw came in and said: 'Here, sir, you'll never guess who I've just been talking to. A reporter from the *Sun* who's come all this way just to tell the world about our glorious exploits.'
Mace said: 'You mean the battalion shagging itself stupid in Kaunas?'
Simon settled in a corner, pulled his coat up round his ears and tried to sleep. He was owed about twenty hours' sleep, he reckoned. His head buzzed; when he tried to think, he felt his mind clogged with exhaustion, his thought processes pushing their way through treacle.
It was no use. His brain wouldn't work properly, but it wouldn't stop either. Mace was boasting loudly about his sexual exploits, starting from when he was ten. It would take till Orenburg before he got through secondary school. Simon could sense Chaffinch worrying about his dinner.
Ryazan? Sergeant Hoodless had said it was the danger point. Why?
'One look at my weapon,' Mace was saying, his audience riveted, 'and you should have seen her fucking tits spring to attention . . .'
Simon wondered how Kate Delacroix was. He wondered, puzzled, where she was.
He decided to go and look.

THREE

She was in the dining car, drinking vodka with the Russian officer, Andrei, and a group of his men.

Her face was flushed. She smiled up at him and said: 'Hello, soldier.'

'Hello,' he said, sitting down. Andrei passed him a glass.

'I don't suppose there's tea?' said Simon.

Tea, tea, they laughed. Andrei spoke to a soldier, who went off in search of tea.

Simon said: 'Andrei, I wonder if we could have a talk?'

'Drink first,' said Andrei.

'Yes, have a drink,' said Kate.

'You do realize,' Simon said, 'it's just after eleven-thirty in the morning?'

'Is it? Is it just after eleven-thirty in the morning, is it?' She put her arm round the soldier next to her and said: 'Hey, this is my granddad. What do you think of my granddad?'

'Andrei, when do we pass through Ryazan—?'

'He is, honestly. He's a *ded* – a granddad. It means he's been in the army for more than eighteen months, and is fully authorized to bully the others about.'

The soldier grinned toothlessly: he'd clearly been well bullied himself at some point.

'Two hours,' replied Andrei.

'Do you expect any problems?'

He gave Simon a look of irony. Kate laughed.

'Ryazan,' said Simon, 'is the headquarters of the 14th Airborne Division, right?'

Andrei said: 'Is it?'

'Come on,' said Kate. 'It's not a state secret. Can you fix a plane to fly us out?'

'If you like,' said Andrei.

'Oh, I like. My God, imagine landing at Heathrow in a 55 Firefox.'

'Will they let us through the station?' said Simon. 'Are they loyal?'

Andrei raised his glass and drained it.

'Yes,' he said after a moment, an ironic look on his face. 'They're loyal.'

Kate said: 'He means loyal to Russia.'

Andrei said: 'Have a drink. Pour the man a drink.'

'Andrei's done a tour in Kurdistan,' said Kate. 'Have *you* done a tour in Kurdistan?'

'Everybody's done a tour in Kurdistan,' said Simon, 'except for me.'

That explained Andrei's good English. The Federal troops in Kurdistan had been integrated in the NATO command structure, just as they had been in Bosnia.

Anna was coming down the aisle, Gates behind her.

'Any luck?' said Simon.

She shook her head. 'If I can help at all . . . I don't know how, but . . .'

'You've done first aid?'

'With the volunteers . . .'

DOSAAF: the old Soviet children's society that assisted the army, airforce and navy, and tended the gardens of war graves. Seventy five *million* children had gone through DOSAAF, Simon had read somewhere. It had taught a million teenagers a year how to drive. First aid with DOSAAF would have included battlefield wounds.

The Russian soldiers were looking at Anna, expressionless, but somehow conveying hostility. She was standing close to Gates, a defiant look on her face.

Simon stood up. 'All right,' he said. 'Gates, you go back to section HQ. Come on, Anna. Let's go and find out. I'll talk to you later, Andrei, if that's all right. Before we get to Ryazan.'

'OK, that's fine.'

A Russian soldier said something quietly. Anna gave him a quick glance then looked away, her face suddenly flushed.

'Bye bye,' said Kate, amused.

Simon leaned down to her. 'There's another reporter on this train. One of my chaps came across him.'

'No, there isn't. *I'm* the only reporter on this train.'

'Sorry,' he said happily.

'The only Western reporter anyway.'

Simon led Anna away down the corridor.

'I'm the last Western reporter out of Moscow,' she shouted. 'Right? OK? We're all agreed on that? We're agreed, are we?'

Yes, yes, the soldiers around her all agreed.

Art Finkel had awakened when they stopped at the clearing in the forest.

He had looked out at the little dachas in the birch trees, and thought how peaceful they looked.

Then the refugees had started to drift past, their possessions in cardboard boxes and plastic bags; some of the women in tears, the men grim and white-faced, the children silent and exhausted.

It was the same as fucking everywhere he'd ever been.

At least, in this case, there were no machine-guns pumping bullets into them, no rockets blinding them, no mortar fragments slicing their limbs, no appalling politicians organizing conferences on their behalf in Geneva; no sign, thank Christ, of UN peacekeeping negotiators or internationally famous Foreign Correspondents of the Year.

Just Art Finkel, freelance hack currently working for the *Sun*, watching them, powerless to help, but not inclined to make their suffering worse by parading in front of them in a stylish macho battledress and doing a *piece to camera* . . . not inclined, he told himself, to make a trade out of crocodile tears.

At one point, during the terrible night, peeping cautiously out at the sea of huddled bodies in the corridor, he had considered letting some of the little children into his compartment – letting them tuck themselves into the opposite bunk.

The voice of reason had prevailed. *Get involved and you're done for!*

The train was moving, the last of the refugees were disappearing amongst the dachas. He tried to sleep again, but couldn't. His compartment had been damp and chilly when he had entered it in the wee small hours, and it hadn't warmed up much since.

It was nearly midday. He was hungry. He had food in his case, but, being an old campaigner, he preferred to live off the land.

He got up and cautiously opened the door. The corridor was clear of huddled bodies.

He walked back through three carriages. One of them had its compartments filled with boxed files. He'd have been tempted to poke about if he'd been able to read Russian, and if the doors hadn't been locked. He came to the kitchen of the diner and peered in. A girl sat peeling grey potatoes into a plastic bucket. A cook in stained white coat and limp hat was slowly pouring grey meat, swimming in grey gravy into an aluminium container.

Art passed on.

The conductress who had given him tea during the night was locked in an embrace with a man, the two of them squashed between her stove and her samovar. She was a strong healthy-looking woman in her thirties. The man's massive hands were playing over her firm thighs, his face nuzzled her bosom, which was as capacious as Mother Russia's. She might well, he thought, have been the mother of Sonia, his favourite tart from the Embassy Rooms Casino.

They stopped and looked at him.

He asked for breakfast in five languages, including Serbo-Croat and Kurdish.

She waved him towards the next carriage.

He went through into the dining car, which was empty except for a group of Russian soldiers at the far end.

A girl was with them, playing cards. She was speaking in Russian; they were roaring with laughter.

He sat at an empty table decorated with two pink carnations in a fluted green vase. A 1920s-style menu card, looking like the cover of an Agatha Christie novel, said in English: '*Welcome to the Bukhara Express, Your Passport to Romance.*' It offered shirred eggs and Canadian maple-smoked bacon, but he knew there was no chance, no chance at all – not this train, not this journey.

The conductress came, buttoning up her blouse, and he proffered his tickets and she carefully ripped one out, then went away again.

The girl with the Russians said suddenly, loudly, in English: 'Look, I think I ought to go and lie down.'

The soldiers didn't seem to think so. '*Niet, niet* . . .' they protested.

'Yes, I'm afraid so. I'm sorry . . .'

She tore herself away from the soldiers and came down the aisle, a sickly look on her face, not noticing Art until he said: 'Morning.'

She looked at him and blinked. 'Oh Christ,' she said dismally.

The international press corps was united again.

FOUR

12.50 hours. Endless birch forests giving way to forest clearings. High-rise flats over the trees. An hour to Ryazan, at most.

Gallagher was lying on pale blue sheets embroidered with the logo of the Bukhara Express. His chest was bandaged tightly. Over his abdomen the bandaging was looser, as if the person fixing it had been less sure of what to do, or had lost confidence.

He was unconscious. His face was grey, bloodless under its smudged camouflage blacking.

Anna said something quietly in Russian. She went down on one knee and took hold of the hand, puffy and dark purple, that was dangling down to the compartment floor.

An SAS soldier said: 'We bandaged him tight to stop the bleeding. There's shrapnel in his lungs, maybe. We don't think his backbone's broken. He didn't feel as if his backbone was broken. I don't see how he can live with his lungs like that.'

'It's OK,' said Hoodless. 'It's not as bad as it looks.'

On the other bunk, the soldier with the smashed arm leaned against the corner, cleaning his rifle. He was using his bandaged hand to wedge the stock, and his good hand to draw through the wadding.

Hoodless said mechanically: 'You OK, Terry?'

The man nodded.

Simon said: 'There's no doctor on the train. She's asked in every carriage.'

Hoodless said: 'A train full of the Democratic Republic's fucking elite, and not a single doctor.'

'There's four Mercedes car-dealers.' And a film director, he could have added, and the manager of Moscow Pizza Hut, and five directors of the Vladimir Tractor Plant, and the chief accountant from the Moscow American Medical Centre – who had given Gates a leaflet advertising his company's comprehensive Western pharmacy and psychological services for adults and children.

Hoodless was looking at Anna. He said: 'She's the journalist?'

'Russian. Intourist.'

'Intourist. Why didn't we think of Intourist? Trust the heavy infantry.'

Anna looked up, smiled, and said: 'Hi.'

'Hi,' said Hoodless heavily.

'We're coming in to Ryazan,' said Simon. 'I want to talk to my battalion. I want to talk to Kaunas.'

Hoodless said: 'We've taken over the next compartment.' He led the way. Simon wondered what the occupants of the next compartment had thought about being taken over.

'It was a car-dealer in here as well,' said Hoodless. 'Moscow Mitshubi. We kicked the bastard off at Vosresensk.'

'We didn't stop at Vosresensk, did we?'

'We slowed down,' said Hoodless.

A soldier was kneeling on the floor. On the seat in front of him was a powerpad for satellite burst-transmission, a fax machine and an FT radio. The two heavy machine-guns, the belts of ammo, the anti-tank LAW, were piled on the opposite seat. On top of the pile was an XM Armalite grenade-launcher and two Hecker Koch MP 5.9-mil submachine-guns.

Hoodless said: 'Corporal Buck, by the way.'

Buck, a lad in his mid-twenties, looked up and nodded.

Hoodless said: 'An hour to Ryazan, then seventeen hours to Orenburg, give or take, that's what we were told at the briefing.'

He sat down and cradled his head in his hands.

He's all in, thought Simon; he's shattered.

Hoodless looked up and said: 'You all right, are you, Taffy?'

A soldier on the floor said 'I'm all right.'

He was cleaning the 5.56-millimetre rounds of the XM 203 with oily flannel, then easing them into the thirty-round magazine.

'Taffy was with Five Group,' said Hoodless. 'Taffy and Chris. They got the comms gear on board. Para's one of mine – what's left of him. He was my triggerman. Number four gun team. The bloke in the corridor's one of mine, too. I was wondering if there was any way of getting a doctor on board,' he went on, still thinking about Gallagher. 'Eighteen hours to Orenburg. He doesn't look to me like he's going to last eighteen hours – not without a medic.'

'Who are you in contact with? You said Hereford earlier. Are you handling your own operation?'

'Kaunas,' said the man on comms. 'We're being routed through to Kaunas.'

'I want to talk to my battalion, but first I want brigade intell. I want to know which side the 14th Airborne Division are coming down on.'

The man on comms said: 'The satellite's operational at 13.30. There's a civilian comsat, but we can't use it for burst transmission. We can use the HF of course.'

Hoodless said harshly, 'We can do a fan dance naked on the roof if we want to, or we can just top ourselves and save the buggers the trouble of finding us.'

'Only a suggestion,' said the man on comms.

'I've got my orders,' said Hoodless. 'We don't call anybody.'

A pause.

Simon said: 'I don't suppose there's anything we can do, anyway. We can hardly take on an airborne division. What about you lot? Is there anything we can do to help?'

Hoodless looked at him vaguely. 'You've no medic?'

It was tiredness. Simon said quietly: 'If I did have, he'd be here. I'm going back to my men. Come and find me if you want anything, all right?'

Hoodless nodded.

Anna was investigating the unconscious man's wound, gently loosening the bandages from over his chest. The blood had dried, black, solid, crusting the bandages, but the centre was stained yellow.

There was another wound across his stomach.

As she teased the bandages apart Simon saw something dark and shiny, and moving.

Intestines, he realized, horrified. Gallagher moved his head restlessly, his body suddenly convulsed.

Fresh blood spread suddenly, a crimson stain. Blood and liquid. The intestines heaved upwards.

Dear God . . .

Anna pressed down with her hands, pushing the intestines back, murmuring to herself in dismay.

The man with the injured arm, Terry, was watching with casual interest, the way he might if he were back at Hereford and was cleaning his rifle with half an eye on a TV daytime quiz show.

Simon said: 'Anna?'

She looked up and said: 'Can you send Verniho to help me, please?'

He was puzzled for a moment, then he nodded.

He walked slowly back down the train. The air was warm with the mingled fragrance of peat smoke from the cast-iron stoves and tea essence from the samovar.

The Bukhara Express! Escape to the warm south, to romance and excitement, in the manner of a bygone age . . .

He could smell Gallagher's excrement, and urine, and blood.

Corporal Pullin had the section cleaning their rifles.

Mace said: 'Sir, Ferney's not had his milk.'

Ferneyhough was seventeen. He would not reach eighteen for another two days. According to army regulations, he was still supposed to drink a glass of milk with every meal.

'You've not had your milk?' said Simon, frowning.

Ferneyhough's face flushed with indignation. 'How can I have me milk, sir—'

The others broke in. 'Give him his milk. It's bloody not right.'

'He'll tell his MP, won't you, Ferney?'

'I wish you fuckers'd shut up.'

'Language—'

'What'd your sister say, Ferney?'

'Ask Mace—'

'Me? Me? I never fucking touched her—'

'Look, just shurrup, you lot.'

Simon said: 'I'm very sorry about you not getting your milk, Ferneyhough.'

'Honestly, sir, I'm not bothered about milk, sir.'

'But you ought to be. You ought to have told Corporal Pullin,.' said Simon. 'You come with me.'

'Go and get your milk, lad.'

'Go on then, Ferney . . .'

'It's only another two days, sir.'

'Ferneyhough!'

Bewildered, he followed Simon's beckoning finger. Outside the compartment Simon said. 'Leave your weapon here with Corporal Pullin. Go back, right to the end of the train. There are five carriages. At the end of the last carriage there's a soldier on sentry duty. He looks like a Russian, but he isn't. Tell him I sent you. You'll find Anna there. Give her what help you can. I'll send some food along when it's ready.'

Kate Delacroix was nowhere to be seen. Beddoes was in Section HQ immersed in a copy of *Practical Computer*. Colour-Sar'nt Gough had his head down, his parka pulled up round his ears.

Simon went forward into the dining car.

Andrei was alone, smoking, looking out of the window. On the white cloth was a pot of caviar, a bottle of vodka.

'My men have eaten caviar,' he said, 'for the first time in their lives.'

'Ryazan?' said Simon, stubbornly, wearily. 'Tell me why we can't re-route to the south.'

Andrei took a pencil from his pocket, scored a rough map on the tablecloth. 'Moscow, Ryazan, Kuybyshev, Orenburg, the Kazakhstan border. OK?'

He slashed arrows pointing down from the north.

'Second Army at Moscow. At Vladimir, 4 Motorized Infantry Division, 6 Guard Tank Army. Moving down in support of the General.'

He drew arrows pointing upwards. '46 Motor Rifle Division. Rubbish, OK, but thirteen thousand strong – two hundred and eighty-seven tanks and one hundred and fifty combat vehicles, closing the gap, joining up with their friends. OK, understand?'

The Bukhara Express was fleeing along a corridor.

'You want to go south? You want us to kill all the bastards in 46 Motor Rifle Division? Yea, OK, let's do it, if you NATO boys help us.' He gave Simon his ironic look.

Outside there were more high-rise flats over the birch trees, open spaces, a children's playground covered in slush.

'Fifteen minutes,' said Andrei, 'to Ryazan.'

FIVE

'Ryazan,' said Kate Delacroix.

'Right,' said Art, looking out at the dreary suburbs.

They were in his compartment, swapping notes, each trying to establish, covertly but with certainty, that the other had not managed to send a story to London in the last twelve hours.

Kate said: 'The train goes on to Samarkand. We don't. There's an international airport at Kuybyshev. We get there in under nine hours.'

'You want to fly Aeroflot? You are prepared,' Art said, amazed, 'to fly Aeroflot *internal*?'

'We don't have to fly Aeroflot. We can *hire* a plane.'

'In Russia? What sort of plane? Anyway, what's wrong with Samarkand? It sounds all right to me.'

'For God's sake, we're not on holiday.'

Youth, youth, thought Art, trying to remember a time when he too had been young, keen, and conscientious; and to his surprise, yes, there was a dim and distant age when he might have been described as such . . .

But he wasn't going to leave the train at Kuybyshev. He looked out of the window again.

Sleet-covered fields, little plots of land. Dachas so small they looked like garden privies. It was cold and horrible and unfriendly.

Kate, sitting on the bunk bed opposite him, said impatiently: 'Well?'

'I don't know about hiring a plane. I don't know what my lot'd say about hiring a plane. I'm features and they don't like squandering money on features.'

'Yes. OK, *I* hire the plane. I fly out on my own. You want me to tell your newsdesk where you are?'

'No.'

'OK.'

'Listen,' said Art, wishing he had never met this fearful hag, this pouting hackette. 'You leave this train and plunge into the middle of Russia, and you're out of your mind. Private plane? What sort of private plane? Do you seriously think they've got executive jets standing by waiting for you to turn up with your Amex card? You think they've got stewardesses with glasses of freshly-squeezed orange juice? Listen. Anybody in Kuybyshev with a jet has jetted out days ago – not that there ever *was* anybody.'

She leaned forward and spoke slowly and clearly. 'We send a message on INMA.'

'What?'

'A request for a plane, on INMA.'

'What's INMA?'

'Shit, International Marine Satellite. How the fuck do you get your story through, Art?'

'I put my phonecard in the little slot, and when it says dial I dial. Then I wait for a voice to say "Hello".'

'Primitive, huh?'

'I remember you now,' said Art. 'You used to be one of those little girls in the Groucho Club who show their tits and go round the corner to get cigarettes for you when the bar's run out.'

'What,' she said cruelly, 'is the Groucho Club?'

There was a knock on the door.

She said: 'You've got a friend?'

'Not here, I haven't,' said Art, thinking for a wistful second of the landlady of a certain pub in Manchester.

Kate got up and opened the door.

'Oh,' she said, 'it's you. Hi.'

She returned and sat down. 'Lieutenant Simon Morrell of the Royal Mercian Regiment,' she said. 'Art Finkel of the *Sun*.' She seemed amused, and laughed to herself.

The officer came in. 'You're the journalist?' he said to Art.

'*I'm* the journalist,' said Kate. 'I just told you, he's from the *Sun*.'

'Are there any other British on the train?'

'I don't know,' said Art, honestly.

'I'm liaising with the train commander. If you've any problems, you'd better make an approach through me. I don't know if Miss Delacroix has told you; we expect to be in Orenburg at 05.00 tomorrow morning, and we hope to leave the train at that point. That is confidential, by the way. We're trying to arrange an airlift from there to the British Gas complex in north-east Kazakhstan.'

'Good,' said Art warmly. 'You can rely on my cooperation.'

'I don't know what MoD will say about two journalists.'

'MoD will be delighted,' said Art firmly. 'Get on to Sam Tugwood in the press department. If Sam's on board, it'll go as smooth as silk. Would you care for Glenfiddich? A Bacardi? An Old Kentucky Bourbon?'

'No thanks. If we stop at Ryazan, don't leave the train. If there's any trouble for us, keep out of it. Just get clear of the station, and try to get a car to Kiev. You have a map?'

Art said: 'I have a map.'

It was one that had all the Novotels in the world marked on it.

'Here's some money. Coupons.' Simon passed a bundle of notes to Art.

'What about me?' said Kate. 'Don't I get any?'

'Share them between you.'

He glanced quickly out of the window, then looked at Kate and said hesitantly: 'Well, I expect it'll be all right, but if anything happens, good luck.'

'Good luck,' she said, not looking at him.

He left.

'You told me Samarkand, not Orenburg,' said Art reproachfully. 'You didn't mention Orenburg. What if I'd been asleep at five o'clock tomorrow morning?'

'It doesn't matter, because we're getting out at Kuybyshev. At least, I am.'

'Oh what a tangled web we weave,' said Art, 'when first we practise to deceive.'

'Oh, shut up.'

'You don't think,' said Art, 'that his "Good luck" sounded a little bit like goodbye?'

She was staring out of the window, a blank look on her face.

'Orenburg,' said Art. 'It's somewhere I've never managed to get to somehow. What's at Orenburg?'

She didn't reply. After a bit she turned suddenly: 'So where's all this booze, then? All this Glenfiddich stuff?'

'Never mind, pussycat.'

'I don't want it anyway. I'm off alcohol. I had some aircraft brake fluid and it's done something to my insides.'

She lay back on the bunk and closed her eyes. 'Oh God, I feel ill.'

She looked ill. Her hair was lank and muddy red. Her freckles looked like blotches. Her skin had a sort of sweaty sheen.

She looked ill and innocent and, to Art at least, sexy.

Ryazan. In the traffic control centre, rail officials watched the news bulletin on Tula TV, listened to the rumours on the streets, drank coffee and smoked.

Rail traffic was cut by half. Tanks from 14th Airborne Division Regiment were said to be heading into the city, though whether in support of the Federal Republic or of General Kotelnikov, nobody could be sure.

Second Army was in Moscow – you could believe *that* because Tula TV, loyal to St Petersburg, did not mention it, but the BBC World Service did.

Moscow television could only just be picked up in Ryazan. Channel One, dead for several hours during the night, was showing *To Kill the Thirteenth* – a 1992 action movie about a returned Afghan war veteran who stumbled on a desert camp where communist terrorists were training for a coup d'état.

What this meant, nobody was sure.

Channel Nine was showing the British sci-fi serial *Jupiter Moon*. Channel Ten was showing an old hockey match, the Isvestiya Cup: West Germany versus Sweden. The resurrection of Starwars? Capitalist against capitalist? The minds of the Ryazan rail officials puzzled over the meaning behind this, the message that was being sent out to them.

At 12.35 came word that the Ryazan Satellite Communications Centre had closed down on orders from St Petersburg.

At 13.35 it was rumoured that units of the 4th Motorized Infantry

Division, based at Vladimir and supporting Kotelnikov, were heading south to Ryazan, and would be in the city within six hours.

The Bukhara Express was due in ten minutes.

The officials had a fax message before them. It was from the Bukhara Express itself, and it was explicit.

The train was not stopping, either for passengers to alight or to board the train.

The officials had tried to contact Moscow Traffic Centre – the traffic centre that controlled the biggest rail network in the world, stretching from St Petersburg to the Sea of Japan.

Moscow Traffic Centre was closed.

The Bukhara Express was five minutes away.

The consensus was to stop the train – to wait for 14th Airborne Division troops to arrive, to listen to what the commander of the Airborne Division had to say. (Ryazan was an airforce town; every family had someone who worked at one of the six air bases.)

But the last orders from Moscow were clear.

They were in writing. They said that the Bukhara Express must be given priority over all other traffic.

But these orders were twelve hours old, said the doubters.

At 13.40 the divisional networking traffic manager said he felt ill. He got up hastily, and went home on sick leave.

His deputy hesitated. He was a democrat who would shortly be a closet democrat, and shortly after that no sort of a democrat, or anything else, at all.

At 13.45 the Bukhara Express went through Ryazan central station, its blue and gold coaches dusty and travel-stained, its yellow reading lights shining softly in each discreetly-tinted window.

It went through at a restrained but purposeful fifty kilometres an hour, slow enough for watchers on the platform to distinguish soldiers crouching with their weapons along the length of the dining car, to note the stubby muzzle of a machine-gun, the curiously-shaped barrel of a Carl Gustav 84-millimetre anti-tank weapon pointing out of the open window of the last carriage . . . And the odd, ugly, aluminium wagon rattling along in the rear.

The Bukhara Express went on its way.

At 14.10 the 14th Airborne Division declared for General Kotelnikov.

Ryazan station was closed.

SIX

NATO ACE Forward HQ, Kaunas, Lithuania, 19 March

Littlehales was attached to *Catchphrase*. His boss, the Chief-of-Staff Joint Intelligence Central Europe, gave him the news over breakfast.

'Somebody's got to get them out of the mire,' he said.

Littlehales said, 'Yes, sir,' but knew he was being posted to a ship that was sinking, or had already sunk.

'You've met Biggin?'

'Yes.'

'He's SAS but attached to one of the JIC standing groups. He's a good man.' He added, by way of apology: 'It won't do you any harm working with Biggin.'

He and Biggin worked all morning. In the afternoon they were called to the Secure Room.

'It's funny,' said Biggin, the high-flyer from the Joint Intelligence Committee, 'how the phrase "The colonel wants to see you" strikes as much terror now as when one was a junior subaltern.'

'OK,' said Hoepner abruptly, as they entered. 'Where are they?'

'Six hours from Kuybyshev, sir,' said Littlehales. 'The Americans have them on satellite.'

'Any trouble in Ryazan?'

'No, sir.'

'Anything in their way?'

'There's a motor-rifle division, the 46th, moving up on Tula, but the train's in the clear. There are no pro-Kotelnikov forces that we know of between them and the Volga.'

'And the men on the ground? The men who were left in Moscow?'

'Woods near Vyazma.'

'Cut off?'

'Yes, sir,' said Biggin.

'Shit,' said Hoepner.

It was raining. They could hear it rattling sharply against the windows, gusted by north-east winds. Luftwaffe met reports showed snow coming down from the Arctic. Langdon and his men would be in the cold somewhere, out in the cold and wet, dug in, the wounded in the Land-Rovers.

Hoepner stood up. He lit a cheroot, walked to the window. He said: 'I never liked this one. I never thought it worth the risk. Long-range desert patrols, SOE raids on France, it's all romantic elitist nonsense. What's it all for? What's it all supposed to prove?'

A clerk, sitting in the corner, tap-tapped into his machine. Littlehales wondered why he bothered. It was all going on tape.

There were two other men in the room: Brigadier Rosewall, who was Hoepner's chief-of-staff, and the Dutch commander of the Rapid Reaction Force's F-16 air wing.

'The British haven't got the big battalions any more,' Hoepner went on, 'but they do have their special forces, their military intellectuals, their James Bond mentality, yes?'

Biggin looked at the far wall of the hut, absorbed in an old Red Army poster that taught a conscript soldier, in six easy stages, how to tie his foot cloths over his boots.

'I remember Schwarzkopf,' said Hoepner, 'had the same trouble in the Gulf.'

Biggin said: 'General Schwarzkopf was generous in his praise of SAS operations, sir.'

'Afterwards,' said Hoepner. 'Afterwards, he was. And it was a long time ago, major, and in a very different country.'

Rosewall said: 'All right, they're in Vyazma. How do we get them out?'

Biggin said: 'A Puma with full air cover.'

Hoepner returned to the table, sat down.

'Paul?'

The commander of the F-16 wing said mildly: 'We agreed to respect the integrity of Russian air space.'

'We'll be in and out before they know it's happened,' said Biggin. 'They haven't got control of the Moscow MD radar network or Military Satellite Command.'

Hoepner said: 'No. If we go in, we play it by the book. They must know of Langdon's existence by now. They must know he's there.'

Littlehales said: 'We've told them through the Ukrainians. We've said they're British embassy staff.'

'You think they believe that?' said Hoepner. 'You think they believe EC diplomats are kitted out with GPMGs, LAW missiles and L42 sniper rifles?'

'We did say diplomatic *protection* staff, sir,' said Littlehales. 'We didn't say diplomats. We didn't claim they were trade secretaries and their families.'

'What happened to the real embassy guards?' Hoepner looked down at his file. 'What happened to "D" Company 1 Battalion Royal Mercians, Major Innes-Chator?'

'Crossed yesterday,' said his Rosewall. 'We're keeping them locked up.'

'Locked up?'

'Pretty well.'

'Right . . .' The ruthlessness of the English, when playing secret games, always impressed Hoepner.

The Dutch commander of the fighter planes said: 'What makes

you think Kotelnikov's people will cooperate and let us pull them out?'

'We're not asking them to cooperate,' said Biggin. 'We're telling them that a Puma with full air cover is lifting out a small party of our diplomatic protection staff who were caught up in the Moscow fighting. The only cooperation we want is for them to sit on their arses and not to try to shoot us down.'

Hoepner stood up again, returned to the window and looked out, as if seeking illumination in the wet, grey afternoon. 'Even the Kurdistan troops are going over,' he said. 'We were relying on the Kurdistan brigade. For God's sake, they've been part of NATO for six years.'

'The Red Army marches. Arise, O Motherland,' said Littlehales quietly.

The clerk looked up, his fingers stilled.

Hoepner said: 'I beg your pardon?'

'A song, sir. Number one in Arkhangelsk.'

Biggin said: 'Langdon and his men – we need to move quickly. He's got two dead and a dozen wounded. If he's taken, the consequences will be appalling.'

'The entire stupid venture,' said Hoepner, 'should never have happened.'

Silence.

A plane could be heard taking off: a transporter. Perhaps the plane taking *Catchphrase* personnel to the British Gas field in Kazakhstan: the men and the computers and the signals equipment. The Eurocopters were already there, they'd moved up from Cyprus the previous day.

The rain was turning to sleet. Littlehales could see it sliding slowly down the window. It was starting to go dark. He remembered the advice given to him once by a staff captain at Sandhurst: the three essential military maxims: *Never get parted from your kit. Never try to communicate through a tank RT system. Never invade Russia.*

'OK,' said Hoepner, 'get on with it. Get it organized. All right, Paul?'

The Dutchman nodded. Hoepner went on: 'You say the train is approaching Kuybyshev?'

'Yes, sir,' said Biggin.

'Your precious cargo, your booty, all secure?'

'They've got it, yes.'

'Guarded by just a sergeant and a handful of men, two of them wounded?'

'Yes.'

'Can the sergeant cope?'

'He only has to sit on a train.'

'Once it's east of the Volga, it's outside my area of responsibility. When will that be?'

'Another five hours.'

'Good,' said Hoepner. 'Something to look forward to.'

* * *

They were dismissed.

Outside, Biggin walked quickly to a nearby office, picked up a phone and spoke quietly into it. Littlehales followed him.

'The C-in-C is not a happy man,' said Biggin. 'But, then, he doesn't know what's in that wagon from Perm. Let's talk in your office.'

They went out into the driving sleet.

'How long's Hoepner got to go now?'

'Another month,' said Littlehales.

'What happens to you?'

'MoD.'

'You've been G2 for a long time.'

'A lifetime,' said Littlehales. 'Can the sergeant really cope?'

'Christ knows.'

'There's an officer with the Royal Mercians.'

'With the what?' They were hurrying between the Nissen huts. Biggin's head was bowed into the wind.

'The embassy guards on the train.'

'I'd forgotten about them.'

'Their battalion adjutant hasn't. He wants to know if their OC is going to be back in time to organize a cocktail party.'

'Oh,' said Biggin. The Royal Mercians were no concern of his. Then he said: 'Who is their OC?'

'Morrell. A lieutenant.'

'We'd better look at his file.'

SEVEN

Ryazan to Kuybyshev. Six hundred kilometres through the Russian heartland, through the endless pine trees of Mordovia, the fairytale forests of Russian folk myth . . . Home of Baba Yaga the witch, the Snow Queen and her magic rabbits.

They slowed to pass wagons loaded with logs. They clattered over a bridge crossing the Sura.

Blue-and-gold coaches, inky-blue river, yellow-washed March afternoon . . .

Art was writing a prospective colour piece for the *Daily Mail.*

This is the last great train journey, he wrote. *To be saved up for, looked forward to, kept for when you've done the Trans-Siberian, the Canadian Pacific, the Chicago to Sante Fe.*

St Petersburg to Bukhara, via Moscow, Tashkent and Samarkand!

The scent of the pines and the peat-burning stoves, of the tea in the samovar.

The smell of money in the first-class diner.

The Royal Mercians were asleep, collapsed, zonked out. They had spread through both compartments. Mace had won two hundred and fifty pounds off Chaffinch at pontoon. They had had their dinner. Now they were having a kip.

Simon stood outside in the corridor, talking to Colour Gough and Corporal Pullin.

'Rations?'

'I've a box of Mars bars,' said Gough, 'otherwise it's smoked salmon and caviar. They'll moan like buggery.'

'We'll be at Orenburg before tomorrow morning.'

'That's not before supper tonight, though, is it, sir?' said Pullin.

Gough brooded for a moment then brightened. 'I'll tell them it's smoked salmon and chips, but the chips are in Orenburg,' he said. 'That might keep them quiet.'

'OK,' said Simon shortly, not much interested. 'You both know about the lads at the back of the train? The wounded bloke that Anna and Ferneyhough are looking after?'

'Sir.' Pullin looked at him intently. Infantry soldiers were curious about the SAS, known as the 'Nutters' or occasionally the 'Secret Squirrels'. Mace was the one who wanted to join them. Corporal Pullin was the man they might have been willing to accept. Pullin was quiet and calm. He was battalion marksman. His movements were slow and deliberate, but if necessary he could move fast.

He was twenty-three. He had been promoted to corporal before he was twenty. He was intelligent, and would take his sergeant's exams soon. The ideal SAS candidate was not a killer, a fanatic, they said, but a small-team player with a penchant for Arabic or Chinese.

'The sealed wagon we acquired during the night,' said Simon quietly, 'stays on the train to Orenburg. From there it's being airlifted to Kazakhstan, to the BP oilfield. God knows what aircraft they'll use – a Yank C47, I suppose. With luck we'll swan through Kuybyshev without any trouble, but if we get stopped anywhere, if they need help, we'll have to pitch in.'

Gough said: 'You want the lads stood to, sir?'

'No, there's no need for that. But you'd best keep them off the pop.'

Pullin said: 'Not many of them like vodka. Reckon it's a fart's drink.'

A curious look was passing over Gough's face. 'As it happens I've managed to get hold of a couple of cases of vodka,' he said. 'One for the sergeants' mess and one for the officers' mess back in Rheindahlen. Fixed it with the Russian cook general.'

'That was good thinking, Colour.'

'You have to be on your toes. I've managed,' he added, as if on an afterthought, 'to fix a few tins of caviar as well.'

He was a born fixer, the El Supremo of the storeroom, a 'secret squirrel' of a different sort. His den in Rheindahlen was filled to the brim with unlikely bits of equipment, long-forgotten stores. Anything you wanted, Colour Gough could provide – an Inkerman Day buffet for the colonel, or a couple of strippers for a soldier's twenty-first birthday thrash. He was a BAOR man, born and bred. A bit past this sort of soldiering.

Ferneyhough came along the corridor. He looked pale and shocked.

He said: 'Bloody hell, sir . . .'

Mace, coming out of the compartment, said: 'Oi, oi, where've you been, Ferney?'

'Mace!'

'Sir?'

'Where are you going?'

'Shit, sir.'

'What?'

'I'm going for a—'

'All right, get on with it.'

Mace went off, whistling loudly. Simon made a mental note to zap him for the most unpleasant duty he could find in the next few days.

Ferneyhough, his voice odd, strained, said: 'His insides are spilling out. I could see them.'

Simon thought: I shouldn't have sent him; he's only seventeen.

'You could see them?' said Pullin. 'How could you see them?'

Ferneyhough said: 'She wants plastic bags.'

'What?'

'Anna wants plastic bags. For his insides.'

Gough said: 'Christ.'

With a high standard of fittings, adequate toilet facilities at either end of the carriage, and smiling, attentive conductresses, this journey is a 'must' for all who enjoy SAGA tours, concluded Art, thinking of the firm-thighed conductress, permanently coupling with her weedy lover in the recess behind the samovar.

He bylined and catchlined it, filed and stored it, moved straight on to his next piece. The life of a freelance was brutish: a relentless, dreary grind. True, he was currently on contract to the *Sun*, but who could say when the bastards would cross him off the payroll – missing, presumed drunk?

He scrolled up his theatre notes from Moscow. He had a commissioned piece to do for the *Guardian.* He still did quite a lot for the *Guardian.* He looked back to his days as a *Guardian* staffer as Paradise Lost. Sometimes, in his dreams, he re-lived that fatal day in the Seventies when he had stood up in the London newsroom and – swaying a little, for it was just after lunch – had said: 'The day they appoint a fucking woman news editor is the day I leave.'

Goodbye, Art.

He hadn't even heard the word feminist before 1975.

Midnight, he tapped on to the little green screen, *at the old Mossoviet Theatre in Majakovskogo Square . . .*

On the opposite bunk, Kate Delacroix snored loudly – then started, opened her eyes, and groaned. 'Is there anything to drink?' she asked. He pointed to a bottle of mineral water.

Troubles or no troubles, this is where Muscovites are flocking to see Vanda Butlerov's Lolita.

Did I say Lolita?

This nymph-child is no Barbie doll. This nymph-child moves and talks like a rocker. Disillusioned, emancipated, as cool and bubble-blowing as any breakneck roaming any street of any modern Russian town . . .

He looked out of the window. There were no bubble-blowing breaknecks in evidence in this part of Russia.

Sleet was falling. The train was slowly passing a row of shacks. Outside one of them, a young woman in a dirty pink plastic jacket was bending over a small vegetable plot, using a hoe to scrape the ice from the ground, seeking plant tops underneath. By her was a small pile of frost-blackened greens. She looked up at the train and watched it go past.

Kate had stretched out again and closed her eyes.

'Aren't you going back to your soldiers?' he said.

'Why? Can't I stay here?'

'If you pay your wack,' he said. 'It cost me fifteen hundred coupons.'

'I'm sure,' said Kate, her eyes closed, 'that the office will be happy to pay.'

Yes, they were rich buggers in television. He wished he'd said two thousand.

Many see this Lolita as a searing yet subtle and ironic judgement on the GDE – the Great Democratic Experiment, as the Moscow foreign community calls it – on the raw greed and unhealthy passions that are unleashed in a society without dignity, a society without order, a society without discipline . . .

No, he had never lost his *Guardian* touch, not in all his tabloid years . . .

Anna said, her voice calm, the panic controlled: 'When he coughs, they come out from his stomach.'

She lifted the bandage. Simon looked.

'I need something to cover them, to hold them when he coughs, so that no more can come out. Something that will not dry them.'

An SAS soldier, sitting opposite, said: 'She's a bloody marvel, aren't you, Anna?'

Anna said: 'He has to go into a hospital. I can't do anything. I try to help the sergeant, but there is nothing we can do.'

'Where is Sar'nt Hoodless?'

'Having a kip next-door,' said the SAS soldier – then to Anna: 'He'll do you when he wakes up.'

'I don't care,' said Anna. 'He's stupid.' She was crying, quietly.

In the galley fridge they found packs of Siberian gravalax sealed in polythene. They carefully cut off the plastic film and washed it. The plastic still smelled of fish, even after they had soused it in disinfectant from the first-aid pack.

Anna placed the plastic over Gallagher's ruptured abdomen. She covered it with a sterile dressing and a loose bandage. When he coughed she pressed gently.

Simon said: 'His lips. Look at his lips.'

There was a froth of pink blood dribbling from his mouth. His breathing was shallow - more shallow than it had been.

Anna said: 'His chest. His lungs. I think what is wrong with his lungs is more serious than down here. I think down here he has damaged his stomach wall, but it will repair if we do not infect it. But his lungs are I think more serious. I think he is dying because of his lungs. I think he is drowning in blood.'

Simon went into the next compartment.

'Wake him up.'

The SAS soldier they called Taffy looked up at him with open hostility.

'What for?'

'Don't you fucking well say "What for?" to me—'

'It's all right.'

Hoodless was pulling the blanket back from over his face. He slowly sat up, his parka sliding to the floor.

'I don't want to interfere—'

'Well, don't then, sir.'

Simon hesitated a second, then said: 'Gallagher – he's dying. He won't make Orenburg.'

'You're a doctor, are you?'

'You've got to get him into a hospital at Kuybyshev.'

'No.'

'I say yes.'

'He's not being left here to be tortured. He's not being put on TV. You saw what they did to our blokes in Baghdad—'

'Have you told Kaunas about us? Because if not, I'm going to raise them on my own HT set.'

'We sent a signal at 14.00.'

'And?'

Hoodless looked up, expressionless.

'And nothing. You're in the middle of a fucking operation, sir. Now, just fuck off out of it, OK?'

EIGHT

He came looking for Simon an hour later. It was almost dark. They went out into the corridor.

Hoodless stared out of the window. The train was creeping through an endless pine forest. By the track, stout women railworkers were hewing at the gravel with pickaxes. Why they should be doing such a thing, and with such vigour, at such a time of day, Simon could not imagine. They wore black headscarves, grey padded jackets, shiny yellow plastic waistcoats.

'Canaries,' said Hoodless, seemingly amused. 'Waddling about. Bloody hell.'

'Do you want help?'

Hoodless nodded. After a moment he said: 'He's dying. He's definitely bloody dying.'

'What does Kaunas say?'

'Casevac at Orenburg. Lift him out by chopper. But I'm the one with the responsibility. They can't see him. That woman you sent's a tartar. You should listen to her.'

Simon said: 'See Colour-Sergeant Gough. He'll get Royal Mercian insignia on to Gallagher's uniform. I'll get the Russians to radio ahead for a doctor to be waiting at Kuybyshev station. We may even be able to persuade him to come on board, and treat your man between Kuybyshev and Orenburg. At the very least, he can treat your man in the station while the engines are being changed.'

Hoodless said: 'I want one thing clear: we're not leaving him behind. He's not being interrogated by KGB bastards, no way.'

It was a fixed idea, something for him to hold on to.

'You wouldn't wish it on him,' he went on. 'Not if you'd been through interrogation. Four days, and they nearly fucking broke me; they came fucking close. If they can break an SAS bloke, they get a medal.'

Joint Services Interrogation. Jamie Pendred, the senior subaltern in Simon's battalion, had gone in for it. Kept naked in a concrete cell, blindfolded, stood hands splayed out against a wall, fists slammed into his kidneys . . . they hadn't let him have a crap for three days, till in the end he'd crapped on the floor while two women interrogators watched . . .

The KGB might be gentler, but not much.

'He won't be left in Kuybyshev. We'll have a word with Lieutenant Bulygin, the guards officer, about a doctor. OK?'

Hoodless looked out of the window. After a moment he nodded. 'Might as well see what he says.'

* * *

Andrei said: 'You tell me who these men are, I'll fix a medic.'

Hoodless said: 'Who we are? We're NATO.'

'Well,' said Andrei, ironic, 'I'd guessed you were not traffic cops on a fraternal exchange.'

Hoodless said: 'It's your government we're working for, mate.'

Andrei said: 'You say that, *mate*, but how do I know that?'

Hoodless: 'You had your orders.'

'Ministry of Foreign Affairs. A fax from the Ministry of Foreign Affairs. A *diplomat* sent to Kazan to see me off, to tell me I *might*, just *might* be asked to take an extra carriage out of Moscow. Well nobody asked that, and nobody said anything about NATO, and I don't work for the Foreign Ministry.'

'A doctor, Andrei,' said Simon. 'Can you fix a doctor? There is a man seriously wounded.'

'In Russia,' said Andrei, still in his ironic voice, 'I do not think that is anything to get excited about.'

'Jesus,' said Hoodless in disgust.

'What are you doing here? What are you doing in Russia?'

Hoodless stood up. He said: 'Forget it. Forget we spoke.'

'This train is under the orders of the Presidential Guard. Everybody on it is accountable to me.'

'Nobody's arguing,' said Hoodless.

'You are Spetznaz?'

'Yes, Spetznaz,' said Hoodless.

'English Spetznaz operating in Moscow?'

'It's a crazy mixed-up world,' said Hoodless. 'Don't worry about us.'

He left the diner.

Simon said: 'A British soldier is wounded and needs medical assistance. I am making a formal request. I will put it in writing.'

Andrei said: 'And who will you send it to – your *formal request*?'

A pause. He smiled.

'OK. For you, Simon. In view of your *formal request*.' He stood up. 'Come with me.'

They went forward from the dining car. They went through two carriages filled with boxes of government files, through a carriage being used by the guards soldiers, through a door into the cab.

Every surface was covered in a thin film of warm oil. Droplets of oily condensation were suspended from the roof. Ahead, through windows swept by a massive wiper, the track curved through the forest.

The driver – thin, long-hair, plastic fake-leather jacket – sat with his hand on the dead man's handle. A Russian soldier, clerical branch, Transport Corps, dozed over the radio.

Andrei spoke to the transport clerk, waking him abruptly. The clerk spoke into the phone. After a moment he passed it to Andrei. As he did so, he gave Simon a look: incurious, unregistering. His eyes were glazed and empty as he leaned back against the warmth of the engine.

The smell of hot diesel oil was sickly, musky, and curiously sweet. Simon was not surprised.

If grass from Afghanistan, the golden cargo on the Golden Road, could not be obtained on the Bukhara Express, it could not be obtained anywhere.

He turned to look at the driver. Was *his* expression one of mere boredom, or was he, too, stoned?

Andrei handed the phone back to the clerk, and said something in an undertone. The clerk shrugged and inhaled his cigarette, then passed it to Andrei, who took a lungful and stared out of the window at the curving, endless track.

'Well?' asked Simon, his voice raised over the noise of the engine.

'That was Kuybyshev. A doctor will be waiting.'

There was a pause.

'It's OK?' said Simon. 'No problem?'

'No,' said Andrei, then, after a moment: 'They told me local militia are inspecting trains. MVD – you know? Interior troops.'

'Right.'

Andrei again took a lungful of smoke.

'What did you say? Did you agree?'

Andrei looked at him. Suddenly he grinned.

'I told them I'd shoot the first MVD bastard who tried to climb on board.'

NINE

'Do you know,' she asked them, in the gloom of the dining car, 'what the Russian soldier has been described as?'

They didn't.

'A primeval force,' she told them, 'in European history.'

She had trouble translating primeval, but when she had managed to, the Russian squaddies grinned and poured more vodka, and told her about life in barracks.

Reveille, they said, was at 06.00. You had five minutes to scramble into your boots and trousers, run to the lavatory for a quick piss, then get yourself out of the barrack doors.

By 06.05 you were running across the parade ground, through the mud, along the metalled roads, through the forest paths. Apart from trousers and boots, you were naked to the rain or snow. On the arms and chests of other men, dangerous men, were the tattoos of the mafia: the coiled snakes, the dragons.

Among the NCOs, the *praps*, there were still veterans of Afghanistan. Their tattoos, when you saw them, were of the Kabul clan, of the Kandahar brotherhood.

For an *Afghansi*, the third toast of any drinking session was always a silent toast. A toast drunk standing to attention. A toast to those who had not come back.

They had pride, the *Afghansi*. They still walked with their heads held high. They had not, in truth, wanted to come home. Afghanistan might have been hell for the conscripts, but for the professionals it had been one great killing field.

Second Shock Army, they said, was officered by Afghanistan veterans. Brezhnev was their hero. Gorbachev, if they could get hold of him, they would hang. Yeltsin – their army group newspaper told them every day – was a dirty Jew from Yekaterinburg.

'That's a lie,' said Kate. 'Not that it matters. Not that he'd have cared.'

Forty minutes of hard exercise. Twenty minutes to wash and make your bed, and also the bed of a 'senior' conscript. An inspection. By seven o'clock you were marching to the mess hall. Breakfast was *kasha* porridge, two pieces of black bread, one piece of white bread, milkless tea and three lumps of sugar.

The sugar you handed over to a 'senior', telling yourself that, after six months as scum, you would graduate to a *cherpak* – a server of food – and after eighteen months you would be a *ded*, a grandfather, a 'senior' whose bed would be made for him, and who would extort sugar lumps from the scum beneath.

In its last act, in its last appeal to the loyalty of the army, the Federal government on 16 March had again promised to eradicate institutional bullying: *dedovshchina*.

Not fucking likely!

Not until you were out of the army yourself. Not until you'd done your six months kicking shit out of the new scum!

'Do you wish you were with Second Army now?' Kate asked. 'Do you wish you were with the Army of Moscow?'

They looked at her, smiling slyly, offered her caviar.

They said they missed their goldfish. Every floor of their Guards barracks at Kalinin had an aquarium on it: a tank of fish for each company of one hundred men.

Russian army psychologists, they said, believed an aquarium helped relieve stress and homesickness. It had been hoped to cut down on the number of conscripts who committed suicide.

It had not worked.

Suicide by shooting, they told her with grim humour, was the only form of protest permitted by the Red Army.

'Do you sympathize with General Kotelnikov? Do you think the march on Moscow was justified?'

They still smiled slyly, amused, not being taken in, not born yesterday.

One of them poured more vodka. Another dipped a spoon into the tin of caviar, and gobbled it up.

There was no doubt about it. If Kotelnikov appeared in the diner and ordered them to string up all foreigners and Jews, these boys would have her and Art Finkel and the rest of them dangling from the chandeliers in no time at all.

The Bukhara Express sped eastwards towards Kuybyshev.

TEN

Buzuluk, Bashkir ASSR, evening of 19 March

Prosvirkin made his aide-de-camp drive the car. He told him their destination was Kuybyshev public library, which was only a short distance from the railway station.

He did not dare to pack a bag. He had sent the two known spies in his unit – both of them lazy, stupid, dregs of the GRU pool – to a nearby town to negotiate the sale of pigs. But still he did not dare pack a bag. There might have been another spy he did not know about.

'The library,' he said.

His ADC nodded, unsurprised.

Prosvirkin had often used the library when writing his book. The girl assistants had helped him to check his facts and figures. Was it on 29 April or 30 April 1945, he would ask them, that the 1st White Russian and 1st Ukrainian Fronts had almost collided?

On what day, he would ask, did his own division get into the hippopotamus house, and fire at Berlin's famous flak towers?

They would sift through the regimental histories.

For much of his account, though, he had relied on memory. You couldn't expect regimental histories to record how a nineteen-year-old Suvorov cadet saw T-34s prowling the Unter den Linden, an ox roasted in the Pariserplatz! Or how the Berlin night was filled with shellbursts, and light from burning buildings reflected off clouds that were tinged with yellow sulphur smoke. How Russian troops broke into a hospital and drank ether. How terrified, naked women were pursued along a roof top until they jumped to their deaths . . .

They were in Kuybyshev. It was still only 19.00 hours. The train, he had been told, would not arrive before 22.00.

The streets were lit; there were people about. Women were clearing snow even as it fell. An organized place, Kuybyshev, as befitted the second most important military centre in Russia.

Up on the hill, high over the Volga, he could see the red light on the High Command HQ communications mast.

What coded messages would be passing back and forth at this moment, he wondered! What coded embassies would be coming in . . . soothing, polite, persuasive missives, love-letters from NATO, from Petersburg, from the Frunzenskaja Embankment in Moscow!

The generals would be sweating it out, worrying over which way to jump. The high-up military always bore the brunt of it. During Stalin's great purge, thirty-three thousand senior officers had been executed in one year alone. Krushchev had sacked five hundred *generals* in a single day! Reducing them from the pampered luxury of the Paradise Group – the exclusive officers' club from which he, Major-General Prosvirkin, Afghanistan hero, the last serving officer from the Fall of Berlin, had been excluded – to grinding poverty.

Let the generals sweat. Let them jump when they heard a footstep in the corridor, while they waited for the crash of the door, the NCO with the submachine-gun. *By order of General Kotelnikov, Commander Second Shock Army, you are sentenced to death for crimes against the people of Russia* . . .

The car was approaching the library. Prosvirkin looked at the thick, red neck of his aide-de-camp. The man, he felt sure, was too stupid to know what was happening.

The car pulled up. The aide-de-camp sat staring ahead, listlessly.

Prosvirkin had his greatcoat on, his briefcase in his hand.

The library was open, thank God. It was one thing he had forgotten to check on.

'When I have worked, I will go to a cinema. Pick me up at 23.00.'

He had never stayed so late in Kuybyshev before. Surely the aide-de-camp would look surprised, startled, resentful at being kept hanging about for hours?

No, the man was a blockhead. He would probably go to a cinema himself, after cadging a meal in the nearest army canteen.

The car pulled away. It was snowing quite thickly. Prosvirkin looked at the warm, yellow lights of the library. The assistants were friendly, young and good-humoured. They gave him tea, often sweetened with a dollop of blackcurrant jam (for he was a favourite), and listened avidly to his stories of Berlin, of the dead hippopotamus he had seen with a mortar-shell stabilizer stuck in its side . . . of the bunker room where he has seen an SS general with his arms around a beautiful girl, both of them dead, a champagne bottle on the floor.

'A boy of nineteen, seeing all that!'

'A boy from the farm,' he told them. 'A boy who grew up thinking Smolensk was the centre of the world!'

They laughed and called him a poppet.

In truth, he had been sophisticated by the standards of the Army of Berlin. He had seen men from the Uzbekistan Army Front take lightbulbs from their sockets to carry home, in the belief that they would somehow light up without electricity.

He hesitated. It would be pleasant to spend an hour in the warm, to go to a cinema even . . .

He turned away. He could not go to the railway station yet. The Bukhara Express was still over a hundred kilometres to the west, but there was an officers' club where he could sit and pretend to get drunk.

He was a veteran of Third Shock Army at Berlin, of 103rd Airborne Division in Afghanistan, an elderly widower of seventy-two, heading into the unknown.

ELEVEN

They were approaching Kuybyshev.

The train was slipping discreetly through the satellite town of Syzran, with its power station and its floodlit cement works; slowing to walking pace as it passed empty commuter trains in the dark railway sidings.

It was 21.00, and snowing. The train was sixteen hours out from Moscow. An hour behind schedule.

'Well?' said Kate Delacroix impatiently.

'Well what?'

'Well, are you coming or not?'

'You don't understand. I'm features, not news. I'm an arts correspondent.'

'You really intend to go trundling across the Urals on a train, while I fly out to Kiev?'

'That's it, pussycat.'

But he looked out of the window and shivered. Nobody had previously said anything about the Urals. His pocket map – *Novotels of the World* – showed a great yawning chasm between European Russia and Beijing. How long would it take him to get home? What would the shits on newsdesk say?

The chill winds of Russia were as nothing, he knew, compared to the chill winds of Wapping. Immured in Manchester, he had avoided many an executive axe in the long years since he and Shiny White had joined the *Manchester Guardian* (or the *Guardian* as it had just become) as trainee reporters back in 1963.

Nineteen-year-olds earning nineteen guineas a week! The first miniskirts! The long, long, long, bare legs of the copy typists. Cilla Black singing 'Anyone Who Has a Heart' . . . Milly, whose boy Lollipop made her heart go clippety-clop, or possibly pitty-plop . . . they really knew how to write songs in those days.

Shiny hadn't been as bald as a coot then, of course; he hadn't actually been shiny at all. Neither had he been running a guesthouse at Lytham St Annes.

Art hadn't looked up Shiny for donkey's years. Were there still land-yachters on the muddy sands at Lytham? Were there still goldfish in the pools in the Lowther Gardens? Was there still tea in the wooden café, outside of which the wallflowers were such a treat in the spring?

'Art?' said Kate, 'Are you there, Art?'

'Yes,' he said.

He sighed deeply. The train was entering dreary dark suburbs. The snow was falling quite thickly.

'Kuybyshev,' said Kate, 'where I get off. Your newsdesk will tear your balls off for this.'

'What's new, pussycat?' he said, with renewed nostalgia.

Now that really had been a great film. Peter Sellers. He'd seen it at the Odeon with a long-legged girl reporter from the *Bradford Telegraph and Argus*.

The Royal Mercians were crowded into Section HQ. Four of them were on each top bunk, the rest jammed up on the seats underneath.

Gates said: 'Pass it round, then, and hurry up. We haven't got all day.'

Foster passed round the mess tin. Each man drew out a slip of paper.

Anna, pausing in the doorway, said shyly, 'Hi, everybody.'

Henshaw said: 'Come on, Anna. You pick one out for Ferneyhough.'

'What?'

'Pick out a ticket for Ferney. Come on, Anna.'

'No, not me,' said Anna, drawing back into the corridor.

'Anna!'

'Come on, Anna!'

She went back down the carriage.

Lacy, on stag, curious about the noise, said: 'Hello, love. What are they up to, then?'

'Picking the short straws,' said Anna. 'They wanted Verniho to have one. No way is Verniho getting shot.'

She went back to the end of the train. Ferneyhough was sitting by Gallagher, holding up his head, giving him water.

Gallagher's bluish lips opened; water dribbled over his mouth.

'He's drinking some of it, Sar'nt,' said Ferneyhough.

Hoodless, sitting on the opposite bunk, was looking at Gallagher carefully.

'Keep his feet up, higher than his head,' he said. 'It helps his circulation.'

'How is he?' Anna said quietly.

'He'll be fine,' said Hoodless. 'He's tough as old boots is Para.'

Gallagher's eyes were on Anna as the water dribbled down his chin. She knelt and took his hand in hers.

'It's sweating again,' she said. 'His hand sweats, but it is cold.'

'Yes,' said Hoodless. 'It's what you'd expect.'

Gallagher's head fell back; his eyes closed.

'It's the morphine,' said Hoodless. 'His body won't take the water because of the morphine. It gives him a terrible thirst, but it doesn't let him drink. The doctors won't have it, but I've seen it a dozen times. Funny stuff, morphine. You all right, lad?'

'I'm fine, Sar'nt,' said Ferneyhough.

'Go back to the others,' said Anna. 'The captain wants to talk to you all. I will be all right here.'

Ferneyhough looked at Hoodless.

'Well, go on then,' said Hoodless. 'Do as you're told.'

In Section HQ, Gates said: 'Right, it's twenty quid a ticket, and the Colour-Sar'nt wants it paid up now.'

Chaffinch said: 'Mace? Lend me twenty quid of my money back.'

'*Your* money?' said Mace. 'What do you mean, *your* money? It's my money, I won that money fair and square.'

They paid up and opened their slips of paper.

'Bear witness that I am taking one for Ferneyhough,' said Gates. 'This is Ferneyhough's ticket that I am opening now . . .'

He unfolded the paper.

' "Friday's Child".'

Simon came in.

Gates said: 'Taking a ticket in the Colour-Sar'nt's sweep, sir?'

Simon said: 'What's it for?'

'Cheltenham Gold Cup.'

'It's not Gold Cup, is it?'

'Tomorrow, sir.'

'How much?'

'Twenty quid.'

'Bloody hell. Yes, OK. Keep one for me. Right, listen in. We are coming into Kuybyshev. The train will stop for an hour, perhaps two hours. Now, you all know that there are other British soldiers on the train. Two of them are injured, one of them severely.'

They were staring at him.

'We are trying to get a doctor on board. We will also be getting a different engine. While we are in Kuybyshev, nobody leaves the train without my direct authority. Is that clear? This is a country falling into civil war. It's plunging over the edge, and it's happening bloody fast. You've been watching the television news?'

They nodded. Beddoes had been getting a satellite fix whenever the train stopped.

'Kuybyshev is Russia's number-two military command headquarters. If there'd been a nuclear war with the West, the government and military top brass would have moved here, into a command complex built in the cliffs along the Volga. It's also the headquarters of the old Bosnia Brigade. All this means that it's loyal to the government – the legal government in Petersburg. But people are nervous. They are liable to overreact. Nobody is going to take kindly to foreign troops wandering about, even if it is only Mace looking for the nearest fag machine.'

He paused. Mace looked pleased.

'So nobody leaves the train unless I say so. But if anything goes wrong, if for some reason the train is stopped from leaving, then we'll be finding ourselves some other form of transport. Pack your Bergens. I want to be able to evacuate this coach in thirty seconds.'

TWELVE

Kate went looking for Andrei.

She wanted to say goodbye, to give him her number in London. In her opinion it would be a long time before he would be able to return to Russia. Any Federal officer who escaped to the West would have a death sentence on his head. A young officer of the Presidential Guard would need all the help he could get, if he wasn't to end up soldiering for Iraq or serving pizzas in Camden Town.

Andrei wasn't in the diner. Russian soldiers were buttoning up their greatcoats, checking their rifles. She hesitated, then went back down the train. She looked into the Royal Mercians' compartment. The soldiers were sitting with their Bergens packed, playing cards.

'Look, thanks for everything,' she said warmly. 'I want you to know I'm incredibly grateful.'

'That's all right, ma'am,' they said, looking up at her in surprise.

'Take care and have a good journey, yeah?'

'And you, ma'am.'

'Do you know where Lieutenant Morrell has got to?'

They didn't.

She looked into the next compartment, Section HQ, and said thank you to Beddoes and Colour-Sergeant Gough, who were listening to the radio. Then she went back down the train. The corridors were empty. The passengers from Moscow, the capitalist elite with their Ministry of Interior passes, were keeping their doors locked. None of them, it seemed, were interested in Kuybyshev by night.

She reached the end of the fourth carriage and found a small crowd of people: the girls who had manned the samovars. They were packed and standing by a door, chattering in high humour, putting on lipstick, pleased to be home at last.

Beyond them was Simon, staring out of a window, an anxious look on his face.

'Hi,' she called.

He looked round, startled.

'These samovar girls,' she said, pushing her way through to him, 'don't they remind you of airline stewardesses at the end of a flight? Duty-frees stored away, passengers all attended to, little overnight bags packed.'

He laughed, a look of surprise on his face.

He was all right, really. She'd been a bloody awful cow.

'I want to say thank you—' she started warmly, and then said: 'Good God!'

The buildings by the track had fallen away. Above the train there now soared a web of girders decked with red lights. Beneath them was black water, a tugboat bobbing along with a light on its stubby mast.

They were crossing the Volga, in places half a mile wide as it flowed south to the Caspian Sea. The neon lights of downtown Kuybyshev were massed along the opposite shore.

The train slowly moved out, over the black waters.

'Do you realize,' Simon said, 'we're as far east as Iran?'

'What a life,' she said, 'you soldiers lead.'

'You've said it. One exotic place after another. Bints falling over themselves for us.'

'Ah, yes,' she said. 'Soldiers have bints.'

The train clattered slowly off the bridge. In the misty March night they looked down on streets lit by sodium lights, a sports ground, skaters on an ice-rink.

She said: 'Thank God we're back to normality.'

'It's an illusion. Thirty per cent of the population were at starvation level in February. Up until last week we were still flying food aid in to Gorki.'

'Yea, right.'

The suburbs slipped past. An illuminated advertisement for German fruity drinks that nobody could afford anymore.

'I really want to say thank you—' she started again, but at that moment Corporal Pullin came pushing his way through the samovar girls, calling: 'Mr Morrell, sir!'

The samovar girls did not make it easy for him. 'S'cuse, s'cuse . . .' he said. The girls called out, spoke loudly to each other, and laughed.

'I wonder what they're saying?' said Simon.

Kate said: 'You want to know?'

She leaned up and whispered in his ear.

'I thought so,' he said, trying not to look shocked.

Pullin said: 'Sar'nt Hoodless would like a word, sir.'

'Tell him I'm on my way.'

'Sir.'

The girls had crowded closer. 'Now, come on, girls,' said Pullin, 'make way. Come on now. Don't be daft.'

They uttered cries of Slavonic despair and mockery as he pushed through them.

Kate said: 'Sar'nt Hoodless? Who's he?'

'There are some other soldiers on the train.'

'NATO soldiers?'

'Yes.'

'Where on earth did they spring from?'

'They were caught in Moscow, just like us. I'd better go,' he said reluctantly, clearly not wanting to go at all.

She said: 'Listen, I want to say thanks.'

'Thanks?'

'You've been great.'

'That's all right.'

'And I'm sorry. I'm sorry I've been such a nuisance. I'm sorry I haven't seemed grateful. I was just so ill, and I'd messed my job up, and I'd behaved so stupidly and there wasn't anybody else I could take it out on—'

'Thank me when we're airborne from Orenburg. In fact, if you like, you can thank me properly by letting me take you out to dinner in Istanbul.'

'Istanbul?'

'There's a little place I know by the Bosphorus.'

'You soldiers don't half get about. What would we be doing in Istanbul?'

'NATO Eastern Command. Debriefing.'

'I'm going to be debriefed?'

'If,' he said, smooth as butter, 'you give me half a chance.'

'Well,' she said, surprised.

The train jolted, and he put his arm out to steady her.

'Dinner in Asia,' he said, not taking his arm away, but rather moving it round her shoulders to protect her from further jolting. 'Fresh mackerel grilled over a brazier while the sun goes down over the Golden Horn.'

'No, listen,' she said, as the samovar girls jostled her up against him. 'I'll take you out to dinner in London.'

'London? I don't want to wait till London.'

'The Caprice, Joe Allen's. We'll go to the Groucho and sneer at that louse Finkel.'

'Dinner with me first,' he said firmly, 'in Istanbul.'

'I'm not,' she said, with a tight smile, 'going to Istanbul.'

The train was pulling into the vast cavern of the station. A sign said Kuybyshev Grand Central.

Simon said: 'What?'

'I'm not going to Kazakhstan.'

'You've got no choice.'

'Sorry. I get out here.'

'You can't,' he said. He had taken his arm away.

'Look, Simon, you've been great,' she said earnestly, 'but I have got no possible reason to go on a long train journey. There's a Reuters office in Kuybyshev. There's a BBC stringer – I've even got her phone number. I've a girl friend who lives here, a girl I was at university with—'

'How will you get out of Kuybyshev? How will you get home?'

'They'll fly a plane in for me.'

'A plane?' he said, incredulous.

'Yes,' she said, wishing they weren't pressed so close together, trying to push herself back a bit. 'From Kiev.'

'A plane flown in from Kiev, for you? The misery Russia's going through, the sick people, the starvation . . . and they'll fly a plane from Kiev just for you?'

'I'm a reporter,' she said. 'A television reporter.'

'You're a selfish bitch.'

'Right,' she said, upset. 'You've seen through me at last.'

'You are not,' he said coldly, with certainty, 'leaving the train here.'

They were alongside a platform. Outside there was a huge buffet-bar, the size of the BBC Club bar in Portland Square, and about as comfortless. A few men were drinking, watching television behind the counter.

He turned and pushed his way through the samovar girls.

'For Christ's sake,' she yelled, 'don't be so bloody childish.'

'Ooh, ooh,' wailed the samovar girls, who had had a terrible journey to Moscow, but had come back safely, and were in high spirits, and glad to be home.

The train pulled to a standstill. Small children were walking alongside, offering up bunches of tulips, carnations, single roses. She went back to Art Finkel's compartment and banged on the door and, when he opened it, said; 'This is your last chance.'

'Go away,' said Art. 'I want to lock the door.'

She had no coat, no belongings.

'Can you give me some of that money?'

Art reluctantly handed over five thousand coupons. 'I want a receipt.'

She scribbled one. 'See you,' she said, handing it over. 'Have a nice trip.'

'Oh, all right. I'll come for a walk on the platform,' he said, made daring by her adventurous nature. 'How long do we stop here for?'

'How the hell would I know? I've stopped here for good.'

They left the train. Simon and Andrei and a British soldier she did not recognize, presumably this Sergeant Hoodless, were further down the platform, talking to two civilians. There was an ambulance drawn up. Two medical orderlies with Red Cross armbands and blue uniforms were getting out a stretcher.

'I wonder what's going on?' she said, but Art had already disappeared into the buffet-bar. She ran after him. He was pointing at a bottle of Heineken beer, and calling 'That's it, sweetness. That's the one.'

'Art? There's an ambulance meeting the train.'

He said: 'I've drunk too much spirits these last two days. I need to wash out my kidneys. It makes my skin go pasty when I stay too long on the hard stuff.'

'British soldiers and an ambulance out there,' she said. 'What's going on?'

Art was busy drinking, at the same time waving his hand to order another beer. He neither knew nor cared.

Kate made for a telephone. She had her contacts book, and in it the number of the BBC stringer.

The phone wasn't working.

She went outside the buffet, looking for another phone, or for a way off the platform.

She avoided the Bukhara Express and went round the corner and along the next platform. This part of the station was tiled with mosaic murals from Stalin's day: Moldavian farmers bringing in the harvest, plucking the vines. There was a picture of a hydro-electric scheme, a dammed valley, brown-skinned peasants with white teeth and merry smiles sitting by corn-stooks.

It was damp and cold. The murals were dirt-stained and cracked. It could have been New Street Station, Birmingham, before privatization, except that there was no litter. This was a city, like Moscow, where Western 'packaging' was unknown, where even a piece of used brown paper or an old cigarette carton had some value.

She found a row of phones, all smashed; the glass littered the floor.

She'd have to take a taxi – take a chance.

She went back to the buffet, pushed open the door, shouted to Art: 'OK, wish me luck.'

Art said: 'Don't do it.'

'I'll phone your office.'

He was saying to the girl behind the counter: 'Sandwich? Sand – wich?'

Kate ran to the escalator. She was behind the last of the samovar girls, who were muffled now in shapeless coats and carried very old plastic bags and looked just like everybody else, and not a bit like British Airways stewardesses on their way to a four-star hotel.

She reached the foot of the escalator. Two soldiers, Lacy and Henshaw, moved in front of her, blocking her path.

'Out of bounds, miss,' said Lacy.

'Twenty-eight days in nick,' said Henshaw, enjoying himself, 'unless you come quietly.'

THIRTEEN

The doctor was in the SAS compartment, examining Gallagher. Anna was translating, struggling with the medical terms. There was no electricity – the train's engine was not running. Anna and Hoodless held torches, as the doctor cut the bandages away from Gallagher's chest.

The doctor was a young man, late twenties perhaps. His face screwed into a grimace as he revealed the wound. He spoke rapidly, in a low voice.

'He says you must let him take Gallagher to hospital.'

'No,' said Hoodless. 'Patch him up. He'll be all right. Tell him about Orenburg.'

'He says there is nothing at Orenburg. He says you are crazy. Orenburg has nothing compared to Kuybyshev. There is a military headquarters hospital here, an officers' hospital, the best in Russia.'

'I tell you he'll be all right at Orenburg,' said Hoodless firmly, the way a tourist might say to Arab beggars: 'I can carry my own suitcase, thanks. I know where I'm going.'

'You're stupid. You're so stupid. You know that?'

The doctor was taking the bandages from Gallagher's abdomen. He was gently peeling back the plastic film from the stomach wound.

'Stupid!'

Anna knelt down and took hold of Gallagher's hand. He was semi-conscious. He gave a sudden cry. She spoke to him in Russian, softly, tears in her eyes.

Hoodless stood and watched, his face set. 'He'll be fine in Orenburg,' he repeated. 'We can't leave him here. It's not an option.'

The doctor spoke.

Anna said: 'How much morphine has he had?'

'Three syretes,' said Hoodless. 'He mustn't have any more. It doesn't matter about the pain. He can stand a bit of pain, can Para.'

Simon, who had been standing in the doorway, turned and went back to the platform.

The Russian guards were deployed down the length of the train, five metres between each man, the two NCOs standing one pace behind them. Their blue uniforms were immaculate, their white gloves spotless.

Nobody would guess, thought Simon, that they'd been smoking grass for the past fifteen hours, that they were all as high as kites.

At the back of the train an SAS soldier stood in the shadows, next to the wagon from Perm, a Hecker Koch MP 5.9 automatic submachine-gun in his shoulder.

Andrei was walking up and down outside the buffet, smoking a cigarette.

'There's a problem,' he said.

'About Gallagher?' said Simon. 'About the wounded man?'

Andrei shook his head.

'Do they still want to inspect the train?'

'Yes. Come with me,' Andrei said abruptly. He led the way to the escalator. They went up it. They crossed the station booking hall. Andrei pushed open a door.

Rail officials in animated conversation suddenly stopped and stared at them with outright hostility.

Behind them were MVD militia youths, their hair close-cropped in the old Red Army way, the way of the Moscow *Lyuberi*.

Yes, there was a problem, thought Simon.

Andrei was the problem.

He looked like a czarist officer out of *Dr Zhivago*. He was speaking loudly, coldly, with unconcealed contempt.

A rail official reddened and replied aggressively.

Andrei pointed at Simon. The official shrugged.

Andrei said: 'They won't let the train leave the station. They insist on coming on board to inspect the passengers and documents. They want to know about the injured man. I've told them we are carrying high-level NATO personnel with diplomatic protection. They still will not let us go. I have told them that anyone who comes near the train gets shot.'

'Oh Christ,' said Simon dully.

Andrei said: 'I'd *like* to shoot them, actually. Whether they come near the train or not.'

He turned to the rail officials. '*Zheltoe gavno*!' he shouted. 'Yellow shit,' he helpfully translated for Simon.

'Don't,' said Simon, 'annoy him.'

'Annoy him? I'll shoot him.'

'Don't keep talking about shooting.'

The rail official spoke in rapid Russian.

Andrei replied, thumping the table with his fist. The MVD militia youths watched, expressionless.

Simon said: 'I don't understand. You've got clearance from the President's office. You've got the papers. Why won't they accept them?'

'They say Cossack tank units loyal to General Kotelnikov are moving north. They say they will cross the line to Orenburg before we can reach it.'

Simon froze.

'It's been on television. Everybody knows.'

'Oh Christ,' said Simon again.

'Apparently they moved at dawn from their barracks at Saratov and Stalingrad.'

It took a moment for his words to sink in.

Simon said: 'From their barracks *where*?'

Simon opened the compartment door.

'Well?' he asked.

The doctor was replacing the sterile dressing on the chest wound: a wound that seemed so small, so innocuous.

Anna said: 'He says he must operate or Gallagher will die. He says there is bleeding inside.'

Hoodless said: 'He doesn't leave the train. He'll be all right in Oren—'

'For Christ's sake stop saying that,' snapped Simon.

Hoodless tensed.

Anna said: 'He says the blueness round the mouth and the nails means the lung is hurt inside . . . I don't know, I don't know the words.'

'Pneumothorax,' said Hoodless.

Simon realized that he had known what was wrong all the time.

'Perforated membranes of the lung. Air's bubbling out of the wound, you could see it when it happened. It'll collapse in the end.'

Gallagher was staring up at them, – uncomprehending, Simon hoped, though his eyes were open.

Hoodless went on: 'The air's got between the lung and the membrane, you see. The lung can't expand properly because there's air taking up its space.'

'Where did you learn all that?'

'Worked as an orderly at Hereford and Cardiff,' said Hoodless. 'Surprising how many stab wounds you get at Hereford and Cardiff. There'll be blood collecting in the pleural cavity; that's another reason why he's so thirsty. Anna, ask the doctor if he'll come to Orenburg with us.'

The doctor was watching them, trying to divine what they were saying

Anna spoke to him. He replied urgently.

Anna said: 'He says if Gallagher does not go into hospital *now*, he will die. He will not get to Orenburg alive.'

The SAS signaller appeared in the doorway.

'Kaunas on the line, Sar'nt.'

Hoodless went. A moment later he returned. He said to Simon: 'They want to talk to you.'

'Kaunas?'

Hoodless nodded.

Simon went into the next compartment, into the SAS armoury. Two SAS men were resting. One said: 'Do you want us to go?'

Simon shook his head: he couldn't care less. He took the handset.

'It's secure?'

The signaller nodded. 'Racal Merod, the latest.'

Simon spoke into the handset: 'Yes?'

It was Littlehales. His familiar voice was surprisingly comforting.
'You found it, then?'
The train he meant, presumably.
'Yes.'
'I've got the OC to talk to you.'
The OC of what?
A voice he did not recognize said: 'Simon?'
'Sir.'
'I want you to take command there. Give the second unit all the support necessary.'
The second unit must mean the SAS.
Simon said: 'There are hostile armoured units moving north from Stalingrad.'
'From where?' said the voice, startled.
'It's not a joke,' said Simon. 'They've changed the name. Have you information about the troop movements?'
'We'll come back to you.'
'Can I abandon the equipment?'
'No.'
'Can we use other forms of transport?'
'Why should you need to?'
'We are being refused permission to proceed.'
A pause.
'We will arrange clearance. In the meantime stay with the equipment, whatever happens. You understand?'
Christ!
'There's a man needs hospital treatment,' said Simon, 'His condition is critical.'
'Yes, we know.'
Another pause.
'Use your judgement. Do the best you can.'
Shit! Well, thank you and goodnight.
Lieutenant Morrell was authorized to use his best judgement . . . Not our fault he fucked it all up, is it?

He spoke to Hoodless in the corridor. 'I'm to cooperate, but I'm in charge. Any problems from your side?'
'No,' said Hoodless. 'They told me.' He sounded relieved.
Simon said: 'Gallagher is going to hospital. I want to talk to you and your men in thirty minutes. Tell Colour-Sar'nt Gough to replace your sentry on the wagon.'
He said to the doctor: 'Cossack armoured units are heading this way. There have been outrages: people have been killed: Westerners, Western-sympathizers, Jews.'
Anna translated. The doctor nodded gloomily. The Cossacks were notoriously anti-semitic: but then, for that matter, so was everyone in Russia.
'He is a Jew?' he said, indicating Gallagher.
'Not that I know of, but I can't leave a British soldier here in

Kuybyshev. Not under these conditions. You must bring him back. Operate, then bring him back.'

Anna translated.

'He understands?'

'Yes,' she said.

'You have four hours. It will be a risk, but it can't be avoided.'

A warm railway compartment was not a bad sick-bay; many soldiers had experienced worse.

'Do you have the drugs you need?'

The doctor replied: 'We are a High Command military hospital. We have all the drugs we need.'

'Can we give you money? Coupons? Gold?'

'Gold?' said the doctor, amazed.

Simon said: 'Twenty gold sovereigns when you return him.'

Each SAS man, he had learned, had twenty gold sovereigns in a belt round his waist.

'I do not work for money. But thank you.'

They carried Gallagher out to the ambulance. Anna climbed into it behind him.

Simon said softly, 'Anna?'

'I'll be OK.'

'I don't think this is a good idea. I don't think you ought to leave the train.'

She had become one of his charges, somebody he had to protect, to carry to safety. Already, in the back of his mind, he had worked out how he would wangle her on to the American transporter at Orenburg.

'I'll be OK,' she said. 'Don't worry about me.' But he knew that she wouldn't be at all OK if anything went wrong – that her link with the Royal Mercians would condemn her to death, if the madness sweeping up the Volga found her in Kuybyshev.

She smiled and touched his hand – which was a bit daring of her, because she was still frightened of him.

'I'll be OK,' she repeated.

The orderlies closed the door.

The ambulance drove off.

In the transit mess at Kaunas, Littlehales said: 'We won't hear any more for a couple of hours. I'm off to get some sleep.'

Biggin, slowly drinking a Scotch, reading Morrell's file, said: 'How the hell did Morrell get the nickname "Oops"?'

'Is that in there?' said Littlehales, surprised.

'No. I was talking to a chap from his battalion. Nick Chard.'

Littlehales said. 'When Morrell was a subbie at Aldershot, a NATO bigwig came round to inspect his unit's position on exercise. The colonel asked him to sight the SF gun. Morrell pulled the locking lever, and the barrel fell off.'

'Fell off?'

'Then he smiled at the bigwig and said, "Oops!".'

'I see,' said Biggin.

After a moment, and a sip of scotch, he said reflectively: 'I hope he doesn't drop anything in Russia.'

FOURTEEN

It was midnight. The station lights were dimmed, the buffet was shut. The Federal Guards, their AK-M assault rifles crossed, were standing stiffly to attention, all along the length of the Bukhara Express.

Somewhere a bell rang out, a Russian cathedral bell, harsh and Asiatic, far above the underground cavern of Central Station.

Royal Mercian soldiers emerged from the train, shivering in the damp cold.

A Russian *praporshchik* shouted a command. The Federal Guards clicked to attention, turned, goose-stepped down the platform to the front of the train. Another command from the NCO, and they disappeared into its interior.

'All right,' said Colour-Sergeant Gough. 'Spread out, five paces apart, just like they did.'

'D' Company, 1 Royal Mercians, moved into position.

Simon looked round at the faces of the SAS.

'Gallagher will be brought back at 03.50. If the train is still being refused permission to leave, we have two options. One is to abandon the train and its cargo, and head for the Kazakhstan border, commandeering whatever transport we can lay our hands on. The other is to take over the train, the signalling and points, and get the train out ourselves.

'That's the preferred option. Our route is cleared, the Bukhara Express comes this way three times every week. Once we are gone, it is unlikely that anybody in Kuybyshev will care enough to try to stop us further down the line. In any case, this is the last major city before Orenburg. Has anybody anything to say?'

Hoodless said: 'We can operate the signalling box, so we can clear a line for ourselves. Talbot's an expert – that right, Sandy?' A soldier nodded. 'But we'll have to move fast. Once they cotton on to us, we either give up or start shooting.'

'Agreed.'

Corporal Buck said: 'What about the Russian troops moving up from the south?'

'Intell are finding out all they can.'

An SAS soldier said: 'And the Russian troops on the train? Whose side are *they* on in all this?'

Andrei was smoking, alone, in the unlit, unheated diner.

Simon sat down. He said: 'Andrei, once our man is brought back from the hospital, we must get out of Kuybyshev. I know you've called Petersburg, but Petersburg may have other things to worry about.'

Andrei said nothing. A pale light fell through the dirt-encrusted windows on to the cold white cloth, the dark-blue onyx menu-holder, the tiny gilt flower vase.

He took up the vase and turned it round in his fingers, holding it by its stem.

'My men have eaten caviar,' he said, 'for the first time in their lives.'

'I know. You told me. Did they enjoy it?'

Andrei thought for a moment, then nodded.

Outside, a family could be seen leaving the train. A man in his fifties, with his wife and two teenage daughters. They scurried across the platform, through the swirling snow that penetrated the cavern of the station. They struggled up the dead, unmoving metal escalator with their suitcases.

For several hours the passengers had agonized over what to do next. Some had huddled in their compartments, watching news bulletins on their Walkman television sets. Others, the bold ones, had gone and watched television in the buffet, standing there defiantly in their French skisuits, their English overcoats, flashing their Rolex watches, and drinking vodka and Moldavian beer. (Art Finkel had already bought all the foreign beer, together with a dozen jars of peculiar bottled black vegetables labelled PPP.)

Those who could not hide their terror had shouted at Andrei, the man charged to carry them to safety. The woman in the pink shellsuit, Madame Vostrotin, had broken down and wailed; but everyone was used to that by now.

By midnight most families had abandoned the train. They had secured transport, presumably at a cost.

'150k to Kazakhstan,' said Andrei, amused. 'All that way to go, in the middle of the night, only to be turned back by the Kazakhstan border guards.'

Kazakhstanis, he said, had little love for Russia, the nation that had conquered them, taxed them, persecuted their religion, conscripted their young men, and used their land as a vast nuclear testing ground.

'What makes you think they won't turn *us* back, too?'

'We have thirty men with assault rifles,' said Andrei, ironical again, 'and if that doesn't work we threaten them with the English "Spetznaz".'

'OK, but how do we get the train out of Kuybyshev?'

Andrei said: 'Listen. On Monday I received orders. The Bukhara Express had been commandeered from Wagons-Lit. I was to escort a hundred important people and two coaches of Ministry of Finance documents out of the Moscow region, away from General Kotelnikov's army. I was to take them to Tashkent – from there good air links, eh, to the ski resorts? To St Moritz, perhaps, or are we too late for skiing? The French Riviera maybe? Topless girls and casinos?'

'Skiing, I should think,' said Simon. 'It's a bit early for the beach.'

'Later I received a further order. Not from the Frunzenskaja Embankment, not from the War Department or Army Intelligence – this time from the Foreign Ministry. An order that an extra wagon might be attached to the train during the night in Moscow, and it would accompany us to the south.'

'So everything's going to plan,' said Simon. 'We've got the extra wagon; now we just have to get out of here.'

Andrei said: 'I wonder who gave the order about the wagon? I wonder why it is so important? I wonder why I suddenly have English "Spetznaz" on my train?'

'Well don't ask me,' said Simon.

Andrei looked at him speculatively.

'Look, Andrei, I'm not going to be caught here by Cossacks. I'm going to use my men to take over the signal box and clear the line.'

'You'll be killed,' said Andrei. 'And the train will still be here.'

'Who will try to kill us? The MVD militia?'

'The militia . . .' He smiled scornfully.

'You, then?'

Kate appeared at the end of the diner. 'Right,' she shouted, 'so how much longer does this bloody charade go on for?'

Simon closed his eyes.

'I am going to get you thrown out of the army,' she yelled.

He jumped up in a sudden fury. 'Haven't I enough to worry about,' he shouted, 'without worrying about you being debauched by Russian bloody militia?'

'Debauched? What the hell of a sort of word is that?'

'Hey, let's be friends,' said Andrei. 'Sit down. Come on, you two.'

'Debauched?' she marvelled extravagantly, standing there in the dark at the end of the carriage. 'Dear God, the man said "debauched".'

'You are the most selfish cow I have ever met.'

'Hey, hey, come on,' said Andrei.

'There's a girl,' shouted Simon, 'a Russian girl, who's been nursing one of our soldiers for the past fifteen hours, and what do you think about, what do you care about—'

'How dare you! How dare you say that!'

'It's bloody true, that's why—'

'I don't know anything about a wounded soldier. Did anybody ask me to nurse a wounded soldier? How dare you!'

She was coming down towards them, between the tables. There were tears of rage glinting in her eyes.

Simon said: 'Nothing but trouble. Nothing but trouble from the moment I first saw you. I wouldn't have believed anybody could be so utterly self-centred, so utterly self-absorbed.'

'I'm a professional journalist trying to do a professional job!'

'Well my professional job at the moment is to try to keep you alive. Get back to your compartment, stay there. Bother me again and I'll lock you in, with a sentry on the door.'

'You wouldn't dare—'

'Lacy!'

'Now hang on,' said Andrei. 'Sit down. Come on, come on.'

'Lacy!'

Lacy appeared, running, startled.

'Sir!'

'No,' said Kate. 'No you can't. Look, don't be stupid . . .'

Simon was breathing quickly.

Beddoes, from the other end of the diner, called cautiously: 'Sar'nt Hoodless, sir. He's got Kaunas on the line.'

Lacy said: 'Sir?'

Simon turned to Andrei.

'We've got to get out of here, Andrei. There's two motorized infantry divisions coming up the road. There's a tank battalion moving to cross the Orenburg line. Your head's on the block, mate. You're the fucking ex-Presidential guard. You're the one on the losing side.'

He went out of the dining car.

Andrei looked sour, then said: 'Vodka?'

She shook her head and sat down.

'That man . . . that man . . .'

'Forget about it.'

'What a bastard! What a sodding bastard!'

'He's under a lot of stress.'

'And what the fuck am I under?'

'It's modern life,' said Andrei, pouring her a drink, 'modern living.'

'It was *his* fault! It was all his fault! If he'd let Sergei into the embassy, none of this would have happened, but he's a pious sodding pig and Sergei's probably dead because of him. How dare he call me self-centred! How dare he!'

'He's not,' said Andrei, 'your lover then?'

Simon said to Kaunas: 'Gallagher is undergoing an operation at the military HQ hospital. He will be returned in two hours. The local MVD militia support Kotelnikov, and won't let the train leave unless they are allowed to search it. The train commander won't do anything without word from Petersburg or from Kuybyshev Army Group high command.'

Biggin replied: 'We're doing what we can. Protect your cargo. We'll come back to you.'

Simon did not feel any great hope, any infusion of confidence. But nothing could be done until Gallagher returned. He was becoming philosophical. He went to Section HQ, curled up under his army coat, and went to sleep.

At 02.00 Chaffinch woke him. He jerked awake, tense, his heart thumping.

'Yes?'

'A Russian general, sir.'

'A *what*?'

Snow was still spatting against the window. The compartment was bitterly cold. The samovar girls had long gone, so nobody was lighting the peat stoves any longer.

'A general, sir. A cloak, epaulets, medals, everything. Do we let him on?'

'Where's Andrei – Lieutenant Bulygin? – the Russian?' he added as Chaffinch looked at him, uncomprehending.

'Don't know, sir.'

'All right, I'll come.'

'Do I leave him standing there, sir?'

'Yes. Tell him I'm coming,' Simon snapped, struggling into his coat as quickly as he could.

'How?' asked Chaffinch.

'What?'

'How do I tell him? I don't know the Russian for—'

'Oh, never mind.'

The Royal Mercian sentries were huddled in their parkas, their rifles covered in protective waterproof sheaths. The Russian general was standing stiffly near the foot of the elevator. He was small, not more than five foot six.

Simon went over to him and saluted. The salute was returned.

'Do you speak English?' asked Simon.

The general – and he really was a general; a thick crust of gold shone below the wide blue cap-band of an infantry officer, and there were five stars on his epaulets – looked at him blankly.

'English?' repeated Simon.

'A little.'

He was old. He had a brown face wrinkled like a walnut; sharp, beady eyes. He reminded Simon of the ancient brigadier in charge of the Royal Mercian museum in Shrewsbury.

Simon indicated the train, extending his arm in welcome.

'If you come on board, sir, I'll get somebody to show you to the train commander.'

The general looked at him for a moment, then moved stiffly towards the train.

In the corridor they passed Hoodless, standing still as stone. The Russian general went past him, and forward into the dining car.

Hoodless said: 'Who is he?'

'No idea.' Simon turned and called, 'Chaffinch!'

'Sir?'

'My compliments to Lieutenant Bulygin, tell him he's got a visitor. Tell him top brass.'

'Sir.' Chaffinch rotted off.

Hoodless said: 'I'm not happy.'

'Happy?' said Simon. 'Dear God.'

He looked at his watch: he had slept for nearly an hour.

There was a noise outside: a vehicle, lights. The ambulance was coming slowly across the track and up a ramp, snow now turning to slushy rain in its headlights.

'Right, let's get him on board. Corporal Pullin!'

The doctor was speaking rapidly, from the moment he jumped down, presumably imploring them to be careful, presumably disclaiming responsibility for what might happen if they were not.

Gallagher was unconscious. They lifted him carefully, a blanket held up to protect him from the sleet, and carried him towards the train.

Andrei came up the platform, a startled look on his face. Behind him were two railway officials smiling nervously.

'We've got clearance to move.'

'What?'

'The train must go *now*. Immediately.'

'Jesus . . . OK, get him in. Get him in. Colour-Sar'nt Gough!'

'Sir!' Gough came running.

'Get the men on board. Do a head count.'

'Sir!'

The doctor was holding out medicines, syringes and tablets, speaking urgently . . . what the hell was he saying?

Andrei was talking to the rail officials.

Simon said: 'Hang on. Wait, doctor. Hang on. Where is Anna?'

The doctor looked at him uncomprehending, tried to point to the carriage with Gallagher inside it.

'No. Anna, Anna! The girl!'

The doctor was saying something. Simon shouted: 'Andrei!'

Andrei hurried over. 'The line to Orenburg is cut by Cossacks. We're too late. We will have to go north.'

'Anna! Ask him where is Anna.'

Andrei spoke. The doctor replied briefly. Andrei said: 'She is being kept in the rail police office. She has a Moscow residence permit. She should not be in Kuybyshev.'

Simon said: 'Which rail police office? Where is it? Is it near the station?'

Andrei spoke again. 'It's part of the main office – the office upstairs where we went before.'

'Sar'nt Hoodless! Corporal Pullin!'

'This train has got to go,' said Andrei. 'This train has got to go *now*. There is no time to wait.'

He took three SAS men with Hecker Koch MP submachine-guns and three Royal Mercians with SA-80s. Hoodless had the XM 203, a deadly weapon that combined an M16 Armalite with a light-weight single-shot grenade-launcher and fired a 40-millimetre bomb.

Simon himself had his Browning pistol, his 9-milly – a weapon useless except for suicide, some officers sneered, but it could be bloody useful at close quarters. He noted, as they dashed to the escalator, the faces of Kate Delacroix and her seedy journalist friend peering out from a compartment window, two reptiles illuminated by candlelight.

FIFTEEN

They crossed the booking hall at a run, the Royal Mercians fanning out to take up positions on either side of the police department door.

The few Russian civilians in the hall stood and stared at them, mostly apathetic, some mildly curious. Simon glanced quickly round him. Banners hung down from the high ceiling, from the vaulted glass roof: dirty, pollution-stained adverts for Tula Beer and Gorki television videos, and flags in the Russian national colours.

An MVD police officer, looking idly into the window of the small station shop, shouted at them angrily, then ran off into the night.

Simon opened the outer office door and went in, Hoodless and his men behind him.

Four militiamen were sitting at a table. By the time they had looked up, their eyes widening with surprise, Simon and the SAS were pointing submachine-guns at their chests.

Simon moved quickly across the room, Hoodless behind him. He kicked open the door to the inner office.

Three policemen, relaxed, slouching – settled in for a night of questioning.

Anna sitting at a table, nervous, her face tense with strain.

'OK, Anna. Get up and come with us.'

A policeman reached for his gun. It was in a white plastic holster, thrown over the back of a chair. His fingers fumbled with the cover stud.

Simon said, 'No! *Niet, niet!*' and pointed with his pistol.

The policeman hesitated, indecisive.

'Anna, come on!'

She stood up. A policeman grabbed her, pulled her down, shouting in Russian. Simon fired over his head, into the corner of the ceiling. The policeman yelled and dropped Anna and fell back.

'Let's go, Anna. Let's go!'

They went back through the outer office, out into the booking hall. There were whistles blowing from outside the station. The clatter of boots echoed from a covered, stone-pillared walkway that ran alongside the building.

They ran to the escalator. Hoodless, the man with the XM 203 grenade-launcher, remained at the top, facing out into the station, ready to do some damage. The rest of them clattered down the stairs.

They were almost at the bottom when they heard a fusillade of shots from above, and then the massive, deep thud of the grenade bomb that Hoodless had fired up into the glass roof of the booking hall, and the stunning explosion that followed.

Two SAS soldiers knelt, pointing up the escalator with their submachine-guns, covering Hoodless as he came down.

Andrei was running across the platform, his eyes wide with shock.

'Fucking hell!' He must have been spending time with Kate Delacroix to be picking up so much of her vocabulary. 'What have you done? What did you do that for?'

'Let's get out of here.'

From the booking hall above came the delayed crash of masonry collapsing, shouts of warning, yells of anger.

Andrei ran back up the platform towards the engine.

'OK,' said Simon, 'let's go. Come on, Anna!'

They piled on the train. Only the two SAS soldiers remained in position at the foot of the escalator. Next to the buffet, the rail officials who had given Andrei permission to leave stood staring at the men with their sub-machine guns.

Simon spoke into his personal radio. 'Tell me when we're ready to go.'

Andrei's voice: 'Signal's still red.'

'Oh, Jesus . . .'

The two SAS men were firing now, firing up the escalator – a loud continuous crack of sound reverberating round the cavern of the station.

'Andrei, we've no time—'

'I didn't start a war. You started a war, you crazy madman!'

How long would it be before the MVD police cottoned on, before a grenade came bouncing down the escalator? Or perhaps they wouldn't have grenades – not in a small police station staffed by half a dozen coppers. Shit, the SAS men were diving for cover—

The explosion was stunning. A grenade's effect depends on the softness or hardness of the surface it lands on. In a ploughed field, damage will be minimal; in a concrete bunker it will be devastating.

There were many tons of concrete in Kuybyshev Central.

Simon was thrown back across the train corridor and slammed against the wall. Every window of the carriage was shattered. Outside, smoke covered the platform.

He pulled himself to his feet. His head was full of noise; he couldn't think. Inside the train, men were running down the corridor with the machine-gun. Henshaw was positioning it, Lacy bringing an extra ammo belt. Colour Gough's voice came from a great distance away, calmly ordering the rest of the Section to take up positions, to cover the platform, and the escalator that was just visible through the smoke.

The two SAS soldiers had taken cover in the buffet. They must have jumped in through its smashed windows. Their submachine-guns were again trained on the escalator steps.

Another grenade, clattering out of the escalator tunnel, rolling across the platform. Oh Christ—

This time he ducked down with his hands over his ears.

Another explosion.

He looked up to see Hoodless jumping from the train and running to the escalator. Hoodless knelt and aimed the XM 203 up its tunnel, then fired. He dived to one side before the blast of heat and the shower of razor-sharp metal fragments could catch him.

'Andrei?' Simon called into his radio. 'Andrei? One-four to . . .' What did he call the Russians? 'One-four calling Lieutenant Bulygin . . .'

He could see that one of the three Russian rail officials was dead, caught by one of the grenade blasts, his body thrown against the buffet wall.

There was no sign of the other men.

Andrei's voice: 'OK, we're going. Simon? Are you OK? We're going now.'

Simon lurched across to the window. He yelled hoarsely, gave a thumbs-up sign. Hoodless waved back, jumped out from cover, and again fired up the escalator tunnel before running back to the train.

The other two SAS men climbed out of the buffet window, and ran back across the platform. The train was already moving as they swung aboard.

The Bukhara Express was leaving Kuybyshev Grand Central platform five, as it did three nights a week, every week of the year.

This time it was four hours behind schedule.

A police car, its light flashing and siren wailing, emerged from the vast goods yard east of the passenger station.

Simon watched in fascination as it swung round towards them.

It jolted down a cinder track in the darkness, its headlights bouncing up and down, its wheels throwing up clouds of slush and spray, trying apparently to reach a crossing ahead of them and put itself in their path.

Was the policeman inside angry, brave, or just overexcited, Simon wondered. He leaned, exhausted, against the outer wall of the bombed-out coach, the sleet splatting in on him, broken glass at his feet.

'Keep him in your sights,' said Gough.

'He keeps bouncing up and down . . .' said Henshaw, gunner on the GPMG.

Did the policeman think he was in a Moscow gangster movie? Was he hoping for a medal for bravely foiling the *Amerikantsy* mafia? Or did he really want to end up dead inside the mangled wreck of his Skoda?

Some such reflections must have entered the policeman's mind. A moment later he stopped his car, its red light flashing slowly and sulkily, its siren reduced to a low resentful whine.

He sat, talking into his radio, and watched them as they disappeared into the night.

PART THREE
ACROSS THE URALS

A half savage people who have been regimented without being civilized.

Marquis de Custine, on the Russians, 1839

ONE

NATO ACE Forward HQ, Kaunas, Lithuania, morning of Wednesday 20 March

Biggin bumped into Littlehales leaving one of the accommodation huts.

'Morrell,' he said, 'the man who dropped the gun barrel.'

'Yes?'

'He's blown up a railway station.'

'Christ.'

'Not a small one. A big one. Kuybyshev. Perhaps he said "Oops", I don't know.'

Biggin disappeared into the darkness. Littlehales went across the windswept concrete to the cookhouse.

It was nearly 06.00. He had been awakened at 05.00 by a sergeant bearing a mug of tea, together with yesterday's satellite pictures from NORSCAN, overnights from the CIA and the Chinese, and summaries from NATO combined intell, MI6, GCHQ Cheltenham, and Ukrainian Intelligence.

Ukraine intell was considered the most reliable. They still had agents operating through aid agencies in Gorki, Arkhangelsk and Novosibirsk, although their aid office in Yekaterinburg – the next major city ahead of the Bukhara Express on its new route – had been ominously silent for the past twenty-four hours.

The cookhouse was almost full: Dutch and Belgian aircrew from the F16 wing, British and German soldiers from Third Army brigade, RAF helicopter crew, admin and intelligence personnel who had worked through the night, SAS men lifted out from Russia. In front of Littlehales an SAS trooper in filthy camouflage combat gear scooped up half a dozen fried eggs from a greasy hotplate. In his turn, Littlehales shovelled brick-coloured sausages on to a piece of bread. He took butter from a huge bowl, got himself a paper cup of tea, and sat down. A clerk, hurrying through the cookhouse looking for officers on his list, gave him a copy of ACE Rapid Reaction Force's morning intelligence report.

It was timed at 05.30. It said that Kotelnikov's forces now controlled the north, from Murmansk and Arkhangelsk across to Ust Usa, and down to the Mari ASSR, including the cities of Kirov, Kazan, Perm and Gorki.

The Democratic Government retained the loyalty of a small group of military regions closest to the west: Baltic MD, which now included St Petersburg; Minsk MD; Smolensk and Bryansk, and Kuybyshev where the old Bosnia Brigade was based.

The situation, mused Littlehales – he was something of a military historian – was almost the exact reverse of what it had been in 1919–20, when a Czechoslovakian army had controlled the Urals and most of the Trans-Siberian railway.

He remembered that he was now concerned totally with intelligence relevant to the Bukhara Express, which was heading towards Yekaterinburg. He flicked through the light blue pages, and read:

No overnights from Yekaterinburg.

Assessment Summary 22.00 19 March unchanged as follows: Miners in the Urals and Siberia have gained more that most from the so-called 'Freedom Decade'. They have repeatedly gone on strike. They have become experts at bringing their plight to the attention of the West. Since March of last year they have been paid in 'privilege' coupons.

Yekaterinburg was Yeltsin's power base. In Russian terms it has a liberal democratic tradition. Its local police have fought successfully against mafia influence.

Miners are said to have tried to link with Siberian workers in support of the Democratic Government.

These attempts are believed to have failed.

There are reports of famine.

There are unconfirmed reports of a shoot-out between miners and MVD police.

During the past twenty-four hours Cossack tank armies have moved north-east from North Caucasus MD towards the Kazakhstan border, Kuybyshev, and Yekaterinburg.

Despite fears amongst the working population, Urals MD can be expected to declare for Kotelnikov during the next forty-eight hours.

The Bukhara Express had perhaps twenty-four hours to get through Yekaterinburg, through the Urals.

Why the hell were there no reports out of Yekaterinburg?

He flicked through the remainder of the sitrep. It had a footnote from Amsterdam, from the CIA who were busy checking up on Kotelnikov's past.

In 1987 Kotelnikov had been a military attaché in Brussels. He was rumoured to have had an affair with a Dutch girl from Tilburg. He had been in his early fifties at the time. The girl, it was said, had been eighteen.

There were now other rumours, said the CIA. Rumours of orgies at the Soviet military mission residence. Of athletic young Russian girl gymnasts, recruited to the Soviet Army's Central Sports Club, travelling abroad as Kotelnikov's 'aides'. Of Belgian girls persuaded to join in the fun.

American newspapers were obsessed with facts, so they'd be cautious about this sort of stuff. Littlehales assumed the CIA would instead peddle it round Spain and Italy, feed it to the London tabloids. *Kinky Kotelnikov! Moscow is reeling under revelations that the man who has vowed to clean up Russia is a two-timing heartbreaker with a taste for three-in-a-bed sex . . .*

'Art Finkel, where are you?' Littlehales might have said, had he known of Art's existence.

TWO

Bukhara Express, western Urals, morning of Wednesday 20 March

> *For many decades, Moscow pop artists tried to create for themselves a distinctive cultural world.*
>
> *Even now, people think back with affection to the old Moscow Rock Laboratory.*
>
> *'OK, in the end it was imitation Camden Lock,' I was told by blond, attractive Toni, lead singer with Asia Asia, 'but it sheltered and gigged every long-haired guitarist in town. Who cares if the lyrics reminded you of Jethro Tull and Fairport Convention?'*

Who cares, indeed, sighed Art.

His mind wasn't really engaged. Moscow's Rock Laboratory was an experiment that had – unless Kotelnikov was into the hard metal revival – finally failed. Second Army's general staff were not going to boogie the night away to Jethro Tull soundalikes.

He went back through the story and crossed out 'blond, attractive' to save the *Guardian* sub-editor a job.

Why was he bothering? He had missed the *Guardian* deadline for Saturday arts features. (His *Novotels-of-the-World* map showed him to have passed through two time-zones since leaving Moscow. It might be glad happy morning in the Urals, but it was midnight on the Grays Inn Road.)

In any case, he didn't see much prospect of finding a payphone that would like his Amex card, or his fax – not in the next hundred years or so.

A yak stared at him from a rocky outcrop.

Or perhaps it wasn't a yak.

Brown uplands, waterlogged, reedy. Long drifts of ice and snow. A huge white sky.

Occasionally they passed wooden houses, plonked down in isolation, in the marsh, like monopoly houses abandoned by a careless child.

The door opened. Kate Delacroix came in and sat down.

'Hello,' he said, glad of the company, but fearful that she would play Cher and Patsy Cline tapes on the little sound system she had bought off the distressed manageress of Moscow's *Zolotaya Roza* perfumery. 'I don't suppose you know where we are?'

She shook her head.

'Or when we're going to arrive at anywhere?'

She shook her head again. Her red hair was dull and unkempt. Her sallow skin was yellow and greasy-looking. She slumped back in her seat, and after a minute pulled her knees up to her chin. During the early hours, in the cold, she had cried a lot, snuffling to herself between sobs.

'How about some Patsy Kline, then?' he said, wanting to cheer her up.

She shook her had.

Perhaps her period was starting. Art knew that most female reporters on assignment took the pill to avoid having periods, not to mention babies; perhaps she didn't have any pills. He didn't fancy her chances of buying a box of Tampax, not out here.

'What,' she said, 'are you thinking about?'

'Nothing.'

She looked at him suspiciously.

'Are you hungry?' he asked. 'Have a gherkin.'

On the table by the window were the jars of PPP vegetables he had bought at Kuybyshev station.

This, however, was not the extent of his pantry. Somewhere he had cheese crackers, Swedish rye biscuits, tins of liver-pâté sausage. Kate had seen the crumbs, the evidence.

'I'd rather have some biscuits,' she said. 'Haven't you any pâté and biscuits or anything?'

No, he lied. Only gherkins.

'But those are not gherkins, Art.'

'Yes,' he said. 'They're very nice gherkins. You don't have to worry about them being black. It's the taste that counts.'

'But they are pizzles, Art.' She was cheering up, reviving.

'Pardon?'

'Smoked pigs' pizzles in brine. A speciality of Kuybyshev. Have you been eating them? Have you been eating pickled porker pricks, Art?'

She went, after asking him to reflect on what he thought PPP stood for.

He looked out for awhile at the relentless landscape, not believing her. But there was an unpleasant aftertaste in his mouth. He looked doubtfully at another jar, that he had previously assumed to contain pickled onions.

Kate went back to Section HQ and smiled in a friendly way and sat down and said, 'Hi, I'm back.'

She took an interest in a game of pontoon, and listened to Colour Gough talking about his planned marquee franchise. He was due to leave the army in six months.

'It's not the *marquee* hire that makes the money,' he explained. 'It's the *ancillaries*. Are the guests going to sit on the floor? No, they're going to want little white tables – twenty quid a time – and chairs – a tenner each – and the bride of today wants her marquee to be flower-decked and ruched in apricot or peach or cornflower blue.'

He had a small pack of material samples, and would value her opinion.

'You see, miss, an individual franchisee can only *economically* specialise in one colour, because if you have, for example, apricot ruche lining, then your artificial flowers and pole ribbons and other accoutrements will be coloured accordingly. But what will be the colour choice,' Gough went on anxiously, 'of the bride of tomorrow?'

'Blue for a girl,' said Kate. 'What's for breakfast?'

They went to the dining car and ate from the Federal Guards' rations. They were given bowls of *kasha*. (What, the British soldiers demanded to know, was *kasha*? She said it could either be described as wholemeal organic oatmeal porridge, or as a thickish form of pigswill.)

It was served with black bread. There was milkless tea from the samovar. She shared her thoughts on pigswill with a Russian soldier. He joked: 'If we took a pig to our mess hall, it would faint.'

Lacy said: 'What happened to that fishy stuff? I was quite taking to it.'

The beluga caviar had been all eaten, or had been hidden away.

Two passengers, a middle-aged couple, came into the diner and asked for food. The Russian cook general, a bowl of *kasha* in his hands, told them there wasn't any.

At mid-morning the train drew into a siding. Snow was beginning to fall gently from the white sky. Wreaths of fog crept out of the small, rocky ravines, the abandoned surface mines.

Kate looked out of the window and watched Simon and Andrei climb up by the track and walk back and forth along a ridge of spiky moorland grass.

'He's a major-general,' said Andrei. 'I've had to attach two men just to look after him. General Vladimir Stefanovich Prosvirkin. He's been commanding a skeleton division at Buzuluk. He says he's been ordered to join this train. I wouldn't know. Do you want to meet him?'

'Not really,' said Simon.

He avoided top brass on principle. No good, he had found, ever came of inviting their attention. He had dropped a gun barrel once and ruined his army career.

'No,' said Andrei gloomily. 'I don't blame you.'

'You are still train commander?'

'Assuming your "Spetznaz" agree,' he said in his ironic voice. He looked round. 'The Urals, eh! You can get snow till the end of June up here.'

'At this rate,' said Simon, 'we'll be here to watch it happen.'

They were waiting for a goods train from Ufa to pass. At the front of the train they could see the driver speaking into a phone by the track. The SAS signaller, Talbot, was standing by him. The Bukhara

Express had radio phones in its cab, and could talk to Kuybyshev (not that it was going to) or Yekaterinburg (if Yekaterinburg would answer) but Ufa was an old-fashioned sort of place, as befitted the last town on the most easterly edge of Europe.

Simon said: 'Will we have trouble in Yekaterinburg?'

'I've no reason to suppose we *won't* have trouble,' said Andrei, and smiled, pleased with himself.

'What about here? Will we have trouble here?'

'They'd been stopped now for ten minutes. He was worried that Andrei – whose responsibility it was, for God's sake – had not sent out a clearance patrol, or posted sentries on the nearby high ground. He could see the Russian guards all cosy inside the dining car, sitting in a fog of cigarette smoke.

'You don't think,' he said delicately, 'we ought to throw out a screen?'

'Why? We're not stopping for long.'

No, thought Simon, and if 7th Guard Tank Army came over the horizon, a screen of a dozen infantrymen armed with rifles would not stop them.

A British soldier leaned out of the train and waved and called, 'Sir!'

'Good luck with your major-general,' Simon said, going back towards the train. 'Be nice to him. It could be the making of your career.'

'If my major-general had a career,' said Andrei, a cynical Cossack, 'he wouldn't be on the Bukhara Express.'

THREE

It was Kaunas calling. Biggin, the new man in charge of *Catchphrase*. The SAS major.

'Kuybyshev Central Station,' Biggin said. 'Tula TV is blaming its destruction on Western terrorists.'

'It wasn't destroyed,' said Simon tensely. 'We had to get one of our people out of custody.'

A pause. Simon hoped to God he wasn't going to have to explain about Anna.

'How is your wounded man?'

'He's stable. We have drugs. But his condition could deteriorate at any moment, and we have no doctor.'

'The cargo?'

'Secure.'

'We have a new RV for you.'

'Will there be food?'

'Christ,' said Biggin, 'I don't know.'

He sounded harassed. Rearranging a train timetable in the middle of a Russian civil war was enough, his tone implied. It was unreasonable to expect ration packs thrown in.

'We'll find our own grub.'

'Yes . . .' Biggin sounded doubtful now. 'Try not to shoot the place up.'

Simon took down the new RV.

'Get there and stay there,' said Biggin, 'till we can clear you through Yekaterinburg.'

Simon went into the next compartment. Gallagher was conscious. 'How are you feeling?' Simon asked. Gallagher looked at him, puzzled.

Hind, the man with the injured hand, said: 'Strong as an ox, aren't you, Para? Sar'nt'll have you beasting recruits up the Skirrid by Saturday.'

Gallagher smiled, but with an effort. He was wedged in the bunk, lying on his back.

Anna was changing his chest bandages, gently replacing the sterile dressing.

'Such a little hole,' she said.

His wound, newly stitched, was healthily red and angry.

'Your wife will be pleased, Para,' said Anna.

'Wife? What wife?' said Hind. 'He's no wife, have you, Para?'

'No wife?' Anna teased. 'Not even a little one tucked away?'

Gallagher smiled feebly.

'He's no wife, not bloody likely,' said Hind, a dog with a bone. 'A wife is what he needs, isn't it, Para?'

Gallagher's eyes closed.

'Now come on, Para,' Hind went on, 'don't be shy about answering questions, you daft bugger . . .'

'Hush,' said Anna, 'hush.'

Gallagher's stomach had been stitched up. The shrapnel had been removed. The membrane of his lung had been sealed, the blood drained from the pleural cavity.

There was a danger it could collect again, but hopefully not before he was safe in a NATO hospital.

Antibiotics, rest and warmth, the doctor had said; these were the essentials.

He was as tough as an ox. Anybody less like an ox would have died.

They were still in the siding at noon. Ufa traffic control said the goods train had been delayed. The television news was full of chaos and crisis, but up here, on the broad, black Urals, everything was cold and quiet and peaceful. If they'd had food and fuel, thought Simon, they could have sat out the entire war.

Art Finkel had been for a wander along the corridor. He came back and said: 'There's a Russian general on the train. God knows how old he is. That Anna girl told me he was in Berlin in World War II. These food coupons are useless.'

Kate said: 'Talk to Simon.'

'Who?'

'Lieutenant fucking Morrell.'

'Oh, your officer friend,' said Art.

The compartment smelled. The entire train smelled sweaty and stale. He decided to go for a breath of fresh air. 'I'm sick of this train,' he said. 'I've had enough.'

She didn't reply. She was lying with her eyes closed. She looked as if she could do with a breath of air herself – to put some colour in her cheeks, as Art's mum used to say.

He climbed down and stood by the track. He breathed in fresh, damp air, and shivered. He walked up to the front, to the engine, and peered ahead. Low hills, moorland with spiky grass, a bit like the Pennines round Rawtenstall and Bacup, but without the ramblers. Deeply unimpressive. He looked up at the cab. The driver, a thin-faced Russian, looked down at him. Art smiled and gave a friendly wave. The Russian stared for a moment then cautiously waved back.

Art walked quickly back down along the train, his Churchill brogues scrunching the gravel, trying to warm himself up. At the end of the train he reached the container wagon that was stuck so incongruously on the back of the Bukhara Express.

'*Niet*,' said a soldier in Russian uniform, popping out from nowhere, standing in his path, waving his rifle.

Art pretended not to understand. He tried to walk round the soldier. The soldier pushed in front of him, keeping him away from the train, holding up his rifle.

'*Niet, niet*,' he said.

Art wondered why a squaddie with an SA80 assault rifle and Boots thermos poking out of his pocket was pretending to be a Russian. He peered past the squaddie's black fur hat, with its badge of the 19th Ryazan Airborne Assault Regiment.

'*Niet, niet*!'

He noted the red seals on the wagon, noted that it was refrigerated and hummed quietly.

'*Niet*! *Niet*!' said the soldier. 'Don't you fucking understand your own fucking language? Go on, bugger off.'

Art said: 'You have a flair for languages, my friend. A few more years of practice, and I promise you will speak English like a native.'

Kate said: 'So what were you doing out of the train, anyway? Christ, you've not gone and clogged up the loo with bloody crisp packets have you?'

'How can I clog the loo up? It's only a frigging hole, there's track underneath. I wanted a little walk, that was all.'

'You didn't say anything to me about a little walk.'

'Dear God I can go for a walk without asking you, can't I? I don't come trotting after you when you go with your soldier boys, do I?'

The international press corps did not like to be separated, not when it was out and about on an assignment. Its constituent parts became uneasy and fretful.

Kate said: 'I'm starving. What about those cheese biscuits?'

'I haven't got any cheese biscuits.'

'Oh, come on, come on . . .'

'I bloody haven't!'

Kate said: 'OK,' and relapsed into silence.

He said: 'You didn't seem very surprised. Did you know there were English soldiers dressed in Russian uniform?'

'Yes. I know quite a lot about them actually.'

'You didn't mention it to me.'

'Didn't I? I must have forgotten.'

There was a pause. He looked at her. She smiled.

He got up and unlocked his case, and took out a packet of biscuits. She munched for a while.

'Well?'

'They're SAS,' she said.

'Disguised as Russians?'

'That's what Lacy and Chaffinch tell me.'

'SAS . . .?' breathed Art, his news antennae, redundant during his long stint on the *Independent*, his endless sojourn on the *Sun*, now quivering.

'And the refrigerated wagon?' he asked. 'For Christ's sake, you don't send the SAS to Russia to hijack a few sides of beef.'

'I don't know about that,' said Kate. 'I didn't know it was refrigerated. Have you been looking at it? What do you think's inside it?'

'How would I know? H bombs? Some sort of secret weapon that could destroy the world?'

'Oh,' she said. 'Boy's stuff.'

She guzzled biscuits and went to sleep, looking more contented now, a dusting of crumbs on the down above her upper lip.

An hour later Art had a flash of inspiration.

FOUR

I agree that these are very interesting memoirs of a Cold War Officer in the old Soviet Army, and you give us valued insight into Moscow post-Yeltsin society, but with regret I have to tell you that the Russian military-memoir market is presently a real dog . . .

In his compartment at the front of the train, sipping tea brought to him by an awkward young soldier, Prosvirkin read again through the fax sent to him from America – sent to him by Miss Tuttbinder.

It made sad reading.

She wondered how relevant were his observations on the use of tanks and mortars in set land battles. She found nothing new in his account of the Warsaw Pact invasion of Czechoslovakia, or the Airborne Division's seizure of Kabul. She concluded: '*I am very sorry not to be able to be more enthusiastic. On a more positive note, our friends at Dovstoy Agency, St Petersburg, tell us you have been a personal friend of General Kotelnikov, and that you have first-hand verifiable evidence of Kotelnikov's corruption, cruelty, and sexual proclivities . . .*'

Nikolai Alexandrovich had never been corrupt.

Cruelty? What cruelty?

That business at Tashkent tank school, presumably. As commandant, Kotelnikov had devised what he called the slit-trench test. Tank crew were ordered to dig a slit hole in the ground. While they did so, a tank slowly approached. They had one minute thirty seconds to dig their hole and lie down in it. At that time the tank passed over them. They were told that if their slit trench was narrow enough they would be safe, the walls would not crumble.

The test had been abandoned after the fourth, or perhaps the fifth fatality.

But Nikolai had not been *deliberately* cruel. He had been training his men, toughening them up. Cruelty! When Kabul had fallen, there had been fifty executions a night in Pul-i-Charki prison, and the Afghan Army's 26th Parachute Regiment had been annihilated. It was Nikolai who took over and stopped the killing!

There had been sex, of course. Nikolai had been a senior general, a member of Paradise Group. But how did she expect first-hand verifiable evidence of *that*? Did she think that he, Prosvirkin, had been invited to take a video camera with him to the Zhukovska dacha on the ridge over the Moskva River, when Nikolai Alexandrovich's famous 'parties' had taken place?

Did she think that he, Prosvirkin, had been given a turn with one of the girl dancers from 4th Army Group's entertainment troupe?

'Please contact me,' wrote Miss Tuttbinder, *'with a synopsis of contents on the above lines. I feel sure we can come up with something really exciting.'*

He drank his tea.

He had more than Miss Tuttbinder to worry him. He thought about the telephone call he had taken from the Frunzenskaja Embankment.

The Department of War, he had been told, was preparing for a handover to Kotelnikov. Even those departing to St Petersburg were acting civilized, agreeing to leave the computer programmes intact. Second Shock Army was *their* army, for God's sake! Kotelnikov had been runner-up for the Supreme C-in-C's job in the days before the last Democratic putsch . . .

The caller had said: 'There will be a train tonight at Kuybyshev. Take my advice: be on it. It should be safe. It is carrying Rybakov's pension.'

Rybakov was Supreme C-in-C, now assuring the world from St Petersburg that the Russian Armed Forces would remain loyal to the democratic ideal.

What pension? And why did he, Prosvirkin, have to flee?

'There's a hit-list. Your name is on it. Perhaps it's because you were involved in arms sales. Perhaps you know too much about Kotelnikov,' said the caller, sounding like a gangster. But, then, they were all gangsters in Moscow nowadays.

I'm an old man, thought Prosvirkin; an old frightened man. I never got beyond major-general. I should have stayed retired, I should never have accepted a posting after the putsch. I should have stayed where I was, in obscurity, teaching civil defence at School 105.

But then he remembered the horror of those days, the one-room flat in the outer suburb of Kazan, the three trams he had to take each day to get to the school, where the headmaster barely tolerated him and the children laughed at him.

The military memoir market, said Miss Tuttbinder, *is presently a real dog . . .*

His own pension was 500,000 roubles a month, and was now worthless.

He had fled the devil he knew. What sort of devil would Miss Tuttbinder turn out to be?

The compartment door opened. It was the lieutenant, the officer of the Guard. He carried himself well. He reminded Prosvirkin of Nikolai Alexandrovich in the early days.

'Can I get you anything, General?'

Prosvirkin shook his head.

'The goods train is approaching. We expect to be moving again in a few minutes. We have had a rendezvous given to us. About thirty kilometres from Yekaterinburg.'

Prosvirkin felt the need to show his authority, his command of the situation.

'We will reach the RV on time?'

'As far as I am aware, General.' He hesitated . . . 'There is a sealed wagon attached to this train. A wagon from Perm. I do not know what it contains.'

Prosvirkin looked at him.

Andrei said: 'I assume it is correct to remove it from Russian soil?'

'Those are your instructions.'

'Yes.'

'Guard it well.'

Andrei said bitterly: 'It already has a guard. English.'

'Ah, yes . . .'

Back in 1995, Rybakov had gone to the English Defence Studies College at Fulham, a year-long attachment for brigadier-level high-flyers. It was widely felt that that was when he had 'gone over'.

Prosvirkin remembered talking to him one day, soon after his return to Moscow. Rybakov had enthused about English dogs. English dogs were different from Russian dogs. 'You could pat any English dog you came across,' Rybakov had said forcefully, 'and the dog wagged its tail. Could you ever trust a dog in the Soviet Union? Well, could you?'

Clearly that was why the Soviet State had crumbled.

He said: 'You know your destination?'

Andrei said: 'Tashkent.'

Prosvirkin nodded, as if in confirmation.

Tashkent . . . another fifteen hours perhaps.

He felt relieved that Rybakov was not sending his pension to Peking.

Andrei found Simon. He said: 'The sealed wagon, I think it's loot. What do you make of a country where the Foreign Minister is a thief? What do you "Spetznaz" think, eh, of getting themselves killed to save a thief's money?'

Simon said: 'What sort of loot? Gold?'

Andrei shrugged.

'You'd hardly need,' reflected Simon, 'a wagon that size for diamonds.'

Andrei said: 'I need a drink.'

It was 17.30, but already dusk was falling.

Hoodless was with the SAS sentry, the two of them nestling between the last coach and the refrigerated wagon. They were smoking cigarettes, cupping them carefully, not to prevent their giving a target to snipers – it was not yet dark enough to show – but to stop the wind from burning up the thin dry Russian tobacco too quickly.

In the distance, up ahead, a train appeared: a diesel, moving slowly, hauling a long line of open wagons filled with coal.

Hoodless and the sentry slipped out of the shadows, swung aboard the Bukhara Express.

The goods train rattled past. The Bukhara Express driver and the

SAS signaller altered the points, turning an iron wheel covered in thick, grey grease.

The Bukhara Express, in its turn, moved forward.

An hour later they passed through Ufa. It was, thought Art, the most depressing place he had seen in his life. It sat under dark clouds of pollution from blackened factory chimneys. Yellow buses with broken windows were covered in grime. As they moved slowly through the centre, he saw a grey-brick, grey-cement building with the sign in English: *Hotel Tourist.*

Then they were back on the moors, the land gashed with raw earth that was blood red, winding upwards into the mist and sleet. At 18.30 it was dark. They passed a stone, by the track, that had at some point in the past been painted white.

Nobody in the train noticed that they were no longer in Europe: that they had crossed the highest point of the Ural's spine, that they were now in Asia.

FIVE

The train had stopped. The sign by the track said *Kilometre mark 1879*, noting their distance from Moscow. Simon shone his torch at the concrete sign, then at the darkness around them.

'Black as a badger's bum,' said Hoodless.

Andrei lit a cigarette, and Hoodless flinched and moved fractionally to one side. In the SAS, death by passive smoking was defined as getting shot when the berk next to you struck a light.

It was nearly midnight. They were in yet another siding. Nothing could be seen except for the vague loom of hills on either side of the single railway track.

The diesel engine shuddered and died. The train's lights faded to a thin yellow glow.

'This is the place?' asked Andrei.

'Yes,' said Simon. Satellite Navigation Aid confirmed the map references. They were at the RV.

'Cold as a witch's tit,' said Hoodless.

They climbed back into the train. They went into the SAS armoury to check on the map. Andrei looked around – his face telling nothing of his thoughts – at the weapons piled on the bunk, the Russian army uniforms, the satellite communications gear.

'We're two kilometres from a small village,' said Simon. 'Less than a kilometre from the Perm Highway. Hills all round us; what looks like mine workings. So we sit here and wait. OK, Andrei?'

Andrei said: 'Wait for what?'

'Kaunas are calling us at 22.00.'

'Kaunas . . .' Andrei looked down at the map. He seemed lost in thought.

'I think I'll go and have a look around,' said Hoodless. 'Take a quick shufti.'

'I'll come with you,' said Simon. 'Andrei?'

Andrei shook his head.

They climbed through leafless deciduous trees, a plantation of some kind. They emerged on to higher ground. Looking through night glasses, they could see that the Bukhara Express was in a natural cutting, a fold in the lie of the land.

Beyond it, falling away into blackness, were the broad eastern slopes of the Urals.

Behind them were rocky outcrops, some of them man-made. These hills had been mined since the fifteenth century. They were stuffed full with every mineral from iron and salt to gold and chromite.

Kate had given him this information. They were the only words she had spoken to him during the past twelve hours.

'That's interesting,' he had said to her, making an effort.

She had given him a look and wandered off.

'We ought to be able to see Yekaterinburg,' he said. 'It's a city with a million people, we ought to see the lights.'

In the east, though, there was only darkness. Sleet was still falling. The wind came from the north, and was persistent.

'I'll put a man up here,' said Hoodless. His words were an uneasy compromise between a statement and a question. He was SAS, wanting to do his job, the things he was trained to do.

'Talk to Colour Gough,' said Simon decisively. 'Organize stags. Thirty minutes – we don't want them to freeze to death.'

Hoodless said: 'What about the Russians?'

'Sod the Russians,' said Simon shortly.

It was no use trying to involve the Federal troops. Their idea of sentry duty was to huddle inside the train, smoking pot.

Could anybody blame them, he thought wryly. How would British soldiers feel if they were in a train stuck on the Westmorland fells, escorting a load of currency-speculators and the C-in-C UK Land Forces's pension in a mail van? He imagined being their officer: trying to dig them out of the buffet, away from their cans of McEwan's, to guard the train against attack by the revolutionary burgers of Penrith.

'That officer of theirs,' said Hoodless, 'he worries me.'

'Why?'

'I don't see that his interests are necessarily ours.'

'Don't go and knife him,' said Simon, only half joking, aware of what the SAS could do if pushed.

They returned to the train. In the sick-bay, Gallagher was sleeping. Ferneyhough and Anna were reading a paperback together, politely waiting for each other to finish reading before they turned the page. The book was about a German punishment battalion on the Russian Front.

'You'll be able to write you own soon, at this rate, Ferneyhough,' said Simon.

'Sir?' said Ferneyhough.

'Anna, what do you know about Yekaterinburg?'

'Pardon?'

'It's where the Czar died isn't it? Didn't the Bolsheviks drag him off the train there?'

'Maybe,' she replied cautiously, as if he was trying to extract a state secret.

'Come on. Intourist organized tours to Yekaterinburg. I know they did: I saw the adverts.'

'I was Moscow Intourist. We were top-grade. We didn't worry about anywhere out here.'

Hoodless was feeling delicately over Gallagher's chest. He said: 'Ferneyhough, any pus starts oozing out, I want to know. You've been told how to feel the glands in his neck?'

'Yes, Sar'nt,' said Ferneyhough.

'Don't worry about Para,' said Anna protectively.

'I don't, love,' said Hoodless, 'not with you looking after him.'

It was 22.00. They went next-door, into the armoury.

The SAS signaller was on the HF set. The call came through. This time it was Littlehales.

He said: 'You're at the RV?'

'Yes.'

'The cargo?'

'Secure.'

'Your wounded man?'

'His condition remains stable. When can we proceed?'

'Not yet.'

Simon said: 'We have rations for perhaps one day. We are out of heating fuel. I request a helicopter evacuation.'

Littlehales said: 'We can no longer overfly so far north from Kazakhstan.'

There was a moment's silence.

Littlehales said: 'For the moment, the best thing is for you to disappear.'

Simon exchanged a look with Hoodless, who was crouched at his elbow, listening.

'We're in a train,' Simon said, 'covered in blue and gold lettering.'

Littlehales said: 'It's a big place, Russia. To some extent it's a question of not bringing yourself to anybody's attention – avoiding blowing up railway stations, that sort of thing.'

'How are you going to get us out?'

'Through Kazakhstan, as before. Nothing's changed.'

'What is the situation in Yekaterinburg?'

'We don't know.'

'I repeat, we are out of food and fuel.'

'We will move you as soon as we can.'

Simon sent out a clearance patrol. He wasn't going to let his men sleep until the area had been checked; he was a professional soldier in a professional army. Corporal Buck and three SAS soldiers recced one kilometre in each direction.

Colour Gough rostered sentries, gave out the password. Before the train settled for the night, he called his lads together. When he spoke, there was a note of steel in his voice that took even Mace by surprise.

'My guess is that we're on this train for another two days. Two more days and nights without bog rolls or running water. I sympathize. I understand, even. But this train compartment is *indescribable*. It's a filthy stew, it's a fucking disgrace. At first light, assuming we're still here, Lacy and Mace will look for water – a stream, a pond or something. The rest of you will tidy this place up. There'll be a kit inspection at 09.00. From now on, both compartments will be used for sleeping, and the dining car will be used as a recreation area, sharing with the Russians. Got it?'

'Yes, Colour-Sar'nt.'

'Any man here,' he went on, calmly, slowly, 'caught smoking hash will be court-martialled. I guarantee they'll end up in Colly, and not for fourteen days – for a year minimum. There'll be no going on Officer's Orders, no mitigating circumstances. You'll be banged up in the glasshouse. Understand?'

They understood.

'Can't we even have a drink?' asked Chaffinch, possibly the only man in the Section who wouldn't miss it if he didn't get legless twice a week.

'Now, I never said you couldn't have a drink,' chided Gough. He would as soon have tried to stop the sun in its path as stop a soldier drinking. 'But have some sense. Pace yourselves. One glass an hour . . .'

They looked at him.

'Be *sensible*. Remember, you're not in the Kiwi at Bulford. You're in the middle of Russia, and there's a lot of nasties out there, armed to the fucking teeth.'

At midnight Simon went round the sentries. He forced himself to go out, even though he was shivering with cold and could easily have left it to Gough and Corporal Pullin.

He walked along by the track. He could hear sobbing from one of the passenger compartments: Iulia, the daughter of the woman in the pink shellsuit, crying herself to sleep, as she had cried for most of the day. He wondered what was the matter with her – other than being hungry and cold and terrified – but was not tempted to inquire.

Subdued music came from the compartment occupied by the film director. His women, Simon had learned, were called Nina – dark and Byzantine – and Olga. They were both on Andrei's passenger list as music industry executives.

He passed the diner. He was surprised to see Kate's face through the dark window, to see that she was talking to someone. Reptiles having a midnight conference, he joked to himself sourly, passing on towards the front of the train.

SIX

Andrei and Kate sat in the empty diner, a bottle of vodka between them.

'Listen,' he said, holding her hands together gently. 'Listen.'

'I am listening.'

'My men are good soldiers.'

'I know.'

'They came from the airborne divisions. They were part of the elite even *before* they were selected for the Presidential Guard.'

'Yes.'

'You understand what it means to be selected for the Guard?'

'Yes. No. I'm tired. We'll talk in the morning.'

'You must understand what it means to be in the Guard.'

'It's an honour. A great honour.'

'The greatest honour there is.'

'I believe you.'

Soldiers came into the diner: English soldiers back from stag. She pulled her hands away. The soldiers muttered 'Sorry, ma'am' as they passed. Melting snow fell from their parkas on to the pale tablecloth.

'I am an officer of the Guard.' He took her hands again in his. 'I am the train commander. But in truth I command nothing.'

'That's not your fault,' said Kate. 'That's our fascist friend.'

'What am I going to do? What am I going to do, eh?'

Do about what? She wanted to sleep. She didn't know what he meant.

He let go of her hands, poured vodka, lit a cigarette.

She said: 'It's boring, but knocking that stuff back won't help.'

He drank, throwing the spirit to the back of his throat, closing his eyes.

She said: 'Andrei, I do know how real men drink vodka.'

The English soldiers were sitting at the far end of the diner. They had lit a spirit lamp, were starting to play cards.

'What's this blind man's pontoon, then?' she heard one say. 'I'll show you,' she heard Private Mace reply.

Andrei opened his eyes and said: 'Three young lieutenants come back to their battalion from military college, OK?'

'OK.'

'The first one comes to see the colonel. The colonel says, "Did you get top marks in your military exams?" The lieutenant says, "Yes,

Colonel." The colonel says, "Splendid. You are now a platoon leader." The second lieutenant comes back from college. Again the colonel asks, "Did you get top marks?" "No, Colonel," says the lieutenant, ashamed. "Never mind, you will be a platoon leader, and you will learn!"

'It is midnight before the third lieutenant turns up. The colonel is undressed for bed, and is angry. "Well?" he says. "Did you get top marks at military college?" "I didn't get any marks," says the third lieutenant, very drunk, "but I've got a car waiting outside full of women and vodka."

' "My God!" shouts the colonel to his batman. "Get my uniform! Tell the men we've got a new chief of staff!" '

He crashed his vodka glass down and laughed.

'I expect,' said Kate, 'it's funnier when you're actually in the army.'

'No, it's not funny,' said Andrei. 'It's what they made us into. It's what they made out of the army, the best army in the world.'

'Hey,' she said gently, 'come on.'

'I am going crazy.'

'You Slavs, why do you always get so emotional?'

The soldiers at the end of the diner wanted a drink. 'Go on, ask her,' she heard one of them say in an undertone. 'No, I'm not asking her,' said another. Private Mace said: 'Go on, tell her we saved her fucking life.'

'The Red Army,' said Andrei, 'was the army that defeated the fascists. It was the army that held the Germans when everyone else gave way. The army that lost more than a hundred and twenty thousand men at Stalingrad.'

'It wouldn't have done,' said Kate, 'if your political officers hadn't been shooting them in the back.'

He tensed.

'I'm sorry.'

There was silence.

'War!' he said suddenly. 'You know the Russian word for war?'

'*Voyna*.'

'*Voyna*. . .'

He breathed the syllables. '*Voyna* means war,' he said, 'but it means more than war. It means desolateness.'

'Desolation.'

'It means heartbreak,' he said. 'It means terrible loss. *Voyna* is what every Russian dreads. We know you English love war. Your soldiers say they have had "a good war" – Andrei imitated a British officer. Kate laughed suddenly – 'but we Russians cannot have a good war. It is not possible to have "a good loss", "a good heartbreak", "a good *voyna*" . . .'

He was a young man close to despair. Close to tears. A soldier whose beliefs had taken a hard pounding these past days.

'Listen,' she said. 'Listen to me. I love Russia. I love the Russian people. I love your music, your literature—'

'Yes, yes . . .'

'Listen!' she said passionately, holding his hands now, tightly between her own. 'When I first visited Moscow, I was seventeen. When I landed at the airport there were video screens in the arrivals lounge, sponsored by some Jap firm. In England they'd have been playing pop videos, mindless, stupid, *loud* videos, on the assumption, the *democratic*, populist *Daily* fucking *Star* assumption that everybody is either brain-dead or likes listening to screeching freaks.

'But at Sheremetyevo, Andrei, the videos showed the Moscow Philharmonic Orchestra playing Bizet and Stravinsky. And in Moscow itself, people with nothing to live on, their savings wiped out by hyper-inflation, were still buying flowers. And, in the subways, people with only a few roubles between themselves and starvation were buying books – not trash but real books: novels, books of poetry, books of economics.'

She stopped.

He was staring at her intently. She went on: 'Russia is a country where people still believe in something, Andrei. We don't believe in anything in the West – nothing worthwhile, not anymore.'

Private Mace called: 'Here, miss, if you don't want to finish that bottle . . .'

There was silence.

One of the soldiers laughed, embarrassed.

'I must go,' she said.

'Go?' He smiled faintly. 'Go where?'

'It's late. I must sleep. Have you got Hitler's corpse in a refrigerated wagon, Andrei?'

He looked at her blankly. Then he laughed loudly.

(Private Mace's voice: 'I told you he was going to score. Didn't I tell you he was going to score?')

'Hitler's corpse? You think the Commander-in-Chief is sending Hitler's corpse to the West?'

'So what is it? Gold?' She stood up.

'I don't know, Kate. I don't care.' He also stood up.

Nothing was said. Only by the faintest movement of his hand did he indicate the way to the front of the train, to the carriages of the Russian soldiers.

She shook her head, turned, and went towards the back of the train.

He followed her.

'Night, ma'am,' called one of the English soldiers.

She went along the corridor of the Royal Mercians' carriage and through the carriage filled with documents, and into the next coach. She stopped outside the door of Art's compartment. Andrei was behind her. She turned.

'No,' she said.

He put a hand round behind her neck, pulled her towards him and kissed her.

After a few moments she pulled away, turned, and went into the compartment next to Art's, that had been unoccupied since Kuybyshev.

He followed her in, locked the door and pulled down the blinds. He had brought the vodka, but she took it from his hand and put it down on the floor. Then she quickly took off her jumper and jeans and lay down on the bunk, shivering on the pale blue Bukhara Express sheets.

He leaned over her and kissed her again, running his hand down her body. She shivered uncontrollably. He started to take off the rest of her clothes.

She helped him with the buttons of her shirt, it being the only shirt she'd got, and with the hooks on her bra.

She lay naked. He stood up and looked down at her.

He started to unbutton his tunic.

She watched him, her heart thudding.

It might not be possible for a Russian to have a 'good *Voyna*', she thought, but this soldier wasn't having an altogether bad one.

SEVEN

There was a glass of tea and a small portion of *kasha* for each soldier for breakfast.

'Make the most of it. This is the end of soft living,' said Colour Gough.

Snow had fallen again, and still fell: a slushy, wet snow; huge flakes that splatted on the windows. A steady wind from the north piled it into drifts.

Another twenty-four hours, Simon reckoned, and the train would be buried. Even now it was doubtful if they would be able to move.

Perhaps, he thought grimly, this was what Biggin meant when he said he wanted them to disappear.

Sentries trudged up out of the cutting, to the top of the neighbouring high ground. In an interval when the snow had stopped, they saw a road in the distance. They reported lines of lorries on it, some filled with coal, others with people in the back. The sentries watched them through SAS binoculars. They reported that the people were covered in sacks to keep the snow off.

At midday the Royal Mercians ate Russian army macaroni, which had in it a few flakes of dried fish.

The supply of peat bricks for the stoves was now exhausted. In Gallagher's compartment a hexamine stove burned to keep the temperature up, but there were only a dozen hexamine blocks left.

Of the three families still on the train, one couple – the Pastnovs – were found to have not eaten anything at all for twenty-four hours, while the Vostrotins were eating from suitcases full of tinned meat and fruit and packets of Swiss baby rusks.

Simon said to Andrei: 'You're train commander. Make them share it out.'

Andrei said: 'They want capitalism; they've got it. This is how it works in the West.'

'Appeal to their better instincts. Appeal to their common decency.'

'You are insane. You are mad,' Andrei marvelled.

'Put a gun to their heads.'

'Now you're making sense.'

He seemed more friendly, thought Simon, more relaxed. 'Go on, Andrei. You can't let the Pastnovs starve.'

Andrei went into the Vostrotins' compartment. There was shouting and wailing. Pink-shellsuited Mrs Vostrotin burst into tears and clutched her fat girl, Iulia. Her husband chain-smoked with his head in his hands.

Andrei came out.

'We are trying to murder her little child,' he said, 'to feed a gang of degenerate confidence tricksters.'

'You Slavs,' said Simon.

'People always say that,' said Andrei.

Food was handed over to the Pastnovs: a timid, middle-aged couple who had run a joint-venture property development agency in Moscow, and were now adrift and helpless in the raging Russian storm.

Food was also taken – 'requisitioned,' said Andrei, savouring the word – for Gallagher, although he was presently restricted to sugar and water.

'Now, something for my general, my top hat,' said Andrei, taking more tins out of a suitcase, more packets of rusks.

'Top brass,' said Simon. 'If I had top brass on board,' he added, thinking of Brigadier Grenfell, 'I'd enjoy watching them starve.'

Andrei reached for another suitcase. Mrs Vostrotin howled. A Russian guard quietly pressed the muzzle of his rifle against her throat.

The film director and his girls never asked for food. Drugged up to the eyeballs, Simon presumed; satiated on sex.

'What,' said Art, when Kate came back from the dining car, 'have they got to eat down there, then?'

'Macaroni and fish flakes. You wouldn't like it.'

She seemed nervous, he thought. Edgy. She jumped when anyone passed the door. She muttered 'Oh Christ,' to herself when she thought he wasn't listening. She had a blush of colour in her cheeks and a funny sparkle in her eye.

'OK,' he said, carefully munching a water biscuit spread with pâté, 'so Ivan the Wonderful doesn't reckon it's Hitler. What would he know? Who made *him* the great brain?'

'Shut up about Hitler. Perhaps it's works of art or gold bullion or the Romanian crown jewels – and it might well be the Romanian crown jewels, everybody knows they've had them stashed away in Moscow since 1919. What is this thing you have about Hitler?'

'I suppose,' said Art, 'it's the fact that crown jewels don't need refrigeration – don't rely on a temperature of minus-twenty, the way Hitler does. Or it might be the fact that the only Russian general alive *who was in Berlin in 1945* is presently travelling on this train.'

'Art, there is no Hitler's body. You've worked on the *Sun* for so long your brain has gone soft.'

Art had finished his biscuit. He looked hungrily at the bottles of PPP vegetables. 'Care for a pickled onion?' he said casually.

She looked at him.

'Why?' she asked. 'Do you have any? Or are you referring to these pickled testicles, these pigs' balls we find before us?'

'Shit,' said Art.

There were crumbs on his jumper. He pressed his tongue against the wool, lifting the morsels off like a patent crumb-remover.

'You are so vile,' she said. 'You are so *gross*.'

'I'm tired out,' said Art. 'I was up half the night listening to some soldier shagging his tart.'

Kate blinked.

'Time I believe,' said Art, closing his eyes, 'for a spot of Egyptian PT.'

Soon he slept.

By midday the snow had stopped but the wind blew insistently, penetrating the train, equalizing its temperature to that of the ground outside. The English soldiers exercised in the corridors to keep warm. Andrei's men started stripping the rosewood panelling from the Czar's imperial coaches, pulling out the cherry veneer so carefully restored by Wagon-Lit in Paris.

The wood burned in the stoves with a terrible smell of varnish, sending up wreaths of thick black smoke.

Hoodless, standing outside by the track with Simon, said: 'That's naughty, that is. That's way out of order. That's giving our position away.'

'We're not in a snow-hole. We're on a train,' said Simon shortly. 'And if anybody's looking, our position is blindingly fucking obvious.'

Walking up and down the corridors to keep warm, he was stopped by one of the film director's girls. It was Nina, the dark, Byzantine one. She said, 'Hi,' and asked him into their compartment.

He hesitated.

'Hey, come on,' she said. 'Come and have a drink. Come and say hello.'

'I'm sorry we haven't been able to get to know each other,' he said politely, following her into the compartment and sitting down.

All three of them spoke English. The director, who was from the Moscow Film School, seemed relieved to have somebody to talk to who wasn't Nina or Olga. Simon asked what sort of films he made. He said contemporary films, new-wave, erotic, with violet colours and a spiritual hue. He said they could not be shown in the West because he could not afford to shoot on Kodak film.

'That's a pity,' said Simon politely.

Even the *fartsouchiki*, the black marketeers, could not get real Kodak film, said the director. He had heard that the army had Kodak film, though. Did Simon think the army had Kodak film?

Olga, pale white hair and orange lipstick, poured Russian champagne in wide-topped glasses and handed it round. There was no lavatory paper in Russia, she said. Even the *fartsouchiki* could not get lavatory paper. All the lavatory paper in the Federation was imported from Lithuania, and the Lithuanians had refused to supply any more because the Russian government wanted to pay in roubles. 'But we're the ones giving *you* the toilet paper,' the puzzled

Lithuanians were supposed to have said.

Nina was knocking the cheap, dry tobacco out of a cardboard cigarette tube, and replacing it with something else.

'Uzbek grass,' said the director. 'Better than Afghanistan grass. More patriotic.'

'Right,' said Simon. Olga, gently but insistently, was pushing him up against the seat, moving his hand so that she could sit on his lap.

'No, I'm sorry . . .'

He imagined Mace wandering past on his way to the bog.

Olga shrugged and sat opposite. Nina lit her cigarette and took up a glass of champagne. Slowly she exhaled smoke on to the top of the glass. It sat there, a dense, white layer over the champagne.

She smiled and passed it carefully to Simon.

'Drink and breathe in at the same time,' she said, looking at him with her green eyes.

The director said: 'OK, action.'

Olga said: 'What's going on?'

Nina said: 'Psychos are building a bonfire under the bridge.'

'Why?'

'To prepare for the overthrow.'

'Overthrow of what?'

'The bridge.'

'What is the root of all evil?'

'The Bolshoi Theatre.'

'How do we get rid of it?'

'We release the energy of an orange seed.'

'Who possesses the energy?'

'The CIA.'

'Cut,' said the director.

Simon put down his pretend camera. They all laughed.

Prosvirkin was huddled in the cold, reading Miss Tuttbinder's fax. 'Is it true,' she concluded, 'that you and General Kotelnikov were friends? That he came from the same village as yourself?'

He wrote now: *Yes, we are from the same village, though Nikolai Alexandrovich is four years younger than I. We were both at the Moscow Suvorov, both high-flying captains at the Frunze Academy, both heading, in the Sixties, towards the General Staff.*

Yes, we were friends, though Nikolai was too young to serve in the Great Patriotic War. In my mind's eye I see him when he was fifteen.

I see the War Memorial, high on the hill, with snow flurrying from the north. I see Nikolai on guard with his red scarf blowing in the wind, while from the radio speakers inside the granite hall comes the sound of the Red Army choir singing: 'Arise O Motherland!'

I see him, erect and proud, his frozen fingers holding the flag of 211 Pioneers.

The pioneers were the largest youth organization in the world, apart from the Boy Scouts. In my view they were infinitely superior to the Boy Scouts, for they did not indulge in political indoctrination, beyond, at least, teaching Soviet Youth an awareness of the sacrifices made on their behalf, of the price paid by their grandfathers and their grandmothers to defend their country.

Nikolai Kotelnikov was brought up to be a patriot, to love his country.

But, of course, we were all brought up in this way.

It is difficult, now, to understand why we should have turned out as we did, and why Nikolai turned out as he has.

The compartment was slowly warming, a faint heat coming from the old iron pipes. A soldier brought him tea from the samovar. He savoured these, his last days of luxury and ease.

EIGHT

It was 15.00 and all Royal Mercians who were off-duty were crammed into Section HQ.

Kate was there. So was Anna – she'd been dragged from Gallagher's bedside and told to enjoy herself. Outside, a satellite dish was being held manually on the roof of the coach, aiming towards a point in the western sky. Sentries on the distant quarry rim looked down in amazement to see Foster, who had drawn the short straw, crouched like a black gargoyle on the coach's ridge.

In Section HQ the screen cleared for a second, and a cheer went up.

'I must go back to Para,' said Anna fretfully. 'Hey, come on, you guys.'

'He's all right. He's got Ferney, and Ferney's all right because he's got the favourite,' said Corporal Pullin kindly. 'You're here to collect his winnings, Anna, to stop us spending them all.'

'Here you are, Anna,' said Chaffinch. 'You can have a leg of my horse. A leg of Selsey Warbler.'

'And mine,' Mace said. 'You can have a leg of What a Mistake. You're on to a quarter of my winnings now.'

'I am?'

'Yea, so come here and sit by me. That's it, you can squeeze in. That's right.'

'And a quarter of my winnings,' said Chaffinch jealously. 'A quarter of Selsey Warbler. You can sit by me if you want to.'

The picture flickered. Foster was cursed for not holding the dish steadily. The screen cleared, the commentator's voice came with sudden clarity: 'A fine sunny day here in Cheltenham . . .'

'You all right, ma'am?'

A tear was trickling down Kate's face.

'You can have a leg of my horse, ma'am. Parson's Pleasure,' said Henshaw awkwardly, thinking that Kate had perhaps been hurt to be left out.

Kate leaned over and kissed him, and said, 'Sweetie.'

Henshaw looked stunned.

Kate was sobbing and smiling at the same time, being back in England, a sixth-former curled up in the warm, in the common room of her Cheltenham school, eating toast and reading a Joanna Trollope or a Jilly Cooper novel.

'And a leg of mine,' said Chaffinch. 'I've still got three left.'

'And it's Sky Pilot in the lead from Aldhelm Boy and What a Mistake . . .'

The picture went again. The satellite, New Astra, was almost on the horizon, way over distant Bulgaria.

There were roars of rage. A Russian Guard, who was approaching the doorway with a hammer in search of wood for the stove, retreated in alarm.

Simon and Hoodless were in the armoury with the SAS signaller, who was crouched over the fax machine.

It was spewing out intelligence reports.

At Moscow State University students had thrown up barricades against Second Army. The English-language *Radio Maximum* was back on the air, repeatedly broadcasting the students' demand for a bill of rights that would guarantee freedom of speech, freedom of association, freedom to travel, habeas corpus.

A monument to liberty was being built with wire and plaster at the front of the huge, monolithic university building. Buses and cars had been turned on their sides in the approach roads; concrete blocks were positioned to deter tanks.

A French news team had flown in by helicopter from Kiev. As the helicopter had taken off again, it had been shot down in flames by a Russian fighter. Burning fuel had fallen on students below, setting their clothing alight, burning their skin.

There were echoes of Prague in 1968; of Tiananmen Square in 1989.

The French news team was sending pictures out by satellite; the drama was being watched live, hour after hour, in every country of the world that had a TV station capable of arranging a quick contract with the French television company.

The company's shares had doubled in value in twelve hours.

The SAS signaller said: 'They forget we've no spare fax paper. When this roll's finished, that's it.'

NATO intell reports timed 16.00 covered the Volga basin and the Urals. The majority of Federal Army units were remaining neutral. A hundred thousand miners were on strike in the Kuznetsk basin in western Siberia. Other miners were said to be on strike in Norkuta, in northern Siberia, but this latter intelligence was of no interest to the Bukhara Express.

It was western Siberia that they had to pass through, to reach safety.

There were no reports on Yekaterinburg.

Simon, who had a headache, said: 'Can't we go round the bloody place?'

'Not without going back down to Ufa.'

'Well, we either move this train or send a party to one of the villages for food.'

'I don't like the sound of that much,' said Hoodless.

'No,' said Simon, 'I didn't suppose you would. I have to ask myself if I sodding care what happens to some Russian nob's loot.'

'What you have to ask yourself,' said Hoodless, 'is whether you mind some locals stringing you up from a lamppost.'

'Lamppost,' said Simon, with nostalgia. 'There's something comforting about a lamppost. I'm sending out a patrol at dawn tomorrow. Two of your men, five of mine, and six of Andrei's men if he's willing to cooperate.'

The fax machine had stopped. The signaller said: 'Kaunas coming through on the HF, sir.'

Littlehales, the intelligence expert, said cautiously: 'You've seen the summaries?'

'Yes.'

'Everything's changing. Have you any food left?'

'Very little.'

'Yekaterinburg's the problem. We don't know what's happening there. It's reverted to being a closed city, the way it was in Soviet times. You won't find it in the NATO briefing, but the Chinese are talking about a scarlet plague running down the settlements of the eastern Urals.

'Scarlet plague?'

'Don't ask me,' said Littlehales. 'The medics have never heard of it. They think it might be a form of bubonic plague spread up from Armenia, or it could be some sort of radiation disease. Can you send out a reconnaissance patrol?'

'Tomorrow at dawn.'

Simon went outside with Hoodless and they checked radioactivity, which was three times the recommended levels.

'Nothing to worry about,' said Hoodless, looking through the sleet and mist to the scarred, weeping rock-faces beyond the trees. 'Six times is danger level; that's what we're told.'

'I dare say half the minerals round here have natural radiation,' said Simon, trying, without success, to remember if potash, aluminium, and asbestos were radioactive.

He found Andrei at the end of the dining car, in the gloom lit only by the whiteness outside.

He was sitting with Kate, their heads together. There was a vodka bottle on the table. They were deep in conversation, which was very nice, Simon thought, for some.

He joined them. 'Sorry to barge in.'

'Hi there,' said Andrei easily.

'Oh, hello Simon,' said Kate brightly. 'Long time no see.'

Andrei said: 'Have a drink. You're a very privileged man. This is definitely the last bottle on the train.'

'Actually,' Kate said, in an odd chatty voice, 'I think my friend Finkel has a bottle or two stashed away. He has a bag that clinks. He takes it everywhere with him: clink, clink, clink. So how are you, then? I saw you talking to that Nina.'

Simon ignored her. He said: 'Andrei, I want to send a patrol out.

Will you provide five men and an NCO?'

Andrei hesitated, would have said no, then looked quickly at Kate and said: 'OK, Why not?'

Kate said: 'I can see that this is army talk, so I'll leave you to it. Can I get past, please?'

'Dawn tomorrow?' said Simon, as if she wasn't there. 'They can look for food supplies, try and get information. Have you heard of scarlet plague?'

'No.'

'There's talk of an outbreak of it in Yekaterinburg.'

Kate, icy now, said: 'It's in a book by Jack London. Scarlet Plague is what wipes out the human race – or most of it. Jolly good luck to it, that's what I say. Now, will you fucking move and let me get past?'

NINE

Hoodless swung down from the train.

'OK, got your weapons?'

'Yes, Sar'nt,' said Lacy, looking nervous. His SA80 was held at the ready, his bony hand tightly gripping the dark green handle.

Corporal Pullin, next to him, also had an SA80. Each man had three hundred rounds in his webbing, green and black cam cream wiped over his face and hair.

Hoodless looked them over critically.

Their equipment had been taped to stop it rattling. Their field trousers were tied at thigh and ankle to reduce slack that could snag on branches or rocks. They wore Russian army caps to give a blurred, soft head outline.

Hoodless nodded, satisfied. He said: 'Welcome to the SAS.'

'Otherwise known,' said Corporal Buck with a deadpan face, 'as the Savage And Sadistic.'

Buck had the heavy snipe-sight. He had taken off the infrared sight and was clipping on the standard optics.

The four men would form an overwatch team. They would position themselves out on the flank, to provide covering fire for Simon's main group.

Chaffinch and Mace would accompany Simon, Anna, and the Federal Guards. While they waited for the Russians, they stamped on the ground to warm their feet. There was a heavy, wet, yellowish mist, although visibility was reasonable, up to five hundred metres.

Andrei came down the side of the train, leading a file of six men, just as Anna jumped down from the SAS carriage. She was wearing Gallagher's Russian Army camouflage jacket, still ripped by shrapnel.

She said: 'Good morning, everybody.'

'Morning, Anna.'

Andrei said: 'What is she doing? Where is she going?'

Simon said: 'We have to have an interpreter. It was you, her or Miss Delacroix.'

Andrei said, quietly marvelling, 'Miss Delacroix . . . ?'

Kate was peering out of a window, further down the train, inspecting the morning. She smiled hesitantly and waved. Simon waved back awkwardly, not sure if she had been waving at him or at the world in general.

Colour Gough was handing round Mars bars, the last of his reserves, the only rations the patrol would now carry. The Russians looked at them interestedly. If there was a black market handy, thought Simon, they'd be trying to flog them off.

Andrei said abruptly: 'Do you want me to come with you?'

'I thought,' said Simon, 'that you couldn't leave the train.'

He started to wipe the optic sights of his SA80. They had a habit of steaming up as warm air from his face condensed on the glass. 'No, it's all right,' he continued. 'You're train commander. We'll make for the farm, and, if that's no good, the village. Expect us back in six hours maximum. Right, lads?'

'Sir,' said Mace and Chaffinch.

'OK, Anna?'

She nodded.

'This must be a bit different from being an Intourist interpreter.'

'Yea,' she said, startled.

Hoodless had already led his patrol away. They had almost disappeared, filing up through the melting snow.

'OK,' said Simon, hitching up his Bergen, firmly grasping his SA80, nodding encouragingly to his soldiers and to the six Russian Guards. 'Let's go.'

Andrei walked back along the gravel next to the train. Kate was still at the window, watching the soldiers climb up the hillside.

'Simon must be the only man in Russia,' said Andrei, 'who thinks that Anna was ever an Intourist guide.'

Kate said: 'Oh?' Then she added: 'There's nothing so wonderful about naivety.'

'Naivety? What does that mean?'

She shook her head, shivered, and closed the window.

Art said: 'I'm not happy. What we want to do is get to the nearest sodding city and book into the biggest sodding hotel. I've been playing silly soldiers for long enough. What time is it?'

'Eight-thirty.'

'Is there any tea?'

'No.'

'Any breakfast?'

'Only what you've got in your bag.'

'I'm not a kid anymore,' Art said, ignoring that one. 'I'm not one of your shit-hot graduate reporters. They shouldn't send features men on this sort of job. This sort of job's for keen bastards. When you get to my age, you need a few comforts.'

'Do please shut up . . .'

'I've done my share, haven't I? I've done my share of doorstepping in my time. My God, four days and nights on the Killickmoor kidnap, and in February, too, with a chest infection.'

'For Christ's sake,' she said wearily.

The door opened. It was Andrei.

'Don't even think about knocking,' said Art. 'Didn't they have doors on your house?'

Kate said: 'Oh, do, *do* be quiet . . .'

Andrei looked intently at Kate, then wandered off.

'Well shut it, for Christ's sake!' Art yelped. 'I wasn't brought up in a barn, even if you were.'

Andrei had gone. Kate stood up and went out after him.

'Yes, well, never mind me. You just go off for a nice shag . . .' he sneered.

He nearly added that it was all right for some; nobody ever offered *him* one – but stopped in time. He knew you stood with your back to the wall when the Yanks were around, but he was a bit vague about the sexual proclivities of the Russian army.

He closed the door, and sat huddled in his coat. Through the window he watched a British soldier, going on sentry duty, climb up into the mist. He wondered what sort of food the patrol would come back with. They were hardly likely to encounter a Sainsburys or an Oddbins.

For a while he watched his breath floating across the compartment in little clouds. He wanted to relieve himself but wasn't going near the lavatory at the end of the carriage, which was now vile beyond belief: worse than the lavs on the night train from Holyhead when it finally reached Euston.

He wanted a cup of tea. He badly wanted a cup of tea. He thought wistfully of the samovar girls who had got off at Kuybyshev. What had happened to that magnificent conductress and her bony lover?

Eventually he left the compartment and walked down the corridor, past the compartment wherein he assumed Ivan the Wonderful was shagging Kate, and climbed out of the train.

He then walked back down the track, coughing in the raw air that tasted of chemicals. He reached the container wagon and approached it. He inspected the red seals on the sliding door, gently tried the padlock and bolt.

There was no noise, no vibration, so the refrigeration plant was not on – it didn't need to be, not in this weather.

He looked at the smooth-as-satin aluminium. His mind wandered back to accounts of a summer's night in old Berlin . . . Eva Braun biting the potassium cyanide capsule, Hitler shooting himself in his right temple; their bodies doused in petrol, burning to a symphony of gunfire and exploding grenades.

Or not doused in petrol at all.

Abandoned, instead, in the bunker.

Why should anybody organize a cremation when death was raining down from the skies, and the Russians were just round the corner?

Come on! Was it realistic? Would *you* mess about giving a Viking funeral to a former head of state, now dead, with the savages from the steppes only two streets away and loping purposefully in your direction?

Were they now, Eva and Adolf, lying a few feet away from him, on a bridal bed of crushed ice?

Had the Führer been perfectly preserved for more than half a century?

And what about Blondie the dog?

'I thought I frigging well told you to frigging well frig off,' said a voice.

'You know,' said Art, 'you're English is getting better and better. Somebody must have been giving you lessons. Thing is, chum, your officer was telling me about what's in this wagon. Bit of a facer, eh? What did you make of it when you found out? Your officer was going to arrange for me to have a look, but he went on patrol and must have forgotten. Have you seen inside, yourself? Do you think he'd mind if we had a look now?'

The soldier raised his gun. 'Perhaps you'd like to go and ask him,' he said. 'Smartarse.'

TEN

They had walked for the best part of an hour through the rocks, skirting a tarn of black oily water. Up here, the ground was shale; what soil there was was thin and peaty.

Hoodless's overwatch patrol was somewhere out on the flank. The mist had thinned. Simon tried to find them through his binoculars, but they were nowhere in view.

Which was as it should be. First-class snipers were the most feared men on the battlefield, moving elusively from cover to cover, able to pin down entire units of enemy troops or take out high-value targets like senior officers or radio operators.

Simon looked round, panting, to see how well his group was keeping up. His own men were desperately unfit. After a month at the Moscow embassy and three days on a train they were wheezing and puffing like old walruses. NATO soldiers consumed, in active service, the best part of four thousand calories a day, and his lot had gone on consuming four thousand calories a day even when they were stuck in an embassy and then on the Bukhara Express.

They were getting fat and lumpish, he thought severely. What they needed was a good-natured NCO to beast them along a forty-mile route march with full Bergens on their backs.

The Russians, he was pleased to note, were puffing and panting the same as everybody else, sweating out the effects of grass and vodka.

Anna was hopping from rock to rock, occasionally saying: 'Come on, you guys,' to the English; ignoring the Russians.

She was very pretty, he thought, seeing her for the first time with colour in her cheeks. Slim, absurdly attractive in Gallagher's combat jacket.

'OK, come on. Keep moving!' he called, leaping forward despite his Bergen, setting a brisk pace despite the awful stitch in his side.

Hoodless was waiting on a ridge. He appeared from nowhere, popping up out of the rocks like a genie. The other three members of his patrol appeared behind him. Lacy and Corporal Pullin were sweat-stained and fighting for breath, their heads bleeding, their trousers cut at the knees.

'Leopard crawl,' said Hoodless, 'over stones like razor blades. It's what sorts out the time-servers, the day-release cases from Broadmoor. OK, lads?'

Pullin and Lacy nodded, grinning.

Simon looked down from the ridge through his binoculars. Behind him he could hear Chaffinch saying to Lacy: 'Your hand's cut, Stephen. You ought to put something on that.'

Below was a featureless plain with the Perm Highway snaking across it. Closer were fields, a cluster of farm buildings, a village.

Hoodless, also scanning the scree slopes through his binos, said: 'Two hundred half left, seven o'clock, by a boulder.'

It appeared to be a barn, and by it a badly improvised tent. A dozen or so figures, some of them children, round a fire in the snow.

More refugees.

It was like looking at old news footage of Bosnia, of the last days before the relief of Sarajevo – of Kurdistan.

The people down there were more likely to demand food than be able to supply it. But they might be able to give him information.

'All right,' he said after a moment. 'Let's go down to say hello.'

They filed down the scree. They did not try to approach covertly. They were, after all, friendly soldiers seeking help in a friendly country.

They were thirty people, many of them old. They were from the village of Sputnik Mira, a *kolkhoz* collective built in the mid-Seventies and named after one of the early 'peace' satellites. Sputnik Mira had fifty workers, and a similar number of pensioners. Two days ago, the village had been taken over by mafia. The population had been ejected, forced out at gunpoint. Some had gone towards the Perm Highway; the others had come here, up on the hillside. They had been lucky not to be killed.

Simon remembered the words of prophecy from Marshal Kotelnikov, made a month before he launched his coup: 'One more year of democracy and there will be warships on the Volga, and armies will wander the steppes, living off the land.'

It had been a self-fulfilling prophesy.

The mafia were still in Sputnik Mira. The people in the barn were waiting for them to go. The previous night they had gone down and scrounged food, hanging round their own village like dogs.

The *kolkhoz* had potatoes and swedes, carrots and cabbage, a hundred-head herd of cattle. The mafia had a truck to take stuff away, but seemed in no hurry.

The *kolkhoz* leader spoke volubly. Anna shook her head in dismay, in sympathy. The women of the group crowded round her, pouring out their tales of woe.

'How many mafia are there?' asked Simon. 'How many gangsters have taken over the village?'

Fifteen, perhaps twenty. They weren't sure.

'Armed?'

Yes, of course. Armed to the teeth. A middleaged woman burst into a loud tirade of complaints. Her eyes were red and puffed, the skin beneath them grey parchment. She wrung her hands, an action Simon had never actually seen before. She gave the impression of being roused from exhaustion to a last burst of energy.

'She cannot go on any longer,' said Anna. 'For months there has been nothing to eat but potatoes. The mafia take the rest; they take everything: the meat, the milk. The villagers work for nothing. The mafia take everything. There has been no sugar since the New Year. Sugar is in the mafia hands. The mafia in Yekaterinburg issue ration cards, but refuse to give them to farmers on the *kolkhoz*. She blames Perestroika. There was no organized crime before Perestroika. It's what everybody says,' Anna turned to Simon. 'It's very true, I think.'

The woman sank to the ground, crying, her head in her hands.

'Just thank God you don't live here,' said Anna wisely.

'Tell them I have to know how many gangsters there are. Tell them I must know *for certain*.'

Twenty, they said; definitely twenty. Mafia from the city, not from Pervouralsk, the nearby town, but from Yekaterinburg.

'Ask them if they know what is happening in Yekaterinburg.'

They knew nothing, cared less.

A young boy started to cry. The other children, half a dozen of them, looked at the soldiers silently. Chaffinch said: 'Here you are, love.'

He was holding out his Mars bar to a small girl. 'You'll like this. You like chocolate, don't you?'

Shit, thought Simon. He had been anticipating the first bite from his own Mars bar at 11.00.

Never fraternize. Never identify with civilian problems. It's not your job. It lessens your efficiency and increases your vulnerability.

'Chaffinch,' he said wearily. 'Chaffinch, you prat . . .'

'Oh, come on, look at her, sir . . .'

'All right, give it to her. Anna, tell her to share it out with the other children.'

One Mars bar wouldn't go far among seven children. Mace did not have the look of a man about to be suddenly overcome by a generous impulse. Simon handed over his own Mars bar.

He told the Federal Guards that he was going to get food from the village.

The Guards nodded listlessly.

'Sunray to Four-Two,' he said into his personal radio. 'Come down. I want to talk.'

Hoodless, when he arrived, said: 'Why not let them load the truck? We can take it out with the MP once it's away from the buildings.'

'Time,' said Simon. 'They might stay where they are for a week.'

'Buildings are dodgy,' said Hoodless.

'I'm not taking in an assault team. I'm going in to get food, preferably by negotiation.'

'I don't see that it's our business. If we'd tried to stop every Kurdish village being buggered about, we'd still be there now.'

'We are there now,' said Simon. 'And it's food for us that I'm after.'

'I don't like it.'

'Listen,' said Simon, 'I should be in Kaunas, organizing a cocktail party. Don't think I'm enjoying this. Where do you want to make your approach from?'

ELEVEN

He took his group in under cover of a culvert running alongside the dirt track.

They passed a generator building, and used it as a shield to cross to the first of the concrete village houses. There was nobody in sight. They slipped past two ancient wooden cabins with grime-covered windows. There was churned, half-frozen mud everywhere.

The Russian guards took refuge in the lee of one of the cabins, hidden from the farm, and stood together. One guard kept his rifle at the ready; the others lit cigarettes. Evidently they intended leaving it all to NATO.

Simon stared back at them bitterly.

'Anna,' he said. 'Tell them we don't move until they do. OK?'

She nodded and called out in a low voice.

The guards' NCO gave an order. His men slowly put out their cigarettes, carefully put the butts in their pockets, then moved forward to join the Royal Mercians.

There was a silage clamp with old tyres on it. To be classified as an old tyre in Russia, you had to be a *very* old tyre. These were not only bare to the canvas; the canvas itself was in shreds.

Posters were stuck to a wall. On one, under some writing, was a picture of Samantha Fox.

(In the train, before they reached Kuybyshev, Kate had told him all about the relationship between Samantha Fox and Russian male fantasy. When she had been a student in Moscow, every Russian had known the names of two Englishwomen: Margaret Thatcher – universally believed to have had a torrid affair with Gorbachev in his Black Sea dacha – and Samantha Fox, the Page Three pin-up.

Now Margaret Thatcher was forgotten. But Samantha Fox's bosom still featured in a hundred press advertisements; her smile still dangled from a million key-ring fobs.)

Anna looked at the poster. 'It's an advert for the Pervouralsk beauty queen contest,' she said. 'They had a beauty contest on International Women's Day, two weeks ago now. A shame we missed it. I bet we'd have laughed.'

Mace said: 'Remind you of Belfast, eh, Chaffey?'

'Not really,' said Chaffinch. 'Belfast was depressing.'

'Hear that, sir? Chaffey's made a fucking joke,' said Mace, impressed.

'Be quiet,' said Simon.

They rounded a corner. Before them was the village centre. A two-storey concrete building: the Soviet.

There was an overwhelming smell of cow dung. Cattle sheds ran along an entire side of the square; they could hear livestock moving about.

Four men were loading a truck.

'Remember, we are Allied soldiers seeking to buy food,' said Simon. 'Be pleasant. Smile.'

'Sir,' said Mace.

A man saw them, said something. The others stopped and stared.

Simon said to Anna: 'Tell them . . .'

He paused. Anna said: 'Yes?'

We come in peace and friendship? Is there a café open?

'Tell them we want to buy food,' he said lamely.

'He says there is no food anywhere. The country is in terrible crisis. But he's got a story to tell you. A story from Yekaterinburg.'

'Say I'd be pleased to hear it.'

Yet again he was drinking vodka; this time vodka with a curious taste.

The mafia boss was looking thoughtfully at his glass. He spoke.

'When a Russian dies,' translated Anna, 'a glass of vodka is poured to refresh his soul on its journey into the next world. In forty days the spirit has evaporated; the glass is empty.'

'Tell him there must be many glasses of vodka standing in Yekaterinburg,' said Simon. 'Tell him it is a sad story.'

'That wasn't the story,' said Anna.

The concrete-floored room was empty of furniture but for a table. The boss sat on one side of it. He was big, bulky, fleshy, with a round moon of a face. Two men with pistols stood behind him. Simon and Anna sat on the other side, with Mace and Chaffinch standing at their backs. A very drunk man sat in the far corner of the room, by the iron stove.

This was the meeting room of the Soviet. There was a smell of woodsmoke and wet rags.

The boss was speaking.

'Listen,' said Anna. 'The radio in the morning says: "It is six o'clock. Our glorious Democratic president is waking up, and we also are waking up." Then the radio says: "It is six-thirty. Our glorious Democratic president is cleaning his teeth, and we also are cleaning our teeth." '

The boss stopped to make sure Simon was following. Andrei also liked to communicate through allegory: perhaps it was the Russian way. Simon tried to look gripped by the tale. He wondered what Hoodless was doing.

'At seven o'clock, the radio says: "It is seven o'clock. Our glorious Democratic president is having his breakfast, and we are all saying *bon appetit*." '

The boss laughed, a big belly-laugh. Not a man who had missed his own breakfast.

'That's a good joke, I think,' said Anna.

More vodka was poured. The boss apologized because it was made with meatbones. He held up the bottle: bits of bone were still there in the bottom of it.

'Should I be drinking this, Anna?'

'How would I know. I'm from Moscow.'

A real sophisticate.

The man was speaking again.

'Vladick – his name's Vladick,' she said. 'The drunk is the village mayor. He calls him the *ataman*. These mafia are from the south, from the Don.'

'Yekaterinburg,' said Simon. 'Ask him about Yekaterinburg.'

The man looked serious, shook his head, spoke tersely.

'He says it is very bad. There is no food in the city. There is no food anywhere. That is why he told you the story; it is the story people tell each other today in Yekaterinburg. The people are ill. The free market has collapsed. He wants to know where we have come from.'

'Tell him an army unit over the hill. A big unit.'

The man nodded, incurious, apparently accepting the explanation.

'Ask him,' said Simon, 'why he has evicted people from their homes.'

'They have not been evicted. They are telling lies. They have been holding back food from the markets, and have run away because they are ashamed. The people in Yekaterinburg are starving because the *kolkhoz* are keeping back livestock and vegetables, hoping for bigger profits. They live well here because they have food. The farmers ran away because they are guilty. Because their crime has been discovered.'

She turned to Simon and said judiciously: 'It's true what he says about farmers. It's what everybody is saying: farmers ought to be shot; they're all greedy; they care for nobody but themselves.'

'Never mind that,' asked Simon, happy to postpone a discussion of Anna's political views to a more leisurely moment. 'Will he sell us food?'

'There is no food to sell.'

'Tell him there must be food. Potatoes, vegetables?'

The man shook his head. If he had food, he would give it to them as a gift.

'We don't want him to give it to us. We want him to sell it to us.'

What were they offering? Weapons? The man's eyes were on the SA80s.

No, said Simon. Dollars. American dollars. The man shook his head. Dollars were only useful if you could spend them; only of value while the parallel economy prevailed.

'Gold,' said Simon. 'We can pay with gold.'

He held out a sovereign, newly minted.

* * *

Two men staggered in with a huge metal tray. On it were twisting, shiny ropes of intestines, huge sheets of purple liver – God only knew what sort of creature it had come from.

'What about beef?'

'They can't kill the milking cows. They are numbered. They are *very* valuable.'

'Vegetables,' said Simon, turning away from the coil of intestines, thinking nauseously of Gallagher's gaping stomach. 'Ask him again about vegetables.'

Yes, there were potatoes, swedes, shredded carrots . . .

'Five sovereigns worth.'

'How many kilos?' asked Anna.

How the hell should he know. As much as the men could carry.

'Leave it to me,' said Anna. 'OK?'

She went with the boss. Simon sat, exhausted.

After ten minutes she returned. 'OK, they're filling sacks for the boys. Small sacks, not to weigh them down too much. I asked about the truck, but they're out of fuel. That's why they're stuck here. You're sure we don't want any of that meat?'

'I suppose we could take some liver.'

'It's good for you, liver. Makes your hair shine.'

'Sir . . .' said Mace quietly.

Simon glanced round. Men were filling in, lounging against the back wall. Several of them had guns: Kalashnikov AK-M assault rifles. This was not supposed to happen: the Russian guards were supposedly guarding the entrance.

'Where are the Russian guards, Anna?'

'They're helping fill the sacks.'

'Christ . . .'

In his pocket was his personal radio.

His hand had already pressed the 'send' button three times, the prearranged signal, before the mafia boss came back into the room.

He heard a gentle click behind his shoulder: Mace's safety-catch moving to 'automatic fire'.

'Don't,' he said quietly. 'Don't even think about it, Mace.'

'Sir.'

They had at least ten Kalashnikovs at their backs.

Anna said: 'I think we should get out of here. I don't like the feel of things.'

'Try to be natural. Try not to look alarmed.'

The boss sat down. Now everything about him was hostile. He spoke quickly, staring coldly at Simon. He didn't look as if he was telling funny jokes.

'He says he's been talking to the civilian authorities in Yekaterinburg. He is sorry, but the food cannot be spared.'

'Tell him we only need a small amount.'

'He says no.'

'No food, no gold.'

'For the food he wants a hundred sovereigns.'

'I don't have a hundred sovereigns.'

'A hundred sovereigns. He has been checking on their value. He made a mistake before.'

'He's making one now – tell him.'

Anna said quietly: 'I don't like this, captain. Perhaps we'd better give him the money.'

'I don't have a hundred sovereigns. Tell him that. Say no food, no gold. Tell him other soldiers will be here soon.'

The man smiled quickly.

Anna said: 'They have been talking to the men outside. The Russian soldiers.'

The mafia boss spoke again.

'He says our soldiers must hand over their guns.'

'I'm damned if we will!' said Simon in sudden anger.

Mace said: 'Sir—'

The boss shouted.

A shot rang out, incredibly loud in the confined space. Something heavy pitched into Simon's back, knocking him forward.

It was Chaffinch.

Then the window caved in. There was a crash of broken glass, an ear-shattering burst of automatic fire, and the almighty crack of a thunderflash. A black figure was tumbling in like a ball, straightening and rolling as it hit the floor.

Simon grabbed Anna and pulled her down. Beside them Mace rolled sideways, turning backwards, his SA80 on automatic, spewing bullets in a continuous burst.

Anywhere else, of course – anywhere they were being serious, like say in Kurdistan, clearing out a nest of bastard Iraqis, or in Northern Ireland – the SAS would have cooked off a grenade by pulling the pin out and waiting two seconds before tossing it through the window, and going in behind it with automatic weapons pumping out death at stomach height.

But they were only visiting, still trying to be polite.

So they set off thunderflashes instead of real grenades, and raked the ceiling with their Heckler Koch MP 5s to give Simon's group time to get out of the field of fire.

Five seconds, perhaps, had passed. Through the cloud of cement dust he could see three mafia men lying dead or seriously wounded. The boss, Veadick, was on the floor, trying to press his massive body into it. Chaffinch was lying wide-eyed, a hand skewed round against his back, drenched with blood.

A mafia man by the stove started to move his hand.

Kill a moving man. It does not matter *how* he moves, what he appears to be doing. A man who is moving is a man who is *thinking*.

A bullet in the forehead, a bullet in the right breast, a bullet in the left. It was just as Simon remembered it from the manual, as a cadet on the computerized firing range at Sandhurst. *Now, sir, we can do better than that, can't we . . . ?*

He got the gunman a split second before Hoodless's MP 5 opened up. The forehead, the right breast, then the left.

Eight seconds since Hoodless had come through the window.

The man fell over the stove. A gush of blood from his chest sizzled as it hit the hotplate.

Yes, Sergeant-Instructor, we can do better than that . . .

TWELVE

'So you think they're OK?'

'Yea, I think they're OK.'

'I'm not so sure. Nobody out there's going to know that he's a young officer and a gentleman. They won't know he's just a sort of learner. Not that he'll ever be anything else – men never change; not if they don't have to. That man is so *untouched* by life, it's unbelievable. It's not just the army's fault, either. I dare say his mum looked after him at home; then, at university, I expect girls fell over themselves to cook his meals and iron his shirts. They do it because they want to please. Girls always want to please.'

'I think it's the way of the world,' said Andrei, not sounding distressed.

'But then, of course, *then*, when the rest of us were thrown out of university into the cold hard world of supermarkets and laundrettes, he just slipped effortlessly into the *army* – and it's just like being back at school, with puddings just like mum's; and just like at university, with a batman instead of some willing slave of a girlfriend to make his tea; and people are jumping about saying "Yes, sir," and "No, sir". That man, Andrei – that man has not had to cook himself a meal in *twenty-four years*.'

She stared out of the window of the diner. After a bit she said: 'You really reckon they're all right?'

He nodded.

'I'm so hungry.'

'You want something to eat?'

'There isn't anything.'

'The woman with the tins,' said Andrei, 'I think she has stuff.'

'No, it's OK. I want tea more than anything. A glass of tea and a hot shower.'

She stared out at the weeping walls of the quarry, the slowly swirling mist. 'Something should have been done to get us out of here by now. I'm starting to feel scared. How are we going to get out of here, Andrei?'

He was staring at her, thinking about sex.

'No,' she said. 'No way.'

He smiled sadly, not without nobility; the young Russian officer caught up in the tragedy of his bleeding homeland.

It was starting to go dark. Another day nearly gone, she thought in sudden panic.

'Why isn't he back by now? You don't think something's gone wrong, do you?'

He was still looking at her, thinking about sex. Dear God, men would never change – not any of them.

Art had four miniatures lined up in a row, next to the pickled gherkins. He did not expect the patrol to return laden with groceries; he did not anticipate them emerging through the mist burdened with honey-roast hams and hot rolls. These miniatures were to be his meal of the day. He had saved them until Kate had gone off with her Russian boyfriend.

One was sherry, and was his starter. Two were Irish Cream, now prized as a source of combined alcohol and nutrition. The fourth, cognac, was for afters.

At that point, he felt, he might be woozy enough to crunch a gherkin.

A sound. The door rattled back. It was the small dark Russian girl with the green eyes: the music industry executive.

'Hi,' she said.

'Hi.'

'You know where the officer is?'

'No.'

'You want to come to our compartment?'

'No, thank you.'

She had an American accent. She was looking at his miniatures.

'You want to trade those for something?'

Like what?

Her eyes were fixed on the Bailey's Irish Creams.

'Like me?' she said.

Christ!

It was different in Russia, of course. There was a Moscow joke about the girl who was hauled before the magistrates and asked: 'How can a girl of such good family, whose father is in government, whose uncle is a professor, be a prostitute?' And the girl shrugged modestly and replied: 'Just luck, I suppose.'

A Moscow newspaper had published an article on the degrading life of a hard-currency whore, and been swamped with letters from girls asking where they should apply to join. An opinion poll had given dollar prostitution as the first career choice of sixty per cent of Moscow's teenage girls.

'So, what do you say?'

Art was thinking about it.

'You want to come to our compartment for a party? You know Olga? You like her? You like me?'

He looked her over. He remembered Sonia, his favourite. This one had the same sort of smile, though she didn't have Sonia's tits. He wasn't seriously tempted.

'No thanks. Not today,' he said.

She smiled and went.

He told himself he hadn't washed for three days, and she might well have not washed for four months, that it was freezing cold, that he hadn't eaten a proper meal since breakfast yesterday. He told himself that what was worth having on a warm deep shagpile carpet in suburban Manchester was a different kettle of fish on a cold bleak train in the Ural mountains.

He didn't tell himself that he was getting old.

Christ, though, these Russians!

After a moment he opened his miniature bottle of sherry and tucked in.

In the cab of the huge TAN 75 diesel, the driver leaned back in his shiny plastic seat, staring out of the raked windscreen. The Russian signaller, a cigarette in hand, sat sideways by the telephone, also staring into space.

The door rolled back.

Gough said: 'How do, lads. Everything all right?'

The signaller ignored him. The driver shrugged, uncomprehending.

Gough sat down, and lit a fag of his own from his last packet of Benson and Hedges NAAFI full-strength, the sort you couldn't get for love or money in England these days. The cab was warm – the driver ran the engine for ten minutes every hour.

'How are we off for fuel? Diesel?'

They ignored him.

He could have done with a cup of coffee. He liked a big steaming mug of milky coffee in the afternoons, about this time, round about four o'clock, when he'd finished his stores audit.

Only another two months now, and he'd be out of the army. He was a days-to-do man. 'They can't send me there . . . They can't make me do *that*' went up the cry of the days-to-do men whenever anything arduous was in the offing. 'Not with my days to do . . .'

So what was he doing in the middle of fucking Russia?

He started to think about his plans for a marquee franchise. He imagined being out with his lads, putting up a green-and-white striped marquee on a nice green lawn somewhere. He imagined roses, real ones, on the mellow-brick wall of the house.

They'd all stop for coffee at half-ten in the morning, and again at four in the afternoon. It would be a routine, a rule of the firm. Coffee from a thermos, in a rose garden on a nice summer's day in Hampshire . . . unless, of course, the lady of the house (he vaguely imagined the lady of the house as being Mrs Temple, wife of the colonel of the 1st battalion) asked them into the kitchen for coffee and biscuits at the scrubbed-pine table . . .

The driver muttered something to the guard, who passed him the cigarette. They both looked dirty and grubby and unwashed, and bored out of their skulls.

But then, everything was filthy here, thought Gough. People's clothes, people's skin. OK, the diesel left a gritty, oily deposit over everything; that was understandable. But outside was filthy: even the snow seemed to have a yellow tinge as it came down, and the rain was the colour of dishwater.

He settled to thinking about Hampshire again. He might take up fishing in the Test. In his mind's eye there came a sylvan view of meadows and little woods, a sparkling river, the top of a green and white marquee peeking over the distant trees.

'Colour-Sergeant!'

He hurried out of the cab. Henshaw was by the window. The sentry from the high ground was leading a line of figures, some of them with sacks over their shoulders, slowly down the side of the quarry. Two of the men were carrying an awkward shape that Gough knew instantly – from his days in Kurdistan, in Northern Ireland – was a wounded man, or a corpse that was not yet stiff and cold.

THIRTEEN

'Well?' said Biggin.

'Mafia gangs from the cities are raiding villages, killing, raping, taking food. We've been in a skirmish. One man is wounded.'

'What happened?'

'They came behind us. He was shot in the back. I've got them, though. I've got the blokes who did it.'

'You've killed them?'

'No. Four men were killed, but not the one who wounded my man. I've got three men under arrest.'

'You've brought them back to the train?'

'Yes.'

'Your man – how bad is he?'

'Bullet in his upper back, clear of the heart and lung, as far as we can tell. He's lost a lot of blood but he's conscious and can feel his limbs, feel the nerves. To be honest, it was my fault,' went on Simon, too honest for his own good. 'Your blokes baled me out when I got in a bloody mess—'

'Save it. Do you have food?'

'Yes, but we were spotted when we were returning to the train – a tracked reconnaissance vehicle, possibly MVD militia, but everybody seems to have military hardwear. They left us alone, but they saw us. Our position is not safe.'

'We faxed details of a signal-box. Have you seen them?'

'The signallers are looking through them now.'

'It's computerized, ex-Swiss Federal Railways, and controls 370 track kilometres on the Trans-Siberian. It's 15 k from your present position. You and your men will stay with the train. We're going to casevac your wounded and bring out the two journalists and the Russian general.'

Simon said: 'There's a reasonable landing zone half a kilometre from here.'

'You know what's reasonable?'

'Yes,' said Simon.

'Give us a precise RV. Give us the NavStar readings.'

Simon read out the readings.

Biggin said: 'Do you have naptha flares?'

'If we had, we'd be burning them to keep warm.'

'Show what light you can, at 03.00.'

'What are you sending? How many can you take?'

'Euro XD. Eight personnel maximum. There'll be a second helicopter, but only for back-up.'

The standard Euro could seat twenty to twenty-four in emergency flying at sea level. The XD was the new long-range version. That must have been the cause of the delay, thought Simon; they'd have had to get the machine to Kazakhstan, within striking distance of Yekaterinburg.

'As well as the three prisoners, we have nine Russian refugees on the train.'

'I don't understand about the prisoners. What do we want them for?'

'I have their guns. One of them attempted to murder a British soldier who still has the bullet in his back. Forensic will be able to identify the gunman. We will need both helicopters.'

A slight pause.

'You're the OC,' said Biggin. He gave Simon a new RV, west of Yekaterinburg.

Hoodless, who had been crouched next to him, said: 'You shouldn't have said that about us baling you out. You were the one who put me out as overwatch. You did everything by the book, and you did it bloody well. It was those Russian lads who let you down.'

'I should have left somebody at the door.'

'What were the Russians there for?'

'To carry potatoes.'

'They'll have you for saying it was your fault. They'll have that on your record.' He added: 'I've been crunching numbers.'

'Yes,' said Simon. 'So have I.'

Two Euro helicopters could lift out Gallagher and Chaffinch. There'd be room for Kate and Art Finkel, and for the Russian refugees and the three prisoners.

That left one place. Who would he give it to: Major-General Prosvirkin or Anna?

Perhaps he could talk the RAF into counting the child Iulia as an extra who didn't count.

He went next-door. Gallagher was asleep, his breath shallow and fast. The smell in the compartment made Simon gag: there was no hot water on the train, no antiseptic other than Chanel Number 5 perfume commandeered from Madame Vostrotin. There was nothing with which to wash Gallagher's body or his bandages.

Ferneyhough had finished reading the German war novel. Anna was saying: 'Don't you dare tell me the end, Verniho! You should have waited for me. You're a bad boy.'

'They escape and go home,' said Ferneyhough.

'Verniho!'

'To build a better Germany: a Germany not only worth dying for, but worth living for.'

'Oh, Verniho . . .'

Simon said: 'Anna.'

She looked up, smiled quickly. 'Hi, captain.'

'We are lifting Gallagher out tonight by helicopter. Will he be OK?'

She nodded.

'We're all going, sir?' said Ferneyhough.

'No. Just the wounded and the civilians.'

Anna was looking up at him, suddenly very still.

'You're on the list, Anna,' he said. 'Don't worry about that.'

Andrei appeared in the doorway. Simon said, 'I want to talk to you. Where shall we go?'

They left the train. It was dark now.

Simon said: 'I was depending on your men, and they just walked away. They let a gang of murderers come up behind us. They went scrounging for food and vodka. They couldn't even be fucking bothered to leave *one man* to guard our backs. They're not soldiers, your men, Andrei, not professionals. They're arseholes. Rabble. They're dirt, they're the dregs.'

He turned and swung back up into the train.

Colour Gough said: 'I've told them to shoot if the bastards move an inch. The fat one's screaming his fucking head off.'

'They're going to Kazakhstan tonight,' said Simon. 'I want eight men, now, to lay out the LZ.'

The three mafia gunmen were on the floor of a compartment, piled on top of one another, their hands bound behind their backs. The boss, the big man, was on top, screaming obscenities until Gates hit him round the head with the butt of his rifle. The man at the bottom of the pile cried out, once, in pain, his voice rasping as he fought to breathe under the crushing weight above him.

The man in the middle kept quiet – thinking, perhaps, that he was the lucky one.

Chaffinch lay on a bunk in Section HQ, his arm and shoulder bandaged, his face white, his eyes wide open with shock and as big as saucers.

'Well, you've been in the wars now, my son,' said Colour Gough, then, after a moment: 'What the fucking hell am I going to say to your missus?'

FOURTEEN

The landing-zone was a small plateau, boggy in places. They cleared it of large rocks. They established five points for lights: in the shape of a T with its stem pointing into the wind.

They needed flares. They tried filling cooking pots with gravel and diesel, but the diesel oil would not burn. They punched holes in aluminium pots and stuffed them with paper, wood shavings and diesel. These burned, but for only a few moments. They had torches, but the batteries were low.

The Russian civilians were told to get ready to move at 02.00. An hour before that, Simon found Kate, who was curled up asleep.

He said: 'Come with me, please. I might need an interpreter. The bloke's English is poor, and all those girls can talk about is sex.'

He led her down the dark corridor, into the compartment of the film director.

'Hiya,' said Nina, smiling up at him.

'Hi, captain,' said Olga.

Simon said, 'Hello, girls,' and threw the director a Kalashnikov rifle.

The director looked down at it, startled.

'I want you to guard three men on the helicopter,' said Simon. 'Mafia gunmen who tried to murder one of my soldiers. The rifle isn't loaded, but they won't know that. Do you understand?'

The director looked confused. Kate, half awake herself, started to translate—

'Yea, it's OK,' the director said. 'I understand.'

He weighed the rifle in his hands, grinned and nodded. Olga and Nina looked at Simon admiringly.

'You girls are all ready?'

'Yes, captain.'

'Somebody will come for you.'

He turned to go.

'Bye, captain.'

They looked at Kate in a calculating way.

She followed him back down the corridor. 'I don't understand. Why can't *you* guard them? Aren't you coming? Aren't you coming in the helicopter?'

'If I was in barracks,' said Andrei, sitting opposite Prosvirkin, in the quiet compartment at the front of the train, 'I would make them run in gas masks until they collapsed.'

'Why should your men help NATO troops to take food from the mafia?'

'Because soldiers do not let other soldiers be shot in the back. Because the mafia are scum.'

'Ah . . .' said Prosvirkin, sipping tea.

A blue candle in a silver shell burned on the small table between them. It had come from the diner. In normal times, as the Bukhara Express sped across the Kazakhstan plains, passengers dined by candlelight, entertained by ethnic musicians.

'The mafia are scum . . .' said Prosvirkin gently. 'And General Kotelnikov is going to wipe the mafia out, to restore the honour of the nation, the honour of the Red Army.'

'Yes.'

'And you are thinking more and more that the General is a hero, and that you are fighting on the wrong side?'

There was silence. The compartment was warm. It was the only warm compartment, apart from that occupied by Gallagher, on the train.

'You are thinking that Perestroika, has brought with it both the corruption of the mafia and the corruption of the spirit?'

'It is what everybody says.'

'Yes, I have thought it myself. I fought with the Red Army in the streets of Berlin. I led the assault on the president's palace in Kabul. But under democracy, under Perestroika, I sold arms to the Middle East. I supplied tank regiments to rich Western tourists, so that they could play what they called wargames. And, yes, I received American dollars for this in a private account.'

After a moment Andrei said: 'It has been common enough.'

'You are thinking that soldiers of the Red Army were not corrupt? That they did not betray their comrades, their friends? But the Red Army was riddled with corruption from top to bottom, my friend, from the generals with their teams of girl athletes, to the *praporshchiks* stealing money from recruits.'

Andrei was staring at the tablecloth. 'One has to believe in something,' he said.

A cliché. The young always thought in clichés.

'You would be proud to be a senior Red Army officer?'

'Yes.'

'One of the *vasti*, the powers that be? You would like to be able to bump civilians off Aeroflot flights, to have an officer-driven Chaika, to have half the road reserved for your use? You want privileged shopping from the *voyentorg* on Kalinina Prospekt?'

'No—'

'Women? Sex? You want to select the prettiest girls from the signals units, and make them into your personal shooting-team: supple, slim girls who have no choice but to obey your every command? Take them at weekends to your dacha in the Lenin Hills and train them personally – two, even three at a time?'

Andrei stared at him.

'You've heard of Paradise Group?'

Andrei nodded.

Prosvirkin smiled bleakly. 'Paradise Group . . .' He drank his tea. He said, crisply, 'The time has come to take the stars from your eyes. The general staff were always more drunk and degenerate than the Politbureau. They were tolerated because the Red Army was the janitor of the people. Because it guarded the Soviet prison.

'If it was less corrupt then than under Perestroika, it was because the opportunities for corruption were fewer. If it stole less, my friend, it was because in those days there was less to steal.'

They sat in silence.

Andrei said: 'General, why are you on this train?'

'Perhaps my purpose is to say to you what I have just said.'

'You think I should let the British helicopters come?'

'You have no orders not to do so.'

'You will fly out yourself?'

Prosvirkin nodded.

'You think it is my duty to cooperate with the NATO troops, and take the train to Tashkent?'

'Those were your orders.'

'Will you confirm those orders to me?'

'A corrupt senior officer of the Federal Army, fleeing in the night?'

There was a pause.

'In times such as these,' said Prosvirkin, 'I advise every man, who can do so with a clear conscience, to obey his orders and not to think too much. It is a mistake, if I might say so, for a subaltern to think too much.'

Andrei stood up. He saluted. 'I honour the hero of Afghanistan,' he said. 'I honour the hero of Berlin.'

'In Berlin,' said Prosvirkin, 'I was a boy. I sat in the zoo, and cried over a dead hippopotamus.'

Andrei turned in the doorway. He said: 'They want to take three gunmen to the West.'

Prosvirkin looked surprised. 'Why?'

'For shooting the English soldier. The English officer has arrested them.'

'I hope his superiors will be pleased.'

'Do I let them be taken out of Russia?'

'It will save you three bullets,' said Prosvirkin. 'But it's up to you.'

FIFTEEN

Soldiers helped the civilians to climb up the sides of the quarry, through the thin birch trees, their feet slipping on the oily shale.

Madame Vostrotin cried out in the dark.

A soldier said: 'You're all right, love. I've got you.'

'Iulia, Iulia!' cried Madame Vostrotin.

Behind her, Iulia replied, wearily.

Art and Kate scrambled up slowly behind the Russians. There was no baggage allowed, Art had been told. He wondered how long it would be before those Federal army buggers crept into his compartment and started rifling through his case. They'd be in there by now, if he was any judge of human nature. Well, they were welcome to the pigs' pizzles; he had the last of the miniatures in his pocket.

There was a slithering noise next to him. Kate yelped in the darkness, grabbed at him and swore foully. She was in a bad mood again. It was all up and down with her these days; something to do with the boyfriend he presumed

'Well, fucking help me, for Christ's sake!'

He felt sorry for the bloke she ended up with, he really did.

It took them half an hour to reach the plateau. They stood in the cold and dark. It was windier up here, and after a few moments they all moved, on a common impulse, towards the shelter of a small rise in the ground.

'Foster . . .' said Gough.

'Colour?'

'Stay with them. Don't let them get lost, or we'll need a fucking sheepdog to get them together again.'

On the far side of the landing-zone, sprawled on the ground face-down, with their hands tied behind their backs, were the three gunmen from Sputnik Mira village.

Simon briefly flicked on his torch. The thin beam of light traversed their faces.

Buck, standing guard, said: 'Proper mafiosi. They'll be taking a contract out on you for this, sir.'

'They're welcome,' said Simon grimly.

The gunmen were lying exhausted, breathing heavily. They had been made to haul sacks of potatoes and vegetables across four kilometres of mountain. They had been savagely beaten up. Their faces were bleeding, their bodies bruised. One of them looked as if he had a broken arm: it lay bent on the ground at an unnatural angle.

The boss, Veadick, was panting laboriously, his face turned sideways on the peat; dirt over his lips. The torchlight showed clotted blood gluing up an eye that was swollen to a slit.

Hoodless loomed up out of the blackness.

Simon said: 'Kaunas doesn't want them. They'd rather I just released them – let them go. But they know too much about us, and I'm damned if I'm taking them back on the train.'

Hoodless said: 'There is an alternative.'

'Well, I can't think of it.'

There was a pause. Hoodless said: 'No. Perhaps you're right.'

They turned away. Behind them, the gunmen lay on the hillside, waiting to be shot.

The aircraft, said the fax from Kaunas, needed a landing-zone fifty metres in diameter, with thirty-five metres cleared to ground level.

An empty helicopter can land vertically: a helicopter fully laden behaves more like an ordinary aircraft, and takes off at a shallow angle.

The Euros would come down in succession. The maximum ground slope they could handle was fifteen degrees.

A gunship of some description would be overhead.

Kate and Art were huddled up next to the Vostrotins. Prosvirkin was by them, wrapped in his cloak. A Russian guard, one of the *praporshchiks*, stood stiffly to attention beside him.

'You are a journalist?' Prosvirkin said to Kate after a while.

'Yes,' said Kate.

'It took a very long time,' he said slowly, politely, 'before the West understood that the helicopter is not an aircraft.'

'Not an aircraft?'

'Not an aircraft but a tank.'

'Right,' said Kate, her eyes straining in the dark to see Simon. She thought she caught a glimpse of him some distance away, bending over Chaffinch.

'What is the purpose of a tank? Why does it exist? It exists to take territory and hold it. An aircraft cannot do that. You remember what the American bomb crew used to say in Vietnam, as they swooped low over the jungle? "Now it belongs to us," they used to say. Then, as the plane passed, "Now it belongs to them." But a helicopter can hold ground because a helicopter is a tank of the air! It has the same firepower, the same ability to hold ground that it has captured. No worries about minefields! No worries about rivers to cross!'

'What's he saying?' asked Art, shivering.

'He's telling me about tanks.'

'Oh.'

'Now he wants to tell me about his time in Afghanistan.'

'Why?'

'How the hell should I know? He's an old soldier.'

'Ask him about the container. Ask him about the last days of the Third Reich.'

'Piss off.'

She walked away. Prosvirkin spoke again, this time addressing Art.

Art said: 'Don't worry about it.'

Prosvirkin nodded blankly.

Nina came past. Prosvirkin spoke to her. She turned to Art and said: 'You're a media correspondent, yes?'

'I am,' said Art, 'the culture correspondent of the *Sun*.'

'You want to know about a major-general's life in the Red Army?'

'No.'

Prosvirkin spoke again.

'OK, you want to hear about General Kotelnikov's sexual perversions? From a guy who was actually there at the orgies? If this would interest this American woman, would it interest you folk in England?'

Art looked quickly around. Kate had disappeared. He had this one to himself.

Kate said: 'I'm sorry. I'm so sorry.'

'It's OK. It's all right.'

'No, it isn't all right. Listen, Simon. Please, listen . . .'

The clouds were parting, there was a watery moon that should help the choppers; help them or frighten them off. There were distant lights tonight, for the first time, down in a far valley.

She was talking about Moscow, about her driver, Sergei.

'I blamed you, you see. I blamed you for him dying. I blamed you so that I wouldn't have to blame myself. I lay in the doorway of the Aragvi and cursed you to hell for not letting him into the embassy, not letting him through the barrier.'

'I could have let him in. They were evacuating politicians and bankers. I was letting all sorts of people through that night.'

'No, it wasn't your fault. It was me. He wanted money to go to Tula, to go to his family. He had a wife and three children in Tula. I could have just given money to him, but I said he had to take me to Red Square first. He didn't want to go. He told me I was crazy. He told me it was too dangerous. All he wanted was a few coupons for petrol. Oh Christ . . .'

'You're sure he was killed?'

'I saw it happen. I saw them do it. I've pretended I didn't. I've pretended he might have been all right. He was trying to stop them from attacking me. Sergei – and now Chaffinch. I don't know what I'll do if Chaffinch dies . . .'

She started to cry.

He took her in his arms, thinking that this was how it was supposed to have been in Moscow, how he had imagined it . . .

He held her, felt her body shivering, held her more tightly.

'Well now, William,' said Corporal Pullin.

Chaffinch sat on the stony ground, his teeth chattering with shock. Lacy was on one side of him, Ferneyhough on the other. An extra parka was over his head, protecting his back from the wind.

'He bloody shot me,' said Chaffinch.

'Yes, William,' said Corporal Pullin.

'I wasn't looking.'

'No, you weren't. How are you feeling, then?'

'Not very well.'

His shoulder and back were bandaged with a field dressing; his right arm was useless and strapped to his side.

'Where's Mace?' said Chaffinch. 'He said he'd give me something.'

'You don't need anything. You'll be tucked up in a hospital bed before you know it.'

'I ought to have something.'

'I wouldn't trust Mace, if I were you, Chaffey,' said Lacy. 'He only said his brother-in-law was a vet so they'd send him on a first-aid cadre. Anyway he hasn't bloody got anything.'

'Can't he give me a paracetamol?'

'Wait till you're in Kazakhstan. Nice civvy hospital for oil workers,' said Corporal Pullin soothingly – then to Lacy: 'Can he stand up?'

'Not without us holding him.'

'Give him a drink of water and some chocolate.'

'He gave his Mars bar to a kid, didn't you, Chaffey?' said Lacy.

'Yes,' said Chaffinch, his teeth chattering away.

They ought to have given him morphine for shock. Even half a syrete would have helped, but the morphine was reserved for Gallagher.

Gough said, quietly: '02.45, sir.'

'Yes, I know.'

Everyone was quiet, tense.

Andrei had thrown his men out in a screen, protecting the landing-zone from the north. The Royal Mercians and SAS were positioned round the landing-zone itself. The machine-guns were set up. There were no jokes, not even about the fucking RAF.

Now Gallagher was carefully carried up from the train. He had been injected with morphine and was dead to the world. Anna was with him, and two SAS soldiers.

At 03.20 the helicopters were heard, a distant drone from the south-west. Behind them was a different, deeper throbbing noise. Simon joined Hoodless and the SAS signaller behind a rock where the radio had been set up.

Hoodless had been testing the wind, viewing the line of approach, using a compass together with satellite navigation readings.

Now he composed a signal. Simon held the torch, and remembered the words of the instructors at Sandhurst.

Encode, decode, keep it clear, keep it accurate. Remember that in 40 seconds a Russian BM-21 rocket-launcher can deliver 14 tonnes of high explosive or chemical agent on to your position.

'Sir,' said Hoodless formally, handing over a sheet torn from Simon's pocketbook. The message read:

Code-name:
LZ Eagle
Location:
FOUR-SIX ROMEO PAPA ROMEO NINE-THREE-ONE-THREE
Open quadrants:
OPEN TWO-SIX-ZERO DEG TO THREE-FIVE DEG AND FOUR-THREE DEG TO ZERO-TWO-TWO DEG
Recommended track:
FOUR-FOUR-ZERO DEG
Obstacles:
HIGH GROUND ZERO-NINE-FOUR DEG ONE KM

Simon said: 'LZ Eagle?'

'We had to call it something,' said Hoodless defensively.

The SAS were boy scouts, after all.

The signal was sent. The radio's range was only 10k, but to anyone who might have intercepted it, their location was now precisely revealed.

'OK,' said Simon, 'light the flares.'

'Light the flares!' shouted Corporal Buck.

Black oily smoke was whipped by the wind.

A soldier with the StarlightScope said: 'Two Euros. Another aircraft further out. Looks like a Hercules.'

'A Spectre,' said Hoodless. 'AC-one-thirty, the U version.'

The ultimate gunship. From this moment on, any Russian vehicle moving in the landing-zone area, be it a hostile AFV or an innocent commercial traveller wending his weary way across the Urals, could be taken out instantly. The Spectre's 25mm cannon was linked to sensors that allowed its crew to read a car licence plate at 14,000 feet and shoot through clouds, at night, at two targets simultaneously. Its 105mm shells could penetrate several floors down into a building. It was stuffed with radar-jamming equipment. The C-in-C US Special Operations had described it as the most advanced surgical weapons system in the world.

Hoodless started to speak into the radio. There was a burst of noise, then a voice: 'In position now. Leader One descending.'

The Euros were slowly spiralling downwards, just visible in the near-darkness.

Simon ran across to where the passengers were lining up. He shouted: 'Remember to go in *exactly* when you are told, and to go *exactly* in a straight line towards the aircraft. It you go to either side you will be caught in the jetwash from the engines. Do you all understand? Kate, do they all understand?'

They all understood. Madame Vostrotin had caught hold of his hand, and was trying to make a speech.

Kate said: 'They want to thank you. They want to give you a gift.'

Someone shone his torch. The Vostrotin child, Iulia, was holding something out to him. It was a watch.

Simon, bemused, said: 'Thank you.'

The Pastnov couple clapped. Nina put her arm round his neck and kissed him on both cheeks. Olga, the blond, kissed him on both cheeks, then on the mouth.

Art said: 'Thanks for everything.'

Kate said tightly: 'Well, cheerio, then.'

From above, spotlights suddenly bathed the landing-zone in white light.

A soldier was running towards him, 'Sir, they can't come down. There's too much wind.'

He ran over to Hoodless behind the rocks.

Hoodless said: 'They're dropping ladders. We'll have to move fast.'

'We can't send Gallagher up a bloody rope ladder!'

Hoodless had his hand clamped over his headphones, trying to keep out the whine of the helicopters. 'And he can only take five people in each heli.'

'Give it to me.'

Hoodless handed over the headphones and microphone.

'This is the OC of the landing-zone,' said Simon, speaking slowly, pitching his voice high, as he had been taught. 'I've got two wounded men and fourteen civilians.'

'We haven't the fuel. Give me your priority cases. Personnel only, no weapons. We'll take the wounded first.'

The first Euro came down, its rotors screaming as the wind buffeted it, its searchlight bouncing round the landing-zone and the hills and sky like a disco spotlight.

A harness snaked down. A soldier beneath caught hold of the guide rope. Chaffinch was being clipped in. In seconds the chair would be winched up into the night.

But they could never put Gallagher in a harness! He was flat on his back, his stomach carefully bandaged to avoid the slightest strain.

'Who's next, sir?' said Gough.

Kate, Art Finkel, and the major-general were waiting.

Behind them the Russian civilians were in a line ready to go. Madame Vostrotin was clutching her Iulia. A soldier was confiscating a suitcase her husband had somehow sneaked up the hillside.

Kate was looking at Simon intently, her hair blowing in the gale of wind from the Euro's jetwash.

Now Corporal Pullin and Lacy were pulling forward the three mafia men, their hands roped behind their backs.

How the fuck would *they* get up a rope-ladder?

Colour Gough said: 'Who's going, then, sir? We can only send nine of them. Who are we sending out?'

SIXTEEN

NATO ACE Forward HQ, Kaunas, Lithuania, night of Friday 22 March

Littlehales was listening to Radio Maximum.

It was the same girl who had broadcast from the studio in Arbat Street, the girl who sounded as though she was sixteen and taking her GCSEs.

Radio Maximum was now transmitting from Moscow State University. Every few minutes, between records, the girl read out the words used by Yeltsin during the abortive coup of 1991: *You can erect a throne using bayonets. But you cannot sit on bayonets for long. Clouds of terror and dictatorship are gathering over Russia. But they must not be allowed to bring eternal night. Our long-suffering people will find its freedom once again – for ever . . .*

The girl went on: 'Are you drinking a toast to Papa Stalin, tonight, General? Stalin means steel, but remember his real name was *Dfjugashvili*, which means dross . . .'

Then music: *US in Concert*. Littlehales listened nostalgically, then pressed a pad to get Radio Moscow.

Tchaikovsky: *Swan Lake*. Earlier there had been Chopin, music to putsch by.

Somebody had once said: 'For Russia, Chopin is not music; it is a diagnosis.'

Biggin came into the hut.

'One wounded soldier, eight Russian civilians, and the Russian major-general that the CIA are after.'

He poured scotch, held up the bottle to the clerk, who brightened, pushed forward a paper cup and said huskily: 'God bless you, sir.'

'I wonder,' said Biggin, 'why he didn't send the reporters out?'

'Soldiers out last, shits out last, I imagine,' said Littlehales. 'It's probably his plan for a new world order.'

'I'd worry about his career,' said Biggin, 'if I thought he had one.'

Littlehales said: 'There's been a lot of fuss over the girl reporter. Her television company knows that Royal Mercians went into Moscow to find her. I keep getting faxes from MoD press office. The newspaper bloke's people seem fairly relaxed, they don't seem to have noticed he's missing.'

Swan Lake faded out.

'Shame,' said the clerk, chattily. 'I was enjoying that.'

Littlehales wondered why Biggin had given him scotch. SAS

egalitarianism or something, he supposed.

Radio Moscow: a woman with an English accent, something from *Watch with Mother* in the Fifties, said: 'Here is the news from Moscow at 01.00, 23 March. In the Congress of Deputies, General Kotelnikov has announced that, in keeping with Paragraph Seven of Article 127 of the Constitution of the USSR . . .'

'Whoever would have thought,' said Biggin, 'we would hear those words ever again?'

' . . . told deputies that authority had lost the confidence of the population. Hope and enthusiasm had become apathy and despair. There had been malicious mockery of the institutions of state. In such a dark and critical hour, he had felt duty-bound to accept the invitation of those deputies who had appealed to him to restore legality and law and order. General Kotelnikov promised to wage merciless war on the criminal world, and to end the tyranny of the mafia . . .'

'Papa Stalin,' said Biggin. 'You know they're calling him Papa Stalin?'

Littlehales said: 'We danced round the lion when it was not yet dead.'

Later in the night, two men joined them in the hut. One was Langdon, his face bloodless and drawn, his arm in a sling. The other man was a brigadier from Joint Intelligence Committee, London.

The brigadier said: 'When do they reach the signal-box?'

'Three hours, sir. Just before dawn,' said Littlehales.

Langdon said: 'I want Hoodless made OC.'

'Change, counter-change, chaos,' said the brigadier.

'I want Hoodless made OC, and my men pulled out. I can't have them tied to a sodding train commanded by a subaltern from the infantry. It's fucking bizarre. It's a fucking nightmare.'

The brigadier said: 'They've got the container. They'll be through Yekaterinburg by dawn.'

'I don't care a fuck about the container. I never did. We should have swapped food-aid for it, not thieved it.'

'We didn't thieve it. It was for sale,' said the brigadier, pouring himself whisky, 'and we bought it. From the wrong person, perhaps, under the wrong circumstances, but you people were happy to go in there and fetch it out. Anyway,' he added, 'it's out of your hands.'

Biggin kept quiet. Littlehales studied the sitreps coming in from Norway, from the Murmansk border.

The brigadier said: 'What's happening in Moscow?'

'Kotelnikov addressed forty deputies, sir,' said Littlehales, 'just before midnight. The text of his speech is being read out. We don't yet have intell's analysis. We are picking up transmissions from Radio Maximum. The 14th and 17th tank regiments are still surrounding the State University. Students are making speeches. The French television crew are sending out pictures.'

'It'll be another Tiananmen Square,' said Langdon.

'Yes, Major,' said the brigadier. 'I read the papers, too.'

They went through details of the pick-up from Kazakhstan, the airlift to the British Gas oilfield.

Langdon was there out of courtesy, thought Littlehales. He no longer had a part to play; the game had moved on.

Littlehales and Biggin were to leave Kaunas at 07.00 in a VC10.

A VC10! The oldest plane in the fleet. They were slipping down the priority list. They were being thrown back on RAF resources. NATO supreme command was getting bored with the British Government's little games.

Outside, Biggin breathed the cold air blowing from the pines. It was 05.00, but already there was a smell of fried potatoes and bacon wafting from the cookhouse.

He said: 'Hoodless? *Should* we try and make Hoodless the OC? He's SAS, after all. He's been trained for this sort of operation. It'll cause a devil of a row. What do you think?'

Littlehales said: 'Can he do any better?'

'Better than a subaltern who's being kicked out of the army for incompetence?'

They plodded towards the accommodation huts.

'No, we'll leave it,' said Biggin, after a few moments. He added: 'To be honest, I think your bloke Morrell is doing rather well.'

PART FOUR
THE DZUNGARIAN GATES

I, a citizen of the Russian Federal Republic, on entering the ranks of the Armed Forces, take the oath and solemnly promise to be an honourable, brave, disciplined, and vigilant soldier . . . If I should break this solemn oath, then let me suffer the severe penalties of Russian law and the universal hatred and contempt of the Russian people.
Soldier's Oath of Allegiance, Russian Federal Army

ONE

Bukhara Express, Yekaterinburg, early morning, 23 March

Few operations officers would choose a train as the preferred way to move special forces discreetly and swiftly through enemy territory.

A train cannot move, in safety, unless it has registered its route with a traffic-control centre. It must stop when it is told to stop, or risk a collision. It is utterly vulnerable to attack by tanks, mortars or rockets. Small children can disable it by putting rocks on the track. It cannot take evasive action or alter its route. It is large, difficult to camouflage, and can be easily tracked from the air.

But nobody should overlook the sheer size of Russia. Even without the Ukraine and Kazakhstan, it is twice the size of the United States of America.

How many satellites and helicopters do you need to find a train you believe is in Texas – when it might just as easily be in San Francisco or New Jersey? When you have no access to railway traffic-control networks outside Washington DC?

Russia's railway network is the largest in the world. It has 140,000 kilometres of track. In the late Nineties it still carried an astounding *forty-five* per cent of all world freight tonnage.

Two days after the fall of Moscow, Moscow Traffic Control's writ still only ran in areas controlled by Second Army. The new government did not have access to the national satellite surveillance network, and the planes and helicopters of 14th and 15th Airborne Divisions had other things to think about than a train carrying rich capitalists to the West.

It was, nevertheless, a sign of the importance of the container from Perm that, by the afternoon of Friday 22 March, officers from Kotelnikov's Chief Intelligence Directorate were examining the bombed-out train in the siding at Khodynskoye, and interviewing the commanders of those Second Army units that had overrun the airfield and railway.

By the evening, they were hearing, from witnesses, the words 'Bukhara Express'.

In the hour before dawn on Saturday 23 March the Bukhara Express was in a siding ten kilometres west of Yekaterinburg, next to the signal-box on the junction with the Trans-Siberian railway line.

In the signal-box itself, Talbot, the SAS royal signaller, stood in front of the huge curved hemisphere of diagrams and circuitry.

'What we're looking at here covers 828k of single track under signals,' he was saying with enthusiasm. 'That means four hundred and fifty points and around twelve hundred possible routes to choose from. These are the buttons that set the defined route. They activate points as necessary, with clearance of relevant signals, providing – *providing* – that the route is safe to set. Route setting *can* be automatic,' he went on, without pause, 'but the scope is restricted by the intricacy of traffic flows. That's why it's normally confined to railways where trains run to a consistently-repeated pattern over short distances. If you think *just for one moment* of the multiplicity of routings in and out of a junction like Crewe . . .'

Simon listened dumbly. A train buff. Dear God, five more minutes and he'd be going on about the Aberystwyth and Barmouth Light Railway.

'It was like this, of course, on the old Euston to Glasgow Central,' said Talbot rapidly. 'That was why they brought in the junction optimization technique. Any of you speak English?'

The three Russian signals operators, two of them female, had been finishing their night-shift when the party from the Bukhara Express knocked politely on the door.

'Amerikantsy?' said one of them now, bemused.

'Bloody Welsh, lover!'

'Yes, all right, Talbot,' said Simon. 'How does it work – no, I don't care a shit how it works. What do we *do*?'

'We key our four-character description into the track-circuit berth, sir, and in theory it will find us a line and stay with us as we pass from one circuited section to another—'

'Can anybody change it? Once it's been set?'

'An operator, manually.'

'How do we stop him?'

'It's more likely to be a her, actually.'

'Talbot . . .' said Hoodless.

'Well, let's see. Basically the signals won't clear for any route until the apparatus has automatically detected positive resetting of any points involved. We're talking about failsafe: the universal rail engineers credo—'

'Talbot!'

'We disable the entire fucking system.'

Now they were on the main line; the line of the Trans-Siberian. The carriages were rocking and heeling over as the train rounded huge bends. They swept past small wooden stations. In the dawn they passed a lake and watched geese fly up in alarm, up into the pink eastern sky. They rattled round the northern suburbs of Yekaterinburg.

Simon went down the train, sought out Kate and Art.

'I owe you an explanation,' he said, sitting down on Kate's bunk. 'You deserve to be told why I didn't send you out on the chopper. I had to choose the most vulnerable, those in the most danger. If the

Russian civilians had been arrested, they would have had it. You'll agree with that, Kate? They'd have disappeared to the camps without trace. You people might have an unpleasant time, you might be put on trial, sent to prison, even, but it would be a political matter. You would not be forgotten about. You would have somebody fighting on your side.'

Art looked at him blankly. Kate nodded.

'I wanted Anna to go,' Simon continued. 'I wanted Anna to go instead of the Russian general. Generals are fair game in my book. He'll have sent many a poor sod to an early grave in his time.

'But Anna wouldn't go. She's a nurse – well, she's done some first-aid – and she wouldn't leave Gallagher. So I let the major-general go instead. Kotelnikov's people would have shot him, I think, if they'd caught him.

'I didn't think either of you would have wanted to fly out to safety, knowing that it would have meant someone like Madame Vostrotin or Iulia, was having to stay in Russia.'

He smiled hesitantly.

Kate said: 'Yea, right.'

Simon sat for a minute, looked vaguely expectant, then got up and left.

Art said: 'Do you want a gin?'

'Tonic?'

He shook his head.

They drank gin and water, a miniature each, silently absorbed in their own thoughts.

The Royal Mercians were in cheerful mood, glad to be moving again, joking about the mess of shredded carrots and turnip which Foster and Henshaw had boiled up for them to eat, but refusing the potatoes that were a greyish yellow and had a peculiar smell. Simon, finding no carrots left, cursed them foully and ate the potatoes and felt ill. He went down to the end of the train. Hoodless was just going into Gallagher's compartment. Simon heard him say:

'So how are you then, Annie?'

'Anna! Anna! I keep telling you Anna!'

'All right, don't get your feathers ruffled' – a pause – 'Annie.'

Hoodless being frivolous? Simon was shaken. He went into the armoury for a lie down.

Now they were leaving the eastern suburbs. The door of the armoury opened.

'I want to show you something,' said Kate.

'What?' he said, half asleep.

'Please? Oh, come on, please. Hurry!'

He followed her, down the corridor, into the carriage that had been bombed out at Kuybyshev.

It was one of the coaches from the old Russian imperial train, refurbished and restored in Paris. It had been decorated with old sepia photographs behind glass ovals. Some of them had been smashed, the photographs sodden by the rain and snow. Others were intact. Photos of the pre-Bolshevik days: a middle-class family having a meal outside their dacha . . . a steamboat on the Volga . . . Moscow's Yaroslavl Station in 1911 . . .

A photo of a girl of about eighteen, sitting in a sentry-box. She looked terrified. The sentry-box number, behind her head, was: *Siding 37, Yekaterinburg.*

'Anastasia,' said Kate, softly. 'That's blood on her white blouse. She tried to escape, and the Bolsheviks caught her. They photographed her like an animal they had trapped.'

They both looked out of the open windows, out at the cold dawn, at the dreary, crumbling buildings. Had they already passed Siding 37?

The train was leaving Yekaterinburg. The place where the imperial family had been murdered.

As Hoodless would have put it, the Romanovs' last RV.

TWO

They were sailing through a sea of dead grass.

By the track there were still drifts of snow, but, through it, pushing upwards, could be seen the pale green swathes of a new season's growth.

Hoodless lay sprawled back, his mouth open, snoring. Simon watched him and wondered about him – about his dedication, his obsessive commitment. He was a former gunner, the son of a sergeant wounded in the Falklands: this much had been revealed. A divorced man – a son aged four, a daughter aged three – he now lived in barracks at Hereford.

What was it that made men want so passionately to belong to 22 SAS? To push their bodies to the very limit of endurance. To perfect the craft, the *art*, of killing?

Many, it was said, were well-read, civilized romantics. Hoodless didn't seem to be a romantic. He didn't have the look of a man carrying the works of Rupert Brooke or James Elroy Flecker in his ammo pouches. But presumably not all SAS soldiers were gentlemen adventurers with a taste for romantic verse. Presumably there was a fair sprinkling of the coarse and the brutal, the bull-headed patriots who just wanted to wear the red beret with its *Who Dares Wins* badge, to belong to 22 Special Air Regiment, to belong to the best, the very best there was.

The door rattled back.

'Tea,' said Kate.

'There isn't any tea.'

'No? What's this, then?'

It was hot and it was fragrant. He put it to his nose and inhaled and felt dizzy.

'Sucky sweet?'

He said: 'Pardon?'

'You suck a sweet in your mouth while you're drinking. It's instead of sugar. Here.'

She offered him a sweet. 'It's from the Russians. They've been hoarding, the buggers. I twisted Andrei's arm.'

He felt nauseous. He handed the glass to her. 'You have it.'

'I've had mine. This is yours.'

'I don't really want any tea, thanks.'

She looked at him and sighed. 'Right. OK, don't have it. Sergeant Hoodless? Tea? It's teatime. Oi, wake up, dozy-chops.'

Hoodless stirred, took the tea, muttered his thanks.

Kate smiled and left.

Simon spat out the sweet, on to his hand, wondered if he ought to offer it to Hoodless, but decided that delicacy forbad.

Outside, the track curved. As he looked out, the dying sun caught the dusty green of the twin-diesel engine, the gold lettering on the coaches, vivid and sharp against the dark, almost black waves of grass.

Then the track straightened, and the train was back running like an arrow across the plain of Ishim, into the rich, magenta darkness of the East.

Traveller's Tales, he thought, his mind torn between the beauty of the scene and the worrying rumbling in his stomach.

Hoodless finished his tea and said: 'Bloody hell, I needed that.'

Simon looked down at the map. 'We're coming to a place called Tyumen. It's where the Trans-Siberian express trains pass each other. According to Talbot, we ought to stop there until morning. That would get us into sync with the Trans-Siberian's usual timetable. There might be a doctor. There might be food.'

Hoodless nodded. He had gradually accustomed himself to accepting Simon's authority.

'I didn't think much of those potatoes,' he said. 'They tasted peculiar.'

'Yes,' said Simon, his stomach moving in a peculiar way. 'So I noticed.'

On the HF from Kaunas, Littlehales said: 'Why not go on tonight?'

'We think the Trans-Siberian might be coming the other way. It's scheduled to pass through at 02.00. There's only one rail line. I'm not happy about sharing it.'

'We don't believe the Trans-Siberian is running west of Irkutsk. Monday's train was derailed.'

'Wednesday's train,' said Simon, 'might not have been.'

'All right. Tomorrow, first light.'

'Will you have us on satellite?'

'I hope not. If satellites can see you, so can planes.'

It was the first news for Simon that the 14th and 15th Airborne Divisions had declared for Kotelnikov. He went and told Andrei.

Andrei said: 'You OK?'

Simon felt queasy. 'I think I've eaten something I shouldn't.'

'Something you shouldn't? Why, what have you eaten?' cried Andrei, as if he expected Simon to confess to having munched a secret dinner of dead cockroaches.

'Those potatoes, perhaps,' said Simon, who had a taste in his mouth that made him think of straw and horse piss. 'Never mind that. Are you OK for us to stop at this place? Do you know anything about it?'

Andrei didn't.

'I want a doctor to look at Gallagher. Can you try and fix it?'

'You want to stop the train for the night?'

'Yes.'

They were passing cultivated fields. By the track were wooden houses with iron roofs, lights shining from oil-lamps. Some cows in a yard – western Siberia was a huge dairy region, and had been ever since the English wife of a Russian nobleman had demanded butter for her bread, and milk for her tea, over a century ago.

They passed a petrochemical works: a huge, skeletal monster bedecked with lights – a spaceship sitting on a launching pad of green wheat.

'We'll stop for the night, if you like,' said Andrei.

'Cheers,' said Simon. He stood up. 'What about you? Are you OK?'

'I'm just wonderful,' said Andrei in his ironic voice.

Simon grinned, relieved that his comments about the Federal Guards were forgotten, or at any rate forgiven.

He held out his hand. Andrei looked at it in surprise, then shook it.

Simon had thought of apologizing, but had decided against it. Life was too full, moving too fast; already the events at Sputnik Mira seemed a lifetime away.

He went back to Section HQ. Chaffinch, he reflected, would now be in a hospital bed at the British Gas complex in Kazakhstan, warm and well fed, the lucky sod. God only knew where Madame Vostrotin and her sad husband were by now. It was a fair bet that she'd be wailing, he'd be sitting smoking with his head in his hands, the stout Iulia would be moaning. The Pastnovs had relations in Canada. The film director was set on reaching Los Angeles; Nina had muttered rebelliously about Paris; Olga had sneaked up to Simon and asked him for the address of his flat in London. What the hell would he be doing with a flat in London? Taken by surprise, he had given her the phone number of his parents in Ludlow. He imagined her turning up, saying, 'Hi, I'm a friend of Simon's,' and sitting in his bedroom drinking Russian pink champagne and smoking Uzbek grass while his mum cooked her a hotpot and his dad wondered what the funny smell was.

The mafia gunmen would have crawled to the Perm Highway by now, or died of exposure.

The train slowed. The tiny station was built of wood, painted blue and green. On the wooden platform a woman muffled up in a shiny nylon parka waved a flag at them vigorously. They came to a standstill. Simon saw, beyond the platform, a deeply welcoming sight.

'Colour-Sar'nt Gough,' he shouted, 'nobody gets off the train yet. Get everybody together in the dining car!'

When they were assembled he said to them: 'You see that hotel? I intend to make it our billet. While we're here, for Christ's sake don't wander off. Stay within the sentry lines at all times. We will be leaving at dawn tomorrow.'

Women with buckets and mops had clambered on to the train.

Now they appeared in the dining car, with the evident intention of cleaning it. A sturdy woman in her thirties pushed a trolley of peat blocks and tea for the samovars. The civil war was far away, he thought with sudden relief. He felt a surge of affection for the back-of-beyond, for the last places on God's earth.

He climbed down to the platform, with Andrei. Two MVD policemen had appeared. They looked cold and bored, and smiled sadly. He and Andrei saluted them, and they saluted in return. Andrei asked the latest news from Moscow, but there was none.

Moscow lay west of the Urals, as fabulous and unattainable as New York. Here they were more worried about Yekaterinburg. The woman stationmaster said, 'Terrible, terrible,' looking at them with beady black eyes, seeking information, wanting to know what horrors they had passed through.

Simon asked about army units on the loose. There were no army units; only the local MVD interior police.

Further east, Chechens had stopped two trains by putting boulders on the line.

Andrei said to Simon: 'Chechens! You know what I want to do?'

'Yes,' said Simon. 'But never mind that. Ask about beds in the hotel. Ask how much they want for beds and food.'

'Beds and food?' said Andrei.

Anna had come down from the train. 'See if there is a warm room, captain,' she said. 'Somewhere for Para.'

'I don't know,' said Simon doubtfully. 'Ought we to move him? I thought he'd be better where he is.'

Andrei had wandered off. 'Oh God, where's he gone? Anna, ask about beds, showers, food. You negotiate, OK?'

His stomach was moving again: muscular spasms over which he had alarmingly little control.

A man from the hotel was sent for. Anna negotiated. He saw the manager name a price, and Anna fell about laughing. She turned to Simon. 'Roubles or coupons?'

'Gold,' said Simon, who wanted to get to a lavatory.

'I don't think that gold, sir,' said Hoodless severely, materializing in the gloom, 'was meant to book us into five-star luxury living.'

Simon said: 'I don't think it's going to.'

Gallagher would stay on the train. The SAS would stay on the train. Real soldiers didn't sleep in hotels, Hoodless's tone implied.

Well, Simon bloody did.

'Colour-Sar'nt Gough, get the men into the hotel!'

'OK, lads.'

'Mace!'

'Sir?'

'Kaolin and morphine. Have you got any?'

'Kaolin and what, sir?' said Mace, an Anglican vicar accused of drug peddling.

'The pink stuff for the runs.'
'No, sir.'
'You were down as fucking first-aid.'
'Nobody said anything about bringing—'
'OK, go on. Bugger off.'

The Royal Mercians hurried down the platform, glad to stretch their legs, springing about like lambs. The Russian guards looked down at them from the dining car.

Kate looked up as she hurried past. She called: 'Hi, Andrei. See you at dinner. Dinner, Andrei! Dinner!'

Andrei looked down at her and shook his head.

'You're staying on the train? Why?'

But she didn't wait for an answer. There was a cold Siberian wind blowing over the steppe, over the black grasses, and she suspected that there was a strictly limited amount of hot water in the Ishim Tourism Hotel.

THREE

Graffiti on the walls of the lift. A strong smell of dog.

Art was surprised: he had thought the dogs would have been eaten weeks ago. Perhaps it was not dog. On the television in his bedroom was the same South American soap he had watched in the Cosmos Hotel in Moscow. He sat for a while on the threadbare pink coverlet of the bed, trying to catch up on the plot, but really just *sitting*.

Then he hid his clinking carrier bag in the minifridge – rusty, dead, and smelling of very old dead rats – and went down to try to find something to eat.

The restaurant was vast, cold and empty. The green and gold-flecked carpet had a greasy sheen. The walls were dirty orange, the chairs tubular metal. It was so like a Warrington youth club from the Sixties (when he had been local reporter for the *Liverpool Echo*, before he got his job on the *Guardian*) that he expected to hear Pet Clarke telling her sailor to stop his roaming. Indeed, so strong was the nostalgia that he looked round for the curtain that would reveal the Dave Clark Five, with Dave grinning his toothpaste grin as he jiggled up and down on the drums.

A trestle table was covered with a greyish tablecloth. On it were piles of greyish bread. There was a battered aluminium tureen. A Russian wearing a black suit, more of an undertaker than a waiter, stood by it.

The man ladled him soup, grey and fatty, and gave him bread. He carried his food off. Like a wolf seeking a dark corner, he sat next to a shady alcove bearing the sign in English 'TOURISM CENTER' and underneath it '*Welcome to the Flowering Steppes of Ishim*'.

He ate his dinner. A woman carried a dish out and put it on the table. From a distance it looked like a jelly, but when he galloped up close, he discovered that it was a wobbling, glistening chunk of fat. This was no time to worry about cholesterol levels. He spooned a large portion on to his plate.

Kate came in. She saw the food and said: 'Oh God, look at that. That looks wonderful. Real food. D'you know what? I just went to the lavatory in my *en-suite*—'

'In your what?'

'*En-suite*, Art, you have *en-suite's* in Manchester, I believe?'

'I haven't got one here.'

'Anyway, there I was when a man barged in and used the sink as a urinal. Would you believe it?'

Art carried his meat jelly and dry bread away, back to his alcove. As he sat down he noticed something in the alcove's dark recess.

Was he going mad? Was he seeing things? It would not be surprising, sanity being at a premium in Mother Russia.

He looked away. He waited until Kate had got her own soup and jelly. He feared that she was going to join him.

She looked towards him, hesitated, then drifted over to some Russians who had wandered in: the local nobs presumably. Soon she was chattering away in the lingua franca, waving her arms about, showing off.

He waited a moment longer. Then he got up and slipped craftily into the gloom of the alcove.

It was real. It was flesh and blood. At any rate it was plastic and alloy. It was an international payphone.

He picked up the receiver. There was a dialling tone.

'Now I know,' he said to himself, 'there is a God.'

He put his Amex card into the slot. A flashing sign said DIAL NOW.

He dialled the London tabloid that paid for his daily meat and for his mortgage on a link-detached starter home in Chester. After only a few moments of clicking, a voice said: 'Newsdesk.'

A moment later it said: 'Hello?'

Art said, trembling, 'It's me. It's Ark Finkel.'

'Yes?' queried the voice.

'I'm in Russia,' said Art.

'You are?' The voice was surprised. 'I haven't got you down, Art. OK, so what's happening? It's fifteen minutes to the conference.'

The youth, Art knew, was reading down the diary, scrolling it down the screen. If Art wanted his story to go on the agenda (*Russia falls into abyss* tucked under an exclusive about a pop star's verruca operation), he had better stake his claim now.

'I'm in Tyumen.'

'Is that in Moscow?'

'Listen,' said Art. 'Listen to me, you little turd.'

Kate had seen him disappear into the alcove and had wondered where he had gone. For a while she chatted to the mayor, who had come to the hotel to welcome the return of the international tourist trade. Soon it would be May, when the steppes would be in flower. Summer would bring the swallows, but would it bring the Japanese? Two years ago, the town had hosted the sub-group of a small international dairy conference. Western Siberia could produce enough milk and butter and cream to fatten all Russia, they had concluded, as well as exporting to the EC! What did Kate think?

She answered politely. She looked over at Art's table again. He still had not returned to his meal. She felt suddenly uneasy.

She was about to investigate. Then Andrei wandered in and leaned over her, and said in English: 'I'll see you later?'

'Yes, OK,' she said, not really listening.

He looked at the food, turned, and wandered out again. Anna said: 'Poor soldiers.'

'Why?' said Kate.

'No money. The hotel won't let them in without money. The police chief said they should go to the army transit camp at Tobolsk.'

'Ah well,' said Kate. ' "It's Tommy this and Tommy that and Tommy shut the door, But it's Thin Red Line of heroes when the guns begin to roar." '

'Poor soldiers,' repeated Anna gloomily.

Kate jumped up, her eyes having penetrated the darkness – or Art, perhaps, had incautiously moved closer to the light.

She ran across the restaurant. She cried out: 'Give me the phone. Oh please give me the phone!' People stopped eating and stared at her as she disappeared into the alcove. 'Art? Give me the phone, please . . .'

'And I want flying home from fucking Omsk first fucking class, and I want a hotel booked, a real hotel, not the sort of hotel where they serve lumps of pork fat and pigs' pizzles. So what have you done about me, eh? Have you been running Page One stories about me, about your famous foreign correspondent lost in the maelstrom of red savagery? I *know* I'm a freelance. Oh, I *know* that, sunbeam. You don't need to tell me I'm a freelance—'

'Art, Art, please, Art, this is vital—'

'I'm here because you couldn't get a staff man on this sodding job, not without a million-quid insurance, and you were too fucking mean to pay the premium, so you sent me, *me*, poor sodding freelance me . . .'

'Art, give me the phone, please, oh please . . .'

'Do we not bleed?' cried Art.

'For Christ's sake—'

She grabbed at the phone. The lights in the restaurant went off.

'Christ almighty . . .'

The phone went. It did not cut, it became echoey and faded, the residual electricity seeping away.

'Art?' said the voice from London, breathily, a sigh on the wind. Then it was gone.

FOUR

Simon kicked the door closed and dropped his kitbag and collapsed on the bed.

He was alone – with nobody badgering him, nobody asking questions, nobody asking for orders – for the first time since he had awakened in Moscow on Monday morning to a steaming mug of tea and the fateful words: 'The bugger's in Babushkin, sir. Word is we're pulling out by dinner time.'

Now it was Saturday night in Siberia. He was doubled up with stomach cramps and couldn't stop shivering.

After a while, as he lay curled up, his stomach eased and a faint warmth started to spread through his limbs.

There was a quiet knock on the door.

Dear God, couldn't they leave him for five minutes! He'd rostered the sentries and checked the accommodation, he'd looked at the food in the dining-room, debated with Hoodless the need for a machine-gun nest covering the street (and decided against), met the town mayor and, through Anna, made some sort of polite conversation. What else did they want him to do: inspect Mace's footrot?

'Yes?' he called sharply.

'Can I come in?'

He sat up. 'Yes, of course.'

She stood hesitantly in the doorway, then closed the door, walked over and stood looking at him.

'They said you were ill.'

'Gutrot. It must have been those potatoes. I haven't had anything else.'

'Have you a temperature?'

'I don't know. Mace has got the thermometer pads, and I'm not letting Mace near me.'

'You shouldn't be lying there with your clothes on.'

'Well, I'm not taking them off.'

'The number of times,' said Kate, 'I've said that.'

He smiled feebly.

'Well, don't sit there. Lie down if you're ill.'

'No, I'm all right.'

She looked at him thoughtfully, then went over to the wardrobe and poked round inside it, pulled out a blanket, said, 'Catch,' and threw it over to him.

'I don't think that's how Nurse Anna does it,' he commented.

'Nurse Anna's patient does as he is told.'

She walked over to the window and looked out. After a moment she said: 'Finkel found a phone.'

He looked round, startled. 'Working?'

'Until the electricity went off.'

'Did he get through?'

'Yes. He phoned London. He complained about his hotel room.'

'What?'

'To his newsdesk.'

'He didn't talk about us, or the SAS?'

'No.'

'Thank fuck for that.'

'Yes,' she said 'Of course.'

A silence fell.

He said: 'I'm sorry. It's important for you to send a story. I *do* know that. I'm not completely stupid.'

'I don't think you're stupid.' She was staring out of the window, out at the darkness. She turned to face him. 'Simon, when do you think we'll get out of all this?'

'Another day, and we'll be in Kazakhstan.'

'You think Kazakhstan's a safe haven? Alma Ata's had more ethnic riots than anywhere. The Russian population hate the Kazakhs.'

'Well, I don't know,' said Simon wearily.

She came back to the bed and sat on it. He leaned back against the pillow, the blanket round his shoulders. After a few moments she flopped down on the coverlet and curled up next to him.

He said lightly: 'I don't think Nurse Anna would be doing that.'

'Stuff Nurse Anna.'

Her parka hood was sour and smelly. She pulled it away and cautiously laid her head on the pillow, found it clean and cool, and thanked God for small mercies.

He said: 'What would you have said in your story?'

She lay still for a minute. 'I'd have talked about the fall of Moscow,' she said.

'Oh. Right.'

'I'd have said that it wasn't just Moscow that fell, it was the fall of an ideal, a corrupt ideal if you like – an ideal that goes back to the building of St Petersburg, the art collections, the time the aristos all started speaking French . . . The idea that Russia could be something better than a Balkan Asiatic power, the Russians something better than culars and serfs. The idea that the endless agony which is Russia is not *inevitable* – is not *predestined* by some atheistic God.'

'Can you have an atheistic God?'

'In Russia you can.'

'Russia's like an onion,' said Simon. 'The more you peel it, the more you cry. Heard that?'

'It's a good one,' said Kate, who had heard it many times, 'I'll use it somewhere.'

She added: 'I suppose I'd better go.'

'I suppose so.'

She sat up. 'Tummy still bad?'

'Yes.'

She was looking at him. 'I panicked when I heard you were ill. I thought: oh my God, he can't be – what will happen to us? I came running up here.'

'That was nice.'

'No. I was frightened. You need brandy. Brandy for an upset stomach.'

'You've got brandy?'

'I know who has.'

On the flat roof of the Hotel Ishim the sentry – Foster, the 'D' Company marksman – stood huddled in his padded jacket, looking up at the vast Siberian sky. Instead of his SA80, he had an SAS sniper rifle: an American-made Barrett Light 50 which had a killing range of eighteen hundred metres, and could pierce body armour.

Tired of looking at the sky, he looked idly around him through the gun's telescopic sights.

The town was small – little more than a village, really. A wooden station, a concrete-block tourist hotel, a cluster of houses and farms, a wooden church built in 1899 by the Alexander III Fund. Out on the steppe, half a mile away, stood the vast towers of the petrochemical works and the accommodation block for its workers.

A harsh land, a savage land. Snow lay on the ground here for one hundred and fifty days of the year. Temperatures were twenty below freezing for much of the winter, and over a hundred degrees in July and August. Mosquitoes made life a misery in the short summer months.

The town had been hewn from virgin steppe as a place of exile for Polish Jews. In the Bolshevik Revolution it had been a divisional headquarters for the Czechoslovak army that controlled the Urals. The town's moment of fame had come in 1919, when the treasurer of the Imperial Mint had been hauled out of a train here, and murdered by Bolsheviks.

Fifty kilometres north of the railway track was the remains of a Stalinist death camp that had been turned into a Soviet Pioneer Camp in Krushchev's time, and had functioned until 1988.

There was a photograph of it in the lobby of the Hotel Ishim. It showed a ceremony in 1993, attended by one of Boris Yeltsin's junior ministers. The unveiling of a memorial stone bearing the inscription: *Beyond these walls the earth cries out in pain.*

Not exactly Bognor Regis, thought Art. What with one thing and another, he was in a town that had had more than its share of grief.

He said: 'Evening,' to the sentry outside the hotel, Henshaw, who replied: 'Evening, sir.'

He walked down the street, to the railway crossing. Beyond was open land, flat and endless: the steppe. A moon was shining through clouds. He peered into the distance. In a direct line north there was nothing bar a few abandoned (though not for long, he thought) Stalinist prison camps between here and the Arctic Sea.

What would happen if they were caught by the Reds? Kotelnikov wouldn't need to send them to Siberia, would he, not when they were here already?

He imagined the poxy young assistant news editor in London, in twenty years time, saying: *These rumours about a prison camp they've just discovered with Brit soldiers and journalists. It might be true. I remember getting a phone-call, oh bloody years ago . . . thought it was some nutter . . .*

Art stared out at the cold and empty steppe, and thought, as he often did at times like this, with unbearable longing, about his days on the *Guardian*. The deep silence round the sub's table, the friendly clatter of the tea trolley with its bacon sandwiches and its jammy doughnuts . . .

In his first week there, in the summer of 1966, he had worn a knitted tie from Austin Reed and a puce-coloured shirt.

He shuddered; not all memories, after all, were pleasant ones. He turned and walked back, past the hotel, to the railway station. (Foster, still playing with his Barrett sniping rifle, tracked him all the way.) He went onto the platform. The moon threw a pale light on the Bukhara Express.

He walked down its length, past the engine, past the dining car full of sleeping Russian guards, past Gallagher's compartment, where he could see Anna and Ferneyhough reading a book together, Gallagher himself propped up, but leaning back with his eyes closed.

An animal moved on the far side of the track, a slinky sort of animal: a very large cat perhaps, a wolf, or a marmot. There had been marmot in Kurdistan, dozens of them: they had sat on tree trunks watching the press minibus go by, staring in at Art, as Art himself stared out at them.

The SAS sentry was deep in the shadows, between the last coach and the metal container wagon. Art spotted him, the smudge of white under the camouflage cream smearing his cheeks. His gun was black-matt, nothing gleamed there.

Kate told the key-woman to open Art's door. The woman protested, wide-eyed with horror. Kate said that Simon was a senior NATO army officer. Simon said: 'I'm going back to my room.'

'No you're not. Don't be bloody feeble.'

The woman opened the door. They went in. Art's case was on his bed. Kate went quickly and efficiently through it.

Simon sat on a chair and watched. 'What nimble fingers,' he said.

There was a German toffee bar and a packet of nuts covered in milk chocolate. There was half a packet of cheese biscuits. There was a jar of pork liver pâté. Kate marvelled as the riches emerged.

'The sod told me everything was gone. The sod claimed all he had was pickled vegetables.'

The television was on. Simon watched it, a not-unpleasant buzzing noise in his head. It was an English programme with Russian subtitles. 'Do you remember this?' he said. 'I never watched it.'

'Nobody ever watched it,' said Kate.

'What were they all doing in Spain?' he asked.

'God knows,' said Kate. 'Here, have a biscuit.'

He cautiously ate a biscuit.

She was going through Art's clothes. She looked round, found a ballpoint pen by the bedside, poked gingerly through his laundry.

'He kept those cheese biscuits next to his underpants, the cunning bastard. Don't touch anything that isn't cellophane wrapped or bottled.'

'But I've eaten a biscuit. You gave it to me.'

'My God,' she poked and prodded. 'I'm finding out what life is all about, on this trip.'

'What will we say if he comes back?' said Simon.

'All food is impounded,' she said, 'under military law.'

He had never been so hungry in his life. He said: 'I'm going to be sick,' and went into the bathroom, and was sick.

Kate looked in, helplessly. She wondered if she ought perhaps to put a cool hand on his forehead.

'You OK?'

He was retching over the bowl. She hesitated, then decided, being a practical girl, that there was nothing to be done.

She went back to searching through Art's luggage. She found his spare pair of socks. She found a tube of shampoo and put it in her pocket. She prowled round the room. She looked in the minibar (*The obvious hiding place is the best hiding place, eh Holmes?*) and there it was: the carrier that rattled, filled with the booty from the minibars of the Cosmos Hotel, Moscow.

'I've got Cognac,' she called. 'Five-star. You'll be better with some of this.'

Simon was sitting beside the lavatory, leaning against it.

She stared down at him. 'Simon?'

Back in his own room, he lay down on the bed while Kate stood in the doorway saying: 'My God, if you're really ill, we've had it.'

'I give in,' he said.

'Christ, Simon, don't say that!'

He told her to get Mace.

Mace arrived.

'I feel bloody awful, Mace,' he said. 'I'm sweating. I've got cramp in my stomach. I've been sick.'

'What about the runs, sir? Have you still got the runs?'

'Mace, if I were to eat a tin of fruit salad, it would go through me so fast you would be able to stand with the tin under my bum and collect it all back up again.'

A pause.

'Well?' Simon said.

Mace said: 'There's still some paracetamol.'

Anna appeared with the doctor from the petrochemical works, who had been changing Gallagher's dressing. The doctor took Simon's temperature, looked at the whites of his eyes, felt his pulse, prodded his stomach, asked what he had eaten, then said he had toxic food poisoning and prescribed salt and sugar diluted with water.

Anna said: 'Shall I stay with you, captain?'

Kate said: 'That's all right, Anna. I can look after him. You don't have to look after every little creature that's unwell in the world.'

Anna went away. The doctor was talking.

'He says he is more used to dealing with pneumonia and malnutrition,' Kate translated. 'Heart and lung complications. Diabetes and TB. He says the elderly in Yekaterinburg have each on average lost nine pounds in weight this winter. There are no healthy people left. Schools have been closed since January. He wants us to tell the West – to tell the United Nations Health Authority.'

'Yes, of course,' said Simon.

'He says the town is overrun by packs of wild dogs: some of them pets abandoned by their owners who cannot feed them.'

The doctor was looking down at Simon. He said something softly. Kate translated. 'They tell us it is the last winter we will face these horrors. We tell them it is the last winter we will face.'

Simon felt a sudden chill.

He said: 'Tell him, "Thank you". Tell him . . .' What could he say? How sorry they were?

Kate said something. The doctor nodded, smiled wearily. He left.

Mace was still hovering with his first-aid kit. Simon said: 'When we get back, Mace, I'm going to do you.'

'Sir?' said Mace, outraged.

Half an hour later, Hoodless sent a grinning SAS man with two tablets from the SAS medical kit. 'Delhi-belly, blackwater fever – these'll set your guts like concrete.'

They did.

Art was still outside by the train, unaware of the violence being offered to his possessions.

The clouds had cleared. The sky was filled with stars, more stars than ever he saw in Kurdistan even. It was cold and there was a smell of dank vegetation on the wind, but it was champagne after the stench of the railway carriage, the dog-smell of the hotel.

He did not try to speak to the SAS sentry, but each of them was aware of the other's presence.

Art smoked a black cheroot and brooded on the aluminium container. He was a good reporter. He thought there was at least an outside chance that Hitler's corpse was being trundled across the steppes. Rumours about it being in Moscow had been persistent in the mid-Nineties. There was logic in a half-burned body being flown out of the smouldering ruins of Berlin to Moscow, to a land where they had a grisly habit of freezing, stuffing, embalming their dead leaders, and a morbid love of secrecy.

But it was only an outside chance. A hundred to one, say.

It was more likely to be gold bullion in the container, or the last stack of negotiable currency in the Moscow State Bank, or diamonds – Russian diamonds. Russia produced nearly thirty per cent of the world's diamonds in Siberia, and there were Western interests who would happily kill to get hold of them and stop the bastards flooding them on to the world market.

There were people, Art knew, with clout enough to send in the SAS to stop that happening – to arrange a 'transfer' to some vaults in Lombard Street . . .

Or the wagon could contain something totally blood awful. Bacteriological warfare . . .? Everyone knew the Russians had maintained their programme, right through the Gobachev and the Yeltsin eras, in defiance of a dozen agreements with the Americans.

The wagon might contain phials of germs enough to wipe out the population of central Asia. Jesus, that could account for the refrigeration, he thought, picturing the thin delicate glass suspended in mercury. Dear God!

He jumped, his blood thudding in his ears.

On the other side of the track a dozen shadows had sprung to life, running and howling – wild dogs, in a pack, tearing down the railway line for no obvious reason, to no obvious destination.

The SAS man raised his weapon, but did not fire. Rounds were too scarce to waste.

FIVE

It was shortly after 02.00. Simon woke up when the door opened. Kate was standing holding a candle.

She said: 'How are you feeling?'

'Better.'

'A lot better?'

'A bit better.'

My room's full of cockroaches.'

'Pull your bed away from the wall.'

'I have,' she said. 'They've pulled it back twice. Can I come and sleep with you?'

She went into the shower. She yelled and cursed at the coldness of the water.

'It's your bloody soldiers,' she called. 'The moment it's a degree warmer than freezing, they're in there with their Givenchy for Men and their Donald Ducks.'

A moment later she shouted: 'Don't let anybody come in. A man came and peed in the sink in my bathroom earlier.'

He had been sleeping in his clothes. He took them off. If the hotel was suddenly attacked by Russian paras and he was found with his pants off in bed with a glamorous girl reporter, well, it would make a good story for the *Shropshire Evening Star*.

She appeared in the doorway, dripping wet. 'This is the second cold shower I've had. But I didn't have Finkel's shampoo the first time. He favours Marks and Spencer's *Fragrance of Honeysuckle*. Not normally my favourite, I'll confess, but better than nothing. I hope you're appreciative.'

He looked at her.

'Whenever you're not with me,' he said, 'I'm going to picture you just as you are now.'

She smiled. 'You'll enjoy that.'

She reached for one of the Hotel Ishim's paper-thin hand towels and patted herself dry. She slipped into bed next to him.

'Don't be sick,' she said. 'I couldn't bear it if you threw up. That would be the end. That would be the pits.'

He could smell her smell – Kate Delacroix with a background of flowery perfume.

He'd fought his way through a lot for this. He'd been through real pain. He was still going through real pain.

She had found his signal pad, lying on the pillow, and was trying to read it.

'What's this? Your last will and testament?'

'Intelligence. They want to know about economic conditions: morale of the civil population, level of support for the Reds . . .'

'Everybody hates the mafia. The saddest word in the Russian language is Perestroika. The saddest word, that is,' she added, recollecting, 'after *voyna*.'

She blew out her candle. The moon shone in through the dirty window. He put out his hand towards her under the covers.

'You're positively sure,' she murmured, 'that you're better?'

'Positive.'

'Well, that's Nurse Kate for you.'

Afterwards she snuggled her back against him. She slept immediately.

He felt her warmth, and soon slept himself.

Later – an hour later perhaps – he woke up, desperately thirsty, feeling sick again. The moon was still shining brightly through the window. She was lying on her back, breathing softly. Her left breast, creamy white with a brown nipple, was five centimetres away from his eyeball. Never, in future years, would he be able to see a vanilla ice-cream and a flake bar without feeling the twin urges of lust and nausea.

Later again, they both woke, startled by a thumping noise, quiet and sinister, from the wooden sidewalk that ran under the veranda of the hotel.

It was the sentry, trying to keep his feet warm.

She said suddenly, 'I really don't know why you've got so much faith in Kazakhstan.'

'Go to sleep, sweetheart.'

A pause, then she said, her voice amused and entranced: '*Nobody* ever calls *anybody* sweetheart.'

There was a knock. It was repeated with quiet insistence. Kate got up. Simon lay still, hoping to God he would not have to move. She lit the lamp and crossed the room and opened the door.

'Yes?'

'Sorry, ma'am.'

It was Henshaw, his voice horrified.

'What is it? He's feeling hellish,' said Kate.

'Sorry, ma'am,' repeated Henshaw.

Simon called: 'What is it, Henshaw?'

'Train coming, sir. Lieutenant Bulygin said to wake you.'

Simon got up. He told his legs to move, swung them over the side of the bed, sat up, his head spinning.

'You're stupid, you know that?' Kate told him.

'It's dehydration, that's all.'

Andrei appeared in the doorway behind Henshaw. 'Good morning,

I see you're feeling well again,' he said, coming in. His eyes were on Kate, who was wearing only Simon's parka and showing about five miles of leg.

'The train. It's from the East?' asked Simon, pulling on his trousers.

'Yes. Hello, Kate.'

'Hello,' said Kate.

Simon quickly walked over to the window and opened it. He could hear the train now. It was in the distance, the sound carrying over the empty vastness of the steppes.

'God it's cold,' said Kate, getting back into bed, shivering.

'Henshaw.'

'Sir?'

'Call Colour-Sergeant Gough.'

'Sir,' said Henshaw.

'Well, go on!'

'Yes, sir,' said Henshaw, tearing his eyes away from Kate, who had peeled of Simon's parka to reveal, for a split second, a tantalizing, perfect glimpse of bosom before she pulled the blankets up round her shoulders.

Henshaw went out of the room, calling, 'Colour-Sergeant Gough!'

Andrei said, courteously, to Kate: 'I am very sorry to disturb you.'

She said: 'That's all right, Andrei.'

'OK,' said Simon, putting his parka on. 'Let's go.'

Gough was already in the corridor.

'Train coming, Colour. Get the men stood to,' said Simon.

'Stand to! Stand to!' yelled Gough in a sudden frenzy.

They went down the concrete stairs and across the dark lobby, past the tourist display and the charts on the Siberian dairy industry.

Above them, through the thin ceiling, he could hear his men tumbling out of their beds. The two sentries, Lacy and Gates, were standing outside on the veranda.

They could now see the train pulling into the station, next to the Bukhara Express. There was a lot of shouting and yelling going on, and a Federal Guard was running out of the station towards the hotel, calling out urgently.

SIX

Bandits, the new arrivals said, has placed boulders on the line to stop their train. They had been armed with automatics, submachine-guns, AK47 Kalashnikov assault rifles (the MV version with a folding butt stock, Andrei told Simon bitterly, which were supposed to be reserved for the army's elite assault battalions). They had gone through the train and taken everything of value – money, clothes, food.

Four women had been raped, two men had been beaten up; but it had been good-humoured as such events go. Nobody had died, no carriages had been set alight, nobody's finger had been sliced off to liberate a gold wedding ring.

No one was talking yet about a Bosnia situation here, or a Kurdistan horror story. Just the two men with puffed eyes and broken lips and smashed ribs. A couple of dozen minor injuries from shards of glass, a few raped women in their underclothes, gabbling and moaning.

The doctor from the petrochemical works tended the injured. He came to the SAS compartment, pleading for sterile pads. Hoodless reluctantly handed over a few of them: there was precious little now left in the SAS first-aid kit.

On the platform Andrei was arguing with the mayor and the MVD police officers. The mayor waved his hands angrily, pointing at the train with its shattered windows, its distressed passengers. Andrei shouted back at him, pointing at his men.

Simon wondered what the row was all about.

Anna was standing listening, with a broad grin on her face. The women with their clothes torn were shouting and wailing at the MVD officers.

'Ho, ho, ho,' Anna chortled to herself quietly.

'Anna . . .' Simon called.

'Yes?' she said, nervously, a timid deer where he was concerned, as if still fearing that if she displeased him he would say: 'Right, Anna, you remain here.'

'Tell me what they're saying,'

Kate came from the hotel, lugging two plastic carrier bags: the personal possessions she had somehow managed to acquire in the last five days.

'We're off, then, are we?'

'As soon as we can.'

Anna said: 'The mayor wants the captain to kill the Chechens.

The captain says why did nobody find beds for his men last night and give them something to eat.'

'Ah,' said Kate. ' "It's Tommy this and Tommy that and Tommy wipe my arse, but it's good old Tommy Atkins when the guns begin to blarst." Here . . .'

She gave Simon a bread roll. He hesitated, then ate it ravenously, his first food, apart from poisoned potatoes and a cheese biscuit, in twenty-four hours.

Art Finkel came out of the hotel and down the platform.

'Hey ho, Finkel,' said Kate.

'Sod off,' said Finkel.

'Who said it was me? It didn't have to be me.'

'I'll bloody get you thrown out of the NUJ.' He climbed up into the Bukhara Express.

Andrei came over to Simon. 'OK, let's talk.'

They walked down the platform. In the east the sky was lightening.

Andrei said: 'You are not involved this time. This is my work – my job.'

'Why, what are you going to do?' said Simon, alarmed.

'Show you that my men are not arseholes, not the dregs of the bottle.'

'You don't need to show me anything. I lost my temper. I'm sorry about what I said.'

'No, it was a fucking disgrace. My men were a fucking disgrace.'

'Look, Andrei, you don't have to prove anything to me. Your job is to get the train safely to Kazakhstan, or to Tashkent.'

Andrei looked back down the train. Hoodless and Buck were in conversation. They always projected an air of menace, thought Simon irritably. They always seemed to have one eye looking around them. They always seemed on the point of grabbing a weapon and killing somebody.

'The train,' said Andrei, 'or the container from Perm?'

Simon said: 'Well, both.'

'I'm going to set a trap for the Chechens. You keep your men out of it, and keep your "Spetznaz" out of it. I'm giving you an order as train commander. Get your men aboard. We're leaving in five minutes.'

'Here we go again,' said Kate chattily, flopping down with her carrier bags.

Art was busy at his laptop, the early bird that catches the first edition.

Today in Siberia I saw a statistic turn into flesh and blood.

I saw a rape victim, a girl of seventeen, carried off a bombed-out train. The fourteenth train – for those interested in statistics – to be attacked and robbed in as many days. The HUNDREDTH rape victim in this terrified Siberian town since Kotelnikov's proclamation sent the old Red Army marching.

Tyumen is a town besieged.

A doctor – the only doctor in fifty miles – pleaded with me to tell the plight of the REAL Russia to the West.

Dr Seryozha Grachev said: 'We scream silently because nobody can hear. You are the only journalist who was not afraid to come into the heartlands of Russia. God bless you.'

Kate said: 'You're doing a story?'

'No, I'm writing my memoirs.'

'Listen, Art. I needed brandy for Simon, and we needed that food for Gallagher.'

'You only had to ask, flower.'

'You only had to offer!'

He read through his copy: *We scream silently because nobody can hear.* It reminded him of Pilger's stuff from Cambodia, back in the old days – only hadn't Pilger made his name with stories of piles of skulls and child prostitutes?

He went back through his copy, changing the age of the raped girl from seventeen to fourteen.

Perhaps he could compare the Khmer Rouge of Cambodia to the Cowboy Reds of Kazakhstan. It was many years now since he had dreamed of a press award . . . Journalist of the Year, Best Feature Writer, Best Foreign Correspondent. Now, hopes that had died flickered back to life.

Once wolves roamed the steppes, now there are wolves of a different kind.

I looked in the haunting face of that fourteen-year-old girl. I saw the terror in her eyes.

Kate said: 'We'll be over the border in Kazakhstan soon. Steak and chips and a pint of best.'

He did not reply.

'Shall I try and get some coffee?'

His fingers paused. He grunted; a signal she took to be a piggy expression of affirmation.

This is a land where murderers go unchallenged, where rapists walk tall.

Simon looked into the armoury, where Hoodless and Buck were cleaning their personal weapons. 'We're going after the Chechens. He's turning us into a Q-train.'

Hoodless pulled the oiled rag through his rifle and said: 'U-boats must be a bloody menace to Siberia.'

'We're keeping out of it.'

Hoodless nodded. 'We don't have enough ammo,' he said, 'to do otherwise.'

As the sun rose, the Bukhara Express crept out of Tyumen.

In his compartment near the back, Art drank coffee: his own coffee – he was bitterly aware – made with one of his very own Nescafé sachets. At least, he thought, looking out at a great and comforting emptiness, they would soon be across the border. Barring gunships, it seemed unlikely that anybody was going to get them between now and a late lunch.

Kate, still trying to be friendly, said: 'Art, what's a Q-train?'

'I don't know.'

'Oh, come on . . .'

'Q-ship – you mean a Q-ship. Q-ships were allied merchant ships in the First World War,' he said, still cold and aloof, 'fitted out with hidden guns. When the unsuspecting German submarines came on the surface, they sunk them. Why?'

The Federal Guards had four RPD light machine-guns and one RPG 7 – the standard-issue portable Russian short-range anti-tank weapon.

The troopers had their rifles.

Andrei positioned them in the coach that had been bombed out in Kuybyshev. They crouched on the floor, out of sight.

Simon was in the cab. The sickly smell of diesel made him feel queasy again. He opened a small side window, and was grateful for the draught of cold air.

'They probably won't touch us,' said Andrei, preparing himself in advance for disappointment. 'They're not going to attack every train.'

Two soldiers with binoculars watched the line ahead for obstructions.

'If they don't,' said Simon, 'we take the line south into Kazakhstan at Omsk, right?'

Andrei did not reply.

'Well, we can't cruise up and down this line for the next week, Andrei!'

'We take the line south at Omsk. I'd already decided that.'

Simon went back down the train. His own men had been moved to the rear two coaches, and told to keep their heads down.

He had made up his own Rules of Engagement. You do NOT shoot unless your opponent has a weapon and acts as if with intent to use it. You do NOT shoot a person committing an act of theft or assault, unless you are physically threatened.

The SAS soldiers listened, expressionless.

They passed the point where the westbound Trans-Siberian had been stopped.

The Bukhara Express slowed. The steppes on either side were empty. The train filed through a cutting.

All was quiet. The train rattled softly over the rails. Simon stood back in the shadows, scanning the low hills on either side.

He stiffened.

'Henshaw . . .'

'Got him, sir . . .'

Simon watched for a few moments, then slipped into Kate's compartment.

'Did you see?'

'What?' said Kate, peering out of the window.

'On the hill. A bloke on a horse.'

'A bloke on a horse?'

'You sound,' said Art sourly, 'like a music-hall routine.'

'A bloke on a horse,' said Kate again. 'How romantic.'

'Waving a submachine-gun,' said Simon. 'Stay where you are and keep your head down, unless you want to be shot.'

Kate said: 'I want only one thing in life. Just a two-man Betacam crew, a satellite transceiver, and a live insert into the One o'clock News as the bandits come charging over the hill on horseback, whooping in a colourful sort of way.'

'That's it, is it?' asked Simon.

'That and a powder-blue designer battleblouse.'

'Bloody television.' said Art.

Sitting on the compartment floor he was busy again at his laptop.

Today I escaped from Kotelnikov's bloodstained kingdom in a Q-train guarded by Royal Mercian Regiment soldiers and men of 22 SAS.

From the scorched wastes of Siberia we travelled east in a convoy with such enormous firepower that the bandits, the mafiosi, were too cowardly to attack us.

Responding to the urgent pleas of the civil authorities, we had diverted from our route south to Kazakhstan and were continuing on the Trans-Siberian towards Novosibirsk.

They watched us from the hills, and we watched them in return. We waited for them to attack us, but some sixth sense warned them that we were no ordinary Trans-Siberian express.

On a rise of ground, a man on a horse raised a rifle in a romantic, primitive but stirring acknowledgement that on this occasion we were too much for him and his gang of brigands—'

'Shit!'

The brakes squealed. Simon's radio buzzed.

Andrei's voice said, 'Obstruction—' Then the corridor window behind Simon shattered in splinters.

'Keep your heads down, both of you. Colour-Sar'nt!'

'Sir!'

Simon was gone. The train was slowing to a halt.

'Christ,' said Art, his head down.

'Art, look at that!'

'Keep your bloody head down. You heard what he said!'

'For shit's sake, look!'

He quickly looked. A four-wheel-drive jeep was bouncing along by the track. Men in the back were dressed in a mixture of army uniform and civilian gear: an officer's fur hat over a Pepsi-Cola sweatshirt; Afghan skin jackets. The train was stationary now. More men were jumping up from the side of the track – from the ditch.

A crash of automatic fire.

'Get down!'

The window shattered. Art fell back to the floor. Somebody was knocking the remaining glass of the window away with a rifle butt. Art was turning to crawl towards the door when a man came swinging in.

Kate yelled: 'Get Simon. Art get—'

The intruder's hand was at her throat, pulling her up, wrenching at her body. Art was trying to pull him off. The man turned and swiped viciously with his gun. Art fell over backwards. There was a shot so loud that for a second it stunned her mind. The man slumped on top of her. Blood gushed over her eyes, over her nose. She wanted to scream but did not dare open her mouth for fear it would fill with blood. She wriggled frantically, stretching her head to one side, away from the thick, pulsing liquid.

She saw Gates in the doorway, his rifle in his hand. Then Simon was there with him. She could hear Art yelling in rage about the fucking army always being fucking late.

She felt the man's hot blood begin to congeal on her face, and suddenly she opened her mouth and gave a long, terrible moan.

Simon was heaving the man's body off her. He was coming to help her. She put out her arms, but he was scrambling past, his gun raised.

Art and Gates helped her to her feet.

'Get her down!' shouted Simon.

As they pulled her back down to the floor there was a massive crack of noise, a sound that turned into a continuous roar, as the Federal Guards at last opened fire.

Simon wiped the blood from her eyes. He said: 'I'm sorry. I don't know why Andrei didn't fire sooner. I'm so sorry.'

'Go to Anna,' she said. 'Leave Gates here. Go to Anna.'

He nodded and was gone.

Art was sitting holding his head, which was bleeding. A lump was swelling on his forehead.

Gates crouched by the window.

'Art?' she said. 'You OK?'

He nodded.

'Watch the corridor for me, will you, ma'am,' said Gates. 'But it should be all right, Mace's at the far end. Bloody hell, look at that . . .'

She looked out.

A truck was on fire. The jeep was on its side, its engine still roaring. At first her eyes sent a message to her brain to say that the Chechens were lying down, lying on their backs or curled on their sides for a snooze or a sunbathe – which all seemed most curious.

If it hadn't been for the frenzy of noise from the jeep's engine, and the crack of bullets, and the oily smoke from the truck, it would have been quite a peaceful scene.

She climbed down from the train and sat on the grass. Art joined her. His face was puffed and red down the left side. One eye was almost closed. He had two miniatures of whisky. He gave her one, and she took it without speaking and drank, swilling the taste of blood from her mouth.

'I want to wash.'

She tried to stand, but she couldn't. 'I've got to wash. I've got to wash!'

'Later,' he said. 'In a minute.'

She was sobbing, fighting for breath, and then sobbing again. She rocked backwards and forwards.

Art put his arm round her.

'You can wash in a bit.'

'Oh God,' she moaned. 'Oh, dear God.'

Simon was walking wearily towards them, over the dead couch grass.

'Kate?'

He flopped down by her, took her hand.

Art said: 'She's a bit shaken up.'

Simon said: 'We'll be moving in a few minutes. I'll come for you. Stay here until I come back.'

Art nodded. 'I'll see she's all right.'

Simon got up and walked to the front of the train. Andrei was standing, a pistol in his hand, talking to his sergeant. He turned, a grin on his face.

Simon said: 'Why didn't you open fire?'

Andrei's grin disappeared.

'We did open fire. What are those?' He pointed to the dead men.

'You waited too long.'

'I'll be with you in a moment. OK?'

'Not really. No, it's not OK. Several of my people were nearly killed.'

'The second vehicle,' said Andrei, 'the truck. We had to wait until it was in range. Now you understand.'

'You waited too long.'

'I don't think so. It might have escaped.'

His expression now was sulky and angry.

Simon said: 'They'd have learned a lesson. They'd have learned to leave trains well alone. You didn't need to kill them all, for God's sake.'

There was a new sound, a sound from the sky, a steady droning. From the back of the train, Hoodless shouted: 'Helicopter!'

SAS men, who had watched the engagement between the Federals and the Chechens with lazy interest, were setting up the heavy machine-gun.

Simon said to Andrei: 'Not much point in us taking cover. We can't hide a bloody train. Let's get moving. Let's get out of here.'

Andrei said curtly: 'We'll go soon.'

'I think we ought to get moving now.'

'There's a problem with the train engine.'

'What?'

'A bullet has severed a fuel pipe. We are mending it. It's OK. Don't worry.'

Simon sat down, put his head in his hands.

When he looked up again, the helicopter was a silver speck in the sky, over to the west. It was unlikely that it had anything to do with them, or had even noticed them.

Andrei had walked over to where the Chechen prisoners, a dozen or so, were lying on their stomachs, their heads down in the grass. Two Federal Guards were pointing their semi-automatics down at them.

As Simon watched, wondering if they were going to bury the Chechens who had been killed, Andrei and the guards prodded the prisoners to their feet. They made them put their hands on their heads. Then they marched them away from the train, up a small rise and over the other side.

Simon realized what was happening, even before he heard the first of the shots. He jumped up and ran towards the rise.

More shots, then a burst of automatic fire.

He reached the top of the rise, gasping for breath, his head spinning from dehydration and lack of food. He shouted: 'Andrei!'

Two of the Chechens had tried to run. Their bodies were a few metres away from the others, which were lying neatly in a row, face-down.

Andrei looked up, his semi-automatic pistol in hand, his face expressionless.

Simon walked back down to the train. He told Art to get Kate back on board. He said to Hoodless: 'Do you realize what just happened?'

Hoodless nodded. His eyes were on the chopper, the silver speck glinting in the distance. 'Reconnaissance, looking for something. I wonder what, though.'

'Will we be implicated?' said Simon.

Hoodless said: 'They didn't use NATO ammo. We didn't see anything.'

'Christ almighty.'

Hoodless said: 'They were using three rounds, just like us. Two in the chest, one in the head. Mind you, we reckon that's for a potentially armed and moving target; that's for dealing with the buggers in South Armagh. It's a bit wasteful when they're lying in the fucking sand with their hands tied.'

Simon said: 'Get that machine-gun on the train. We're moving now.' He turned away.

Andrei and his two guards were coming back down from the rise.

Hoodless said: 'We'll have trouble with Ivan before we're finished. I have told you that.'

Simon said: 'My men have got forty rounds each. The Russians have got at least five thousand rounds per man.'

'It'll be down to the SAS then, won't it?'

* * *

In the armoury, Beddoes was fiddling with his television, which was showing scenes of fighting. He called to Anna: 'What are they saying, love?'

Anna came to the doorway and watched, then said: 'How should I know? You think I am Chinese?'

They were nearer to China than they were to Kuybyshev.

'They had a map a minute ago. It looked a bit like this part of the world.'

The Chinese narrator's voice suddenly gave way to a Russian voice: the original reporter on the newsfilm.

Anna said: '201 Motorized Rifle Division has crossed the border from Tajikistan to Kazakhstan, to support the Russian freedom fighters.'

'What Russian freedom fighters?'

'Against all the dirty Kazakhstanis.'

'Think I ought to tell the OC?'

Anna pondered, flattered to have her opinion asked.

'Yes,' she said judiciously, after a moment. 'I think you'd better.'

SEVEN

NATO Air Base, Ankara, morning of Sunday 24 March

Biggin and Littlehales were waiting to fly out of Ankara when they heard that Russian troops had crossed into Kazakhstan. All flights over Georgia, Armenia, Azerbaijan and Kazakhstan had been immediately suspended by the Turkish government.

'Where did they cross?' asked Biggin, his temper at breaking point.

'A 5k front 200k south from Petropavlovsk, sir.'

'201 Division – what's it got?'

'Don't know, sir,' said the transit section clerk.

'Well, bloody well find out!'

201 Division was Cossack in composition. It had a tank regiment as its striking force, and three motorized infantry regiments. It had a rocket battalion equipped with six launchers capable of firing chemical and tactical nuclear weapons distances up to one hundred and fifty kilometres. It had one hundred and fourteen T82 tanks, one hundred and fifty infantry combat vehicles, and two hundred and twenty one armoured personnel carriers, and it had thirteen thousand men.

NATO intelligence was confident that these numbers were correct. During the winter, 201 Division had been hired to an American television network for a drama series. Payment had been at the rate of ten dollars a day per vehicle, and one dollar plus food per soldier. Thirty nine thousand frozen location meals had been flown into Russia each day from Germany – said the TV company's PR department, proudly – and heated on location in microwave ovens. Not one single meal, claimed the PR unit, had been refused. In four weeks of filming, not a single bacon muffin breakfast or turkey dinner had been left uneaten.

'They're fighting fit,' said Biggin, 'and it was the bloody Yanks that did it.'

'There's something interesting from Rostov,' said Littlehales, who had been going through the intell summaries.

At midnight a crisis session of the Cossack parliament had been addressed by its senior ideologist.

'Like no other community, the Cossacks have preserved in themselves the gene of Russianness,' he had said; 'the psycho-physical potential of a great people whose genetic fund has otherwise been mercilessly destroyed. In the Cossacks the healthy part of the downtrodden Russian people has resisted its perdition, the abomination of desolation.'

American intell had issued a crisp summary: *Moscow is using the Cossacks to ethnic-cleanse the Kazakhs.*

At 13.00 Moscow television carried the story of a woman primary schoolteacher in Alma Ata who had been raped by Kazakh youths, had complained to the Kazakh police, and had been raped yet again by a police officer.

Street interviews in Arbat Street showed Muscovites calling for reprisals. (NATO intelligence scanned the newsvideo eagerly: they were the first television pictures from Moscow since the city had fallen, apart from those sent out by the French crew at the State University.)

On Tula TV there were pictures of a rally by Russian National Unity, the extreme right-wing organization that had been suppressed during the last months of the Democratic government. The speakers were calling for immediate military action against the criminals of Kazakhstan. The crowd replied with the neo-Nazi cry: *Slava Rossii!* – Glory to Russia.

At 14.00 a government statement on Radio Moscow said that all necessary steps would be taken to protect the lives of Russians living in the Kazakhstan capital.

At 14.30, Chinese television reported that the 14th Airborne Division was dropping paras on Alma Ata.

Biggin and Littlehales waited in the transit mess for permission to fly to the British Gas oilfield. Political pressure at the highest level was being exerted to get Turkish government clearance for their flight.

Outside, the sky was filled with American planes: helicopters flying in from the south, from Cyprus; Talon 2 transporters from the northern Med.

The helicopters were Blackhawks, infiltration aircraft equipped with terrain-following radar; and MH-46E Chinooks that could refuel in the air at night and carry vehicles deep behind enemy lines.

The Combat Talon 2s, a line of them – huge ungainly geese silhouetted against the afternoon sky – were modified Hercules planes that could be used to move troops or evacuate civilians. They were said to have enough electronic warfare equipment on board to penetrate the air defences of any country in the world.

It might have been coincidental that the two flights of aircraft arrived at the same time: the helicopters skimming in low and landing like a flock of birds; the Talons slowly wheeling and landing in succession.

Or it might, understandably, have been a deliberate display of American air power.

Biggin and Littlehales stood at the window and watched them land.

Their own RAF jet, tiny and old, seemed to be quietly hugging the wall of a hangar.

On their personal radio they heard a Foreign Office statement from London. The British Gas oilfield in northern Kazakhstan was being evacuated: twelve hundred EC nationals would be airlifted to Tashkent by American transport planes and helicopters.

'Now the Yanks are giving *us* turkey dinners,' said Biggin wearily.

They tried to speak to London, to find out what had happened to the NATO Euros and the Westland Hydra – still sitting, as far as they knew, at the British Gas airfield. Their call on the scramble-net was delayed.

They were still waiting when it was announced from Alma Ata that Kazakhstan had declared war on Russia.

EIGHT

Bukhara Express, Kazakhstan border, morning of Monday 25 March

Simon was travelling in the engine cab. His eyes stared fixedly through the window at the balls of spindlegrass blowing across the track.

The train had spent the night in a siding south of Omsk. They had seen television pictures of Russian paras entering Alma Ata. They had heard on the radio that the British Gas oilfield was being evacuated. They had heard the Kazakh president appeal to Iran and other Islamic Fundamentalist states to send help to his beleaguered country. The SAS fax machine had, unaccountably, sprung to life to produce a French intelligence report that five Iranian kilo-class submarines – highly sophisticated, diesel-powered, bought from Russia in the mid-Nineties – had moved from their base and were patrolling the entrance to the Gulf. A CIS cruise liner was believed to be a possible target.

Just before dawn the fax machine sent another message: a new rendezvous.

The Bukhara Express had moved at first light. The engine's fractured oilpipe had been repaired, but they dared not put on any speed.

They were on the 'cotton route', a single-line track that ran alongside the Kazakhstan border. The steppes were grey-white: undulating waves of stone, pools of sand. Simon's eyes kept closing.

Kate came in. She brought him tea. 'Elevenses,' she said. She sat by him, at the back of the cab. After a while she said: 'They're called barkhans.'

'What are?'

'The sand dunes.'

A pause. Then she quoted:

And day after day the barkhans were rolling
Like silent waves of a stilled sea.
There was only the shimmer of heat left in the world,
In the yellow and blue of the glassy expanse.

'Vladimir Lugovski, a Russian poet. When do you think the RAF will be able to pick us up?'

'I don't know. As soon as we're over the border.'

'I don't know where from. Not if the oilfield is being evacuated.

Where's the nearest NATO base to Kazakhstan? I've been trying to work it out. I don't think there is one nearer than Turkey. Can we overfly Iran?'

'I don't know.'

Nor did he care. Just let the steppes stay empty, let him not look up to see T82 battle tanks bucking over the dunes, armoured personnel carriers flanking the railtrack.

They were travelling south, slowly but steadily, towards their next RV. Let them just keep moving.

Kate said: 'Simon?'

He looked at her and was shocked. Her face was thin, her eyes dark smudges. Her parka was filthy and bloodstained.

He put out his hand. She took hold of it and held it tightly. Tears formed in her eyes.

'I'm sorry,' she said. 'Do you have dreams?'

He might have, if he slept.

She said: 'I had bloody awful dreams last night.'

'I'm not surprised. You'll be OK. Nobody's going to hurt you.'

'That man yesterday. I kept dreaming it, over and over.'

'Nobody,' he said, 'is going to hurt you again.'

'Promises, eh?'

'Believe me.'

She smiled. She gripped his hand tightly. He pulled her to him, put an arm round her. Her hair smelt sour.

'Titian,' he said. 'Isn't that what they call the colour of your hair?'

'No, mine's darker – the French say *Feuilles mortes*,' she said, her face buried in his shoulder.

Dead leaves. Perhaps one day they might go to Paris in the autumn, in which case he would find out if that was true.

She looked up. Her smile had gone. 'Simon, I don't think Para's going to make it.'

It was the first time she had used Gallagher's nickname. It sounded odd on her lips.

He said: 'Not much further to go. Even if the RAF can't pick us up, we only have to keep moving south.'

'I wish you'd go and rest.'

He shook his head. 'No, I'm all right.'

'None of us are all right.'

After a few minutes she moved away from him, got up and left the cab.

They crossed into Kazakhstan in the early afternoon. The border was marked by a wire fence and a sign by the track, put up in the early Nineties. It had the flag of the Kazakhstan Republic on it, but the paint was peeling.

The train had stopped.

'What is it?' asked Simon wearily.

'Water,' said a Russian soldier, also weary.

Simon looked at him. He had not known any of the Russians, apart from Andrei, spoke English.

This one was a *praporschik*, mid-thirties, intelligent-looking. What was he: GRU or KGB? Simon tried to remember what he had read in recent NATO intelligence briefing notes. GRU, the Russian military intelligence organization, was said to be the more effective of the two security organizations, and growing in power. After Yeltsin it had tightened its grip on industrial and technical espionage. It had not been compromised – unlike the KGB, its agents had not sold their secrets to the West. And its elitist military base had helped it to keep its structure intact.

But the KGB was wily and supple, sophisticated and corrupt. It was inevitable that it would have an agent on a train like this. The GRU would be for Kotelnikov. Which side were the KGB on? Their own side, of course, but otherwise who could say.

Perhaps the agent didn't think he needed to fool Simon any longer. Perhaps he was too tired to keep up his guard.

They took water from a reservoir by the track: a huge wooden tank. There was a smell of green water, dank and cold. A pump was worked; the water foamed out. The wind was from the north, and was cold and damp, but as he watched the gushing green water Simon fantasized about stripping off his clothes and standing under the jet, the bubbles bursting over his skin, washing away his tiredness.

'Why does a diesel need water?' he asked suddenly, but nobody replied.

Anna came through to the cab. 'Captain? Kate sent me,' she said nervously.

'Hello, Anna.'

'Come and rest, captain? Please come and lie down.'

The train sighed, rumbled, vibrated, moved forward.

'Cooling system, sir,' said Gull, the SAS corporal with the REME background, dully. 'Have to have water for the cooling system.'

The horizon was a thick grey pencil line.

Russia was so huge, he thought. It went on for ever, and they would go on forever with it.

There was a sign by the track. In English, Russian, and two languages Simon could not identify, it said: *May Peace Prevail On The Earth.*

They were in the old Soviet Union's nuclear testing zone. This land had absorbed more radiation than any other land in the world. Here, nearly five hundred nuclear bombs had been exploded; fifteen tests a year for nigh on forty years.

Somewhere just over the horizon must be the scientists' town of Kurchatov. Not far away, at Navada-Semipalatinsk, the Kazakhstan authorities had mounted a public display of malformed human foetuses, as an example of what the Russian conquerors had done to the Kazakh people. To the south, the Kazakh Tourist Board was trying to entice Westerners to go trout fishing in a lake created by nuclear explosion at the bottom of a ninety-metre concrete shaft.

The dunes of sand were gritty and grey as cement mix. The barkhans were dry as a bone, the soil sour. It was a bloody awful place.

Anna was still standing at the back of the cab.

'OK, Anna,' he said. 'I'll come and lie down for a bit.'

He sank blissfully down on the bunk. The blind was down, the light that filtered in was green, like the water from the tank by the track. He slept.

When he awoke he saw a sentry, Ferneyhough, in the corridor outside, looking in at him anxiously.

He fell back on to the bunk, closed his eyes, tried to look peaceful and content, so as not to worry poor Ferney.

Gallagher was running a fever; Hoodless and Anna could no longer ignore it, or put it down to a temporary setback. A yellow liquid was seeping from his stomach wound, it had a terrible smell. Gangrene, thought Hoodless; perhaps it was gangrene. Gallagher's eyes were bright, his skin hot to the touch.

Anna helped to change his bandages. Hoodless's fingers were deft. She was astonished at how gentle they were.

She looked hopelessly at the stinking bandages they had removed, wondering how she was going to wash them.

'You all right, Para?' Hoodless said, his voice expressionless.

Gallagher nodded but said nothing. He could no longer eat. They were feeding him on sugar and water, but he was finding it difficult even to drink.

'Bloody hell, Para,' said Buck, looking in on his mate, at his fellow member of Four Group gun team. 'You're the only one who's got any grub and you're too fucking idle to eat it.'

Gallagher said: 'Piss off,' but so faintly they could hardly hear him. His massive frame was shrinking, the skin of his arms lying in loose folds.

Out in the corridor, Hoodless swore foully but quietly. Anna leaned against the window, in a breeze that was full of sand and black grit from the diesel.

'It's no good,' she said. 'It's no good.' She was crying. 'If we find a hospital, I will stop with him.'

He said harshly: 'He's not stopping anywhere, and neither are you.'

He turned away.

'John?'

He walked down the corridor.

'Sir? Sir?'

Hoodless was looking down on him. Behind Hoodless, Kate appeared in the doorway.

'He's been asleep for only an hour.'

'I'm sorry about that.'

'For Christ's sake . . .'
'It's all right,' said Simon. 'I'm awake.'
'We're coming to a town. We need another doctor.'

It was little more than a village: a farm commune with blockhouses. There was not even a school. Around it were fields of crops in the desert, the 'Long Idle Lands' first ploughed in the Fifties. The nearest doctor was fifteen kilometres away. He was sent for.

They made a stretcher. They carried Gallagher out and propped him up. There was a field of spring wheat bisected by irrigation channels.

Anna held his hand. 'Is that comfortable? Are you all right?'

He nodded, smiled. He breathed quickly, short panting breaths; perhaps blood was flooding his lung again. The wind was on his stubbly, shrunken cheeks. His eyes were moist.

He said something. Hoodless bent down. Gallagher whispered: 'I should have took that insurance.'

An army pay corps sergeant visited Hereford every six months, urging life insurance on those of the SAS who did not have it.

'Not at those fucking premiums,' said Hoodless. 'Come on, sup up, for Christ's sake.'

Gallagher slowly tried to drink water and sugar. He could not swallow.

'This is it for me,' he said.

'Bloody rubbish,' said Talbot. 'There's a Yank military hospital in Tashkent. I'm fixing a through track, priority express.'

'Bugger that. Hereford,' said Gallagher.

'Hereford it is,' said Buck. 'You're on, chum.'

Hoodless looked down. Gallagher's eyes were focused on another world, as if he were seeking out his hidden enemy, the thing that would kill him.

Hoodless thought of Hereford: not of the hospital, but of the churchyard at St Martins, of the 22 Special Air Service Regiment plot, the rows of white headstones; the Falklands graves along the grey stone wall.

The doctor arrived in an old Toyota truck.

The infection was spreading inside Gallagher's stomach. Septicaemia. Para's groin was swollen, there were red trails across his skin, he was shivering and sweating by turn.

He moaned and then yelled as the bandages were pulled back.

The doctor, a Muslim, brown-faced and alert, said, shocked: 'You must get him into a hospital quickly.'

Simon went back to the train, to the armoury, and called Ankara. He spoke to the duty officer.

'We need a Casevac. Urgent.'

'What's happened?'

'Corporal Gallagher. His condition has deteriorated seriously. He must be lifted out now.'

A pause. The duty officer said: 'We pulled out of the oilfield this morning. The Euros have been taken away from us and redeployed. Your operation officers are en route to Tashkent. We'll speak to the Americans. Give me your NavStar position. Wait out.'

Simon could imagine the chaos. The British Gas field was huge; it was the biggest EC investment in Kazakhstan.

The duty officer came back. 'The nearest American helicopters are in Tashkent. They can't reach you yet. Proceed to the RV.'

Gallagher was sleeping, lying in the sun. They were gathered round him.

Andrei came walking down the track from the front of the train. His men had been buying early vegetables, using Simon's money: tiny courgettes grown under glass.

He shook his head slowly over Gallagher, and tried to look concerned and sympathetic. Simon knew he was wondering why so much fuss was being made over one man, why so much sentimentality was in the air.

Andrei said: 'We're going to get moving?'

Hoodless said: 'No.'

Andrei looked at Simon, then wandered off.

They sat in the warm spring sun and waited.

After ten minutes, Gallagher awoke. Again he gave a terrible cry of pain, then another. Kate put her hands over her ears.

'Christ almighty . . .'

Hoodless took up the remaining two syretes of morphine. He looked up at Simon.

Simon nodded.

Anna said: 'No, no you mustn't . . .'

Hoodless bent over Gallagher, carefully inserted the needle, and said gently: 'I don't know, Para. Intravenous bloody feeding.'

> White on a throne or guarded in a cave
> There lives a prophet who can understand
> Why men were born; but surely we are brave,
> Who take the Golden Road to Samarkand.

It was engraved on the SAS parade-ground clock at Hereford; it was painted on the SAS window in St Martin's church; it was carved in granite on the memorial wall to the Falklands dead.

The Bukhara Express was less than two days' journey from Samarkand.

Para, thought Hoodless, had almost made it.

NINE

They used the local signal box to clear a route forward.

They slipped from sidings to sidings, sometimes only managing twenty or thirty kilometres before having to stop and wait for a slow, lumbering freight train to pass.

Some of the freight trains had more than fifty wagons. 'They're the old four-bogie, eight-axle jobs,' said Talbot, creeping up behind Simon when he was off his guard. 'You wouldn't think it, but it gives them a payload of a hundred and eighteen tons, with an axle-load limit of twenty-two tons.'

Simon moved away. 'You won't see *that* except on the old SZD,' Talbot called after him.

Mostly, the line stretched ahead, straight as an arrow, though at some point before Ayaguz it had swung round so that they were now heading south-west.

In the early afternoon they tried to raise Alma Ata traffic control on the trackside phone, but the line was dead – which was a bad sign, because there was no way of avoiding the Alma Ata conurbation.

In mid-afternoon all rail traffic ceased, and that was a bad sign, too.

Shortly before dusk they came across a vast expanse of water. It was Lake Balkhash, said Andrei, though he spoke a little uncertainly.

The railway track ran alongside the shore. Ahead of them a column of smoke rose into the evening sky. As they drew closer, they saw that it came from a factory at the water's edge. Behind the factory a village straddled the dusty, unmetalled road to Alma Ata.

This was the RV.

A branch line forked away towards the south-east, towards the distant mountains. There was a small hill by the village, little more than a sand dune, but enough to command the country for a mile or so in every direction.

They crept under its lee, into the factory's own railway siding. They sent out clearance patrols and posted sentries. Gough went with Anna and the Russian cook general to barter for food.

Simon and Andrei were in the diner, sitting over a bottle of vodka. It was a wonder to Simon where the stuff kept coming from.

'How are we for diesel?' he asked.

'Half a day, perhaps.'
'We'll have to get hold of some, then.'
Andrei nodded. They pored over the map.
'Where do you think the fighting will be concentrated?'
'Fighting?'
'The war with Kazakhstan.'
'14th Airborne Division against the Kazakh MVD?' Andrei said, amused. 'My friend, the fighting will be over by now.'

Simon looked at the map. It didn't really matter, actually, whether the Euros came to lift them out or not. Another day and they would be in Uzbekistan. They would be safe then. A few hundred litres of diesel, a bit of luck getting round Alma Ata, and they would get there on their own.

That would make the sods at MoD sit up. Moscow to Tashkent in seven days, by the scenic route! Innes-Chator would have a job not saying 'Congratulations, bloody well done.' It would be some time before the cry 'Simon, will you get a *grip*' was heard in the land after this.

Andrei poured vodka.
'Cheers,' he said.
'Do you realize we're nearly there?' said Simon, thinking longingly about an army transit mess, threadbare and uncomfortable, a portrait of the Queen on the wall, a sign saying NO TREATING, a glass of cold beer he could sign a chitty for. 'Jesus, I don't believe it,' he said, drinking the vodka in one gulp. 'We're nearly home.'
'Cheers,' repeated Andrei, using his ironic voice again.

Art had been asleep when they halted. Now he awoke and peered through the window. He saw the emblem PPP on the side of the corrugated-iron factory walls, and thought what a small world it was.

His bottles of vegetables, or animal testicles, or whatever they were, stood on the small table by his bunk. By now all the bottles had been opened and most of the contents had been eaten. Those substances that remained swam around, appearing occasionally against the side of the jar, submarines cruising in their inky element.

During the previous night he had been overcome by hunger and had fished and nibbled. Kate had awakened as he crunched and sucked in the darkness, and had said: 'Whatever you're doing, Art, and I don't want to know, please stop it.'

After the Q-train incident they had moved to the compartment previously occupied by the Moscow Arts Lab film director and his two girls. Art now slept on the bunk where (he imagined in his tabloid fashion) the director had nightly had sex with Nina and Olga, one after the other.

He had tried not to think about it as he lay in the dark, his head throbbing, his damaged eye weeping, rolling pickled onions or bits of testicles round in his mouth.

He and Kate could each have moved to a separate compartment –

there was plenty of room on the train – but they felt uneasy when apart. Each liked to feel confident that the other hadn't secretly found a cardphone or a Reuters satellite TX station. They were, anyway, in a state of shock.

Kate had sobbed quietly in the darkness, when she thought that he was sleeping.

'PPP,' he said now, looking out of the window through his puffed and bloodshot eye.

'And what might that be?' she asked, lying on her back, staring up at the roof. 'Your masonic call sign?'

She spoke without aggression. They had been through too much.

'We're at the place,' he said, 'where they pack my pickled vegetables.'

She looked out. The factory stood by the water's edge. To north, east and south was sand and rock, to the west the grey muddy waters of the lake.

'You can see fields of vegetables, can you Art? Gherkins and onions? Cauliflowers and cucumbers?'

'No, but I can't see pigs either.'

The compartment smelled of sweat. Suddenly she couldn't bear it. She jumped up and tugged down the window, ignoring his cry of protest. She peered out. The air was cold and strangely pungent – a fishy smell, a smell she remembered from a day when she and Sam had walked along the beach at Lyme Regis, looking for dinosaur bones, and found instead a vast flat fish swarming with bluebottles, its belly white and rotting.

'Fishballs,' she said. 'Pickled fishballs. That's what you're eating.'

'I thought they had an interesting texture,' he said, sucking a bit from between his teeth. It was time to stretch his legs. 'I think I'll wander over there,' he said. 'Coming?'

They walked over to the factory. They entered through an open, broken door. A dozen or so women were slowly washing glass jars in water that was covered in blackish scum. They looked at Art and Kate but said nothing. In the next room was a huge, empty vat. Two men were swilling it out. There was yellow slime on the floors, and a terrible smell of fish and of fishy decay.

Art looked at the broken glass on the concrete, at the thick, congealed oil on the conveyor belt.

A man, a cigarette in his mouth, appeared in an office doorway and barked a question aggressively.

'Down, Rover,' said Art.

'Come on,' said Kate. 'We'd better go.'

'Tell him,' said Art, 'that we are European Community health inspectors and have come to see if his hygiene quality merits us awarding him a month's holiday in the Bahamas.'

'You silly sod . . .'

They went outside and walked along the shore. Kate guided him, because it was almost dark and his right eye was still puffed and watery.

'Your stomach must be made of iron,' said Kate. 'I'll say that for you.'

'When you've had my years of experience in foreign parts, flower . . .' he said bravely. 'When you've eaten some of the things I've had to eat . . .'

It was true. The cuisine in some so-called *international* hostelries was diabolical.

'Yes, Art.'

There was an ancient children's roundabout by the shore, its painted, brightly-coloured metal peeling, driftwood piled against it by the winter gales. She tried to make it go round, to jump on it, but it was corroded with salt and rust, and would not move.

'Oh, Art,' she said, 'what a terrible place. Who can have put this here? Do you think the village saved up for it? What can have happened to the children who played on it in the summer time . . . ?'

They had had so little, so very little, under communism, she thought, looking over the water with tears in her eyes (she was crying all the time now; anything set her off) but what little they had had was now gone. *Perestroika* and *democracy* – twin horsemen of the Russian apocalypse.

'I think my PPP vegetables came from somewhere else,' said Art, who had been thinking deeply. 'I think some PPP factories do veg, some do fishballs. There's a Novotel in Tashkent, did I tell you? I looked it up. It's got two hundred and thirty rooms and a Golden Road restaurant, and a swimming pool and steamroom. I think my eye will be better in the steamroom.'

'One more day, eh?'

'That's it, flower . . .'

She looked out over the lake. The light was fading in the west.

'Come on then, you old bugger . . .'

They went back to the train.

The sentry, Gates, who had been watching them playing on the shore, said: 'Password' and Art said: 'Fishballs, my son,' and Gates said: 'People who think it's fucking funny to make fucking jokes about the fucking password get fucking shot in the fucking crotch. Those were the first words, sir, the sar'nt-major ever said to me.'

As they reached the train, Simon and Andrei jumped down and ran out past them.

'Bloody hell, what's going on now?' said Art.

The two men were running up the side of the sand dune. They looked as if they had challenged each other to see who could get to the top first.

Lacy said: 'Coming up the road, sir. 500-half right-six o'clock.'

Simon threw himself down and looked through his binoculars. He pulled out his radio.

'Sunray to Alpha.'

'Alpha, Sunray.'
Hoodless was out beyond the village with a patrol.
'Tank – maybe more following, with infantry support. Get back now.'
It was a T62, old and rusty. The infantry at its heels looked like refugees, dressed in tatters.
But they were armed, and there were a lot of them, and the tank's muzzle was uncovered. Even as he watched, a BMP infantry combat vehicle appeared behind them on the unmetalled road.
He turned to Andrei. 'Well?'
'Kazakhs,' said Andrei. 'An MVD tank battalion.'
'How many men?'
'God knows. The entire regiment might be coming up behind.'
They would swarm like grey rats over the village, the factory, the railway sidings. Behind them, harrying them, enjoying themselves, would be a unit of the 14th Airborne Division, the paras who had dropped north of Alma Ata with their artillery, their tanks, their APCs.
Simon looked quickly towards the branch line that headed towards the mountains.
They had been told to RV at this junction. Were they supposed to take the branch line? Would that be the next order from Ankara – or whatever it was that 'Ankara' had moved itself to? The duty officer had said Tashkent, but it might be Calcutta by morning, he thought bitterly.
The branch line was their only hope – and the tank was approaching it.
He again pulled out his radio.
'Sunray to all units. Prepare to move out.'
Instantly he saw the patrol near the factory run back across the track. They left a rear-man to cover them, then stopped and took up positions to cover the rear-man's own escape. He felt a split second of pleasure that it was all being done properly – a sight less of a pig's arse than they usually managed on Lüneburg Heath.
He said to Andrei: 'We take the other line, right?'
Andrei was looking at the advancing Kazakhstanis.
'Andrei! We take the line to the mountains!'
'The tank will have us in range.'
'It doesn't mean they'll shoot.'
'Why shouldn't they shoot?'
'They're not expecting us. We're just a train. We'll be past, gone, before he's even thought of stopping us.'
'And if we're not? If he gets to the railway line first? You know what they'll do to Russian Federal Guards?'
'Christ, we haven't time to have a debate. A whole fucking army'll be down on us in ten minutes!'
'We can go back.'
'Back where?'
'Karaganda.'
Karaganda, the Russian city in the Kazakhstan desert: an outpost

of the Slavs, more than half a million of them working the coal mines that fuelled the metallurgical industries of the Urals. Karaganda would be supporting Kotelnikov; it would be the first objective of 201 Rifle Division.

His phone bleeped.

'Alpha to Sunray.'

'Yes?'

'All units are back at the train.'

'Roger.'

He turned to Andrei. 'No, we must go south. Your orders, my orders.'

The T62 was already turning round the edge of the lake.

Andrei said: 'You'd risk it?'

'I'd risk it.'

'It's what your NATO people say?'

'It's what *I* say!'

Andrei grinned. 'OK, let's go.'

They slithered back down the slope to the train. The diesel was already humming with life. Andrei ran forward to the engine cab, Simon to the rear. The train was already moving forward as they swung themselves aboard.

'Colour-Sar'nt!'

'Sir!'

'Post the men at the windows. Nobody fires until I say so. Corporal Pullin, Lacy, come with me. Mace, go and tell Miss Delacroix and her chum to lie low, and stay with them. Anna, go with him.'

In the armoury Hoodless and his men were taking the Carl Gustav 84-mm rifle out of its protective greased-paper packing. Jarvis was ripping the XM 203 Armalite from its cardboard transit box. Hind, his face smeared with green and black camouflage cream, his damaged hand still encased in bandages, was checking the ammo feed of his submachine-gun.

'OK, Corporal Pullin, Lacy . . .'

He gave them each a LAW: the British Army's one-shot, throwaway anti-tank weapon that could, with luck, disable a tank at one hundred and fifty metres.

'OK, everybody get in position.'

Now the train was in the open. It had left the protective screen of the factory. The track ahead ran round the side of the lake, alongside the unmetalled road towards Alma Ata.

Before them – halfway, perhaps, between them and the Kazakh tank – the branch line diverged: a hundred, perhaps one hundred and fifty metres away.

Peering out from the bombed-out coach, he could see the T62 in the deepening dusk, and the infantry tramping along behind it.

They were getting closer by the second.

Christ, the train was stopping!

He ran forward along the corridors, past the Russian Guards in the dining car. He saw an open door. Outside, by the track, ahead of the train, Talbot and Henshaw were wielding a sledgehammer.

'Can't clip the points, sir,' yelled Talbot.

Simon jumped down. His radio bleeped.

Hoodless said: 'I can't get them from this angle.'

'Wait out.'

Andrei had also jumped down. He was watching the Kazakhs through his binoculars. He said: 'Bastards! Where do you think they got that thing from? The Alma Ata museum?'

The T62 was perhaps two hundred metres away. It had seen the train now. The ragged soldiers in its wake were scattering into cover.

Clang!

It was Henshaw, bashing at the points.

A Kazakh soldier, an officer presumably, though he was wearing no recognizable uniform, moved forward and yelled.

'Andrei, what's he saying?'

'He's asking who we are.'

Clang

The Kazakh officer was shouting again.

'Now he's telling us not to try to move the train.'

Clang!

Henshaw brought down the hammer in a massive blow. Sparks flew.

Andrei said: 'You can deal with a T62?'

Simon said, honestly: 'I don't know.'

He tried to imagine what would happen if they tried and failed. He pictured what the high explosive charge of a T62 would do to the Bukhara Express.

He ran forward to where Henshaw was wielding the hammer. The points were thick with grease and rust.

'Look out!' shouted Andrei from behind him.

He looked up.

A section of Kazakh soldiers were kneeling, next to the tank, raising their weapons.

Clang!

'Quickly, Henshaw!'

Henshaw raised his hammer again.

From the Kazakhs an order rang out, then a shot cracked.

Henshaw dropped his hammer.

'Christ . . .' he yelped.

Simon stood up slowly and faced the Kazakh soldiers. He moved out in front of Henshaw. His chest was tight. He knew that a dozen angry, defeated, frustrated men, were drawing a bead on him, and any one of them might fire at any moment.

'We are NATO forces,' he shouted. 'We are NATO forces taking passage to Uzbeskistan.'

He was suddenly aware of birds, gulls of some kind, wheeling overhead, attracted by the unusual movement, looking for fish scraps.

'We are NATO forces,' he shouted again. 'We are British soldiers from Russia. We are in transit through Kazakhstan.'

Out of the corner of his eye he saw Mace jump down from the train, take the hammer, swing it back over his head.

Clang!

Simon moved forward, sensing the dozen rifles moving slightly, adjusting their aim.

The Kazakh officer was shouting now, but sounded doubtful. Simon stood his ground, suddenly confident that they would get away with it, that they would be allowed to disappear into the night. He yelled, his voice firm and confident: 'We are British troops. We are making our way to Alma Ata, and from there to Uzbekistan. Thank you for not trying to delay our journey—'

Clang!

'That's it!' yelled Mace.

The wheel screeched as it turned.

Suddenly a volley of rifle fire cracked out – not from the Kazakh troops but from the train, from behind him. Simon fell flat on the ground.

Andrei!

He just couldn't resist shooting the buggers.

Simon jumped up and ran back to the train, aware of rounds zapping into the ground at his feet and ricocheting against the metal of the engine.

He swung up, ran down the corridor, from coach to coach, passing Art, who was sitting on the lavatory floor with his back to the bulkhead. ('That's for aeroplanes, Art, *aeroplanes*!' Kate had shouted, but he reckoned it was still the safest place, down behind the pedestal, away from the flying glass.)

Hoodless had the anti-tank gun on his shoulder, aiming out of the window from the dark recess of the dining car galley. Buck was reading the bearings.

The train was moving forward, heading directly towards the tank.

'It must be a big temptation for him,' said Hoodless. 'Not often a tank gets to take out a train.'

Simon said: 'How often does a train take out a tank?'

'It'd be the first time in the history of the world.'

'Let's make history,' said Simon. 'Fire when you're ready.'

'Get out of the way, sir. Watch the back-blast.'

The Carl Gustav had a ferocious back-blast. On its stock was a printed red warning against firing in a confined space. To protect themselves, they had opened the carriage door on the side away from the Kazakh troops. The windows were all smashed. It was the best they could do.

Ferneyhough was passing round ear-protector sets. Their eardrums would burst without them.

'Engage.'

'Linking set.'

'Phasing.'

Simon could see the BMP now – and another tank, a T-72 by the size of it. Swarming along on either side came the infantry.

'Seventy metres,' said Buck.

'It's a question,' said Hoodless, 'of what to go for. The side of the turret is easier to penetrate, but it's a smaller target than the front.'

He was slowly pulling the handle forward.

'Go for the front,' said Simon, then shouted: 'Stand by with the LAWS. Aim for the fuel tanks.'

'Sir,' said Pullin.

They were at the points. Ahead the Kazakhs must be puzzled, wondering what the hell the train was doing, confident that it must stop before reaching the T62 that straddled the track.

Suddenly the Bukhara Express turned broadside on, like a three-decker yawing into the wind: they were over the points – and on to the branch line.

'Nearly on target,' said Hoodless.

'Colour-Sergeant!'

'Sir!'

'Get ready with phosphorus grenades.'

'Sir.'

'Ear-protectors on,' shouted Buck.

Simon pulled the pads down. He was enveloped in silence. He turned to look out of the window. He dimly heard Pullin cry: 'Watch his turret!'

The T62's turret was swinging, its massive gun was aiming straight at them.

He stared at it, his heart suddenly pounding and his ears singing.

'Fire!' yelled Buck.

The HEAT round spat. The back-blast signature was an explosion of white, burning air that sent him smashing back into the wall. Dimly he heard the LAWS fire. He got to his hands and knees, pulling off his ear-protectors, waiting for the deep crump of the T62's main gun – although had it fired, they would all have been dead before the sound reached the train. He staggered to the window. In the deepening dusk the tank was ablaze, black smoke leaping up from the turret, a cascade of liquid fire pouring down from its severed fuelpipe.

And now the train was swinging back towards the tank, slowly moving across its front as the branch line ran parallel for a short time with the Alma Ata line. They were a ship raking a disabled enemy, thought Simon exultantly, they were the *Victory* breaking the French line at Trafalgar—

'Grenades!' yelled Gough, and the crack of the grenade-throwers was followed by sheets of white phosphorus that flashed in the darkness, and thick yellow smoke that billowed over the burning T62.

Flames shot upwards. The sky darkened. In the sudden bright

light the Kazakh troops were revealed, crawling on the sand, caught like crabs in a beachbuggy's headlights.

The Federal guards poured fire down on them. A few Kazakh soldiers returned the fire, and the BMP's heavy machine-gun opened up, but firing wildly, and at too great a distance.

Then the train picked up speed, and the T62 was suddenly left behind them, and outside was only darkness and the desert. As Simon's eyes became accustomed to the night, he saw the stars reappear over the southern mountains, and felt the night air, cold and clean, on his face.

TEN

Tashkent, Uzbekistan, evening of Sunday 25 March

They had finally boarded a US AC-130H Spectre that climbed to forty-five thousand feet before it slipped, unseen, through Iranian airspace – and then dropped down over the Caspian Sea and into Uzbekistan as the sun was setting.

Tashkent in smog; the sun a huge, magnified red ball as it fell to the horizon. They drank Turkish coffee at the ambassador's residence, a villa in the suburbs. No time for a bath, they washed quickly, the ambassador's car waiting. In the floodlit, security-fenced garden, huge sprays of lilac scented the air. The ambassador had two young children and a Labrador called Bambi who ran round and round with a squeaky rubber bone.

The ambassador was going frantic trying to find emergency accommodation for twelve hundred EC oil-workers, most of them British, all of them his responsibility. 'God knows how long they'll be here for,' he said. 'You haven't any idea?'

They hadn't.

There were no civilian flights out of Tashkent. There was talk of a convoy south to Afghanistan, to Kabul, and then down over the Khyber, but that would mean flying in fuel for the lorries.

Now it was ten minutes to eleven, and they were in the US Army's newly-established advance airbase in the desert, 50k down the M34 motorway.

'If you'd like to come this way,' said a clerk, turning to go without waiting to see if they liked or not. Littlehales and Biggin followed him along the bare concrete passage. The soldier waved them through a door.

The man sitting behind the desk wore a khaki vest which only partially covered a chest of curly reddish hairs. 'Christ almighty,' he said, looking at them in stunned amazement. 'CHRIST ALL MIGHTEE.'

'Good evening, General,' said Littlehales politely.

'Major Biggin. Captain Littlehales. You are seriously telling me that you have misplaced more than twenty NATO soldiers on a train in Kazakhstan? You are seriously saying that you have LOST your boys some place east of Karaganda? Your Defence Department seriously thinks it can send me a fax and not only will I evacuate twelve hundred Brits from your oilfield, I'll also pull your *soldiers* out of the shit? You think you've come to China? You think I'm Aladdin and his magic fucking lamp?'

His eyes bulged. Littlehales waited to be told how American boys from the farms of the Middle West had saved England in 1916 and 1941.

'We haven't much time,' said Biggin, who didn't go in for fancy wordplay. 'The train's 200 k south of Ayaguz.'

'Ayaguz?' said the American incredulously, either because he could not believe they were serious, or because he had never heard of the place.

Biggin said: 'Can you get that far or not?'

'No way,' said the American promptly.

They spent the next two hours in a borrowed office with one telephone line. They did not have satellite comms to Cheltenham; they did not even have a secure means of communication (though presumably the Americans, who hadn't time to talk to them, were not bothering to listen to them talk to anybody else). In the Americans' communications centre they gratefully drank sweet, hot coffee and watched the output of a dozen television channels, from Armenia and Azerbaijan, and the crazy Chechen Republic, from Alma Ata and Kuybyshev, and from Arkhangel and Murmansk in the north.

Only the Baltic states, the Ukraine and Uzbekistan itself – a state so corrupt that the Americans had virtually bought it – were now considered safe from the xenophobic rage: the *Red Terror* as already it was being dubbed by the Western press.

In Yekaterinburg the mobsters had been lynched: horrific reports and photographs were slowly reaching the West. Elsewhere the mob were reinventing themselves into local Communist bosses – just as they had been in the good old days of Brezhnev and Gorbachev.

Overhead they heard the deep roar of the first transport planes leaving with fighter cover for the British Gas oilfield, for the US-Australian Bakyrchik goldfield, for Karaganda and Alma Ata.

At midnight they were back in the ambassador's garden. The house was in darkness; only the security lights shone, illuminating the lawns. They had been given a key, but were sitting in the garden, warm in their parkas, savouring the scent of lilac on the night air. Frogs croaked in a lilypond.

Littlehales murmured:

' "Turn to me in the darkness,
Asia with your cool
Gardens beyond the desert,
Your clear, frog-haunted pool . . ." '

' "There's a boy across the river with a bottom like a peach," ' said Biggin, not to be outdone in the literary stakes. 'They'll have to send 24 Airmobile Brigade.'

'It's committed to at least two places already. So's the Light Infantry, so are the Royal Anglicans. We haven't any other helicopter attack forces, have we?'

'No.'

That was the trouble. The Russians and Americans had air *divisions*. The British had a brigade. *One* brigade. It could be absorbed into an American air division and form only such a small part of it that nobody would notice it was there. They shouldn't really have sent the SAS adventuring further than Eastbourne, not if they were relying on British airpower to protect them.

But Tashkent!

Persia lay to the south, Afghanistan to the east, and beyond Afghanistan lay the Indian subcontinent. They were back on the old imperial stamping ground, back in the land of the Great Game, in that part of the world where England had always counted for something.

Littlehales sighed for what was gone, and would not return. He said: 'The French?'

'Do you seriously believe the director of JIC is going to ask the Prime Minister to ask the *French*?'

Littlehales threw the rubber bone for the dog Bambi.

'Don't do that. You'll waken the whole bloody place up,' said Biggin irritably.

Squeak, squeak, went the bone, as Bambi ran round in the darkness.

Littlehales said: 'I don't know a lot about your set-up. I don't really know how important this all is.'

Biggin said nothing. He was the SIS representative on the Central Europe standing group of the Joint Intelligence Committee. *Catchphrase* had been his responsibility, his baby, right from the start, long before Langdon and the SAS had been brought in.

'At least they're out of harm's way,' said Littlehales. 'At least they've managed not to attract attention to themselves. They're well armed. They seem, somehow, to be able to slip about without causing trouble.'

'And they haven't blown anything up recently,' said Biggin. 'Not that we know of.'

A window opened. The ambassador, trying not to sound irritated, called: 'Are you there? I've got London on the line.'

Squeak, squeak went Bambi's rubber bone.

ELEVEN

Bukhara Express, the Gates of Dzungaria, night of Monday 25 March

The train had stopped.

'What's wrong now?' said Simon, half dozing at the back of the engine cab.

Andrei said: 'The engine.'

'Christ, we're not out of diesel?'

'No.'

The electric light in the cab faded to a dull glow. Before it died he saw an odd, irritated look on Andrei's face. Behind him the KGB man was smiling nervously.

Gull and the Russian engineer climbed down from the cab and again set about repairing the damaged oil pipe, working by a dim torch. They had developed a language of their own by now, a mixed English and Russian vocabulary.

Andrei and Simon climbed down and stood by the track.

Their eyes became accustomed to the darkness. They were by another lake, this one smaller than Lake Balkhash, surrounded by pine trees. There was a village somewhere close by – dogs were barking but no lights were visible. They were in a part of the world where folk went to bed at dusk and rose at dawn.

The train had been climbing for some three hours. All around them were mountains, black silhouettes leaning down broodingly over them. They were in a narrow valley. The air was fresh and clean, smelling of snow.

'I think we'll stay here until morning,' said Andrei casually. 'OK with you?'

'Sounds a good idea,' said Simon, equally casual.

He spoke to Gull. Then he went back to the armoury. He woke up Beddoes and told him to call Ankara. He went next-door and found Hoodless asleep, cuddling Anna. Her eyes opened, black and bright as a bird's in the torchlight. His massive arms round her, Hoodless snored.

Simon said: 'John, wake up,' and was pleased at the way Hoodless started in confusion. He was keeping his *grip* better than the SAS these days.

Beddoes called: 'Ankara, sir.'

It was the duty officer. Simon asked for his operations officer. The duty man said: 'Not available. Have you a problem?'

'Not apart from being stuck up the arsehole of Asia with a battalion of Kazakhstan MVD trying to kill me. What happened to my signal of 23.30?'

'It's been passed on. What are you requesting?'

A hot bath. Kate Delacroix, naked, bringing him a pint of Bass in a silver tankard . . .

'A hot bath,' he said. 'Kate Delacroix, naked, bringing me a pint of Bass in a silver tankard.'

Silence.

'Nothing, Ankara,' he said. 'We are stopped for the night. This is our position.'

The duty officer took their position.

Hoodless appeared in the doorway.

Simon said: 'Gull doesn't think we had to stop the train. I think the Russians decided to stop, but I don't know why. Beddoes?'

'Sir—'

'I want to know of any other HF transmissions from this location.'

'But there's only this set, sir, and the one we brought with us—'

'You don't know that. Don't argue.'

'I told you,' said Hoodless, 'we'd have trouble with the Russians.'

'Yes, all right,' said Simon. 'Has anybody checked up on the bloody news?'

They picked up a satellite transmitting from south of the Hindu Kush. There were pictures of a march through Red Square. Old Communists (the sort they said would never die, and clearly never had) were waving red flags. Then there were pictures of Moscow State University, with students supposedly welcoming the tanks of Second Shock Army. The barricades had been taken down, said the commentator, after the successful assault by MVD security police and the arrest of criminal elements.

'Now for you nightbirds,' said the Singapore continuity girl, 'The movie that made Michael Caine a star: the historical epic *Zulu*.'

'You know, I must have seen that film twenty times,' said Hoodless.

'Don't all the Zulus get slaughtered, Sar'nt?' asked Beddoes.

'Not all,' said Hoodless, 'but a good number.'

'Bloody hell,' said Simon, looking out of the window.

The Russian soldiers had been gathering brushwood from the lake shore. They were lighting fires by the track.

Hoodless cursed.

'It doesn't matter,' said Simon. 'If the Kazakhs are coming after us, they only have to follow the railway. They can't be here before morning.'

'It's not just Kazakhstan militia, is it?' said Hoodless. 'You don't know what sort of buggers are about.'

Soon the buggers came out of the darkness, drawn by the light of the fire: curious villagers, roused from their beds. They offered goods for sale. Cooked rice, flat leathery bread, *Red Star* bubblegum that must have been in stock for a decade or more.

Beer – *kaas*, light and frothy – was brought in a bucket.

The men from the village had been fishing. They offered tiny, silvery fish called *sodak*, and Gough was able to buy a basketful.

Simon threw out a screen of sentries, then the Royal Mercians built their own fire. They impaled the fish on twigs and cooked them like kebabs.

The wind rose. Sparks spiralled upwards. One of the Russians started to play a mouth organ. Other soldiers round him began to sing: Red Army songs, songs of the Great Patriotic War, songs from Afghanistan. Some of the soldiers started to hit sticks against each other, creating a rythmic, military beat.

Hoodless said: 'I don't think we ought to let that lot see what's on the television.'

'What?' said Simon. 'Keep *Zulu* to yourself?'

'I'm not joking.'

'I wasn't planning to ask them all in for beer and crisps.'

They were standing away from the fire, in the dark shadow of the train. A figure approached from the fireside. It was Art, who said: 'Where are we?'

'I don't know,' said Simon.

Art stared at him. 'Well these mountains, what are they? The Pyrenees, the Atlas Mountains, the Appalachians? I don't want you to think I'm losing confidence. I'm not one to interfere. Have I interfered?'

'No,' admitted Simon.

'I haven't said a word. Not even when I was being shot at. But where are we? It's not unreasonable to ask where we are.'

'The extent of Andrei's map,' said Simon, 'was 25k east of the main Alma Ata rail line.'

'You don't know where we are – not at all? Oh, bloody hell . . .'

Kate and Anna were muttering conspiratorially by the fire. As Simon approached he heard Kate say incredulously: 'Ten thousand coupons for a Jap coil?' and Anna reply: 'Yea, and if it's not Jap, forget it.'

'That journalist friend of yours,' he said, 'is half pissed. How are you, Anna?'

'Fine, captain,' said Anna, as nervous as always.

'Poor old Finkel,' said Kate. 'Weak beer and the last of the cream liqueurs.'

From the village, dogs howled.

' "The dogs bark, the caravans pass . . ." ' said Kate. 'Can I kebab you a fish?'

On the other side of the fire, British soldiers started singing to rival the Russians – the Royal Mercian squaddies' anthem, sung to the tune of *Lili Marlene*, heard wherever the regiment had served since the Western Desert in 1942:

Early in the morning,
Company's on parade,
Sergeant-Major's whistling the Donkey Serenade.
Some silly bastard shouts 'Right dress!'
You should have seen the fucking mess.
We are the Royal Mercians
We are a fucking shower . . .

Anna passed him a piece of bread and a fish. 'Captain . . .'

'Oi, that was my fish,' complained Mace from the other side of the fire.

'Tough titty, Mace,' said Simon.

'Yea, tough titty, Mace,' said Anna.

'Officers' perks,' called Mace, not without humour, enjoying chancing his luck.

Simon sat down between Kate and Anna.

After a minute Anna said, uneasily: 'Well, I'll leave you guys,' and moved away.

'She's always doing that,' said Simon.

'She thinks you're going to talk about Intourist. You know she's a tart. Why do you keep embarrassing her?'

'I was trying,' said Simon, his feelings injured, 'not to hurt her feelings by letting her know that I didn't believe her.'

Kate thought about this. 'Men,' she sighed.

'I don't think Sar'nt Hoodless would like her being called a tart. I think he might start breaking kneecaps. I think he and Anna are—'

'Everybody else,' said Kate, leaning against him, 'has known about John and Anna for *days*.'

'Oh,' said Simon. Then: 'If you're so clever, what are your Russian chums up to?'

'*My* Russian chums?' she said, looking round at him, startled. 'What do you mean?'

'Well you're the Forces Favourite. Did they ever mention having a radio transmitter? Not that it matters. Somebody's going to have to airlift us out, and I'm past caring who.'

Art wandered past and saw them, their faces close together in the firelight. He thought how young they looked, just kids really. The Benedick and Beatrice – he told himself, sentimental on *kaas* and liqueurs – of the Bukhara Express.

Sar'nt Hoodless wasn't a kid, or sentimental. He was at the end of the train, standing guard over the refrigerated wagon.

'I don't suppose you know what's in this thing?' said Art, approaching him, finally abandoning subtlety and cunning.

'Something as'll make your ears pop, sir,' said Hoodless.

'Oh yes?' said Art, not appreciating that he had just been given a succinct and fairly accurate description of the wagon's contents. 'Not Hitler's body then?'

'Can I talk to you?'

Andrei had appeared abruptly by the Royal Mercians' fire.

Kate sat up, moving away from Simon, and said: 'Hi, come and sit down. Warm your toes.'

Simon said: 'Yes, come and sit down. Have a fish.'

Andrei looked at Kate.

'Well, I'm not moving,' she said. 'This is my bit of fire. You two can go somewhere else.'

They climbed a grass bank behind the railway line, up through the pines.

Andrei said: 'The wagon from Perm.'

'Is that where it's from?'

'Number 12 Soviet Hero rocket assembly.'

'Christ,' said Simon, startled. 'Don't tell me it's an armed ICBM.'

'You are so short of H-bombs you need to send English "Spetznaz" to steal them? Listen, today the West can buy a Russian H-bomb for five thousand dollars.'

They stopped and looked down. Below them was the dark train, the camp with its two fires, its two groups of men.

'So what is it?'

'You don't know? You *genuinely* don't know?'

'Of course I don't know! But whatever it is, it goes to Tashkent.'

Andrei said nothing.

'They're *your* orders too, Andrei.'

'Things are changing,' said Andrei.

Simon said: 'All right, tell me. Tell me what's in the container.'

Andrei looked at him. 'You have heard the joke about our *praporshchiks*?'

'Oh Christ . . .'

'*Praps*? You know *praps*? What do you call them in your army – the people who thieve everything they can lay their hands on?'

'Colour-Sergeants,' said Simon.

'OK, Colour-Sergeants. There's this story from way back, from Yeltsin's time. President Bush sent Yeltsin a present – a neutron bomb that killed people but left property untouched. In return Yeltsin sent Bush a *praporshchik* – a guy who ignored people but lifted every bit of property he could get hold of.'

'Andrei, what's in the wagon?'

'An air fuel explosive device,' said Andrei, 'known as *Chernobog*.'

They could hear the Russian Guards singing:

> *Slava Rossii. Slava Rossii!!!*
> Glory to Russia. Arise, Oh Fatherland!

And the Royal Mercians:

> Singing balls to your partner, arse against the wall,
> If you've never been fucked on a Saturday Night,
> you'll never be fucked at all . . .

TWELVE

Simon said: 'Get me Ankara.'

'Sir,' said Beddoes, plugging in the batteries.

The duty man, his voice dull with weariness, said: 'You are being patched through to your operations officer.'

Simon sat down, then got straight up again and swung out of the compartment. He jumped down from the train. Hoodless and Buck stood in the shadows.

'*Chernobog*,' he said. 'Did you know?'

Hoodless nodded in the gloom.

'Air Fuel Explosive,' said Simon. 'Right?'

Hoodless nodded again. 'Take out Dudley in fifteen seconds according to the boss. Every man, woman and child.'

'Dogs and cats,' said Buck. 'Elephants in the zoo. I don't know about the killer whale, not if she kept her head under water.'

'It dematerializes water,' said Hoodless.

Beddoes was calling to him. He went back, swinging himself up into the carriage, possessed of a sudden energy.

Littlehales also sounded weary: 'Don't try to pass through Alma Ata. We're trying to find a way round for you.'

'*Chernobog*. I didn't know.'

'It doesn't make any difference.'

'Christ, it makes a difference!'

'You might have to go back to Kulunda. We're trying to find a route that avoids the war.'

'No can do.'

'Explain.'

'There's an enemy force, battalion strength, sitting on my backside. We're halfway up a line into the mountains. Did you get my signal at 23.30?'

'No.'

'Christ almighty!'

'You have to understand, it's chaos. We've only got a five-man team in Ankara, and the ambassador's wife is taking messages in Tashkent. Give me your NavStar reading.'

Simon gave it.

Littlehales said, startled: 'Repeat, please.'

Simon did.

Littlehales said: 'You are on the line that takes you through the Dzungarion Gates.'

'Can you send me a map?'

Pause. 'A *what*?'
'A map,' repeated Simon distinctly.
'Yes, we can send you a map.'
'Shouldn't we have come on this line?'
'No, you're all right. It was the fall-back option. We're still clearing it at a high level.'
This made no sense.
'The Air Fuel Explosive. Is it dangerous?'
'Not while it's sitting in a railway container. Don't interfere with it without NBC suits. In fact, don't interfere with it at all. Where did the MVD troops come from?'
'Alma Ata, we think. We took out a T62 with a Carl Gustav.'
A pause. 'Repeat.'
Simon did. He added: 'We assume they're behind us in battalion strength. Do we move forward?'
'Not till you have clearance. What's your immediate situation?'
Simon said: 'We are halfway up a mountain in a train that has an oilpipe fracture, we have perhaps three litres of diesel left, the Russian guards are going to declare for Kotelnikov at any moment, there's a battalion of Kazakh MVD a few kilometres behind us, the only map we've got is from Private Ferneyhough's *Racing World* pocket diary, and this bit of Asia is on the crease in the middle of the page.'
'I'm closing this line,' said Littlehales. 'It's been open for too long. Wait out.'
Simon leaned back in the seat. Beddoes said: 'Bit of a bugger by the sound of things, sir.'
Five minutes later the fax bleeped.
A map came through.
The lake that gleamed beside them was called Ala Kul, the mountains looming ahead the Ala Tau. One kilometre further up the mountain was a pass: the Dzungarian Gates.
Beyond that lay the People's Republic of China.

Simon went outside again. The fires were dying down. British soldiers were settling round the embers in their dossbags, evidently preferring to sleep in the open than in the railway carriages. He found Kate and said: 'Come with me.'
'What?'
'Well, come on!'
They walked down to the lake. By the shore, where they could not be overheard, he told her about the container from Perm.
'It's way outside the ban, the nuclear ban, the chemical ban, the biological warfare ban. It doesn't use anything proscribed and anyway they can't ban it, as nobody's prepared to admit it exists. It's based on stuff like alcohol and gasoline, mixed with special compounds. It doesn't even use napalm. It's not even new – it's been going since Afghanistan. That was when the Reds first tried it. The Americans had a go in the Gulf. Reports I saw said it didn't work terribly well, although a lot of allied troops are still suffering funny symptoms that

nobody can account for, so God knows what it did to the Iraqis.

'In theory it's got everything going for it. It's green, you see: environmentally friendly. It ought to have a Friends of the Earth approval sticker. You can walk in there sixty seconds afterwards and collect up the bodies. And it's big – it can take out a town the size of Dudley.'

'Dudley?' said Kate. '*Dudley?*'

'The first versions, the Afghanistan versions, were crude. Somebody sprayed a petrol mix out of the back of a plane, and then ignited it. That produced a fireball of sorts by sucking the oxygen out of the atmosphere, and if the spray stretched to the ground, it incinerated up the odd village—'

'Don't,' said Kate. 'What did you say it was called?'

'AFE. Air Fuel Explosive. The Russians call it *Chernobog*.'

'The Slavonic god of evil. Why are you telling me all this?'

'I'd have thought it would be right up your street. Don't you want to make a television programme about it?'

'Simon,' she said, 'you're off your head. You're not thinking straight. Your priorities are getting muddled. How are we going to get out of here?'

After a moment he shook his head, then walked away, back towards he train.

Andrei was sitting by the guards' fire. She walked over to him, sat down, leaned over, staring into the flames. Someone passed her a bottle of vodka. She shook her head.

'Drink,' said Andrei.

She sighed and drank, tipping her head back: just like a bag woman, she thought, with a bottle of meths.

'Cheers,' she said.

Andrei motioned gently towards the train – to the front, to the Russian's sleeping coach. He smiled at her sexily.

'No,' she said incredulously. 'Certainly not.'

The Russian soldiers round the fire were singing a different song now, a slow, sad song of the steppes, about the Virgin Lands, of the pioneers who came east from the cities to plough the soil. Outside the circle of the fire she could see eyes in the darkness: children of the village, with round moonlike faces.

'No!' she said as Andrei took her arm to lift her. 'Get off!'

He let go. He said: 'I want to talk to you.'

'No, Andrei,' she said. 'Unbelievable though it seems, at this moment of crisis in all our lives, you want to screw me.'

He said: 'Listen. You know the joke about the presidential phone calls?'

'I hate jokes. I hate riddles.'

'Listen.'

She swallowed more vodka and closed her eyes.

'One day Brezhnev phoned Reagan. "I had a dream last night," he said. "I dreamt I saw the White House covered in red banners."

'Next day Reagan phoned Moscow. He said to President Brezhnev: "Now I also have had a dream. I dreamt I saw the Kremlin covered in red banners."

'Brezhnev was puzzled. 'So what's so special about red banners on the Kremlin?" he asked. "We always have red banners on the Kremlin. What did the banners say?" Do you know what Reagan replied?'

'No,' said Kate.

'He said: "I couldn't read them, President Brezhnev. They were written in Chinese." '

Kate said: 'OK, so Russia doesn't trust China.'

'It is so easy to *say*. You don't understand.'

'No.' After a moment she said: 'Are we moving again soon?'

Andrei said: 'I don't think so.'

'Well, I'm going to bed. It's all too much for me. If I don't get some sleep soon, I shall die.'

'I hope you didn't go antagonizing him,' said Art nervously.

'Antagonizing him?'

'There's no point in making him mad.'

'OK, Art, you sleep with him. He's stomping up and down out there. He's not going anywhere. He's past being fussy.'

Art looked out. Andrei was a silhouette against the fire, a menacing figure. He had the look of a coiled spring.

'There's an old saw,' he said, 'that's very true, in my experience.'

'An old what? An old *what*?'

' "It's as well to be off wi' the old love—" '

'Oh dear God . . .'

' "Before ye be on wi' the new. Och aye." '

'There's no och aye on it. Piss off.'

'I'm bloody fed up with this,' said Art miserably, the side of his head still puffy and raw, his eye still weeping. 'I've had enough. It's time to go home.'

It was three o'clock in the morning. He was shattered. He curled up on his bunk and closed his eyes.

Later, lying in the dark, he said: 'The container wagon. They're peddling the story that it's some sort of ear-popping machine, but we won't waste our time believing that one.'

'No Art,' she said.

When the door opened he was dreaming about Lytham St Annes. There was sunshine, and the smell of mud and ozone. There were land yachters on the sands, sea pinks and cockleshells in the gardens, and there was Kate, lying on a towel, topless.

He heard a voice say, 'Can you come and talk?' and drowsily heard Kate say, 'OK. Wait a minute.'

Soon he was dreaming of the old *Guardian* newsroom in Manchester, with its huge oak bookcase hiding the cubbyhole of the news editor. It had been a gentlemanly sort of place in the Sixties, full of old lags who growled sexily over *Daily Mirror* pictures of bimbettes ('totties' the poor hacks called them) in miniskirts.

'Bacup is the mecca of black pudding manufacture' he had written in his first ever story. The assistant news editor had told him that 'the mecca of' was a phrase outlawed by the *Guardian* style-book because it was sloppy and overused.

Funnily enough, he had never used the phrase again, not even on the *Sun* where they wouldn't know a style-book if it came with a 44-inch bust and the biggest nipples east of Everest.

Somebody was shaking him.

'What the hell—'

It was a British soldier. Henshaw.

'The OC sends his complements,' said Henshaw, still shaking him brutally, 'and can he have a word?'

THIRTEEN

Tashkent and Moscow, early hours of 26 March

'OK, so you were bringing out an AFE,' said the American general. 'I've had Langley on the line. I've had the Pentagon on the line. I've had my good friend General Hoepner on the line. I'm still getting faxes from MoD, London. Somebody at MoD keeps telling me about Greek Fire. I'm an ignorant Air Force slob, tell me what your understanding of Greek Fire is?'

Littlehales said: 'In the last days of the Roman Empire the Byzantines perfected a ship-borne flame thrower. The fuel is assumed to have been oil mixed with some kind of alcohol and saltpetre. At any rate it was like napalm: it clung to everything it touched and instantly set fire to anything organic – ship's hull, rigging, sailors' bodies. It was the AFE of its day, and was used to terrible effect on the Muslim fleet trying to capture Constantinople in 678 and again in—'

'OK, so what happened?'

'The Byzantines used the Coca-Cola system of security. They mixed and bottled the concentrated liquid *only* at their HQ. It was the most closely guarded secret in the empire. Only one family was permitted to know how to mix the fuel – the incredients, the proportions.'

'Don't tell me . . .'

'The family died – we don't know why. An epidemic of some sort, perhaps. The secret of Greek Fire was lost. The Byzantine empire fell' – Littlehales was aware that he was telescoping the development of western civilization somewhat – 'the Muslims triumphed, Christendom was defeated.'

'You're saying the man who devised the Russian Air Fuel Explosive has died?'

'We are saying,' said Biggin, 'that the prototype Air Fuel Explosive machine now attached to the Bukhara Express is a one-off. It is super-efficient, nobody knows why. Four prototypes were made. This machine, this *one* machine is at least five times more effective than any of the others.'

'That's what your Russian friends told you?'

'Yes.'

'When they were doing a deal to save their skins?'

'There was evidence that the claims were valid.'

'There was evidence that the claims were valid . . .' repeated the general, faintly bemused. 'So you were bringing it out?'

'Yes.'

'Why you? Why the British?'

'I suppose,' said Biggin, 'it was because SIS did the deal.'

'SIS?'

'MI6.'

'OK, James Bond did the deal. You thought you'd go it alone?'

'Yes,' said Biggin wearily. 'I suppose we did.'

'Well, I don't know,' said the general delicately. 'I don't know that we ought to panic. Langley isn't panicking. The US's own AFE might be more advanced than "MI6" thinks. You believe that might be possible? You think James Bond might be out of date on this one?'

'I wouldn't know,' said Biggin.

'There's talk of Kotelnikov being not unreasonable. *A man we can do business with*, as Mrs Thatcher once said. You should never have kicked that woman's butt – anybody ever said that to you?'

'Occasionally,' said Biggin.

'A big mistake.'

'People say so.'

'If she'd wanted something fetched out of Russia, she'd have damned well got it out of Russia.'

'I'm sure she would,' said Littlehales, conscious of his own inadequacy.

'What's she doing these days?'

'I've no idea.'

Biggin said: 'It's no longer just a question of giving the AFE back to Kotelnikov. There are Muslim forces in battalion strength some five hours behind the train, which is approximately one kilometre from the border with China.'

The general's smile faded.

The colonel organizing the rescue said: 'We leave at 04.00. We'll go due north over the desert, then turn east between Karaganda and Lake Balkhash. I want to RV at a place called Burlyu Tybe. We'll need a Sikorsky to lift out the container. The nearest is in Turkey; it's due to arrive at 03.00.'

Littlehales said: 'We're very grateful.'

'There's a total security blackout on this one; a *total* blackout covering *all* radio signals. You can no longer communicate with your people, you understand that?'

Biggin said curtly: 'We understand.'

'This is a US Air Force operation. Any messages for you will be passed on. From now on you are to speak to no one outside the US military structure.'

Littlehales said: 'We really are very grateful.'

'We'll be taking twelve Commanches, supported by four Apache Longbows. You know the Longbow?'

'It's part British,' said Biggin.

'Yea? What part's that? The toilet seat?' He laughed good naturedly.

'We really are very—' started Littlehales.
'Yea, I know you're grateful. OK, let's eat.'

Biggin said, after some moments: 'I suppose we're used to arse-licking Washington.'

Littlehales said: 'Much better than arse-licking the Frogs.'

'Christ, yes,' said Biggin with feeling.

They ate in the all-ranks dining-room. It was just after 03.00 hours. US Army food supplies had not yet arrived from England: the Air Force was living off the land while it waited for Montana steaks and frozen apple pies. A dish of rice and meat was brought in, enough perhaps for six men of moderate appetite.

There were twelve of them present, big hulking servicemen. Each one looked as though he could have eaten the entire platter of food that had been placed in the centre of the table.

Such was the politeness shown, such was the underlying frozen hostility, that the Uzbekistani boy who was serving took nearly a quarter of the food away uneaten.

An Air Force pilot said: 'So what were your boys doing in Kazakhstan to start with?'

'They were the Moscow embassy protection squad.'

'Coming home the scenic way?'

Littlehales laughed.

None of the Americans looked amused. 'Jesus,' said one of them.

'OK,' said the colonel. 'Thirty minutes to take-off. Let's get moving.'

'Well?' said General Kotelnikov, staring down on the darkness of Red Square.

'It's on the border. The Gates of Dzungaria.'

Kotelnikov closed his eyes.

The mistake in the construction of the device could have been minuscule. It could have been in the computer programme. It could have been a millimetre-thin sliver of metal incorrectly milled in the toolroom. It could have been a minute variation in the fuel mix, in the delivery or ignition system.

If it reached the Chinese, they would never know.

'The Americans?'

His aide said: 'We have no information. But the Foreign Ministry is taking a call from Washington, and has alerted us that the message is on a Military Share basis. We think they are moving towards cooperation. Events in Kazakhstan may be out of their control.'

The room in the Kremlin, with its white and yellow Christmas-cake plasterwork, was one of the rooms that Stalin had occupied. It looked out over the Presidium Building and the French cannon captured at Borodino.

The GRU officer who had led the investigation into the disappearance of the device said: 'Yakutov told us the AFE was in Leningrad.'

'Leningrad, Leningrad?' said Kotelnikov. 'You have a budget to change all the road signs?'

'St Petersburg,' the GRU officer corrected himself.

Yakutov, pale, supple, Second Directorate KGB, said: 'It was a government train carrying Ministry of Finance records. We had no knowledge of an AFE being attached. As far as we were concerned, the AFE was being routed round the northern orbital to Petersburg.'

'We should complain to Washington' – this from a soldier: a colonel from the Frunzenskaja Embankment.

'Why should Washington want the Finance Ministry records?' said the GRU officer. 'They compiled most of them.'

The roof of the Ivan the Great belltower was a black mass against the starry sky.

I would like to be on the Lenin Hills, thought Kotelnikov, watching the red navigation light flicker on the spire of the Moscow State University's tower block. In his day, in the Fifties, the university had been a cosmopolitan place, full of cheerful young Africans, Cubans, Chinese . . .

At least in Red Square the freelance photograph booths were gone, the child 'spivs' selling fur hats, badges and Russian dolls were gone, the advertising posters were pulled down, the Coca-Cola neon sign was dead.

A month ago, prime office space in central Moscow had been two hundred and fifty American dollars a square metre – more expensive, they said, than London! What was office space worth now?

The colonel said: 'General? The Bukhara Express.'

'It must not cross to China.'

But how could they stop is crossing to China?

Yakutov, the representative of the KGB directorate that had dreamed up the bizarre 'Miss KGB' contest at the height of appeasement to the West in the early Nineties, said: 'The commander of the Federal Guards will not allow the train to cross to China.'

The GRU officer said: 'You know that?'

'He is patriotic, but confused . . .'

Like all of us, he implied; the KGB playing the honest but bewildered servant of the state, working on its own rehabilitation.

Kotelnikov said: 'How soon can we get there?'

The colonel said: 'The nearest assault helicopters are six hours away.'

'Paratroops?' said Kotelnikov.

'Two hours.'

It was 04.00 in eastern Kazakhstan, but midnight here in Moscow. As Kotelnikov looked down from the window, the bells began to ring out from the Cathedral of the Annunciation. He had not got to bed before 03.00 for a week now. *Uneasy lies the head that wears the crown*, he thought wryly, remembering a Shakespeare production of his student days.

He must learn to avoid nostalgia. A peasant woman brought into the Kremlin for an *Isvestia* photocall had told him: 'Under Papa Stalin I had money to buy food, to buy clothes. The bread was good. What did it matter if the traitors were sent to the camps? What did we know of the camps?'

'Yes, mother,' Kotelnikov had said, smiling for the cameras. But he knew that when Papa Stalin was in the Kremlin she had been young, and in love.

The paras would drop at dawn. He turned and nodded. The aide reached for a telephone.

FOURTEEN

Bukhara Express, the Gates of Dzungaria, 05.00 hours, Tuesday 26 March

On the table was an oil-lamp stolen or bought from the Ishim Tourism Hotel.

By its light, as he came in, Art saw Kate and Hoodless and Anna – and a village man, brown-faced and slitty-eyed, with a fixed smile. Not a man to trust, thought Art the internationalist.

Simon had a map under the lamplight.

'You were asking where we were,' he said. 'The lake is Ala Kul, the mountains to our right are the Ala Tau. Less than 1k up the track and we reach the border.'

What border? Uzbekistan? Iran? How could they have got to a border? Art's head was buzzing.

'China,' said Kate.

'China? You mean as in slow boat to?'

'Sinkiang Province,' said Kate.

'We are on a mountain rail line,' said Simon, 'skirting the Gates of Dzungaria.'

'Well,' said Art, 'thanks for telling me.'

He wondered if he was supposed to go back to bed.

Simon said: 'If you'd like to go to the frontier now, this gentleman has a truck.'

Art looked at the gentleman. Of course he had a truck. And very possibly one of those curved knives with a slit near the hilt for the blood to run down.

'Why?'

'You own safety,' said Simon.

'Simon thinks,' said Kate, in a peculiar voice, 'he might have to fight in the morning.'

Art looked round. 'Fight who?'

Kate said, her voice tight: 'The Russian guards, Art. He thinks he might have to fight the Russian guards. He's fought everybody else, after all.'

Art was aware of the sentry on duty at the door, the way he had held his gun in the crook of his shoulder rather than slung across his arms; of the other sentry at the end of the coach.

'Mind if I ask why?'

Simon said: 'We think the guards are on the point of switching their allegiance to Kotelnikov. One of them's an agent; we know that. Almost certainly KGB. We think they might try to stop us moving the train through the frontier.'

'And you'll fight them?'

'If we have to,' said Hoodless.

Art looked at Simon, and felt something like affection. 'Listen,' he said, 'I'm a lot older than you are. Heroics are for dickheads.'

'Yes,' said Simon, 'I know. But I still haven't a choice. The Kazakh troops will be on us by morning. Either the Russian guards take the train through the frontier, or we take it through ourselves.'

'And shoot the guards,' said Kate, 'if they object.'

Art said to her: 'Are *you* going on the truck?'

'She's going,' said Simon. 'This gentleman will take you, Kate and Anna to the frontier. OK?'

Art shrugged. 'OK by me, squire.'

'You've got your passport?'

Art nodded.

'The visa will cost thirty American dollars; they don't take cards apparently. I'm also going to give you both a loan of fifty gold sovereigns, but not when this chap's looking.'

Art smiled at the Bearded Bandit. Not only a gentleman but a 'chap' – they'd be putting him up for the Army and Navy Club next.

Kate said: 'We'll need the gold to get Anna through.'

Anna opened her mouth as if to speak. Hoodless put his hand over hers and shook his head.

Simon said: 'Anna's more vulnerable than any of us. The Kazakhs would shoot her as a Russian. The Russians would shoot her as a Western collaborator. Also she has no passport.'

'We don't abandon her,' said Kate, 'no matter what. OK, Art? Is that agreed?'

'Don't worry, Anna,' Art said. 'I've got people through borders before now.'

Anna smiled miserably.

Simon was looking at his watch. 'Five-fifteen,' he said. 'What time will the border open?'

Anna spoke to the bandit, but the man did not speak Russian. Curiously enough, his language reminded Art of his long stint covering the Kurdistan War.

Now Anna was waving her pink Mickey Mouse watch – a mistake, Art thought, seeing the way the bandit drooled over it.

The bandit spoke. Art said: 'He says six o'clock,' and was gratified by Kate's look of surprise.

The night air flowed down from the mountains. There were no stars, only moving wraiths of mist. They climbed the grass bank to the dirt road. From quite close by, Art could hear a stream falling down the rocks, down to the water. It reminded him of weekends in the Lakes, of the various newsroom copy-typists he had enticed up to Shiny Bright's cottage near Ullswater.

Below them a few Russian guards were still crouched round their campfire – off-duty sentries perhaps. Kate had muttered something, then disappeared. He could see her now, in the firelight, talking to her Russian officer chum.

She was a girl for the boys all right. She'd kissed and cuddled the English officer lad for a good five minutes, and she'd have been kissing and cuddling him still if he hadn't been called to speak to someone on the radio.

Anna and Hoodless were talking quietly.

'You won't forget me?' he heard her say. 'You won't send me to China, then forget me?'

'If you think that, you deserve to be forgotten.'

She clung to him, crying.

'Hey, now, come on . . .'

Art looked away. Kate and her Russian appeared to be deep in a meaningful conversation by the fire. It was all happening tonight.

A new sound: the lorry chugging up the track from the village. The Russian guards round the fire looked up, puzzled by the noise. The lorry appeared. It was a wooden caravan on wheels, fantastically painted.

'Now, Annie,' said Hoodless, 'whatever happens, you go to Hereford. OK? You go to Hereford, to the address I've given you.'

She was staring at the ground, sobbing very quietly.

'Annie,' he said, 'look at me.'

She looked up.

'Be a good girl, eh?'

She nodded. A tear trickled down her cheek.

The lorry pulled up beside them. The bandit leaned over and opened the cab door.

Hoodless said firmly: 'Go on, love.'

'John . . .'

'In you get.'

She turned abruptly, climbed into the cab, moving into the middle to leave room.

Kate came panting up the slope. 'Here,' she said abruptly. 'Here's my money. I'm staying. Our soldiers have no interpreter without me. Phone my office for me when you get to Beijing.'

Russian guards were moving slowly up the slope towards them. The bandit was leaning across Anna, saying something, being polite.

'For Christ's sake, Art, go!'

He climbed into the truck and closed the door. He nodded to the bandit and shouted 'Go!' in Turkish. Somewhat to his surprise, the lorry jerked forward.

Looking back, he could see Simon jumping down from the train, and Kate turning to walk away, back towards the fire. By him, Anna was silently crying her heart out, not even trying to look back at Hoodless, who had, in any case, melted into the shadows.

He put out a hand to comfort her, and she took it and held it to her face, and he felt the warmth of her tears. As they turned up a dirt track, into the pine trees, the bandit started singing, a crooning, howling sort of song, a song of old Dzungaria perhaps; or something from the Asia Star satellite pop charts.

Art looked again out of the window, back at the train for the last time.

Simon and Kate were standing facing each other – shouting by the look of things. The fire blazed suddenly as Russian sentries threw on new wood. For a moment the light flickered on the aluminium container, and he thought how strange it was that Hitler's corpse should end its days stuck halfway up a mountain on the Chinese border.

FIFTEEN

Dawn, and a pale white light over the Ebi Nor mountains.

A cock crowed in the village.

Visible now on the steep mountain sides were man-made workings: rusted iron towers and buckets, narrow-gauge rail tracks climbing impossible slopes through the pines, crossing the scree, soaring into the high rocks towards the Dzungarian silver mines.

Higher still, the summit ridges of the Ala Tau were already shining in the sun.

In the armoury, Simon put down the handset. 'The Kazakhs are 2k down the line,' he said. 'The Chinese have them on satellite. Our own satellites show Russian planes airborne from Baku. We have an hour at most.'

Gough and Pullin looked quietly stunned. Kate was making tea, boiling up water in the samovar.

Hoodless said: 'What do they say we do?'

'Ankara can't get a response from Tashkent. The signal just comes back "Wait out". They must know what's happening. Last night they said the Chinese border was a last-ditch option. They said they were clearing it at a high level. I know fuck-all about the Chinese.'

'The second biggest economy in the world,' said Kate.

'Well, yes, I did actually know that much. Whose side are they on?'

'In an overview of world diplomacy,' said Kate, 'that might be regarded as a simplistic question.'

She gave him tea.

Hoodless said: 'We're pissing around with a signals unit. We ought to raise Hereford.'

'No, it's too late. We go over the border now,' said Simon. 'I'll go and talk to Andrei.'

'Give me five minutes,' said Hoodless. He left the compartment.

Kate said: 'Where's he going?'

Simon turned to Gough and Pullin.

'We all act normally. You've made that clear to the men? That's understood by everybody?'

Gough nodded. Pullin said: 'Thank you, ma'am,' as he was handed his glass of tea.

Gough said: 'Ammo's the worry.'

He didn't need to elaborate. They both knew how much ammunition was left. Their reserves had been depleted at Kuybyshev, in the Urals, at Lake Balkhash.

They had twenty-eight rounds apiece for their SA80 rifles. Enough for three minutes' worth of close fighting.

Kate said: 'I don't suppose anybody wants to listen to the still small voice of reason?'

Gough and Pullin looked uneasy. After making the tea, she ought to have gone away.

'Jaw-jaw,' said Simon, 'not war-war?'

'Something like that, yes.'

'There's nothing left to talk about.'

'It's *their* train. The Russians. It's *their* wagon. Well, isn't it?'

'Actually I think we've bought it off them.'

'Bought it? *Bought it*? Well, Simon, that's been the story of democratic Russia. It's been the story of the decade. Half the foreign-currency reserves syphoned off into Cyprus banks, half Moscow sold to Swiss real-estate companies, half the airforce sold to the Middle East, the diamond mines at Arkhangel licensed to South Africa, the Moscow telephone exchange run by BT – do you wonder Second Army are heroes? Are you surprised Stalingrad Division refused to defend Petersburg?'

Simon said: 'Can we talk about it later?'

'Will you be alive to talk about it later?'

'I do hope not,' said Simon. 'It'll be worth dying not to have to listen to that twaddle.'

'Right. You know, Simon, you've changed, but it's not been for the better.'

She went out. Gough looked approving, though whether at Simon's comment or hers it was hard to say.

Simon said: 'It's not Andrei that's the trouble. It's that fucking KGB agent. I wish we'd smashed his fucking radio.'

He paused.

'I think it's going to be OK.'

Every second, the armoured personnel carriers were coming up the road to the frontier, the Russian planes crossing the Kazakhstan desert.

He walked out. The light was stronger. There was pink icing-sugar on the top of the mountains; the lake was a dark, steely blue.

Andrei was among the men round the camp fire. Simon walked over and joined him.

'You want some tea?' said Andrei, looking down into the blaze.

'I've had some, thanks. I think we ought to move. Those Kazakhstanis must be coming up behind us.'

'It's OK. You don't have to worry about them.'

'The engine's fixed. Why wait?'

On the other side of the fire a Russian spoke.

Andrei looked up at the sky. He said: 'Look, Simon!'

Two birds were wheeling over the lake. Andrei's men were pointing them out to each other, excitedly.

Andrei said: 'They are famous, the eagles of Kazakhstan!'
'So we move out now, all right?'
Andrei was gazing up at the eagles. 'You have already sent somebody through the border into China?'
'Mr Finkel,' Simon said, 'the reporter. And also Anna.'
Andrei looked at Simon. He said, amused: 'You're taking a Moscow prostitute to England?'
'Actually,' said Simon, stubbornly, 'she worked for Intourist.'
'Oh, *Intourist* . . .' Andrei grinned, then his grin faded.
They looked at each other, embarrassed.
Simon said: 'We have to move over the border. We have to move over the border *now*.'
Andrei looked at him steadily. Then he slowly shook his head. 'No.'
Simon turned and called: 'Colour-Sar'nt Gough, get Talbot and Gull to the engine—'
'No,' said Andrei, then loudly: '*Niet!*'
Russian soldiers suddenly rose from the bushes at the front of the train, kneeling with their rifles covering the side of the track, making a killing ground of the openland that the Royal Mercians would have to cross to reach the engine.
Others made themselves visible in the rocks. A machine-gun nest had apparently been set up there during the night.
Simon looked again at the machine-gun nest.
The barrel of the gun was pointing at him.
Andrei said: 'I'm sorry. The wagon from Perm does not leave Russia.'
'It already has.'
'I don't think so.' His ironic voice. 'You ought to keep up with the news.'
From behind Simon, there was a sudden shattering of glass.
They both turned to see the muzzle of the Royal Mercians' light machine-gun emerge slowly from a train window brushing away a few fragments of glass before settling itself to rest on the metal frame.
Three rifles appeared next to it.
Andrei said: 'Listen, Simon. Paratroops are coming: Russian paras. They are coming now. Don't worry about the Kazakhs. Take your men and cross the border.'
Simon looked at the ground between his feet. He looked up.
'Another seventy years of Communism, is that what you want?'
'Simon, I don't think you are good at politics. Just go – please?'
'The train goes into Sinkiang, Andrei. Your orders and my orders. To deliver it into the protection of NATO and the Russian Democratic Government.'
He could see the Chinese border-post: a wooden tower, a row of Red Flags above the pine trees.
'I no longer accept orders from Petersburg,' said Andrei. 'Or from London. Or from NATO.'
Repeating himself because he was weary and could think of nothing

else to say, and because he knew what would happen if he was to stop talking, Simon said: 'The container goes over the border. It goes through the Dzungarian Gates.'

Again Andrei shook his head.

(Each time he shook it, he rocked; and Buck, up on the hill, cursed softly as the hairline target moved.)

Andrei was speaking again, but his English was now so confused that Simon could scarcely understand him. He was talking about corruption eating the hearts of the Russian people. The worm of corruption, he was saying, the tiny worm . . .

'Maggot,' said Kate, from behind Simon.

He whipped round. 'For Christ's sake!' he yelled, though he had known that she was planning some sort of stunt, some sort of crass stupidity, 'For Christ's sake—'

'Andrei?' she said, ignoring him. 'Are you OK?'

'Maggot, thank you. Maggot is the word. The maggots of corruption.'

'You're not going to the West, Andrei?'

'I am not going to the West. Will you stay here with me?'

'You want me to stay here?'

Simon said: 'I don't understand this.'

'Don't worry, my friend,' said Andrei. 'Take your men and go.' He turned and pointed up the valley, to the distant wooden tower.

('I've got him,' said Buck. 'Just give me the word.'

'Wait,' said Hoodless.)

'Kate?' said Simon.

'Oh God almighty . . .' she said. She sat down on a rock, her head in her hands.

'You're staying here with the Russians? You're staying with Andrei?'

Andrei, out of modesty or politeness, looked away towards the lake, watching the eagles.

'For fuck's sake,' said Simon, bewildered, '*when*?'

'Don't talk to me,' said Kate, 'as if I was a tart.'

('He's looking right at me,' said Buck. 'I've got him now.' His weapon was resting in a V formed by his left thumb and forefinger; his shoulders were level to prevent canting. As he breathed in, then out, the crosshairs moved straight down through the centre of the target between twelve o'clock and six o'clock. 'I've got him now,' he said. His trigger finger applied pressure steadily, until he was just short of firing.)

'You and *him*?'

'And don't talk about him as if he's a fucking ape.'

'Kate, go to the train,' said Andrei.

'No, you stay here,' said Simon.

'Oh God, I don't believe I'm hearing this.'

'Do you love him?' asked Simon.

'What?'

'Do you love him?'

'You're at the point of killing each other, all of you, and all you can ask me—'

'Well, do you?'

Kate sighed deeply.

'Kate!'

'Take your men and go, Simon,' said Andrei gently.

There was a sound, a pulsing noise in the air.

'Planes, sir!' called Gough.

'And me?' said Simon.

Kate sighed again.

'What about me?'

'Russians, sir,' called Gough.

'Are you so stupid that you need to ask? What is it about you that you need to be told everything that everybody else has known for years? Andrei, you must come to the West. You are being romantic but you can't be romantic about Russia. People like me can be romantic about Russia, we can cry over Russia and then go and write books about it, but you can't be like that. You'll be killed. You'll go to a gulag. Jesus, Andrei, you're an officer of the Presidential Guard.'

'Russian paras, sir, coming in to drop. They'll be on us, sir,' called Gough. 'Two minutes at most.'

(Buck said: 'They'll be on us. I'm going to fire.'

'Wait,' said Hoodless.)

Simon said: 'The train's going through the Gates.'

'No.'

'OK,' said Simon. 'We destroy it.'

Andrei looked at him, startled. 'It's unstable. We'd have to evacuate the entire valley. Anyway, it's the only one that works. The only one in the world.'

'Yes,' said Simon. 'That's what they tell me. Well, I'm not going to kill you for it.'

He turned round and fired from the hip, aiming his 9-milly at the explosive charge placed by Hoodless on the wagon door as a last, desperate resort, should the Kazakh forces overwhelm them; and on the hill Buck shouted 'Christ!' and fired his sniper rifle as Andrei leapt back and the explosive charge on the wagon detonated in a cloud of yellow and blue smoke.

Then there was a second explosion, the fail-safe destructor from within the wagon itself, and the air moved and everything on the land moved, and Simon grabbed Kate and pulled her to the ground, covering her with his body as stones, and wood, and soil ran like water towards the container, which burst open to reveal a white and blue ball, the size of a satellite dish, but throwing a bright radiance.

It slowly ascended, and Simon put his head down again, clinging with his hands to the rocks, while his feet were dragged round, his very skin was pulled, and he could not breathe.

* * *

It was gone.

The container from Perm was an aluminium Easter egg cracked open, its jagged edges revealing a blackened interior.

A splash of chemical, yellow. Bits of computer. Bits of glass, blue and purple.

He helped Kate up. Andrei was sitting nursing his head, which was bleeding from a small wound. The Russian paratroops were falling from the sky – the first landing a bare fifty metres north of the train.

Overhead there was a new sound, closer than the Russian transporters . . .

American helicopters, Apaches and Commanches, coming in low over the pine trees, one of them weaving delicately to avoid the Russian paras that were drifting down on the train, others hovering with their red rocket pods aimed downwards.

'Oh God . . .' said Simon. 'Oh, dear God, look at that . . .'

Other helicopters were sweeping round over the water to land on the shore.

'It's the bloody cavalry!' said Simon. 'Andrei, you all right?'

Andrei nodded, one hand on his small, puzzling wound, his eyes glued to the Commanches coming in to roost, and the first stick of American troops tumbling out to form a defensive circle . . .

'Lieutenant Morrell? Lieutenant Simon Morrell?'

The American marine approached cautiously, climbing up from the water's edge. A Russian paratrooper, busy collecting up his parachute, shook his head, uncomprehending.

A village boy offered bubblegum.

'No thank you. No thank you, sir. Not today,' said the American passing on towards the train. 'Mr Morrell? Mr Simon Morrell?'

'Who wants him?' asked Mace, cautiously.

'Who wants him?' said the American, looking at the wreckage of the container wagon. 'Christ, who doesn't want him?'

SIXTEEN

The satellite operator said: 'Sorry, I have no booking from your receiving organization.'

'Booking to follow,' said Kate. She smiled warmly at the American who had let her clamber up into his helicopter.

'You have clearance,' said the operator, 'from the host country?'

'This is Kazakhstan.'

'You know you must have clearance.'

'Clearance will be retrospective.'

It was pointless telling the operator that there was a war on, that the capital Alma Ata was occupied by Russian forces, that Moscow was in the process of invading overland on three fronts. International satellite operators weren't interested in that sort of thing.

She smiled again at the American, whose expression was stern, like a Middle-West preacherman who had found his daughter braless in the back of a pink Cadillac.

'Booking 22.00 hours,' said the operator. 'Tashkent, London.'

'Thank you for your cooperation.'

She gave the phone back to the American and thanked him profusely.

He said: 'That was a mercy call, ma'am?'

'Of course it was. Thanks for being such a sweetie.'

He muttered 'sweetie' as she left the helicopter.

She stood for a moment in the sunshine.

A camera crew would be waiting for her in Tashkent.

They'd get a long, panning shot of her arriving in the lead Apache gunship. She'd be wearing an American body protector, just like the one she lost in Moscow. She'd do a piece to the camera, with the other choppers coming in behind her. She'd interview the American mission commander. She'd interview Simon.

She wished she had a camera now, a little lightweight camera and a satellite dish.

This is Kate Delacroix, live, from the Gates of Dzungaria . . .

The only Western reporter in Kazakhstan! The last Western reporter at the Fall of Moscow!

(She'd forgotten Art – but then, Art wasn't here, was he?)

'Ma'am?'

An American was offering her coffee, real instant coffee, out of a thermos.

She drank. She filled her lungs with the clean, sharp mountain air.

The rhododendrons along the lakeside would soon be out – she could see the buds swelling. She could smell the scent of warm new bracken. She remembered that she had always fancied a walking holiday in the Himalayas.

She gulped more coffee. Life was good. It really was *bloody* good.

She looked round for Simon and Andrei.

They were down by the lake, away from everybody, standing by the shore, throwing little stones into the water.

She smiled and shook her head.

She walked down towards them. She passed the American helicopters: the Apaches with their clustered rocket pods, the Blackhawk infiltrators, the Commanches, the huge Sikorsky surrounded by excited village children.

Overhead, she could hear the drone of choppers that were airborne, warning the Kazakh MVD troops – now less than a kilometre away – to keep their distance.

Machine-gun nests sprouted from behind every tree. Nobody was taking any chances.

She scrambled down to the rail track, and walked past the train, past the twisted aluminium shell of the wagon from Perm, past the coach bombed out in Kuybyshev, past the coach that had been boarded by the Chechens, the compartment where she had been attacked . . .

A man wearing brown cord slacks and a sweater was sitting outside what had been the SAS armoury, speaking into a phone. She'd been told his name was Biggin, and that he was the 'operations controller' of *Catchphrase*.

Next to him was the SAS radio operator, fiddling with the radio transceiver, and a young army officer not much older than Simon, who smiled selfconsciously when she caught his eyes.

'Yes, it's totalled,' she heard Biggin saying. 'He did it personally. I don't know why. I haven't asked him. We lift out in ten minutes. Yes, the girl's here' – he was following her with his eyes; there was nothing selfconscious about this one – 'no other reporters that I've noticed. The paras, by the way, are 105 Guards Regiment. Morale's high. We should never trust Ukrainian intell, I've always said they were playing their own game.'

The paras of 105 Guards Regiment were grouped among some rocks, ostensibly waiting for transport, although everyone knew there wasn't any.

They were Blue Berets, the elite; they came from the Ryazan Higher Airborne Command School that the Bukhara Express had passed only a few days ago. They were sitting in the sun, battle-blouses open to reveal their famous *telniashka* blue-and-white striped T-shirts. They were famous for their virility, their appalling sense of humour, and their toughness.

'Hey, come up here, baby,' one of them shouted to her, in Russian, not expecting her to understand.

'Piss off,' she shouted back, also in Russian.

He looked startled. His friends laughed.

There was some talk of the Americans airlifting them out, down the mountain, perhaps even to Alma Ata.

Washington was being consulted. It would be a peace overture to the new rulers in Moscow.

Nobody was bothering to consult the government of Kazakhstan. Nobody knew quite where it was anymore.

They were still shimmying stones over the water. As she watched, Simon's stone bounced five times before it sank. He waved his arms triumphantly in the air, and Andrei punched him playfully.

Dear God . . .

She stood and watched them. Andrei would go back to his precious Guards Regiment, she supposed, then to the Frunze Academy: the staff college for high-flyers. End up a marshal of the Soviet Union, or on the long walk to the gulag.

'No, it's going to be different,' he had told her. 'This time it's all going to be different.'

Well, yes. Kotelnikov was no communist; the forces he had unleashed were not the forces of communism but of extreme nationalism, of xenophobia (never buried far beneath the surface of Russian society) and hatred of the Jews.

Russia was turning fascist – but with Kotelnikov it would be the fascism of a Franco perhaps, rather than the fascism of a Hitler.

Simon.

Whatever was going to happen to Simon?

She knew, if she knew anything, that his redundancy notice would be revoked, deferred, reassessed in the light of the latest manpower review – whatever they chose to call the real reason, which was embarrassment and fear of adverse publicity. There'd be nothing on the television news about AFEs, of course, or about Gallagher dying, but plenty about Chaffinch and the lads of 'D' Company brought out of Russia by an intrepid young officer.

She'd make sure of the TV coverage. She's make Simon into a hero. They would have dinner at his little restaurant overlooking the Golden Horn. They'd sleep together an awful lot. She *had* thought she did not love him – not in any permanent sense; she was capable of loving anybody for just a summer – but she didn't really know what she thought any more.

She knew he'd never be any good in the army.

They had stopped playing ducks and drakes, and were sitting on a rock, looking out over the lake, talking. She walked down to them through the ferns.

She heard Simon say: 'Well, I'm leaving the army. You could come and join me in Colour Gough's marquee franchise.'

'Yea?'

'The trouble would be, of course, that you'd keep trying to pinch Kate.'

'But I don't need to pinch Kate, my friend. She is mine already.'

'Dear, oh dear,' said Kate, looking down on them. 'What *are* we going to do with you boys?'

A question that was being asked, though perhaps not with the same degree of affection, in MoD, London, and on the Frunzenskaja Embankment, Moscow.

POSTSCRIPT

Sinkiang, Republic of China, afternoon of Tuesday 26 March

Art was wandering through deserted streets, past empty houses half buried in sand, past Buddhist monasteries that had not been used for five hundred years.

Eventually he came to the end of a row of dried mud buildings. He looked out at the desert.

It was called the Taklamakan desert. The name, he had been told, meant: '*You go in, but you do not come out*'.

Yes, it looked like that sort of desert.

He turned and said to the Chinese tour-girl, who was following him at a distance: 'When do we go to the hotel?'

She said severely: 'Not for another hour. What are you doing down here? Who told you to come down here? There are no telephones down here. There are no telephones for forty kilometres. Wait in the chai-house if you want to.'

In the chai-house he took off his shoes and sat cross-legged on the carpet. His socks were stuck to his feet. He remembered when he had put them on – it had been after his bath, sitting in his room at the Cosmos Hotel, Moscow, about a century ago.

He asked, in Kurdish, for a telephone and they laughed tinkly laughter.

They sold him a dish of yak yoghurt. They wore ethnic clothes and tried to sell him a miniature cheese in a claypot – it was worse than taking tea at a National Trust property. When the rest of the party came in, cameras swinging, the tea-girls twittered to the Chinese tour-girl and she leaned over to him and said roguishly: 'They think you are Turkish. They think you are a rich Mussulman from Istanbul seeking a bride. It is true, yes?'

He said: 'When did you say we go to the hotel?'

'You haven't seen anything,' she said angrily. 'You think you are too civilized to need culture? You think it's too boring to see the corpse with a thousand-year-old Persian coin found in his mouth? I think you had better stay here on your own.'

'No, it's all right,' said Art.

'You want us to help you? You want us to take you back to the town? To find you a fax machine?'

'Yes,' said Art. 'I'm sorry.'

'Well, there's no fax machine. I tell you that now.'

She was more of a cow than Kate Delacroix.

Anna was drinking tea and chattering to an American matron from Grand Rapids, USA, telling her how she was on her way to join her fiancé in England, in a place called Hereford.

She was telling everybody this, stating it firmly, with conviction, defying contradiction. It seemed to Art that she was always expecting somebody to say: 'No, you're not.'

They were now part of the Fabulous Silk Road Grand Orient Tour, which had started its journey from Grand Rapids, USA.

He and Anna had gone round a corner in Jinghe – the most godforsaken hole in God's universe – and suddenly there it had been: a pink and blue and silver bus with cameras poking out of every window as if the occupants regarded the locals as baboons in the wild – a judgement which wasn't, in Art's estimation, far from wrong.

They had begged to be let aboard. The German tourists sharing the bus – selfish, Hunnish bastards; my God they'd never change – would have left them in the gutter. It was the Grand Rapids Globetrotters who had made room and given them a hospitable welcome.

'I hear they believe you are a Turkish man,' said one of these matrons, a beady, intelligent old bird, settling by him. 'Of course the Uyghurs speak a language very like Turkish. They came here from Asia Minor over a thousand years ago. They think every Westerner is a traveller bringing news from their ancient homeland. A sad and sorry story.'

'There is a telephone at the hotel, I suppose?'

'Not one that works.'

'No, of course not.'

'But Mr Buchanan has a powerbook with a Satpax 4 satcom terminal.'

'He has?' said Art.

'And a PSI fax modem.'

'Oh,' said Art. 'Do you think he'd let me use it?'

'Newsdesk,' said a voice, young, female – the sort Art loathed.

'Art,' he said. 'Art Finkel.'

'Where are you, Art?'

'Urumchi.'

'Where?'

'Urumchi, in the land of the Uyghurs.'

'That's not,' said Newsdesk cautiously, 'anywhere near Manchester?'

'It was from Urumchi that Mare's Nipple grapes were sent along the Silk Road to the emperor of China's court,' said Art, 'packed in lead-lined boxes, covered with snow from the Mountains of Heaven.'

'Right,' said Newsdesk. '*That* Urumchi. Are you sending us something? I haven't got you down. Actually I'd stay there if I were you. There's some bother over a hotel we booked for you in Omsk. They say you didn't show or bother to cancel. And Al says there's a Russian colonel who keeps sitting in reception and won't go away. Did you really say we'd buy some old tat about Kotelnikov . . .'

Ms Newsdesk was chatty today, one of the kittens rather than the vipers. She droned on. It was around ten o'clock in London, the quiet part of the shift. She'd be having a fag and coffee, passing an idle hour before trecking over to The Boatman for an early liquid lunch.

Art looked out through the cool marble hall to the courtyard. Trellises of grapes were throwing out the first green buds. There were hothouse geraniums, and blossom of some kind, and Anna was standing in the dappled sunlight telling somebody else about her fiancé, and their new home in Hereford.

'So where've you been, old son?' said Newsdesk, fishing for a funny story to tell in the pub. 'Tell us where you've been?'

'I was the last reporter at the Fall of Moscow. Where were you, lassie?' Art sneered.

'Sorry, there's a girl who was last out from Moscow. She's a television reporter. She's quite a celebrity. Kate Delacroix. We're trying to get an exclusive – in fact you're not near Tashkent by any chance?' Her voice suddenly became excited and reptilish.

'I'm at Urumchi,' said Art in a leaden voice. 'Urumchi in the land of the Uyghurs.'

'There's an airport?'

'Yes, but no planes.'

'We'll get one. Give me the name again.'

Art did, but in a tired voice. He knew a plane would be sent. He knew it would go to Uganda or perhaps Ulan Bator, or Uruguay. It would never come here.

Anyway he didn't want to interview Kate Delacroix. His thoughts about her were confused. She was the sort of trendy kid he loathed, but they had got on together, in the end.

She was a professional, he had to admit it.

He dabbed gently at his injured eye, feeling old and vulnerable.

'Hello?' said Newsdesk, then, to somebody else in the office: 'Bugger me, he's gone again.'

'Listen, turdette,' said Art. 'I was the last reporter at the Fall of Moscow. I want that on the record. I want it on the front page. I was doing my job. I wasn't pissing around shagging half the British and Russian combined armies, like some people.'

Newsdesk said she was glad to hear it.

'Hey,' said Anna, coming in from the courtyard, a spray of almond blossom in her hand: 'Come and have something to eat. You're getting thin, you know that?'

Her face was beaming. Before Art had called London, she had called a number that Hoodless had given her. She had been told that he was safe, told to go to the British Embassy in Beijing, told that travel documents were being prepared, that the world was being moved to get her home.

'To get me home . . .' she had marvelled happily. 'What do you think of them saying that, Art?'

Nobody was moving the world to get Art home.

'What's Hereford like? Everybody keeps asking, and I don't know what to say. Can we go to Beijing with the rest of the group? That lady says she's going to send me a wedding present, and there's an "Old China Hands" reunion in Grand Rapids in the fall, and I can take John to it if I like . . .'

Art let himself be led away to the stewed goat and rice.